THE ANGEL REVEALED

The World of Evendaar

Book Five

The Angel Revealed

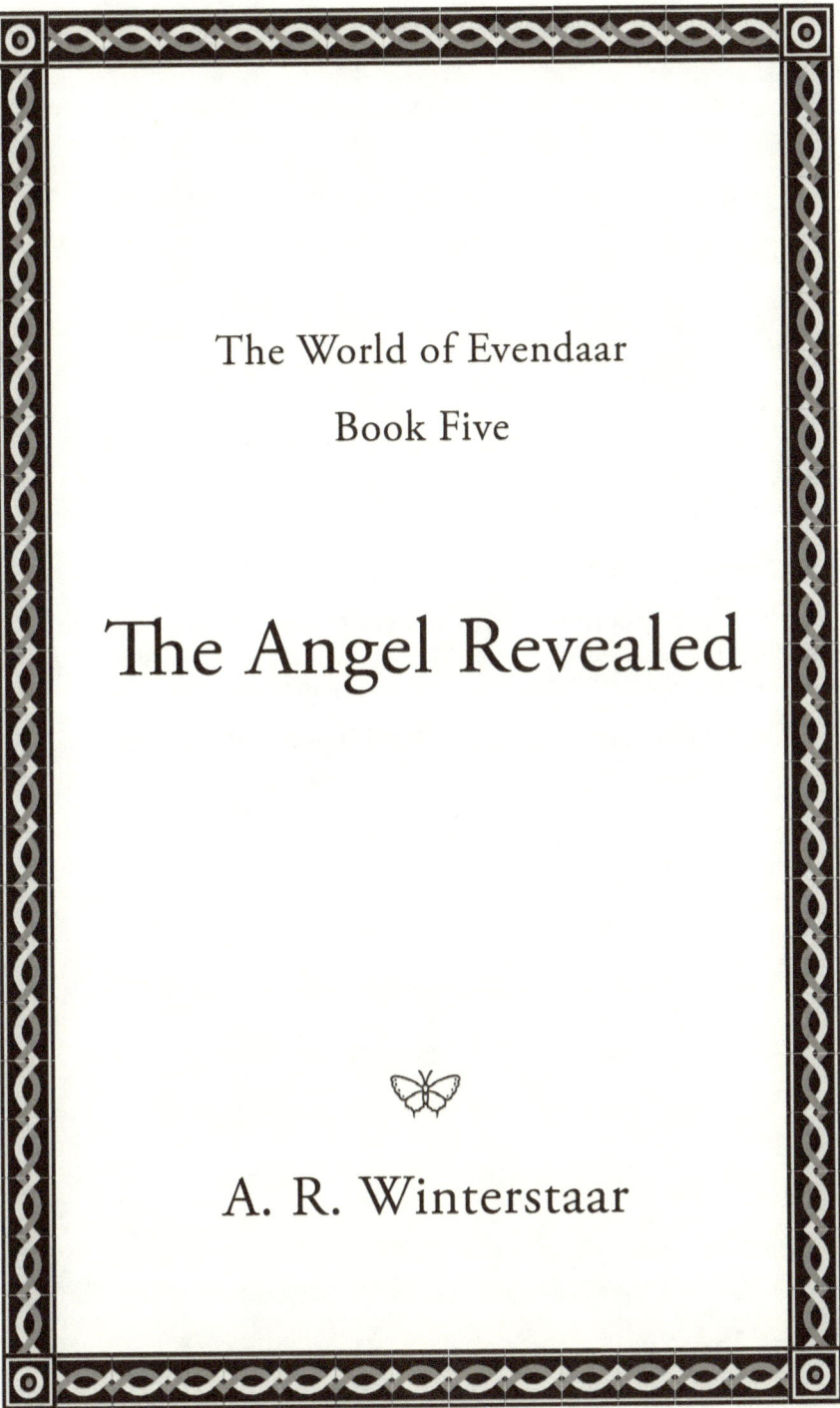

A. R. Winterstaar

Cover Illustration by Anastasia Ward (akward13@live.com)

First edition, March 2022 ISBN-13: 978-0-9914794-1-2

www.evendaar.com

More books in the
World of Evendaar Series:

Book One:
The Child Revealed
Book Two:
The Queen Revealed
Book Three:
The Demon Revealed
Book Four:
The Warrior Revealed

**Discover more by visiting
www.evendaar.com**

For

Z.S.C.

The first star in my sky.

Contents

CHAPTER ONE

"The Words of a Goddess"

Prince Rainold Marchant stood beneath the splintered remains of the great carved doors and surveyed the destruction before him. His reeling senses told him that this was the vast Throne Hall of the Golden Palace, but he had no memory of how he came to be there, nor any idea of why he should have returned to the world of Evendaar. The scents of smoke and dark magic hung heavy in the air. Sweat trickled down his temple. Instinctively, he knew that it wasn't the sun shining through the gaps in the shattered windows that brought a feverish flush to his cheeks and made his heart pound in a reckless tattoo—something was wrong, very wrong.

"What in the name of the goddess happened here?" His voice rang like a bell in the silence, shocking him. His next question was a whisper. "Who is the victor, who the defeated?"

With trembling hands, he smoothed his shirt front, pulled the sleeves of his velvet dinner jacket down over starched cuffs, and twitched his black silk tie straight. Glass and stone crunched underfoot as he made his way up the ruined carpet of the center aisle. He climbed up the steps of the throne dais and nudged a chunk of gilded wood out of the way with his shiny dress shoe. The enormous throne of Unisia lay broken on its side, velvet cushions spewing brown and white feathers.

Pulling out the twist of cloth that he always carried in his pocket, he unwrapped a strand of Queen Adelena's hair and a broken locket, hollow but still carrying the stamp of his son's fingerprint. He closed his eyes and flexed his magic, trying to locate them. But though the magic was there inside him, he couldn't quite grasp it. He chewed his bottom lip, trying to solve the puzzle of this mad dream.

"You!" The shout came from a figure standing at the entrance. He was tall, blond, and very naked.

When Rainold clapped eyes on the man striding toward him, his heart soared for just a moment before he saw his mistake. "Orestes St. Lucidis, you're looking as vivacious as always," he said, hiding his dismay behind a smile. "Any chance your gorgeous twin is coming too?"

Orestes leaped up the steps of the dais and lurched into the prince, grabbing the lapels of his jacket. They were the same height, just over six feet, but Rainold knew better than to struggle with him.

"What've you done?" Orestes hissed, swinging an arm to encompass the chaos of fallen tapestries, broken pews, and still-smoking craters in the stone floor.

"This wasn't me. I only arrived a moment ago." Stepping back, Rainold detached the unwelcome grasp and raised an eyebrow at Orestes's dangling member. "I still, however, managed to get dressed."

With an irritated huff, Orestes flicked his wrist and was wearing a plain white robe, tied at the waist with a rope cord.

Rainold smirked at the pitiful effort. "Very you, darling."

The wizard's gaze went to the cracked ceiling mural above their heads. "What's happened to my beautiful palace?" he asked, then narrowed his electric-blue eyes at Rainold. "And how can you be here?"

Though Rainold knew the throne should've been impossible to lift, he righted it easily and sat down, spreading his coattails on either side of him. "I've decided that none of this is real, darling," he said, his hands twirling elegant spirals in the air. "Probably just one of my more vivid dreams."

"Fool!" Orestes spat. "This is not your dream—it's my vision."

"Whatever it is, I'm just waiting for the good bit to start."

Orestes sneered. "What good bit?"

"There's always a good bit in my dreams," Rainold replied, settling against the ruined cushions, and pretending Orestes's anger didn't frighten him. "My son, Rainere, should be here soon."

Before Orestes could reply, a bright flash of light erupted in the center of the room, and when it had dissipated, a naked woman stood before them. She was eight feet tall, with long, muscular limbs and a cap of short, brown hair. Her face had been carved with a beauty both flawless and terrible.

Orestes gasped and Rainold slid off the throne. They both fell to their knees. "My goddess, Serena!"

The goddess smiled, and without moving, Rainold found himself standing before her. She embraced him, his cheek pillowed on her firm breast. "My son," she whispered, but the power in her voice echoed with all the magic in the universe and vibrated every cell in his body. "I cannot be here long. My angel, Adelena, awoke the dragon Sighmere in his lair. He returned to the Realm of the Gods and keeps me captive."

She released him, and he felt a breeze as Orestes appeared at his side.

"Children, we stand in the future of our ruin." Serena's tears sparkled as they streaked down her cheeks. Rainold saw one fall to the floor and a vine of green erupted through the cracked stone tiles. "All that I have made in Evendaar will be destroyed when Adelena births the god-seed of Dahk'hani."

"My goddess, I know nothing of this," Rainold said, curiosity swamping his reverence. "I've been separated from Unisia for too long."

"I'll kill her!" Orestes shouted, but his mouth was suddenly covered with a sheet of skin stretched tight over his still-moving lips. Rainold stifled a yelp of fear. Truly, their goddess could be as cruel as she was glorious.

"Hush, children, listen to my words, for they will be your prophecy. If Dahk'hani is released from his volcano, then Evendaar will fall, disintegrating like the dust from which it was made." Serena's beatific expression creased with pain, more crystalline tears fell from her cheeks, and a garden of vines and flowers grew at her feet. "I bound my brother under the earth to sleep for an eon, but Adelena has dedicated herself to him, and he has favored her to be his mother."

Orestes's mouth reappeared with a wet, ripping noise that made Rainold cringe. "I'll kill the demon queen! With her life ended, Evendaar will return to the way it was."

The goddess shook her head. Now long, russet locks fell about her shoulders, and her eyes changed from brown to pale green. "Dahk'hani has no awareness that he is the only god left in Evendaar, nor that his duty is to maintain the balance of magic. He loves Adelena and will retaliate against those who wish her harm."

Rainold didn't want to lose his mouth, but there was so much he had to know. "Tell me how to stop Dahk'hani rising," he said. "Could I bind him in sleep again?"

"Dahk'hani is already moving under the earth, and the children of my tribe cannot resist his call," Serena replied. Her hair changed to long, springy curls, and her skin deepened to an inky black. "The oldest of my Marchants have the magic to contain him, but he can compel Adelena to destroy their tribe, then rise on the tide of blood from those sacrificed in his name. Don't let her kill the Eldars. Don't let her kill my Favored—" The image of the goddess started flickering, and she looked over her shoulder as if someone might be coming. "Hurry, my Chosen, you must save Evendaar!"

With another flash of blinding light, she was gone.

Rainold's knees buckled, and he sat with a thump. He felt the stone step beneath him and smelled the scent of honeyed roses. He knew he had just had a conversation with his goddess, but it shouldn't have been possible. "Impossible is for fools," he whispered. "And I am no fool."

Orestes was standing with his arms folded across his chest, his robe bunched up to reveal hairy knees. "I cannot believe that Serena means us to save Evendaar from Adelena," he muttered, a tic jerking his head to the side once, twice. "All along, my brother thought that cursed woman was Serena's Chosen one, but now I know it's me— and another damned Marchant prince."

"And how does Serena expect me to save Evendaar when I'm stuck in my prison dimension?" Rainold asked, his hands fluttering like wounded birds. "And why would she choose you instead of Ohren to help me?"

"The goddess chose me because I am the only man who loves Unisia," Orestes snapped. "More than ambition, more than power, it's my kingdom of Unisia which sustains me."

"Your kingdom?" Rainold climbed to his feet, dusting himself off. "Darling, you won't have a kingdom if I'm not there to help you stop Adelena from killing Marchant Eldars, then letting a god-seed destroy the world."

Orestes's tic flicked his head again, but the madness in his eyes dimmed as he considered the choices before them. "I'll free you, but it won't be easy. I've made some miscalculations, and it's fair to say that I'm not entirely welcome at court."

"But I'm not at court, Orestes." Rainold enunciated each word carefully. "You must come and get me through the portal that Rainere and Adelena left open. You'll just need someone with royal Marchant blood to help you conduct the magic. Are you on friendly terms with my son?"

Orestes remained silent.

Rainold felt relieved despite his predicament. "Well, please find someone else as quick as you can."

Orestes's head twitched to the side again, then he nodded. Rainold thought that was probably the best he could expect from his lifelong enemy.

"Now, how do we leave this vision state?" Rainold said and found himself falling through nothing. He landed back in his own dimension with a nasty lurch of vertigo. He got up off the grass in front of his Gray Palace, a much-modified replica constructed from memory and his own magic.

"Goddess, I hope that animal keeps his promise," he said, climbing the dozen stone steps to the front door. After being imprisoned for one hundred and forty years, he couldn't wait another minute to be free.

CHAPTER TWO

"Weathering Magic"

An unnatural storm raged outside the Golden Palace. Thunder growled and lightning illuminated the night sky with jagged streaks of green energy. Through the open balcony doors, great gusts of wind brought the rain into the palatial apartment of Lord Orgustus St. Lucidis, threatening candle flames and making the wet curtains billow fitfully.

Inside, a battle of words was being waged, and while no man had a solution for the crisis, every one of them had an opinion about the three Marchant Eldars who were, at this very moment, flying over the city of Concordis, screaming their bloodcurdling screams.

Sitting on an overstuffed couch in the center of the room, Adele ignored the men arguing around her. She held Stella in her lap, hardly believing that her two-year-old daughter had recovered from the ravages of the Summer Influenza. Cupping a chubby cheek in her hand, she studied Stella's sky-blue eyes and could see there was now an iridescent band circling each iris. She guessed it was caused by the healing magic in the dragon's tear Stella had been given—the tear Adele had crossed the whole of Evendaar to find for her. Yet, something didn't feel right. She tried to convince herself that she was just overwrought after the long journey, and the ensuing drama since getting home. But in her own body, she could feel the savage force of the dragon's tear that she had also taken, mixing with the magic she had accidentally absorbed from the Ice Mountains tribesman, Jordan Jordansson. It raced around her system, dragging out the leonine gold magic at the back of her neck and the serpentine green that lay coiled under her heart. *I need a Command to lock all this crazy power down,* she thought, *but why've my Chimes gone quiet now?* The Chime Voices usually sang useful Commands and spells endlessly, like a helpful radio station playing in the back of her mind. They also loved Prince Rainere Marchant, singing loudly whenever he was nearby. Yet though her lover was just a yard from her, they weren't even whispering.

God, the poor guy looks as exhausted as I feel, she thought. Rainere was slumped at the other end of the couch, his elbow propped on the arm, chin in hand. His black suit jacket was badly torn and she could see blood staining the dirty bandage on his shoulder—an injury sustained during the mission to rescue her older children, Natalie and Aaron, from their kidnapping by Pere Raven and High Magistrar Orestes. Right now, his glare was trained on High Wizard Ohren and Lord Orgustus as they argued over who could say the most and mean the least.

Adele put Stella down and watched her daughter totter the few steps to grab Rainere's knee. It was always a joy to see her toddler gravitate to the man she loved with the complicated, extraordinary love that defined her relationship with the Marchant prince. The relationship that she had set on very shaky ground the day she left for the Ice Mountains in search of the dragon, Sighmere. *Is he still mine?* she wondered. *Or did I hurt him too badly when I told him he had to stay behind?*

Feeling Stella's touch, the prince pulled the toddler onto his lap and studied her eyes. He raised his head, catching Adele's gaze. He didn't smile, but then she hadn't expected him to. There was a new crisis in the Golden Palace and working out the emotional mess between them would have to wait—just not too long, she hoped.

"Queen Adelena, we need a strategy, and we need it now!" Lord Orgustus's voice boomed over the others. Young, handsome, and pompous, he stood in the center of their group with his hands on narrow hips, shiny boots planted wide. "The citizens are in mortal danger, and we sit here doing nothing!"

"The queen's just returned home this morning on the back of a dragon and then spent the day in prison after being arrested by you, my lord." General Ohrig spoke through clenched teeth. "Give her a minute to get her bearings."

"And she's the last person who can help us, my lord," Ripenzo Shale said, mocking Orgustus's courtly accent. He smirked when all eyes turned to him. "Oh, I'm sorry! Are we supposed to ignore the fact that she never knows what to do?"

Adele warned herself to stay calm, thinking, *We've all been through so much, of course tempers are fraying—Rip's included.* His crooked smile and charm always got under her skin, and though she didn't trust him, he'd also been on the mission to rescue her children. His stolen steward's uniform was ripped and bloody, and he looked exhausted despite his grin.

Determined to use her rusty diplomatic skills, Adele rose to her feet and joined Rip at the open balcony doors. Side by side, they watched the rain falling on the terrace. The faint sound of an Eldar scream carried on the wind and her unsettled magics responded with a wild surge.

"What do you think the Eldars want?" she asked. "As far as we can tell, they keep circling and haven't landed yet. Are they looking for something?"

"Or someone?" Rip bumped her shoulder and grinned like this was a game. "Should we go out and get a closer look, my queen?"

Adele heard the challenge and noted the circles of gold magic spinning around his irises. She knew he was powerful, but could he help her take on three immortal Marchant Eldars?

"Your Majesty!" Lord Orgustus threw his hands in the air as he spun round to face her, his cropped shoulder cape flaring. "We're running out of time."

Adele swallowed a sigh. She didn't see that she had a lot of choices right now. "All right, I'll go into the city and try to kill these Eldars, my lord."

"Easy, tiger! Not every magical creature needs to die!" Rip protested. "Let's think about this a little more."

Adele frowned at his panicked tone. "Then what do you suggest?"

"Do you really need me to tell you why you shouldn't attack three Eldars who will definitely be smarter and more capable than you in magical combat?" he asked, cocking his head to the side in that all-too-familiar gesture of his, like he was trying to read her mind. "Or should I explain why you shouldn't kill *anyone* until you know what they actually want?"

General Ohrig moved to stand at her shoulder. Much like herself, he stank of stale sweat and long days of travel, but his presence made her feel calmer. Even the dragon magic racing through her veins seemed to slow its turns with him nearby.

"The idiot's trying to goad you, Your Majesty," he whispered in a rasp that was so dry, it hurt her own throat just to hear it.

"Go sit down before you fall down, General." She patted his shoulder. "I've got this."

Acquiescing with bad grace, Ohrig smothered a yawn and dropped onto a couch next to Charlie, who flung an affectionate arm around the general's wide shoulders. Dressed in black trousers and a filthy white shirt, Charlie was still covered in grime from his night in Hell after the rescue mission. He caught her evaluating gaze and sent her a cheeky wink before nodding at Rip, reminding her that the man was still talking.

"You are forbidden to kill any more magical creatures in Unisia." Rip flung out his arms as if to encompass the kingdom. "Your bloodthirsty reign of terror must end tonight!"

Adele swallowed a tired sigh, not bothering to explain that she only killed those creatures who tried to hurt her family—there just happened to be a lot of them. To avoid Rip's glare, she took a seat on the couch next to Ohrig.

"All right, Your Maj'?" Charlie asked, concern for her in his hazel eyes.

"Well, I still need to deal with these Eldars tonight before I move on to my problem with the volcano god, Dahk'hani," Adele said, but meant for Rip to hear her words too. Her life was far more complicated than anyone in this room knew.

"Your Majesty?" Rainere's expression was cold, but his gaze still sent a happy tingle down her spine. "I'm not quite sure how Jordan Jordansson fits into this situation. Why exactly did you bring him back with you from the Ice Mountains?"

"Well, that was Sighmere's fault, not mine," she replied, and darted a glance at the bedroom door where the enormous tribesman was lying unconscious, having collapsed after helping her heal Stella. "I'm not sure why, but the dragon forced me to honor the promise I made to Jordansson that if he stole the map to the dragon's cave for us, then I'd take him to Unisia as my guest. But I would like to mention that I made that promise after I'd been recently squashed by QG Bear in a freak melting-ice-bridge accident. I wasn't quite in my right mind."

"I did apologize for that, didn't I, Your Majesty?" Queen's Guard Obearon asked, wincing in embarrassment. "If Dahk'hani's magic hadn't healed you so well, you'd still be covered in bruises."

"Wait! Didn't you actually make that promise to Jordansson after you and Captain Lucky got blasted smoking opiates with the chieftess in that naked blood ceremony?" QG Oleitham asked.

"Oh yeah, Leith's right," QG Owens agreed. "Apologies for the correction, Your Majesty. We just want to keep the timeline right."

Adele was going to advise them to shut up, when Ohrig nudged her in the ribs. "Tell the prince the other thing about you and the boy," he muttered.

"What other *thing* about you and the boy, Your Majesty?" Rainere snapped, green sparks already forming a halo above his head, proof of his growing anger.

"Oh, it's nothing, really." But Ohrig poked her again. She shot him a glare before continuing in a rush, "It's only that Dahk'hani wishes to be reborn, and he wants Jordansson to be the father and me to be the—"

"Mother of a god." Rainere's whisper sounded like a curse.

"I told the god very clearly no," she hastened to add. "But Dahk'hani visited me in a bunch of visions, and I'm afraid he might've interpreted helping me as some kind of binding contract between us."

"There is no way I will allow Dahk'hani to manipulate you in such a manner," Rainere promised, and Adele really wanted to believe him. Instead, she focused on the problem at hand.

"As you can see, Rip, I've already got another crisis on the horizon," she said. "So please just tell me why you think these Marchant Eldars are flying over Concordis."

"I'm sorry, darlin'. Really." Rip smiled his crooked smile and moved to kneel in front of her. "You're a demon, but you act so human, you know that?" He took a deep breath as though bracing himself to deliver the really bad news. "Adelena, your tribe was the first created by Serena, even before she made the humans. In the Temple, you would've been worshipped as a demigod, an angel. In Evendaar they call you demon, but, darlin', you are not who they say you are. I'm sorry but I must tell you that I am the Lost Child of the End of the World Prophecy. I am the true son of Queen Olivia and King Octavius St. Lucidis—and your half brother. I was the one given to the Marchant Eldars one hundred and forty years ago by High Wizard Ohren, but it was you the Eldars wanted, Adelena. You're the daughter of Rainestra, one of the most powerful demons ever to escape the Eeyrie, and King Octavius. If you give yourself to the Eldars, they will return to the Eeyrie, and the whole of Unisia will be safe again. Eating your potent magic will sate their hunger for at least a hundred years."

Whatever Adele had been expecting him to say, it wasn't that. So many questions spun in her head, but only one mattered. "What about my children?"

Rip folded her cold hand in both of his. The dragon magic flared at the contact, causing green sparks to drip from her fingertips, but he ignored them. "Adelena, I think Natalie is a demon like you. If the Eldars knew she existed, they'd take her too," he said. "Aaron is an oddity, an abomination. It's said to be impossible for a demon to give birth to a male anything, let alone a magical human like your son. Stella is completely human and free of magic. I don't understand how she could even really be yours."

Shocked, Adele yanked her hand away. "Stella's mine. I gave birth to her. I held her all bloody and slippery in my arms."

"That's unlikely, but all right." His face creased in sympathy. "Now, I've told you what you need to do if you want to save the kingdom."

Adele's spinning mind stopped on another question. "You want my crown?" she asked.

"No!" Rip looked so horrified that she almost believed him. "Darlin', have the wizards told you that Evendaar sits on the front step of the Realm of the Gods, and that it's a very dangerous place to be? The End of the World Prophecy wasn't for you, it was for me, and I must save the world—*my* world—by protecting the magic that is slowly disappearing from the tribes and creatures all over Evendaar. The longer the most powerful Marchant Eldars in the Eeyrie can remain strong and stable, the longer magic can be sustained at balanced levels here."

"So, I give myself to feed the Eldars, leaving behind my children, and you become king?" Adele felt sick saying it aloud.

"Catshit!" General Ohrig snapped. "I don't believe any of it."

Adele searched but found no guile or treachery in Rip's indigo eyes. "Sweet Christ, Ohrig, he thinks he's telling the truth."

"I promise on my life that I'll make sure the children are safe when you leave. No one will ever get to hurt Aaron," Rip said.

"She's not going anywhere!" High Wizard Ohren shouted. "He's lying, I'm sure of it. It's all lies!" He began taking off the rings that held his old-man disguise charms, dropping them into a trouser pocket. Without the long gray beard and wrinkled forehead, he looked like the twenty-one-year-old man he'd been when cursed with immortality all those years ago. Tall and lanky, with blond curls flopping over his forehead, his chin was narrow and his lips were pink and full. Only his electric-blue eyes remained the same as he glared at Rip.

"We will not offer up the queen of Unisia to the Marchant Eldars." Rainere's voice cut through the discussion, as sharp as a blade. "I forbid it."

Adele wanted so badly to go to Rainere and to wrap herself in his warm arms, but magic was racing in her veins again and she was wracked by a full-body shudder. *Rip wants me to join the Eldars in the Eeyrie and be their magical battery, and Dahk'hani wants me to carry him as a god-baby. Sweet Christ, how do I get out of this mess now?*

"What did the Marchant Eldars do to make you so loyal to them, Ripenzo? Do they support your bid to steal Adelena's throne?" Ohren asked.

Rip sneered. "What did you think would happen when you gave a newborn baby to your worst enemies, Ohren? Did you think they'd kill me?"

"That's not an answer, Rip," Charlie said, angry. He and Rip had survived the mines of Mount Ecrusius together, the hideous labor camp where the gray crystal was dug from the earth and converted into the Gift of Life—an elixir crucial to keeping the immortal wizards of Unisia sane and healthy. "Tell *me* why you would lie about who you were all this time."

"Charlie, I never lied—there were just things I didn't say," Rip explained.

"So, you're an immortal wizard too."

"No, I'm just a magical human like you," Rip said. "I haven't aged because time works differently in the dimension of the Eeyrie.

Whenever I come to Evendaar, it has the same effect on me as on anyone. I might be one hundred and forty, but I estimate that I've only aged about thirty years."

"Then tell us why the Eldars are looking for Her Majesty *now*," General Ohrig demanded. "It's not like she's been hiding herself away. She's been all over Evendaar since her coronation a few months ago. Did you tell them she's home?"

"It was the North Wind," Rip answered.

"What? The wind?" Charlie snorted in derision.

"The North Wind is sentient and a real gossip," Rip told him, perfectly serious. "That's how I found out that Adelena had arrived in Evendaar from Earth, and it's why I encouraged the empress of Sandar to send a delegation to investigate her."

Adele felt the embers of the dragon magic inside her chest suddenly ignite. "You encouraged the empress to send a delegation to Unisia?" she croaked. "Was it also you who *encouraged* her to withhold the Fire Orchid stamens that Unisia needed to make the tonic against the deadly Summer Influenza?"

Rip raised his chin in a defensive tilt. "I wasn't the reason that the influenza struck so hard this year. I couldn't have known—"

Adele stood up, swinging Stella to her hip. "If you hadn't stopped the Sandarians from sending us Fire Orchid stamens, Stella would never have gotten sick," she shouted, her voice vibrating with the force of magic-fueled fury. "I would never have had to leave my children to travel across the world looking for a dragon tear to cure her, and they would never have been kidnapped by Orestes and Pere Raven. Now I've got Dahk'hani demanding a home in my body and this dragon tear messing with my own magics."

"Darlin', I know the truth is awful, but you need to listen to me." Rip did look genuinely sorry as he grasped her elbows and stepped in close. Stella giggled and reached her chubby arms out for him, but he only had eyes for Adele. "You have to go to the Eeyrie. The Eldars need you."

Furious, Adele just stared at him until he dropped his hands and backed away a step.

"And, uh, I almost forgot, I've got a gift for you." He pulled something from the back of his trousers and offered it.

With her free hand, Adele took the wickedly sharp obsidian knife and held it up to the light. Burgundy flecks glinted within the black crystal.

"It's the same one you used to kill the mage in Sandar," he said, grinning like it was something fun they'd done together. "It's ridiculously powerful. If another Sandarian mage ever bothers you, you'll be able to use it on them too because, as it turns out, Sandarians are really vulnerable to obsidian." His grin died as he raised a hand to rub the back of his neck, embarrassed. "Not sure why, but I felt a compulsion to get it back to you. Seems stupid now . . ." he trailed off.

Carefully, Adele put the knife on a side table and handed Stella to High Wizard Ohren, who came in close to collect his favorite little girl. "If he's telling the truth it could ruin you," Ohren muttered only for her ears. "We should get *rid* of him."

Adele felt the pressure of everyone's expectations on her shoulders like a crushing weight. Rip's confession, true or not, was another complication in her already complicated life. "Right, there's been enough discussion," she announced. "I'm going to the city to see these Eldars myself and I'm taking Prince Rainere and High Wizard Ohren with me. Rip, you're coming too."

Charlie was on his feet faster than her exhausted Queen's Guard. "And me, Your Maj'," he said. "You'll need my help to get around the city."

Adele considered it. They used to be the same height, but Charlie was a few inches taller now. Despite his time in the mines of Mount Ecrusius and his near-fatal brush with a Marchant Eldar, the sixteen-year-old looked more like a man than a boy.

"Charlie, no," Rip said, and shook his head. "This could get dangerous, and you don't need to be there."

"But it's true you know the city better than any of us, Charlie," Adele said, throwing Rip a glare. "And I'll need you because my Queen's Guard is staying here."

General Ohrig rubbed the silver and brown bristles on his chin, muttering a string of curses. "And what's the plan, Your Majesty?" he asked, though his expression suggested he didn't expect there to be one.

"I'm just going to spy on the Eldars and learn what I can," she replied. "But if trouble comes, then I'll need men who can defend themselves from magic."

"Your Queen's Guard have done all right so far," Ohrig retorted. "What with the killing of Spider People, ice bears, and dealing with dragons and the like."

"Ohrig, the men are dead on their feet." She gestured at QGs Bear, Owens, Pepper, Leith, and Captain Lucky. They were still dressed in bits of furry clothing from the Ice Tribes tied over filthy gray Queen's Guard uniforms, cheeks windburned and eyes bloodshot with fatigue. "I'll need you refreshed and ready to help me come up with a proper plan when I return."

"I really don't think I should go, Your Majesty," High Wizard Ohren protested. He'd put his disguise back on and waved a hand loaded with charmed rings in the air. "There are certain things about me that just don't hold together beyond the walls of the Golden Palace."

Adele turned her glare on the high wizard and was pleased to see him flinch. "I'm not leaving you home while I go on another adventure, Ohren," she said. "After all, your brother—the high magistrar—and Pere Raven are still at large, and I might need your help if they try to kill me again."

Ohren nodded, reluctantly. "Well, I'm not promising I'll be any help."

"When are you?" Rainere asked, but only Charlie sniggered at the insult.

"Tell me how we can spy on the Eldars?" Adele asked Rainere, closing the distance between them to stand by his side.

"We can access the city through the ancient portals beneath the Golden Palace, Your Majesty." Rainere always used her title in front of others, but the way his lips curled around the words made it feel special. "There's one that will take us right to the Lower District of Concordis. Unless the Eldars land, we should be able to track them through the air." Surreptitiously, he brushed his hand against hers, causing more happy tingles along her spine.

"Don't you want to say goodbye to your children, Adelena?" Rip asked, and his voice carried an edge of desperation though his smile was bright.

"I'm just going to spy on the Eldars," she said, frowning. "I'm certainly not going anywhere near them."

"Fine, fine." Rip raised his hands, as if in defeat. "It's just that—"

"Your Majesty?" General Ohrig interrupted, his square jaw set with that stubborn tilt she knew so well. "If you get yourself dead tonight, I'll never forgive you, all right?"

"I can't have that, General." She found the energy to force a grin. "But it's been my experience that nothing is ever as it seems in this world, and Rip's been wrong before."

"Exactly, Your Majesty," High Wizard Ohren agreed. "You don't have to do anything you don't want to."

Adele could have laughed. She was always doing things she didn't want to do.

"And be very careful, Your Majesty," General Ohrig added.

"Unless I can see a way to fix this myself, I'll be back in an hour," she replied, and with a glance at Rainere, she headed for the door. The quicker she left, the quicker she could finally be with her children again.

Chapter Three

"A Dangerous Demon"

Adele stumbled behind Rainere, almost falling against his broad back, when he pushed open the narrow door to reveal a small but richly appointed bedchamber. She heard him mutter a vicious curse as Charlie, Ripenzo, and High Wizard Ohren piled out of the secret passage after her.

"My apologies, Your Majesty. I forgot that this anomaly existed. If I remember correctly, the doorway was moved over here." Rainere crossed the room to examine a bookcase, poking at it to find the invisible entryway to the portal chamber of the Golden Palace.

"We've been here before." Adele recognized the small room. There was a wooden four-poster bed against the far wall, covered with a navy blanket. In front of the only window stood a large, round mirror on a spherical support. There was a massive wardrobe, so tall it almost touched the ceiling, shoved in beside the bookcase that was worrying Rainere. A small rolltop desk stood in another corner.

"But this is Orestes's bedchamber!" Ohren exclaimed.

"Orestes?" Rainere frowned at the high wizard. "The secret passageways have remained intact since the Golden Palace was built. How did he manage to change the configuration to include his bedroom?"

Ohren was just as mystified. "Maybe it wasn't him who changed it?"

"He's got a very big wardrobe," Adele said, and Rainere gave her a look which she took to mean that he'd already realized this. She'd only had a few moments to explain her plan to him and knew he thought it was very risky and not a little stupid. But she didn't trust Rip as far as she could throw him, and like all of her plans made at short notice, it would just have to do.

"Your Maj, come and look."

Adele followed Charlie to the circular mirror in front of the window. He ran his hands over the frame, fingertips tracing the engravings. "The Boss's scrying mirror," he told her in a hushed voice. "He uses this to find anyone, anywhere in Unisia."

"Could it find him, you think?" Adele asked. The mirror instantly lit up, white shards like static electricity flying across the surface until an image appeared in the glass. A young man who looked just like Ohren was at a desk in a darkened office, scribbling on a parchment. A wardrobe could be seen in the corner behind him.

Adele met Charlie's wide, frightened gaze. "Orestes," he mouthed.

She raised her hand to signal the room, and in a flash Rainere was so close at her back that she felt his intake of breath.

Rip, oblivious to their discovery, was nosing about the wardrobe. "Hey, lads, there's a breeze coming from in here." He opened the door wider and poked his head inside. "Hello! I think this is a portal."

In the mirror, the Boss startled and with another glance to the wardrobe in his office, he threw down his quill, grabbed the parchment and dashed from the room.

"He's off!" Charlie was the first to respond, diving into the wardrobe with Rip right behind him. Rainere shouted an incantation and there was the sound of a body falling with a thud. A moment later Charlie appeared in the mirror, then Rainere could be seen chasing after him through the office.

High Wizard Ohren followed behind Adele as she dashed through the pitch-dark wardrobe, jumping over the prone body of Rip. Her breathing sounded loud in her ears as she brushed past the hanging clothing, then felt the shiver of magic over her skin before stepping out into the ill-kept, dusty office. The walls and floor were bare wooden planks and the air smelled like stale beer. There was a long, rectangular window looking out onto an internal balcony that hung over the main room of the building. The door of the only exit was open, and Rainere was already returning to the room, blood trickling from a cut on his forehead.

"What happened?" she snapped. It had been too much to think that they could catch the Boss in his own house, but her anger still burned hot. He had kidnapped and terrified her children, and he would pay for that.

"Orestes escaped through a portal in the stable yard the moment before it adjusted to another destination," Rainere said. "I saw trees through the darkness—it might've been the Dark Forest, or it might've been a garden at the Golden Palace. Then I was hit by a nasty trap he left behind." Pulling a handkerchief from his pocket, he dabbed at the blood.

Adele clenched her hands, trying to control the dragon magic that was riding her temper in waves of murderous rage. "That is very . . . disappointing. Do you think he was staying in this dump?"

"We're in a public house called The Magician's Wand," Rainere said, tucking his bloodstained handkerchief away again. "This building is owned by Orestes. It's where he was keeping your children and all the others to transport to the mines. We think he ran his whole base of criminal operations in the Slums from here. There are protective wards all over the building and an ancient rotating portal in the yard. I didn't get a chance to destroy it when we rescued the children, but by the goddess, I wish I had!"

Turning away, Adele hid her frustration from Rainere, reminding herself again that everyone had been through a lot. Mistakes would happen. Shaking the green sparks from her fingertips, she sat in Orestes's chair and began searching the desk drawers. She found a carbon pencil and ran it over the parchment sheet that had, she hoped, been sitting underneath the letter he wrote. Thankfully, words appeared with her rapid shading. "It's addressed to Pere Raven." She read the letter aloud: "'Things have changed, Raven. I will free the prince and ensure this nightmare ends quickly. Get the Eldars back to the Eeyrie at all costs. The fate of Evendaar is in my hands. Until I have succeeded you must keep them safe—' He stops there. That must've been when he heard Rip call out."

"What in the hell does my brother think he's doing?" Ohren muttered as he took the letter from Adele. "Why's he trying to protect the Eldars?"

Charlie came back into the room, shaking the rain off his hair. "I've checked the building, and there's no one else here," he said. "But they didn't leave that long ago. I think the pub was open for business tonight, if you can believe that."

"Your Majesty, we should find access to the roof," Rainere said. "See if the Eldars are still flying over the city."

Ohren yelped in pain, then staggered and fell across the desk. His face was gray, and his disguise started flickering horribly, giving way to his natural youthful appearance. "Pere Raven must be the one who called the Eldars to the city. We should go home and come up with a proper plan to catch him," he said, gasping.

Adele took Ohren's clammy hand. She felt an uncomfortable lurch in her gut as her three magics combined, excited by the presence of the high wizard's own magic. "Ohren, what's wrong?" she asked, helping him to sit on the desk chair.

"I'm so sorry, Your Majesty. I tried to warn you that I'd be no help. I really can't be much further from the Golden Palace than this." Ohren put a hand over his mouth as if to hold back vomit.

Adele frowned. Ohren was an incredibly powerful wizard, and she'd never had a reason to think of him as weak before. "At least watch the wardrobe portal for us while we go up to the roof. If we're not back in an hour, then you can return to the Golden Palace." To an impatient Rainere and Charlie, she asked, "Ready?"

Charlie gave her a rakish grin. "Let's go get 'em, Your Maj!"

Taking the lead, it was Charlie who guided them along the corridor outside the office and up a narrow wooden staircase to the roof. He opened the door at the top, and Adele peeked over his shoulder. The rooftop was rectangular, flat, and covered in chunky black gravel that crunched beneath their feet when they shuffled out of the doorway. A dozen brick chimneys and ventilation shafts dotted the wide space, creating a maze, and each was illuminated by two or three green-flame lanterns, casting the whole rooftop in a sickly glow. The rain was lighter now, though lightning still flashed across the sky. The metallic scent of dark magic hung heavy in the air.

"I think the Eldars are controlling the weather," Rainere said, his lips close to her ear. "Which means this might be where they'll land. I'll go scout."

"Oi!" Charlie hissed. "Before you go running off, Your Highness, there's something I forgot to tell you about the Eldars." He shuffled in closer. "There's a word they use, a Command. You'll feel it right in your balls, and you'll want to run toward the one who used it. I heard it when I was on the offering table at the mines. If Rip hadn't held on to me, I would've given myself right to the hungry Eldar."

Adele caught Rainere's gaze. They both knew he'd never been able to resist the Commands the Chime Voices gave her to control him during sex and feed on his magic. She sucked in her bottom lip, worried, but Rainere only snarled, "I'll be fine."

"He's wrong." Charlie seemed very sure of himself. "Adelena, you'll be all right, but the prince should go back downstairs."

Adelena? Since when does Charlie use my first name? She felt a frisson of energy ripple over her skin and scanned the rooftop again. *Something's not right here. There's already too much magic in the air.*

"Hey, guys," she whispered. "Something weird's going on, and I'm not sure it's the Eldars. I feel like we're being watched."

"We're well hidden here," Rainere said as he moved out of the doorway. "Just make sure you stay behind me."

"Darling, I faced down a dragon the other day. Pretty sure I can deal with a couple of Eldars," Adele muttered. She rolled her shoulders, trying to shrug off the sensation of being gripped by invisible hands. "You really can't feel that strange magic in the air?"

But Rainere didn't answer because a piercing Eldar scream made them all cover their ears. Three large forms could be seen flapping against the dark sky. One of them was carrying something in its arms that dangled like a sack.

Triggered by the sound, the wild dragon magic was racing through Adele's veins, filling her abdomen with heat that was intense yet not painful. She stood from her crouch, feeling pulled by the same invisible hands. Rainere threw her a glance over his shoulder. She wondered if he was feeling her spike of lust through the Mark, but didn't have time to communicate with him before there was a sudden, very human shriek and the bundle dropped from the grasp of the low-flying Eldar and fell to the rooftop.

"Sweet Christ, what're they doing?" she whispered.

"Both of you stay behind me," Rainere ordered. "I'll create a shield to deflect any spells they might throw at us."

"No, I don't think—" Adele began, then realized the time for discussion was over when Charlie crept past her to follow Rainere out onto the rooftop, both hunched over, using magic to move faster than she could track through the maze of chimney stacks.

Adele listened for her Chime Voices. Whenever she had been in mortal danger before, they played an eerie symphony in her mind. The music freaked her out, but there was a certain comfort that came from knowing when to anticipate danger. Tonight, however, she felt a very separate, powerful presence breathing down the back of her neck. Praying it stayed out of her way, she moved through the shadows and found Rainere and Charlie huddled under a ventilation pipe. There was just enough room for her to squeeze in next to them. She felt another sharp prickle of foreboding and listened harder for the Chime Voices. But it was the leonine magic at the back of her neck that roared, racing through her blood, and the serpentine magic under her heart that uncoiled, rearing up to her hands. She braced, as ready for action as she could be.

Silently, Charlie pointed to a dark mass on the other side of the roof—the Eldars. The man with them was sobbing and pleading for his life. Charlie pointed to a brick chimney stack a short distance away, then he pointed at her. He pointed to yet another chimney ten yards from it and then to himself. Tapping Rainere on the chest, he indicated that he should stay in the alcove.

Adele was surprised again at Charlie taking charge of the mission. However, she'd promised to spy on the Eldars, and an opportunity to get close to her enemy had to be taken advantage of quickly. Creeping across the uneven surface of the roof, she made it to her new position. From the corner of the crumbling brick pillar, she could see the three Eldars standing in a circle around their victim. They were just as horrifying as Rainere had described. Tall—close to eight feet—long-limbed, and skeletal, wearing identical dark cloaks that scraped like metal sheeting over the gravel. Their elongated faces were hideous, with sharp, pointy chins framed by waist-length black hair and huge silver eyes that glowed in the dark.

She recognized the victim on his knees in the gravel. The portly priest was wearing a filthy brown robe belted at the waist with rope. His bald head gleamed in the pallid light of the green-flame lanterns. "Please, Masters, it isn't my fault," Pere Raven whined, holding his palms up in supplication. "It was Prince Rainere!"

Adele's anger with the priest was strong enough to quench her rising panic at being so close to the monstrous Eldars. The invisible hands gave her a shove, trying to push her out of the shadows. She fell forward on her knees and heard a muffled noise from Rainere but didn't look back to see what he was doing.

One of the Eldars leaned over Pere Raven and began hissing in a sibilant language that Adele couldn't understand. Nor, it seemed, could he.

"Please, Master, slow down," he begged. "You ask me where the 'son' is? Is it Queen Adelena's son? I told you that Prince Rainere took back all the children meant for the mines."

Another Eldar stepped forward speaking more slowly, his hand hovering as if to transmit the questions directly into Pere Raven's head. The priest began sobbing in earnest, tears coursing down his round cheeks. "Why're you here, Masters?" he cried. "Serena help me, I didn't call you. I was meant to meet your emissary, but he's gone. I don't know who you're looking for."

The Eldar hissed another word, and this time both Pere Raven and Adele understood. "Deee-mon."

"The demon queen has returned to Unisia, Master." Pere Raven gasped with relief to have the right answer. "The St. Lucidis dogs have locked her up in Hell below the Golden Palace."

The third Eldar joined in the hissing. Pere Raven looked both terrified and confused as he swung from one Eldar to the next, desperately trying to translate their words aloud. "Whose son came for the sister-demon? Who is bringing you the demon before the god-seed is . . . planted?" Pere Raven asked, hysterical. "Masters, I don't understand!"

Adele sensed Charlie moving behind her. His breath warmed the side of her neck when he leaned in to whisper, "I'm so sorry, darlin', but this is bigger than both of us."

When she turned her head, it was to see not Charlie but Ripenzo, and she felt the heavy vibrations of his power as his arms tightened around her. He heaved her out from behind the brick pillar and carried her, legs dangling, over to the Eldars. "Masters!" he shouted. "It's done."

Bound tightly to his chest, Adele only knew that Rip was taking her away and she lost all control. White-hot and sharp as knives, the magic of the great dragon Sighmere was unleashed.

"Masters, I give you the demon—" The rest of Rip's speech was cut off by his howl of pain as white fire covered her skin. He dropped her, and she leaped away, her gaze on the approaching enemy.

The three Marchant Eldars were hissing and moving in close now. Pere Raven was crawling away. He would die tonight too, but first she had to kill these Eldars. She raised her hands, remembering the words for the hideous spell that had destroyed the Shadow Wasps in the Black Mountains. The magic responded, forming glittering balls of energy in her palms. Oddly, the Eldars moved to stand in a line before her. One even dropped to his knees, head bowed, arms raised.

"Adelena, stop!" Rip darted in front of her.

One of the standing Eldars advanced behind Rip, quick as a snake and hissing just as loudly. She couldn't warn him because she had to chant the spell and the words filled her mind.

"Don't kill them," Rip shouted. "You must go to the Eeyrie to keep us all safe. Trust me, please!"

The Eldar was now towering over Rip, still hissing.

Rip glanced up. "Rainog, don't sacrifice yourself like this. Let me talk to her."

The Eldar hissed, waving his large, bony hands, trying to beckon Rip toward him.

"Dragon flame? She can't have. That's impossible!" Rip looked back at her, his eyes wide. "No! That's impossible."

The Eldar lowered its face close to his. "Ssson," it hissed. "Daaahk'haaani."

IT'S TIME, ANGEL. SERENA'S SERVANTS MUST DIE SO I CAN LIVE. The invisible hands lifted Adele as she swung a ball of magic right at the chest of the Marchant Eldar closest to Rip.

The towering Eldar went up in a bright column of flame, stumbling backward, its mouth open in a silent scream. The other two Eldars rushed to its side, but the flames jumped, and they were all devoured like paper in a bonfire, their bodies disintegrating into piles of gray ash. As shocked as she was, Adele felt a great easing of the pressure on her shoulders. *THANK YOU, ANGEL.* She shuddered as an orgasm swept over her in a flash of exquisite pleasure.

Ripenzo's cry of grief shook her back to her senses. "You really will bring the days of darkness!" he shouted, a cloud of gold magic coalescing as he swung his arms in a series of complicated gestures. "Serena damn you, Adelena!"

With a last wave of his hand, a bright seam of gold ripped open in midair and Rip stepped inside the portal, but before it closed a figure streaked across the roof and jumped in behind him. Rip and Pere Raven were gone.

Then Rainere was there, his arms wrapped around her. "Rip bound me with magic so I couldn't come to you," he said, his voice hoarse with panic. "Tell me you're all right!"

"Rainere." She buried her face in his chest. His shirt was damp with rain and he smelled of warm honey from the touch of Rip's gold magic.

Rainere raised her chin with a finger. "Tell me how you did that," he demanded.

Adele saw the shadows in his deep forest-green eyes as he searched her gaze. *Don't hate me for killing them,* she silently begged. *And please don't hate me for losing Rip.* She looked over to the pile of Eldar ashes, still flickering with little white flames. "It was a spell I remembered," she said. "But this time I built it with magic from Sighmere's tear and . . ." She fell silent as the wind blew harder, tugging at her shirttails and blowing wisps of hair in her face. Within the noise of the storm, she could hear thin voices calling her name.

"Adelena. Prophecy bringer. Adelena. She brings the god. Come to us, brothers, your sacrifice is done."

"It's the North Wind, come to take the fallen Eldars home to the Eeyrie." Rainere pressed Adele against his chest, almost hiding her face with his hand. "Do not speak to it, my beloved."

The wind swirled around the piles of ash and sucked them up into a single, skinny spiral. The twisting cloud moved across the gravel. At the edge of the roof, it split into millions of particles, leaping to join the maelstrom still punishing the sky above their heads, and taking the eerie whispers with it. Rain began to fall on the rooftop in slow, heavy drops.

"It's over for now," Rainere said, and she wondered how he could be so sure. "We should get inside."

Adele was still vibrating from the power of the dragon's magic. She looked at her palms. *Dahk'hani was with me. But why did he want me to kill those Eldars?*

"Do you have control of yourself?" Rainere asked, cradling her hands in his.

But something in his tone made Adele frown up at him, blinking the rain away. "I'd never hurt you, Rainere."

"Then tell me how you did that?" he said. "How did you cover yourself in dragon flame?"

Rainere fears me and Dahk'hani loves me. She shook her head to dislodge the mad thoughts before they could settle in. "I'd tell you if I knew," she said. "But those Eldars wanted to take me, and I wasn't going to let that happen. How the hell did Rip get the drop on us?"

"He must've guessed your plan and spelled himself to look like Charlie," Rainere said, his mouth twisted like he wanted to spit. "I should've known he'd want to protect the boy from confronting the Eldars."

"Yeah, that Rip is a real hero," she muttered, but only because she felt guilty. Rip had been horrified to see the Eldars die—his grief was awful. She pulled out of Rainere's arms and began walking to the shelter of the staircase.

"I just meant that the two of them were friends," Rainere continued as he followed her.

"And Rip was your friend too." She stopped in the stairwell and couldn't suppress the jealousy that claimed her. "Should I be sorry that I made you pick a side, Your Highness?"

In a few quick strides, Rainere wrenched Adele against his chest. His gaze was fierce. "You could kill everyone in the world, and I would still be on your side, Adelena," he growled. "But I will not follow blindly, and I will not be commanded by you. We are equals, remember that, my love."

"Yes," she whispered, feeling relieved. "Always, darling." The dragon magic flared in her chest, warming her in a pleasant way. She took his hand as they descended the narrow staircase, making their way together along the balcony that overlooked the large floor of the pub. Wiping the rain from her face with her dirty shirtsleeve, she surveyed the room from their elevated position. "This place is huge, and pretty nice actually."

"The beer is pleasant," Rainere admitted. "Though the clientele is exclusively Slum dwellers."

She made her way down to the public room floor set with dozens of sturdy square tables and ladder-back chairs. The granite-top bar ran along the wall under the stairs and turned at a right angle down one of the short sides of the rectangular room. Plenty of beer taps were spaced along it, and the wall of wooden shelves behind it was fully stocked with bottles in every color and shape.

"The basement is where we found your children." Rainere stayed close, and she could feel him watching for her reaction.

I can't see this. Adele shuddered, then demanded, "Show me."

Rainere led her behind the bar and through swinging doors into the kitchen. The air was stifling warm, and the three fireplaces were still smoking. There were huge gouges cut out of the walls and scorch marks on the floor, signs of the battle they'd had to rescue her children. But now the kitchen was clean, and trays of glasses were sitting on the damaged countertops. From the scattered piles of aprons and uniforms, it looked as if the employees had been made to leave in a hurry.

"*Cara mia.*" Rainere's voice was gentle as he pointed at the corner of the room. The basement doors had been blasted off their hinges and now rested against the wall, awaiting repair. Her heart raced as she approached the edge of the steps and looked down into the darkness. The magic around the edges of the door snapped at her like loose electrical connections. She recognized the primitive runes engraved on the wall. "This was an interdimensional portal."

Rainere slipped an arm around her waist. "I was lucky that the Boss opened it before the fighting started. I wasn't completely sure I could do it without you."

She stared down into the hole and imagined the screams of her children, feeling their fear as they were hurled down into the void. Guilt settled like a cold weight in the bottom of her gut. *And Rip was the reason I had to leave them to find a cure for Stella,* she reminded herself.

Shaking off the tumult of emotions, she pulled Rainere through the swinging doors back into the public room. "I need a drink, or I'll go insane thinking of my poor babies down there."

"I'm sorry I failed you, *cara mia*." Rainere sat himself on a stool at the bar, misery etched into lines around his mouth. "I was meant to be watching over them."

"You never actually told me what you were doing when the kids were taken from the stable yard. Why weren't you with them?" She watched his face shutter and felt a nasty twist in her heart, wondering what he didn't want to tell her.

He looked away. "By the goddess, I wish I'd got my hands on Pere Raven tonight."

She noted but allowed the change of subject. "Do you think Rip and Pere Raven have been working together all along?" she asked as she went behind the bar and found glasses. She picked a beer tap at random and pulled two pints of a sparkling amber brew.

Rainere frowned. "I can't imagine they were. Rip told me that he only came back to Unisia because he knew your children would be in trouble without you close by, and he was right. He was instrumental in saving the children from the Boss and his Dark Forest Rangers. Raven just took the opportunity to escape us when he saw Rip open the portal."

"Oi! You two!" Charlie was standing on the balcony glaring down at them. "Why in the hell did I just wake up with a bloody sore head in a bloody wardrobe?"

"Is the high wizard up there with you?" Adele called out.

"Nope, he's scarpered." Charlie descended the stairs looking unsteady and holding on tight to the handrail. He took a stool at the bar next to Rainere and accepted a handful of ice cubes wrapped in a dishcloth from Adele.

"Sorry about your head," she said and placed a glass of beer in front of him.

Charlie glowered at her and took a sip. "Where is Rip, anyway?"

Adele slid the other beer to Rainere. He drank half the pint before setting it down, licking the foam off his top lip with relish. "What's this one called?"

Adele checked the tap handle. "Merrills's Bitter Ale."

"It's very pleasant." Rainere took another deep swallow.

Charlie looked from the queen to the prince. "Hello! Anyone going to tell me what happened while I was knocked out?"

Adele thought she should probably do the explaining. "Rip set you up. He swapped appearances with you so he could betray me to the Eldars."

Charlie gingerly pressed the ice to his head. "Typical sneaky Rip."

Adele pulled another beer for herself. "I thought I was so clever asking Rainere to get him out of the way so we could just do this job with the three of us. But even I didn't see through Rip's Charlie-disguise, and normally he can never trick me."

Charlie glared at Rainere over the rim of his glass. "So you're the one who knocked me out."

"It bodes well that you're already walking around. You're tougher than you look, boy."

Charlie snorted at a rare compliment from the Marchant prince.

"Rip opened a portal and disappeared, taking Pere Raven with him," Adele added. She sipped her ale, trying to wash the taste of ashes from her mouth. "He was a little upset with me for killing the three Eldars."

"Go on, then, how'd you manage to kill three Eldars?" Charlie asked, clearly trying to match her composure.

Adele didn't have the heart to tell him she was only calm because she was too emotionally exhausted to feel much right now. But Charlie had been on so many adventures with her and she figured he deserved her honesty. "Dragon magic burst out of me and set them on fire. I couldn't stop it," she said.

"Just like that, eh?" Charlie swilled back the rest of his beer, slamming the glass on the bar. "Now you've killed three more magical creatures Rip asked you not to."

"It all happened very fast," she protested, knowing it was a lame excuse. "I only came here looking for knowledge about the Eldars. I wanted Rip out of the way but I didn't want him gone."

"But you did plan this," Charlie said, and something in his voice made the magic in her respond.

"It was Rip who betrayed you, Charlie, not me."

"But it was your Prince Rainere who actually knocked me out. Who's to say he didn't know it was me in that disguise?"

Rainere's glare could frost glass. "If I wanted to kill you, Charlie, you'd be dead already."

Charlie rolled his eyes at the old threat. "I'm just saying, things might not be as simple as you expect me to believe, Your Maj."

"I might not have told the truth, but I'd never hurt you, Charlie," she said. "As awful as it was to kill the Eldars, what's done is done. Like always, we just have to move on."

"And take the time to throw back a couple of cold beers?" Charlie turned to Rainere. "Shouldn't we return to the Golden Palace to tell them what she did?"

"It can wait for a moment," Rainere answered. Turning back to Adele, his expression was bright with pride. "Her Majesty has killed three Marchant Eldars, and I'd always been told that was impossible." He raised his glass. "To Adelena, queen of the impossible!"

"Impossible is for fools," Adele murmured, remembering another wizard who'd laughed at the word. She raised her own glass in the air and watched the bubbles sparkle up through the ale. After this terrible night, what else did she have to celebrate but more death? The dragon magic in her chest swirled a little in response to her sadness.

Rainere reached across the bar to touch the back of her hand. She could tell he was trying to comfort her, but it just made her want to cry.

They drank silently for a long moment, then she refilled everyone's glass.

"Where did you learn to pour such neat pints, Your Maj?" Charlie asked.

"I worked in pubs and bars when I was a university student on Earth," she replied, putting Charlie's fresh beer down on a tile coaster.

"I still find it hard to believe you had a whole life on a whole other planet before you became queen of Unisia," Charlie said, wonder coloring his voice. The ale was clearly softening him up.

"You and me both, kid."

"And I still can't believe that just this morning you were entering the cave of a dragon by yourself," Rainere said.

"I had the Queen's Guard with me, and they're game for anything despite most of them not having an ounce of magic in their bones. Of course, General Ohrig argues with me every step of the way, but they never stood back when I asked them to do the craziest things. It actually makes my skin crawl to think of everything I did just so we could get home quicker."

She raised her beer. "To the Queen's Guard, the brave men who follow their alien queen anywhere."

The three of them drank, but only Charlie chugged his and asked for another with a cheeky wink.

Adele laughed, glad to see Charlie's anger dissipate. She'd only known him a few months, meeting him for the first time at Belvoir Estate when he'd secretly come to steal the Fire Orchid stamens from her for the Boss. He'd failed at that and instead ended up as a go-between for Rainere and Adele when their relationship was still secret. Charlie might be young, but he was also incredibly brave and very loyal.

"We should still talk about what we're going to do next," Rainere said. "What do you want to tell the court at the Golden Palace?"

"Can't I just hope that everyone will be happy I got rid of the Eldars?" she asked, hazarding a grin. "And while I'm at it, I'll hope that the rest of the Eldars don't come back to Concordis on a revenge mission. How many live in the Eeyrie, anyway?"

"I really don't know," Rainere replied. "But if what Rip says is true about them needing a powerful demon, it won't be long before they come back to claim you."

"Then there's the little matter of Rip saying he's the real king," Charlie added, hiccupping and thumping his chest with a fist.

"We should expect retribution from the Eeyrie, but no more Eldars can be killed, or apparently we risk upsetting the balance of magic," Rainere continued as if Charlie hadn't spoken. "I knew magic was slowly degrading in Unisia but I had no idea it was so widespread. I'll need to do my own research on this."

Charlie set his glass back on the bar with an unsteady *thunk*. "Bartender, another round for all me friends."

Adele threw a dishcloth over her shoulder. "Nope, I'm cutting you off," she said, and laughed at his drunken protest.

Rainere's hands clenched into fists on the bar, looking unamused by their banter. "You should send Jordansson home," he snapped.

Adele quickly lost her light feeling. "Look, Jordansson is just a boy with a lot of ambition. He wanted to get out of his shitty little village in the Ice Mountains and see the world. He also wants to be a father to Dahk'hani and my king. Which is ridiculous, of course."

"Adelena, there's something I should've told you already." Rainere took her hand in his. "The goddess Serena came to me in a vision when I was in Hell. She told me that Dahk'hani was going to make you have his baby and that it would be an abomination. She said that

I needed to protect you from him. She was very clear that you needed me, not this village boy."

"It's nice to know that I'm not the only one getting holy visits," she said, eyebrows high. "Should I be jealous?"

Charlie started laughing. "Ask him who you should be really jealous of, Your Maj. Ask him who he had his hands on when he should have been watching the kids." He belched loudly and his eyes crossed. "Ooh, that's me done."

Rainere stood to catch Charlie as he fell off his barstool. He slumped him onto a nearby armchair, and the look he threw Adele had an accusatory edge.

"He got drunk so fast," she said, wishing she were tipsy too. "He'd only had a couple."

"I suppose it wasn't wise to encourage a boy with a head injury to drink," Rainere said. "But at least we can talk frankly now."

Adele came out from behind the bar and wandered across the room to take a chair at a table by a darkened window. She wiped a cloth over the sticky surface before setting her elbows down.

"Sweet Christ, if only Rip didn't have his big 'I am the real king' confession in front of everyone tonight," she said. "I refuse to believe that I need to live in the Eeyrie. Yet I'm sure Lord Orgustus will take full advantage of the doubt to call himself regent again. Whatever way I look at it, I'm always just going to be the demon usurper sitting on their throne."

Rainere spun the chair opposite Adele to sit astride it. "Darling, why don't we take the children and leave Unisia? You won't have to be queen, and I won't have to watch my back, expecting to see a knife in it every day. We can be free."

His words surprised her and Adele sat quietly for a moment, listening to Charlie's snores and dreaming of a pleasant future with Rainere. "There's always the little problem of the gods' plan," she said finally. "And I have no idea how we're going to get out of this, Rainere."

He took her hands in his. "Then promise me what we face next, we face together. Don't let anything come between us again, my love."

"I promise." She leaned across the table, and for a moment she wasn't sure if Rainere would lean in to meet her. She watched him hesitate and then tilt his head. Their first kiss after the long separation was soft and tasted like bitter ale.

MY ANGEL, THIS IS NOT THE MAN I CHOSE FOR US. Out of nowhere, Dahk'hani's voice smashed into her head and his invisible hands yanked at her shoulders. She whimpered in pain.

Rainere was crouched by her chair in an instant. "*Cara mia*, talk to me," he ordered. "What is it?"

"I love . . . Rainere," she whispered, her eyes still closed against the pressure of Dahk'hani in her head.

NO! HE IS SERENA'S SERVANT. The passion in the words shook her whole body.

"I love you too, *cara mia*," Rainere said, and pulled her hands from her face. "Darling, you must tell me what pains you."

Dahk'hani, please don't hurt him, she begged the god. "Rainere, Dahk'hani is inside—" Her lips pressed closed, her jaw rigid, and she couldn't get another word out.

"Adelena, I will never let it come to that." Rainere wrapped his warm arms around her. "I'll find a way to protect you from the god, I promise on my life and yours."

The invisible hands rippled on her shoulders, and her magics spiked on their own as the shout *HE IS FIERCE AND HIS RAGE IS STRONG,* scraped through her brain. *I CLAIM HIM FOR US.*

"Jordansson was told that he was fated since birth to bring Dahk'hani back into the world, but I'll deny him," Adele managed to whisper, wondering how to communicate with Rainere to let him know the god was in her head and listening to them. "But nothing is ever as it seems, Rainere. Look in my eyes."

Rainere's eyes flashed with jealousy, and the silver circles spun around his irises. "What is it you think I'll see?" he asked.

Horrified, Adele could only think, *For God's sake, can't he feel Dahk'hani through the Mark?*

DON'T BE FRIGHTENED, ANGEL. I CONTROL YOU NOW. Adele felt the god's hands squeeze her tighter.

Rainere stared at her for so long she thought that he might see the deity holding her frozen, but he murmured, "*Cara mia,* one kiss isn't enough. I want all of you."

NOW, ANGEL. WE TAKE HIM.

The dragon magic flared, and Adele knew she couldn't resist it this time. Pulling out of Rainere's arms, she raced up the stairs to the Boss's office. Her thoughts filled with wild images of sex and a crushing need to have Rainere beneath her. Rainere collected the unconscious Charlie and followed close behind her.

Chapter Four

"Taking What Is Offered"

Rainere felt awkward carrying Charlie from the portal wardrobe back through the secret passages of the Golden Palace. Over the course of the last few weeks, he'd developed something like feelings, or at least *a* feeling, toward Charlie. So when he cradled the tall teenager against his chest, he tried not to let the boy's sore head knock against the dusty walls.

The royal apartment was quiet when they returned through the secret passage's door in the queen's bedchamber. Several candelabras were lit to soften the darkness, and the scent of Adelena's signature perfume hung in the air, perhaps sprayed by a night maid to welcome her home. Rainere guessed that she would want to go and find her children soon, but he hoped they wouldn't have to return to Lord Orgustus's apartment, where the unconscious Jordansson slept. It didn't seem like Adelena held any affection for the tribesman, but the threat of Jordansson impregnating her made his teeth grind.

Adelena led the way into the vast bathing room attached to her bedchamber. The light of the lanterns reflected off the polished brass taps and tub, and underfloor heating warmed the tiles pleasantly. "Let's put Charlie on this big sofa by the door," she said and grimaced. "He'll probably need the toilet straight after he wakes."

He laid Charlie down, and Adelena hovered over him. "He looks so young, doesn't he?" she whispered, brushing a lock of hair from his forehead. "Little orphan Charlie. I'd hoped that I could give him a better life than I have so far."

"*Cara mia*, Charlie is not a child." He felt jealous enough to pull her away from the handsome teenager. "And I'm not sure you realize just how loyal he is. He understood that you had no choice in what you did tonight."

Adelena shook off his arms, and he felt a surge of anxiety as he watched her cross the room. The last time he'd had her legs wrapped around him, her gold magic had fought his touch. *But her magic hadn't fought Dahk'hani*, he thought bitterly. He could still remember the violence of her orgasms that had plagued him through the Mark while she was on her journey. *But how can I be in love with Adelena and never make love to her?*

Charlie groaned in his sleep, and Rainere placed a waste bin next to the couch. Charlie's hair flopped over his forehead again. *He does look young*, he thought, *but he is Marchant as sure as I am, and our magic does not allow the luxury of innocence.*

He was distracted by a loud gushing sound as Adelena turned on a shower. The water was tinted pink straight out of the tap, and the steam was scented with a floral perfume. Rainere felt the gravity of lust pull him toward her, watching as she shed her filthy clothes and ducked under the hot water. His eyes traveled her naked back, and there he saw a shimmering line, then another and yet another. It was like a spell diagram dancing across her skin.

"*Cara mia*, let me just—" Fascinated, he reached to touch the lines of light, but the diagram disappeared as she washed it with a handful of sponge. With the dim light reflecting on the bubbles, he thought that perhaps he'd just imagined it.

"Sweet Christ, I can't tell you how much I've missed hot showers." Adele scrubbed soap through her hair and then rinsed it out, eyes closed in ecstasy. "I can't wait to smell good again!"

When his queen groaned, the sound was so carnal that Rainere didn't wait for permission to join her. He kicked off his boots and stepped onto the tiles. *She's thinner,* he thought, running a hand over her narrow ribcage. *That damn journey to Sighmere has worn her out and I'll have to make her strong again.*

Concentrating on his examination, it took a moment before he noticed that Adelena was smiling up at him, her wet fingers already undoing his shirt buttons. Both his body and his magic lurched with excitement. After so long waiting for his lover, she was finally back in his arms.

"I've never forgotten that night in the bathroom at your Gray Palace, Rainere. Do you remember it?" she murmured. "It was just before I left you to go to Belvoir Estate for that stupid horse carnival. That was the night I discovered what I could really do to you." She pressed kisses against his collarbone and pushed the shirt over his shoulders, letting it fall in a wet heap to the floor. "That was the night that I knew what you were for."

What I was for? Rainere paused, feeling a twinge of alarm, but decided to ignore it. "*Cara mia,* let me take you to the bedroom," he said, but Adelena continued kissing his chest, moving to softly bite one nipple, then the other.

He glanced at the open bathroom door and Charlie draped on the couch beside it. It was very unlike her to risk being caught in this way. "Darling, Charlie might wake," he protested, but she just reached back and turned up the water so it pounded more forcefully on the tiles, clouds of steam cascading around them.

Then her hands were on his leather pants, pulling at the lacings, while her tongue chased the grooves of his chest. He closed his eyes, craving the dangerous pleasure of making love to Adelena. When she siphoned the magic from his flesh, the song of Serena rang in his ears, and every moment was pure, unadulterated joy.

The top of Adelena's head barely touched his chin, but Rainere knew her power over him was absolute. Whispering the charm that disintegrated the rest of his clothes into feathers of fabric, he collapsed to his knees, and she pushed him the rest of the way onto his back, crooning words of powerful Commands that she didn't even need. Already conquered by kisses, he was hers.

Rainere didn't feel the floor beneath him or feel the warm spray of water on his legs. Every sense was taken up by Adelena as she swung astride his hips, her hands traveling the skin of his chest like they were trying to claw their way inside. She unleashed her magic and he gasped at the agony. It felt like little knives were cutting him. When he looked down, he saw her fingertips lit with white magic, and the diagram of light shifting over her breasts.

Even in pain, Rainere anticipated the pleasure to come, moaning his relief when a rush of her terrible and wonderful power drenched his brain. The magical orgasm built higher and higher as his own glittering green magic was pulled from his body by Adelena's desire. Pinned to the ground by Commands, Rainere could only turn his head a little. Through half-closed eyes he saw Adelena frantically working the magic out of his chest. *She's going to kill me.* The thought was fuzzy, but Rainere clung to it. *Nothing so dangerous should feel this good.* He became aware there was no song of the goddess singing in his ears, just the sound of his own harsh breathing as Adelena moved over his body. He tried to keep a grasp on his senses. *Adelena . . . can't control the magic . . . so I must.*

Internally, Rainere snatched back a thread of his own magic from his lover. Like a trickle of cold water tracing its way into his mind, he felt the intoxicating lust dilute and found the strength to sit up.

"*Cara mia.*" Rainere's voice was only a rasp, but his grip was strong when he caught up her hands. "Enough!"

Muttering a defensive spell, he watched the war between three magics rage in Adelena's eyes. Her beautiful face transformed into something ugly and unfamiliar as she fought him in a fury of lust. She managed to pull one hand loose and used it to guide his cock inside her. At the sensation of her warm, wet heat riding him, he was undone again. He let her go and fell back on his elbows. Adelena's orgasm was immediate, her muscles rippling around him as her hands circled his throat, squeezing. In exquisite agony, he cried out her name as his own orgasm claimed him.

Gasping for air, Rainere saw the exact moment when Adelena—*his* Adelena—broke through the magic and returned to herself. The hard line of her lips softened to the rosebud that he knew, her cheekbones receded into her heart-shaped face, and the hands around his neck relaxed. She threw herself against him with a sob, their chests heaving together.

"That—that was amazing!" Adelena groaned, and he felt her tongue licking the pulse on his neck. "You were incredible, my love. Just incredible."

Rainere couldn't believe it was over and he was still alive. He winced as sweat from both their bodies chafed his burns.

"Darling?" She didn't like his silence, and he saw the worry when she pulled back. "I was, sort of, gone for a minute. The rings in your eyes are tarnished, but I didn't hurt you, did I?"

After the thrall of passion, Rainere's forgiveness was instant, and he cupped her face in his hands. He saw in that tear-soaked gaze her love for him, strong and true. This was what he believed in. The rest was just magic.

"I never want to hurt you, Rainere." Adelena's colorless tears fell over his fingers, and he wiped them on his stomach, healing the angry streaks of red she hadn't yet noticed.

"You didn't hurt me, darling," he lied. "At least, no more than I like you to."

"There's something you're not telling me," she said, sitting back on her heels. "I don't deserve you, Rainere, not if I hurt you instead of pleasing you."

"*Cara mia*, enough." He pulled her in for a gentle, tender kiss. "I'm naked on the bathroom floor with you, how could I not be happy?"

She finally gave him a smile, and, with a quick glance down, he was relieved to see that her tears had worked their healing magic on some of the welts.

"Darling, there is *something* else inside of me now," she said hesitantly, like he might not have noticed. "It could be from drinking so much of Sighmere's tear, or maybe I was infected when I invaded Jordansson, and now Dah—" She coughed. "I feel so full up with magic—it's screaming around inside, and I can't hear the Chime Voices anymore. They've gone, and without them I have no idea how to control myself."

Rainere gathered Adelena's wet hair off her shoulders, where it splayed in black tendrils. "I will teach you control, darling."

"But Rainere, this magic is so much stronger than me," she whispered, burying her face in his neck again. "You'll need to tell me when I'm being a monster."

"I will," he promised, shifting a little so she wasn't pressing on his burns.

"But how? When the three magics are working, I can't hear myself think. How will I hear you?"

Rainere had no idea. The fact that his internal organs felt like they'd been barbecued wasn't helping his concentration. "If only we knew someone familiar with demons and their magic," he murmured, but he didn't think Adelena was listening as she crawled off his lap and fetched a couple of towels for them from a pile by the sunken bathtub. She spied Charlie on the couch.

"Oh, God, did we just have sex in front of Charlie?"

Rainere felt a stab of fear, wondering how long the magics had been driving her tonight? And how, in the name of the goddess, was he supposed to protect Adelena from magic inside her own body?

He got up off the wet floor and wrapped the towel around his waist. "Charlie is sound asleep, and I'm going to go to bed too." He raised his hands to stave off her protests. "And not because you caused me injury, but because I'm exhausted."

"At least sleep in the Glass Bed. I know it'll cause a scandal, but just for tonight, please," she begged. "I need you close to me." And because she was only wearing a damp towel and a smile, Rainere couldn't resist.

Ignoring his pain, he swung Adelena up into his arms and carried her into the bedchamber and to the great Glass Bed, dropping
her among the dozens of small decorative pillows that were stacked
against the cut-glass headboard. With a wild sweep that made her
giggle, he knocked a swath of cushions to the floor, then rolled himself onto the silk sheets spread-eagled and pulled her to his side. As
soon as his head hit the pillow, Rainere nuzzled her neck, inhaling the
scent of flowers in her damp hair. "I'm so glad you're home, my love,"
he whispered, and then let sleep drag him off.

CHAPTER FIVE

"Then There Was Breakfast"

Adele waited until Rainere's breathing evened out to the big, heavy gusts that told her he was sound asleep. It didn't take long. She carefully moved out of his arms and sat up to examine his torso. The mysterious red streaks were there from earlier, but they didn't look like nail marks or ordinary scratches—the puckered skin looked more like burns. She examined herself for the same marks, but there weren't any. *Of course not. I've hurt him like I always do when the magic goes crazy. Why did I think it would be any better with this dragon magic running the show?* she thought, hating that this time the lust had overwhelmed her to the point that she'd even blacked out.

Never again, though. Nothing is going to make me destroy the man I love, Adele warned all her magics and Dahk'hani as well, if he was still in her head listening. She leaned down, her lips brushing the dark stubble on Rainere's jaw, and then slipped off the bed, scattering more cushions to the floor.

Adele found an ankle-length silk chemise draped over a nearby armchair. She slipped it over her head, then pulled on the matching velvet robe lined with pale pink silk, roses embroidered on the back and sleeves. She stepped into a pair of jewel-green satin slippers with feathered pom-poms on the toe. Smiling to herself, she remembered that just a day ago, she would've rolled out of a canvas sleeping sack still wearing the same stinking clothes and boots.

Tying her damp hair back with a pink ribbon, Adele left the bedroom, closing the door softly behind her. Still thinking about campfires and sleeping rough, the luxury of her royal apartment struck her anew. Her slippers sank into the purple-and-gold carpet as she crossed the expansive living room, dodging groups of over-stuffed sofas and armchairs covered in sumptuous fabrics. The giant, stained-glass chandeliers were still glowing, and vases of fresh-cut flowers rested on every flat surface. The air was redolent with the cit-rusy incense smoke that kept insects from flying in the three sets of open balcony doors. When she looked out, the sky was already a pale denim blue, as if washed by last night's storm and dried by the rays of a fresh sun.

Adele made her way over to the mahogany dining table set into a space framed by a huge bay window. The table was big enough to seat twenty people and polished to a mirror finish. At the head, where she always sat, was a pile of paperwork in Majordomo Tilburn's hand-writing, and copies of what passed for a newspaper in Concordis, usually only a short, scrolled page detailing births, deaths, and mar-riages in the city and a little about any upcoming events or scandals.

She shuffled the colorfully inked copies until a headline caught her eye. "What Will the Usurper Do Next?" There was an illustration showing a frowning Queen Adelena and a dark figure she presumed to be Prince Rainere, with only half a face, lurking behind her. She huffed a sigh. The population of Concordis had never liked having an alien queen foisted on them by the High Wizard Council, and she'd borne the brunt of their hatred for as long as she'd sat on the throne.

"Your Majesty, can I get you anything?"

She had heard the steward, Turner, approach but it was bad form to acknowledge his existence until he spoke. The three stewards of the royal apartment, Turner, Hollis, and Franks, liked to consider them-selves completely invisible despite their garish purple-and-green uniforms and the fact that they remained stationed at one of the two alcoves set in the wall by the front door all day and night.

"Tea and toast would be great, thanks," she answered. She gave her steward a closer look. He had olive skin and eyes so brown they could've been black. "If you don't mind me asking, Turner, are you feeling better now? I'd heard you were unwell while I was away."

A slight frown creased Turner's forehead, and his square jaw flexed. "Your Majesty is kind to inquire," he replied. "I am quite well. I suffered a simple case of intestinal poisoning due to Mr. Shale wanting to steal my steward uniform and take my place on duty to get close to the royal children."

Adele tried to hide her shock at both Rip's tactics and the fact that he'd succeeded. "That was a nasty thing to do," she said.

But Turner was more embarrassed than angry. "It was partly my own fault, Your Majesty," he said. "I'm never sick, so I should have suspected something was amiss when I couldn't get out of bed. A steward must be aware of every person he encounters, and not just in the royal apartment. It is an honored role we perform and learning to recognize nefarious political plots is part of our training."

"Well, don't be too hard on yourself," she said. "Mr. Shale is a particularly powerful wizard. If it's any consolation to you, he won't be visiting anytime soon."

"That is a consolation, thank you, Your Majesty." Turner bowed, indicating that the allotted time for polite conversation had ended. "Tea and toast are on their way, Your Majesty." He returned to his post.

Adele sat back in her chair. She wanted to be angry but an image of Rip's grief-stricken face drifted through her mind, and the guilt returned. *Ripenzo is a liar and wanted to be king of Unisia,* she reminded herself then had to add, *but he did also save my children from certain death, and I can't forget that he rescued Charlie and Leafy from the mines as well. I suppose he was trying in his own way to be a good brother and a decent uncle. If only I could trust him. I'd love to have more family.*

Shaking off her wishful thinking, Adele began to wonder when

Mrs. Ollenby would bring her children back to her. Triggered by her worry, the dragon magic was even quicker to respond than yesterday, activating her two other magics and racing through her veins. Thankfully, she was distracted by the sound of a loud yawn and got up from her chair to see who had been sleeping in her lounge room.

"Lord Orgustus?" she said, surprised as the young lord sat up, rubbing his head and groaning in pain. Then she spotted the glass and empty bottle of Firewhiskey on a low table next to him and answered her own question. "Your panic got the better of you, I see."

Adele had never spoken with Lord Orgustus outside of some very uncomfortable meetings and the occasional awkward dance at a ball. He'd hated her from the minute she arrived in Unisia, and the feeling had become mutual. He finally heaved himself to his feet, coming to join Adele at the dining table but politely waited until she gestured for him to sit.

"Your Majesty, you have my most sincere apologies for the presumption," he croaked, twitching his collar straight and tucking his white shirt back into his trousers. "I couldn't sleep with the screaming of the Eldars and that goddess-awful storm. The Eldars stopped a few hours ago, and I didn't know if you'd vanquished them or they you. Drinking myself into a stink seemed a sensible way to combat the terror. Completely stupid, of course."

Orgustus stopped talking long enough for three maids to approach with an enormous tea set between them. They laid out racks of toast cooked to a variety of brown hues, pots of different jams, honey, and savory spreads, curls of butter served on small, flat blocks of ice, jugs of cold milk, jugs of hot milk, and an enormous silver urn of tea steeped to perfection. The porcelain plates were painted with pictures of flowers and birds, the silverware polished to a high shine. So very far from tin cups and stewed tea made over a campfire. Adele sighed with pleasure and reached for the toast, signaling that they could both begin.

Lord Orgustus was on his second cup of sweet, milky tea when he spoke again. "Aren't there normally a hundred people at your table for breakfast, Your Majesty?" he asked. "I've heard that you like to eat with the entire Queen's Guard and all your children, even the nannies and the high wizard himself sitting cheek by jowl."

Adele spread berry jam in a thick layer on her toast. "I usually have to start my meetings in the mornings, and I wouldn't see the children at all if I didn't include them," she replied.

Orgustus sipped his tea. She could see he was feeling much more coherent now, and his questions would soon start. She honestly wondered what she should tell him, considering he knew too much about her now, thanks to Ripenzo Shale's big mouth.

"If I could be so presumptuous, may I inquire as to the current whereabouts of the Marchant prince, Your Majesty?" Lord Orgustus asked, his pompous tone grating on Adele's nerves as always.

"You know, I generally keep my breakfast meetings informal," she told him. "So, unless you're arguing with me, you don't need to be so polite."

Orgustus snorted and needed a napkin to wipe the spray of tea from his chin. "My apologies, Your Majesty," he said. "You took me a little by surprise."

"And you probably want to get on with it, before everyone joins us." They both looked at the front door to the apartment as if Adele's family or the Queen's Guard might leap through it at any moment.

"Where's Prince Rainere?" Orgustus asked again.

"He's asleep in my bed." Adele didn't watch for the lord's reaction but buttered some more toast.

"And the Marchant boy, Charlie Row?"

"He's asleep in the bathroom."

"And Ripenzo Shale?"

Here Adele hesitated. Lord Orgustus's expression was intent on hers, his cornflower-blue eyes filled with concern, but she knew who he was most concerned for—himself.

"Ripenzo Shale has made a noble sacrifice," she answered, wishing it were true. "He's gone back to the Marchant Eldars and will remain with them, giving them no further reason to leave the Eeyrie. He's given up his right to challenge me for the crown."

"And what of the gray crystal mine at Mount Ecrusius?" Orgustus asked. "Surely we cannot keep that hideous place open? And yet without it, how will we replace our production of the Gift of Life for the immortal wizards? Won't the Marchant Eldars come looking for you again when they run out of the Gift?"

These questions were much easier for her to answer. "The mines will be closed, and I will task High Wizard Ohren to replace the method of production with something much more sustainable. Until then, no one will be allowed to torture and misuse the children of Concordis, no matter the color of their magic."

"On that we are in complete accord, Your Majesty. Wonderful news." He was clearly relieved, and it pleased Adele that they were having their first proper conversation without shouting. They crunched their toast in silence before she saw him fidgeting again. She knew that he wasn't stupid, and he'd quickly examined all the contingencies of her answer about Ripenzo Shale. She braced herself for the obvious question.

"Did Mr. Ripenzo Shale go quite, well, willingly back to his family in the Eeyrie?" Orgustus fiddled with his teacup, not looking at her. "It's just that last night, he'd seemed very much in favor of *you* going to them and I just wonder—"

Fortunately, Adele was saved from having to answer by a bare-chested, barefoot, seven-foot-tall Jordan Jordansson bounding into the room, led by a steward and followed by two maids holding what were probably his shirt, jacket, and shoes in their arms.

"Queen Adelena!" Jordansson strode over to embrace her where she sat. He pulled her chin up with a finger and looked into her eyes, studying them intently. "I did not dream it, then. I went inside you for the spell, and you took my magic for yourself—I can see it right there with the others." He let her chin drop. "How do you feel?"

Adele poured Jordansson a cup of tea, guessing he'd like milk and sugar, while he greeted Lord Orgustus with a friendly punch on the arm and took the seat next to her.

"Actually, I feel awful," she admitted, handing the man his tea. "Your magic is getting mixed up with mine in a horrible way. I'd like to see if I can give it back to you, if you'll let me try?"

Jordansson took a handful of toast and dumped it on his plate. "You must be feeling very horrible to want to return my magic to me." He laughed loudly, elbowing Orgustus in the ribs. "She does not ask for permission normally when it comes to magic. But tell me, please, what do I do with these flat bits of bread?"

Adele pushed the butter and jams toward Jordansson's plate. "Proper food will be here soon," she said by way of apology. After camping together for a week, she knew her friend was always ravenous in the mornings. "Jordansson, I'm serious. We need to get this magic out of me right after breakfast."

Jordansson leaned over and laid a wet kiss on her cheek. "It will not be now, Queen," he said. "First, I have a dream I need to tell you."

"This better not be about Dahk'hani," Adele warned him, and felt an answering jolt in her gut at saying the god's name. "Because you're in Serena country now, Jordansson, and I will not tolerate any talk about what Dahk'hani wants or doesn't want."

Jordansson rolled his eyes as if she were being cute but exasperating. "Dahk'hani's will is my will," he said. "And the dream was very amazing. We must lie together soon and make the child."

"I'm sorry, but that won't be possible." Lord Orgustus was affronted on behalf of Adele. "There is a protocol to these things. If you wish to marry the queen, first you must apply in writing, then she must agree to interviews, your pedigree will be analyzed . . ."

Jordansson blinked as Lord Orgustus listed everything the tribesman would have to do to apply for the position of queen's husband. He looked to Adele, but she just shrugged. This was how the Unisians did everything, with meetings and paperwork until the end of time.

"No, no!" Jordansson clasped Orgustus's arm to get him to stop talking. "I will take the queen to my bed and worship her until a babe is made. I don't need to write a letter. She knows my god wants this."

It was Orgustus's turn to look incredulous. She shrugged again. It was the Jordani way in the Tribe of the Three Sisters—the men worshipped women, and babies were made.

"Jordansson, I'm sorry, but there won't be any possibility of worshipping me," Adele said firmly.

"You cannot ignore a god, my queen," Jordansson replied, just as firmly. "My cock is strong—it won't take long to make a babe."

"The queen has Prince Rainere in her bed right now," Orgustus spluttered. "Did you know that?"

Jordansson gave Adele a knowing wink. "The bad prince," he said and chuckled. "So, you took him back even when he always makes you cry. You told me about him when we shared our night together in the forest. Remember?"

Adele sipped her tea, trying to stay calm. "It's actually none of your business who's in my bed."

"You're right, Queen," Jordansson agreed. "Tell me a night that I can have you when he isn't there. I can wait."

Lord Orgustus choked on his tea for a second time.

Knowing she had to nip this in the bud, she tried to find the words that Jordansson would understand. His King's Tongue was excellent, but he had no idea how different their cultures were. "Jordansson, we're not in the mountains, we're in the Golden Palace. It would be very dangerous for you if I took you up on your offer," she explained. "So I will *never* let you worship me, all right?"

"Not all right," Jordansson disagreed. "How will we make our god-baby without lying together?"

"I don't want to make a god-baby," she replied. "And don't talk about us making anything together in front of Prince Rainere." She held Jordansson's gaze so he would understand this clearly. "He will hurt you, my friend, and I won't be able to protect you."

Jordansson frowned, his white-blond eyebrows scrunching together on his broad, handsome face. "The bad prince is a violent man?"

"He can be," Adele reluctantly agreed. "He's also very jealous."

"Jealous?" Jordansson's eyebrows now went up. "But you own your body. What man can tell you what to do with it?"

Adele thought about this and then felt uncomfortable. "We—I mean, it's complicated. I mean, I'm jealous too, I guess . . ."

Jordansson grinned at her stammering. "It is foolish to think you own a person's body. Every man and woman is free to be worshipped as they want."

Dammit, I hate that he's actually right, Adele thought, and tried to finish the conversation. "But I love Prince Rainere and only want him to worship me. That's my choice, Jordansson."

"It is not the choice Dahk'hani has made for you," Jordansson said, with a wink at a gaping Orgustus like he was a co-conspirator.

"And your god doesn't own me either." Adele lit up when she saw her children enter the apartment behind Mrs. Ollenby and rushed her last words. "I do what I want, with who I want. End of discussion."

"No, it's not the end," Jordansson told Lord Orgustus now that Adele had leaped to her feet and run to greet her children. "It is fate that the queen and I will bring Dahk'hani back to the world. Let me tell you how Dahk'hani told me in my dream last night . . ."

Jordansson's retelling of his very sexual dream was interrupted when Adele and Mrs. Ollenby brought the children to join the breakfast table. She was so happy to hug and kiss them all, the relief of having them safe and whole bringing tears to her eyes. Adele made sure the little orphan Leafy was swept into the joyful reunion with her three children. Rainere had told her he'd taken on her care, and to Adele that made Leafy family. Soon after the children arrived, a long line of servants flowed into the royal apartment pushing silver trolleys piled with breakfast foods and beverages, table linens, and silverware. The table was set for twenty people and heaving with a huge buffet in the time it took to get the children settled on chairs and Adele to find a handkerchief. She held Aaron on her lap. Natalie sat at her side, with Leafy next to her, and little Stella had climbed up on Jordansson's lap as if they were old friends. The children's three large puppies ran around the table, diving between servants and chairs, causing their usual chaos.

"Where's Prince Rainere?" Natalie asked, her voice squeaky with fatigue.

"In the Glass Bed," Adele said, giving her daughter another shoulder squeeze. "It took all night to chase the Eldars away, so he's very tired. Charlie's still asleep too."

Natalie repeated Adele's words to Leafy, as if she might not understand the King's Tongue. Leafy nodded and wrapped a knitted lavender blanket around her shoulders. Adele wasn't surprised that the little girl needed a security blanket after the trauma she'd been through.

Despite the fact that Lord Orgustus had imprisoned Jordansson in Hell along with Adele and her QGs the day they'd returned from the Ice Mountains, the two men seemed to be getting along well now, so Adele gave the children her full attention until her Queen's Guard entered the apartment. They had made their way to the table before the second steward, Franks, could finish announcing them.

QG Bear gave Franks a friendly slap on the back. "At ease, man," he said. "She knows who we are."

"Up already, guys?" Adele was pleased to see her Queen's Guard looking well rested, dressed in clean uniforms, and all freshly shaved. "Didn't think I'd see you this early. Sleep well?"

"I slept like a baby, Your Majesty," General Ohrig replied. "That's to say, I woke up screaming every few hours and needed a stiff drink to fall asleep again."

Adele laughed, but Ohrig had spotted Lord Orgustus at the table, and he raised a bushy gray eyebrow in query.

"Gentlemen, Lord Orgustus is at breakfast with us this morning," she announced, just to get any discomfort out of the way. "And he has been fully informed that breakfast is not a time for politics but for informal discussion and eating bacon."

"I don't like bacon," Aaron said, making Adele smile in surprise.

"But you love bacon, honey."

"No." Aaron shook his head. "Prince Rainere told me that bacon is a pig, and pigs are nice animals. I can't eat animals who are my friends."

"But if you don't eat animals, how will you get big and strong, tiny prince?" Jordansson asked, his voice booming. "You do not want to be so small forever."

"I'm Aaron and I'm four years old," Aaron said and frowned at the shirtless tribesman. "Who're you?"

"Children, this is Jordan Jordansson," Adele said. "He's a very brave warrior and hunter from the Jordani people of the Three Sisters Tribe in the Ice Mountains. He helped me find the medicine to heal Stella. See, that's why Stella likes him so much."

Natalie wasn't impressed. "Why aren't you wearing a shirt?" she asked Jordansson. "I'm six years old and so's Leafy and we know it's not polite to be naked."

"I'm twenty-four years old," Jordansson said, grinning at what he probably thought was a social custom, introducing his age, "And all of the clothes they have given me are too tight and make me hot. I live in the lands of snow, you know."

"I don't like you." Natalie narrowed her hazel eyes at the huge tribesman. "Prince Rainere is my favorite."

Jordansson tilted his head, confused. "But children always like me," he said.

"Natalie, a princess is never rude to her guests," Adele warned, frowning. "You should apologize right now to Mr. Jordansson."

"I'm sorry," Natalie said quickly. But she began whispering with Leafy, the two little girls sending Jordansson dark looks.

Adele wasn't sure what she'd hoped for, reuniting with her

children after such a long time away from them. She understood that what they had endured was going to have a lasting effect, but she also expected them to want to cling to her a little more—at least as much as she wanted to cling to them. But it seemed they were just cranky.

"Your Majesty." Ohrig's call interrupted Adele's worrying. "I take it congratulations are in order for your success in chasing off the Marchant Eldars last night? It must have been easy work if you're looking so well this morning."

Adele took a sip of cold tea.

"I think we found a solution." She dreaded explaining herself to her men, worried, as always, what they would think of her ruthless actions. Sensing fear, her three magics swirled together, causing her vision to blur. She could hardly see the teacup in her hands as green sparks flowed from her fingertips. Trying to shake them off, she dropped the cup, splashing Aaron and making him screech.

"Oh, Your Majesty, let me help!" Mrs. Ollenby was immediately by her side. "Never mind, accidents happen."

Still trying to control the magic, Adele let Aaron wriggle off her lap.

"Your Majesty?" Mrs. Ollenby leaned in, hiding her from the table of spectators.

"Just give me a minute." Adele's voice was rough with the effort of suppressing the violent magic. *They don't listen to me at all! The dragon magic is controlling my green and gold, and I'm just a goddamn . . . vessel.* The thought was frightening, and she tucked it away to consider later when she didn't have such a concerned audience watching her every move.

"Queen?" Jordansson's large hand made her arm look like a twig as he stroked her gently. "You all right now?"

Adele snatched her arm away when the magics surged again. "Thank you, I'm fine." She forced herself to smile down the table at the eight men staring at her. "I'm fine! It's just a . . . complication from the magic I took from Jordansson last night when we healed Stella together. Nothing serious."

General Ohrig beetled his brows over pale blue eyes. She knew he hated mysteries caused by magic, especially when they affected his queen.

"I always knew that Jordansson wouldn't be a good match for you," Captain Lucky said, sounding vindicated. "Imagine if we'd been out in the field and Her Majesty had had this type of 'complication'? It's clear their magics are too different."

"Come on, everyone, eat." Adele waved her hands, trying to dispel the tension that had fallen over her table. "This is our first breakfast that isn't half-cooked porridge sprinkled with grit. Let's enjoy!"

QG Owens laughed. "I'll never miss Pepper's camp cooking, that's for certain."

"Oi! I did my best with you lot of whingers," QG Pepper protested, pretending to be offended, but it didn't last long, and soon everyone was piling plates high and chatting. Once she was sure the men were happy, Adele noticed that the little girls had left the table. She panicked for just a moment before she saw Natalie leading Rainere by the hand from the royal bedchamber. He was already dressed: a black silk shirt, and fine woolen trousers tucked into his boots. Rainere took a seat at the opposite end of the table and sent her his gorgeous half smile in greeting.

"I'm sorry, Your Highness," she called down to him. "I wanted you to get a little more rest, but it looks like Princess Natalie had other ideas."

Rainere pulled Natalie onto his lap with a hug, and she helped serve him tea—black, no sugar—and a pile of fried potatoes with onions and eggs. Charlie was next to come out of her bedchamber, still rubbing his eyes, with Leafy holding his other hand. He found a seat in the middle of the Queen's Guard and took their ribbing about his messy hair and stinking clothes with sleepy good humor.

"Feeling all right, Charlie?" Adele asked. "You can go back to bed if you like."

Charlie took the tea that QG Leith had poured for him, but

his hazel eyes were drilling Adele in a way that made her feel very uncomfortable. "I'm fit as a fiddle," he answered. "How're you feeling, Your Maj?"

"Her Majesty is suffering from a complication with the magic that Jordansson forced on her last night when they were healing Princess Stella together," Captain Lucky informed him. "The very thing that I warned her about not too long ago."

"Lucky, we get it! But now it's done, and I need to get it undone," Adele said. Too well, she remembered the night in the Ice Mountains when Lucky had given her that warning and offered her his own body and magic to fuel her strength. She really didn't feel comfortable reliving that moment with Rainere sitting down at the end of the table. He'd always had a jealousy of Captain Lucky that she thought was oddly misplaced. Lucky was a loyal and deeply moral man who would never even attempt to flirt with his queen.

"Have you told everyone what you did to Rip?" Charlie asked, and his voice cracked a little, though his expression was cold.

"Charlie, why don't we eat first, and then I'll give a full briefing after the children have—"

But Charlie wasn't waiting on niceties. "Then you've already told them you killed those Eldars, did you?"

Every man fell silent. *All right then, I guess I tell them now.* Adele took a deep breath and tried to hold on to the magics rising with her anger. "Last night, Ripenzo Shale made the ultimate sacrifice," she began.

"Come on, my sweet poppets! Breakfast is finished!" Standing up with a clap, Mrs. Ollenby scooted around the table and collected the four children. They protested at leaving their mother until Adele kissed each of them on the head and promised to join them after she was done.

Reluctantly she turned back to the table, only to hear Jordansson ask, "But wasn't he a good man, this Shale? He saved the children from death, no?"

Sweet Christ, shut up, Jordansson! she thought, but said, "You all heard Ripenzo say he thought himself to be the Lost Child of the Prophecy of the End of the World, but where was his proof? He told me I had to go to the Eeyrie to feed the Eldars but, again, where was his proof? He gave us nothing but a bunch of baseless stories and then he betrayed me!"

She took a deep, gasping breath, and her fingertips gripped the table edge tightly. The three magics were trying to ride her emotions again. She couldn't let them take over while she was trying to convince her men that what she had done was right. Even now, the lines between good and evil were blurring, and she was second-guessing herself.

"Shale wanted your throne." Lord Orgustus broke the silence that had fallen over the table. "So you had to get rid of him."

"No, that's not it." Adele tried again to explain herself. "Ripenzo is a liar and a thief and he was working with my enemy. The Eldars I killed will teach those left in the Eeyrie not to underestimate the queen of Unisia again."

"Rip told you not to kill them," Charlie said, and anger trembled in his voice.

"The Eldars are too dangerous," she said, shaking her head. "Even Rip said they'd kill Aaron and steal Natalie from me."

"Rip wasn't your enemy." Charlie stood up.

"He was working with the Eldars." She could only whisper with the effort of containing the magics flaring within her. "I had no choice."

"What the fuck are you talking about? You're Queen Adelena, you have all the choices!" Charlie shouted. "If you'd just worked with Rip, I'm sure you two could've thought of something together. You didn't have to send him back to those monsters!"

Adele didn't realize she was on her feet. She didn't feel her eyes blazing as she pointed down the table, shocking the teenager. "How dare you!" She saw her men flinch but didn't know it was because her voice scraped their ears, shrill and too loud. Her hand lit up with white power, flames licking from her fingertips. "I will not be questioned by a boy!"

Rainere was beside Adele in a heartbeat. "*Cara mia*, calm yourself," he whispered. "Resist the magic."

She felt his arms around her shoulders, squeezing hard, and smelled the singeing fabric of his shirt. She grabbed the magics, mentally struggling as they sought to dominate her. "They won't let me go," she whimpered.

Rainere's lips were on her ear. "Listen to my voice, let it enter your head, and think calm thoughts."

Jordansson said something in his own language that sounded like a prayer to Dahk'hani. Rainere snapped something aggressive back at the tribesman, also in Jordani. But Adele was working too hard on those calm thoughts to be surprised that Rainere spoke the language of the Ice Tribes.

Breath by breath, she came to her senses. Only when she was sure that the magic had quietened did she open her eyes again. She gasped, shocked to see the heavy linen tablecloth was decorated with long, charred streaks and covered in upturned dishes. Charlie was splattered with food and bleeding where a shard of smashed crockery had cut his forehead. "Oh, Charlie, I'm so sorry!" Adele covered her mouth with a trembling hand.

General Ohrig was the first to speak. "That's your *complication*, Your Majesty? Now you can throw firebombs out of your fingertips, and magic explodes from your eyes?"

Adele let out a breath, testing her rein on the magics. "It's made me a little unstable," she admitted in a croak.

"Well, you've always been the master of understatement." Ohrig gave her a wry grin. "Right, grab Jordansson, and let's do this before you get any worse."

Chapter Six

"Unexpected Friends"

Charlie found it hot and stuffy in Prince Rainere's bedchamber. The windows were still closed, and it was clear that the prince hadn't slept in the four-poster bed last night. The black silk coverlet was smooth and the pillows neatly stacked at the headboard. Charlie had spent more time than he liked in this small bedroom next to the royal nursery, usually lying on the daybed under the window, too scared to close his eyes for fear that High Wizard Ohren or High Magistrar Orestes would come for him.

Charlie had grown up rough in the Slums. His entire life he'd known fear and uncertainty, sleeping in doorways and empty cellars. But nothing compared to the discomfort of lying in a luxurious palace on fine cotton sheets and wondering if he'd be allowed to draw his next breath. Prince Rainere called the Golden Palace the Golden Snake Pit, and Charlie understood him too well now. Behind their smiles, no one could be trusted, and he had to stay close to those who would watch his back. He was more surprised than anyone that the man watching his back turned out to be Prince Rainere Marchant himself. Grudgingly, he had to face the fact that he owed Prince Rainere his life. The prince had brought him and Leafy back from the dead after finding them at the foot of Mount Ecrusius, then he had taken a bullet for Charlie during the rescue of the royal children. Charlie's debts were mounting, and somehow, they needed to be repaid.

He thought about all of this as he sat on the daybed, letting the prince administer to the cut on his forehead. Queen Adelena had apologized a half dozen times, but he'd still needed stitches, and Prince Rainere had medical training and a few minutes to spare. "What're we going to do about the big man?" he asked, breaking the silence between them. "That Jordan Jordansson."

"Jordansson is completely incapable of helping the queen," Rainere muttered. "I saw how deep the dragon magic goes—it's in her eyes now. There's no way he can just reverse the spell of healing and get it out of her."

"And he wants to get her pregnant for his god," Charlie added, watching Rainere's expression cloud. "He says he'll help her, but you know he's going to try and get his leg over."

Rainere raised an eyebrow but didn't respond.

Charlie tried again. "You want me to get him out of the way? Make it look like an accident so it doesn't point back to you?"

Prince Rainere turned his forest-green gaze on Charlie, and he knew the prince was taking the offer seriously. He felt a moment of pride that a stone-cold killer like the prince would consider him capable and not laugh at him. But then again, Prince Rainere didn't laugh at much.

"It will always point back to me," Rainere said finally, digging through his chest of medical supplies. "And if I wanted the boy dead, I'd also want the pleasure of killing him myself."

"M'just offering." Charlie huffed at Rainere's ingratitude. "I don't know how she can bear to let him touch her. He's so fucking massive and sweaty."

"I'm sure our queen will keep the touching to a minimum," Rainere said. "This is not about desire, Charlie. She'll do everything she can to get rid of the dangerous magic inside of her but won't risk a divine pregnancy. I know for certain that she doesn't look upon the tribesman with any affection."

But Charlie wasn't listening anymore. He had too many thoughts crowding his mind. Mostly he was furious with Adelena, but because he adored her, it was making him feel miserable. Rainere applied a cold salve to the cut on his head and then the prince slathered some on his own arms. His shirtsleeves were in burned tatters, and there were angry red streaks on his skin. Charlie wasn't the only one the queen had hurt with her magical explosion at breakfast.

"Did you know what she was planning last night?" Charlie asked as he watched the prince wipe his hands on a cloth, then thread a needle with fine stitching silk. "Did she tell you that she was going to go against Rip and kill the Eldars?"

Rainere frowned, concentrating on making neat, tight stitches that Charlie couldn't feel now that the salve had numbed his skin. "He was the one who opened the portal and ran away," Rainere said.

"It just shocks me that she could have so little mercy." Charlie was embarrassed to feel his eyes fill with tears. "Rip isn't a bad guy, and he's her half brother. How could she do that to her own family?"

"And this is why she didn't tell you anything," Rainere said. "She knows you're loyal to Ripenzo, and she didn't want to force you to decide between them."

"I should hate her for this," he whispered. By not trusting him with the truth, Adelena had betrayed him just like Rip had.

The stitches done, Rainere shifted to his knees in front of Charlie and wiped the rest of the blood off his cheek with a damp, astringent-smelling cloth. Charlie recoiled; he really didn't like being this close to the Marchant prince's face.

"You can hate Adelena," Rainere said, his voice soft. "But then you'll find that to live without her is a ceaseless agony. So you will forgive her, again and again and again. It's all you can do because she's your reason for living."

Charlie had never heard Rainere talk like this before, and he'd never seen the prince's expression so unguarded. Pain flickered in the depths of his dark eyes, and the silver rings of magic looked tarnished as they turned slowly around his irises. In this moment, the 145-year-old immortal Marchant prince had revealed just how utterly vulnerable he was.

"Well." Charlie wasn't sure what to say. "If that's how you see her, then you're properly screwed, mate."

Rainere smiled a half smile that didn't reach his eyes. "I've killed men for saying less," he said. "But today I'll put your insult down to the head injury. My advice, Charlie—look to girls your own age. The ones who like to giggle and hold hands. Stay well away from demon queens."

Charlie considered this while Rainere got off his knees and began packing up the medical kit. "You really think it's Jordansson that's at fault here?" he asked, though that wasn't what Rainere had said. "You think maybe Queen Adelena wouldn't have been so ruthless with Rip if she hadn't been overwhelmed by that weird magic of his?"

Rainere shrugged. "I know nothing about how demons function. Only Rip did, and now he's gone. We're on our own."

Charlie figured that was the closest Rainere would ever come to saying that he hadn't wanted Adelena to lose Rip like she had. It wasn't much of an apology, but Charlie took it anyway.

"Well, actually . . ." Rainere shook his head. "No, it's impossible." Then, strangely, the prince smiled, all the way to his eyes. "Impossible is for fools."

"Tell me."

"My father, Prince Rainold, would know about demons," Rainere said. "After all, he was married to Adelena's mother, Rainestra."

"But he's in an interdimensional prison," Charlie said, then caught up. "Oh, but with the high magistrar gone from the court, you think you could break your old dad out?"

"Then I can keep the promise I made to free him in return for helping Adelena with the map of Evendaar." Rainere shrugged off his ruined shirt, opening the wardrobe to pull out a new one.

While the prince stood half-naked, Charlie had a rare opportunity to see his Immortality Curse up close. The tattoo was all sharp geometric lines and intricate floral vines inked over the defined muscles of his back and curled around his ribcage, appearing strangely alive as he moved. With Rainere's hair still so short, the dragon and shield of the Marchant family crest was also visible, covering the back of his neck to the hairline. Charlie dropped his eyes as Rainere turned back to him, doing up his shirt buttons.

"You want my help to go get your dad?" he asked.

"No, you'd be useless." Rainere wasn't one to spare feelings, and he was clearly distracted by his new mission. "I need the balance to Marchant magic, so I'll have to find a St. Lucidis wizard to help me. Rest your head and stay away from Queen Adelena. She has enough on her shoulders without you making her feel guilty by reminding her of your injury." He gave Charlie a hard glare of warning, then turned on his heel and left, slamming the chamber door behind him.

"Useless, am I?" Charlie muttered, punching the velvet bolster on the chaise. "I'll show you who's fucking useless!" But the pain in his head had returned, and just as he decided maybe he could lie down for a bit, there was a knock at the door. Out of habit, he didn't respond but palmed the blade from the holster in his sleeve.

"Charlie?" It was the brunette nanny, Siobhan, who poked her head around the door. "His Highness, Prince Rainere, told me to bring you a pain tonic and a glass of water." She was looking pretty, as always, in her pristine pink-and-white nanny uniform, the apron at her waist pulled tight to show off her curvy figure.

"All right, Siobhan?" Charlie winked and enjoyed her blush. She had only ever rolled her eyes and called him names before today. *Maybe all my hero antics with the royal family are boosting my reputation,* he thought.

Siobhan handed over a small vial of white liquid and a glass of water. She touched him on his temple, and her face crumpled in sympathy. "That looks bad."

Charlie shrugged. "I'll live."

"The queen was really sorry," Siobhan said. She took a seat on the daybed, close enough that he thought she might have something more than talking in mind. "Her Majesty was whispering with Mrs. Ollenby about getting you something to make it up to you. I didn't hear what, though." Her giggle was sweet. "The queen really likes you, doesn't she?"

Charlie knew Siobhan was only a year older than him and hadn't been working in the Golden Palace much longer than he had. *Maybe a girl like her could help me forget Adelena and her fierce magic, and her untouchable skin, and her laugh, her sarcasm, her little secret smiles?*

"You got a boyfriend, Siobhan?" he asked.

Trying to hide her smile, she stood up and brushed down her apron but didn't move away. "Not that it's any of your business, but no, I don't have a fella."

"Do you want one?" He reached for her hand, but she crossed her arms too quick for him to catch it.

"Well, if I did, he'd have to treat me well and take me out properly," she said in her high-handed way. "I'm not a girl who wants trouble for just a night."

That wasn't what Charlie had heard from the palace rumor mill, but he nodded anyway. "Well, I could take you out," he suggested. "When do you get off shift?"

But she only giggled over her shoulder as she headed out. "Gosh, you're persistent, aren't you?"

"If there's something I want," he agreed, but she had already shut the door behind her round rump. The stitches on his head tweaked in a nasty way, so he downed the pain tonic and lay on the couch, wondering if Siobhan could ever really be what he wanted.

CHAPTER SEVEN

"Poor Hospitality"

Adele closed the door of the small bedchamber in the Queen's Guards' quarters and made her way up the dark blue–carpeted corridor to the main salon, where the men were waiting for her after the third attempt at extracting Jordansson's magic. Before facing them, she wiped the sweat off her face with her velvet sash and let the shivers of pleasure fade. She was getting used to the temperature fluctuations of the dragon magic, and the heat felt more comfortable in her veins now, like it was trying to adapt to her.

Yet attempting to separate the white magic from her own body and press it back into Jordansson was like trying to get chewing gum out of long hair. Every time she caught a strand of it, other tendrils of the magic glued themselves back inside her, hiding behind organs and clinging to her bones. The half-naked pseudo-sex with Jordansson was all very weird, and she was starting to feel like she'd crossed the line from magical experimentation into abuse. He'd been so happy to make the first attempt with her. In a room alone with a nice big bed, he had all sorts of ideas about how to make intimate connections. Adele had even laughed along. But by the second time she'd knocked him out, she wasn't laughing, and neither was Jordansson. In fact, he was starting to wear the same cautious, almost fearful expression that

Rainere had worn that morning in the bathroom. Like she was doing things without her own knowledge.

In control of herself again, she stepped out of the doorway into the living room. She had never been in her QGs' quarters before, and she'd been pleased to see that the men were well taken care of when she wasn't traipsing them all over Evendaar, making them sleep in tents on the ground.

The apartment was large and had been decorated with a masculine flair, as befitted the six men who lived there. There was a big central living room filled with stocky armchairs, square couches, and low wooden tables. The corridor off to the right, where she'd come from, led to the row of twelve single-person bedchambers complete with separate tiny bathrooms. To the left of the common lounge was a kitchenette and a rectangular dining table with chairs for twelve. A wall of windows let in the summer sunshine, and a pair of glass double doors led out to a small terrace, where cast iron furniture provided another seating area. By the kitchenette was a large fireplace, and over it was an imposing oil painting of a battlefield scene with scores of men in white uniforms fighting Spiders and other hideous Dark Entities. Following the martial theme, four bronze statues of muscular soldiers, wearing not much more than their weapons, were dotted about the room on marble plinths.

On the far wall, by the entrance, was a neatly arranged collection of portraits of the queens of Unisia from the last few centuries. Uniformly blonde, with vacant eyes and varying amounts of cleavage shown in the same head-and-shoulders pose, every queen was the statuesque opposite of Adele. She spotted Olivia, the last St. Lucidis queen, immediately. She'd been told that this woman was her mother, but she had never noticed a likeness between them, and with good reason. As it turned out, Olivia was Ripenzo's mother, and she could see now that he had her eyes. The late queen also carried a strong resemblance to her older brother, High Wizard Ohren. They had the same high forehead, sharp cheekbones, and golden curls. They also shared the same expression—a smug, yet somehow guileless gaze. She couldn't help but notice that her own portrait had yet to grace the wall.

"No luck again, Your Majesty?" Lord Orgustus called out. He was sitting in an armchair reading a scroll from the pile he'd brought with him to endure the wait.

"Nope." Adele slumped in the doorway of the corridor, still studying the regal portraits. "I thought I had it this time, but then it went haywire. All I did was knock him out again."

General Ohrig crossed the floor from the kitchenette and handed her a tall glass of something cold and fizzy. "There's sugar and salts in it, and it'll make you feel better," he said. "You look like hell."

"Thanks," Adele said, unoffended. She wasn't physically tired, because she'd fed on Rainere's magic this morning, but she was emotionally exhausted and ridiculously aroused. *And now I've got someone else to feel guilty about getting my claws in,* she thought. *Poor Jordansson.*

"Drink up," Ohrig reminded her, and she slurped down the fizzy drink and handed him back the glass.

Hoping fresh air would clear her head, Adele walked out to the small terrace. She saw that a little plot of herbs and vegetables had been built in the garden beds meant for flowers and guessed it was country boy QG Pepper who had made it. Her magic lurched, turning her platonic affection for Pepper into unbridled lust. *Breathe,* she told herself, determined to ignore her unruly hormones. *Surely, I can manage to do that without hurting anyone.*

"Your Majesty, what're you going to do now that your efforts with Jordansson have failed?" Lord Orgustus shouted out to her.

Adele sighed and went back inside to face the mountain of problems she had to tackle today. "Honestly, I've got no idea," she said. "Jordansson's magic doesn't want to leave." Taking the armchair next to Orgustus, she thought she could smell the scent of the gold magic that ran in his blood, all honey and vanilla. She wondered what his skin would taste like and had to shake off another surge of stupid lust.

Lord Orgustus scrunched the scroll he'd been reading up into a ball. "Meanwhile, your citizens are looking for someone to blame for bringing the Marchant Eldars to Concordis. Their likely target will be those with any hint of Marchant blood living in the Lower Districts. I have calls here from leaders in the upper guilds to bring the city under martial law, but what they mean is to have the Lower Districts filled with guards and soldiers of the Ordinary Army."

QG Leith scoffed, "Like those kittens with swords could do anything to quell a Slum riot if there was one. The Ordinary Army are hardly even trained for combat."

Adele rubbed a hand across her forehead, cursing the fact she now had to deal with politics. "I believe the cute name for me on the streets of Concordis is the Whore Queen. I can't see me doing much to relieve tensions when I take my petite, Marchant-looking butt up onto the podium." She gestured at the portraits of the St. Lucidis queens. "That's what the people want to see. Blonde, blue eyes, and big breasts."

"While that is mostly true, Your Majesty," Lord Orgustus said, his eyes darting to Adele's modest bust before returning to her face, "the fact is you are the best queen we've ever had on the throne."

Adele snorted at the compliment.

"You've changed your tune, my lord," Ohrig said, his patience clearly tested by Lord Orgustus and his presence in the Queen's Guards' territory. "Is Her Majesty meant to believe that you've become her loyal subject overnight? Wasn't it you who spread most of this trash about her in the papers to begin with? Now you want to help her? Why?"

Lord Orgustus gaped at General Ohrig. "Your Majesty, are you going to let your man speak to me like that?"

Adele curled up in the armchair, tucking her feet under her. "I'm curious too, my lord."

Lord Orgustus met the gaze of every Queen's Guard and finally seemed to realize that he didn't belong in these rooms with these men. Adele appreciated how he accepted this fact and then moved on. *The man's nothing if not pragmatic,* she thought.

"Your Majesty, why would I waste good money making posters or buying effigies of you just to burn them?" he asked. "When there are so many who are happy to take the credit for doing just that?"

"What the hell?" Adele hadn't thought it was possible in her exhausted state, but she was hurt. "I saw a bunch of the nasty posters, but burning effigies of me? That's horrible."

"Don't worry, Your Majesty." Captain Lucky handed her a cup of tea. "Now that we're home, we'll put a stop to all the propaganda."

Orgustus was already shaking his head. "It's very hard to change people's minds once they've been made up," he said. "And anyway, what would you tell them? That you freed a mythical dragon from captivity below the earth to be with the goddess Serena? Or that you managed to kill three immortal Marchant Eldars with your hands? Who would believe any of the things you've done?"

"You make a fair point, my lord." Adele chewed her bottom lip.

"That might be unbelievable to the public, but we know it's all true, Your Majesty," QG Bear reassured her.

She gave Bear a mock salute. "I couldn't do it without my loyal Queen's Guard."

Lord Orgustus huffed, impatient to continue. "Your Majesty, what you need to do is change *who* the people talk about," he said. "The citizens think you're a bad person, so we need to give them someone who's worse, making you the lesser of two evils, if you will."

"The queen's not evil!" QG Bear growled. "Sure she can be terrifying, but that's because the gods are using her so hard."

The rest of the Queen's Guard grumbled their agreement.

"Thanks for the support, lads." Adele smiled at her QGs. "But Lord Orgustus is right. I must get the people of Unisia on my side if I'm going to stay in the Golden Palace for more than a week. And despite my hurt feelings, Concordis is still recovering from the devastation of the Summer Influenza, which killed thousands of people in the city alone. I need to give the citizens a sense of security—assure them that the Golden Palace isn't falling apart and their goddess-given queen isn't actually a Marchant whore."

Lord Orgustus gave Adele a look that, while not admiring, carried a certain respect for her grasp of the complex situation. "I had thought that a spectacle would be effective, Your Majesty," he said. "It was, after all, what High Wizard Ohren was planning to hold for your coronation. There's nothing like a spectacle to win over the public and give them a different conversation. The people will love to watch as different families come out of the shadows to attack or support you. Ideally, I would suggest a royal wedding, but with the current mood—" He cleared his throat and fiddled with the screwed-up paper in his hand. "We do have your birthday coming up soon."

Adele was surprised. "I only know my birth date on Earth," she said. "I've got no idea when I was born in Unisia."

Of course, Captain Lucky knew right away. "Your Majesty, your thirtieth birthday is in two weeks, on the day of Summer's End."

"I thought I was an Aquarius," she joked, but no one got it. They didn't need the zodiac in Unisia, as constellations held no power like the gods. "Well, let's give the people a huge party, with a music festival and charity drives for those who've been affected by the influenza. I'll formally present myself and the children to the public and see if we can't garner a bit of favor that way."

Lord Orgustus stared at her intently for a moment. "Your Majesty, without wanting to seem too forward, how attached are you to the color of your hair?"

"You are too forward, my lord," Captain Lucky snapped at the same time as Adele let out a gusty peal of laughter.

"I'd look terrible as a blonde," she said. "Anyway, my lord, you're all the blond I'll need, because you're going to spend every minute by my side during this birthday festival, until everyone in the kingdom thinks we're joined at the hip. I'm riding the coattails of your popularity before I get my own."

General Ohrig made a noise of disgust which made her laugh again. "And my handsome Queen's Guard will be the flowers to catch the bees," she added, though Ohrig was properly glowering at her now. "I've got six perfectly good poster boys right here. No point wasting their talent on missions to save the world when I can parade them behind me like the gorgeous entourage they are."

QG Leith chuckled. "Her Majesty makes another good point." He pretended to preen until QG Owens gave him a clip over the head.

"The important thing is to really downplay your connections with the Marchant prince and all that is green-blooded and suspect," Lord Orgustus said. He rose from his seat, excited by this new plan. "Could you possibly keep His Highness very much in the background while we work on your new image, Your Majesty?"

She nodded. "Prince Rainere will be delighted to stay out of the limelight, I can assure you, my lord."

"Then I'm off to find Majordomo Tilburn to organize this extravaganza." Lord Orgustus was already at the door when he turned back to Adele, his brow furrowed again. "How much control do you think you will need over proceedings, Your Majesty?"

"I'm kind of busy." She tapped her heart, indicating the magic. "You plan everything and let me know what I have to do and when."

Lord Orgustus's smile was radiant as he turned on his heel quick enough to make his shoulder cape flare out and left the room.

"What's going on?"

Everyone turned to see a shirtless Jordansson standing in the corridor, his long arms stretching up to hold the top of the doorway. His white-blond hair was wet with sweat, there were dark circles under his normally bright blue eyes, and his cheeks were a feverish red. Adele couldn't take her gaze from the defined muscles of his abdomen, the V shape of them funneling down into his low-hanging trousers.

"Sweet goddess, son, you look awful," Ohrig said, and then looked at Adele. She quickly screwed a look of sympathy on her face and murmured her agreement.

"You want to try again, Queen?" Jordansson asked. His expression begged her to say no.

Adele unfolded herself from the chair, already salivating. *God, I should hate myself.* "I'm so sorry, Jordansson, just once more," she said and led him from the room. "I'll be as gentle as I can."

Chapter Eight

"A Time for Family"

Rainere was irritated as he found himself back at the royal apartment. He'd been searching for High Wizard Ohren for hours, even trekking up the half dozen staircases to the wizard's poky attic office. He'd traveled the secret pathways and then the busy public hallways, but to no avail.

Now he was looking for Mrs. Ollenby, who always seemed to know the high wizard's whereabouts. In fact, she always seemed to know everyone's whereabouts, from the lowliest servant to the most exalted person in the palace. But even she was no help.

"He usually comes to breakfast with the family, and I missed him this morning," Mrs. Ollenby said, inviting Rainere to take a seat on the couch opposite, a book of staff schedules on the coffee table in front of her. "It's unlike him not to be in the middle of things, especially with the queen returned and the children still so upset after their ordeal." She turned the full force of her lavender-blue gaze on Rainere. "Permit me to ask: are *you* all right, Your Highness? You did take a bullet for young Charlie only two days ago, and I can see you didn't get much sleep last night."

Rainere was still in a lot of pain and wondered if perhaps he might have a slow intestinal bleed from the force of Adelena's magic sex attack that morning. "I am well enough," he said finally.

Mrs. Ollenby frowned. It was clear she didn't believe him. "Come and sit with the children for lunch, Your Highness. They've been asking after you all morning and will be so pleased."

"Will Her Majesty be joining them?" Rainere inquired, hating how desperate he sounded.

Mrs. Ollenby gave him a sympathetic smile. "I'll send Her Majesty a messenger, Your Highness."

The day had brightened to clear blue skies, and the heat of summer hadn't yet dropped to the milder temperatures of the harvest season, so it was very warm outside when Rainere followed Mrs. Ollenby out to the terrace, where a long table had been arranged in the shade for an informal lunch. The four children were already sitting with their three young nannies, Siobhan, Caitlin, and Seraphina. The young women immediately stood and curtsied when Rainere arrived. Only the little brunette, Siobhan, was brave enough to catch his eye and send him a smile before she dropped her chin.

He had just taken his seat in between Natalie and Leafy, at Natalie's insistence, when Charlie and Adelena appeared through the terrace doors. They were deep in conversation, and he supposed his soft-hearted queen was apologizing to Charlie yet again for causing his injury earlier at breakfast. But Rainere was soon mollified when Adelena caught sight of him and he felt an intense flash of pleasure through the Mark.

The Mark that she'd drawn on his lower left ribs was a mixed blessing. The spell had been designed by the original Marchant kings as a curse to enslave the wearer, though Adelena had drawn it on him by accident. Their passion had always brought out odd aspects of her demon magic, and he trusted that she had meant to join them in love. He'd wanted to marry her that night, but she'd refused him.

For the children, Rainere reminded himself as he looked down at Natalie, who was still chattering away to him. *It was only ever her desire to protect the children that made her deny me. Now that the worst is behind us, perhaps it's time?* The idea of Adelena wearing the Marchant wedding bracelets made him want to grab her now and take her somewhere private.

"We got your favorite sandwiches for lunch, Prince Rainere." Natalie tapped his arm. "The ones with chicken and yellow sauce. I asked to have them specially, and Mrs. Ollenby got them."

"Thank you, Your Highness." He smoothed a strand of hair away from Natalie's worried eyes.

She relaxed for a moment, leaning against him as if she were too tired to sit up by herself. He met Adelena's gaze over Natalie's head, and saw her worry matched his own. No stranger to violence as a child, Rainere knew just how destructive it could be, how it could change a sweet child into an angry one.

"How did you fare with the tribesman this morning?" He could already guess from Adelena's expression, but he wanted her to focus on him instead of Charlie who had presumed too much by taking the seat by her side at the table.

"Badly," she said, morose. "I sent a bunch of messengers asking for Ohren to come help, but he never showed."

"I also looked for Ohren this morning," he said.

"I'll have to go and find him myself if he doesn't turn up soon," Adelena said.

"Mummy, don't go away." Aaron's little voice came piping from beneath the table, where he was sitting with the three dogs. "Stay here."

Adelena ducked her head under the table. "I'm not going anywhere today, sweetheart. Why don't you come out and have some lunch? Then we'll take the afternoon to do whatever you like."

"And me?" Natalie asked. "And Stella and Leafy too?"

"Yes, let's just have a family day," Adelena said. "I've been away too long, and I missed all my babies too much."

The children exchanged glances. It'd been so long since they had had their mother to themselves.

"Why don't we hang out here on the garden terrace?" Adelena suggested. "No plans and no meetings!"

Of course, at that very moment, the majordomo, Tilburn, appeared, trailed by his two scribes carrying piles of scrolls. "Your Majesty, I have been in discussions with Lord Orgustus, and I would prefer to hear from you about this very expensive birthday celebration."

"Nope, sorry." She gestured at her children. "I'm taking a bit of time off today."

"Time off?" Tilburn apparently didn't understand the concept, but he did understand when Aaron crept out from under the table and pulled at his sleeve.

"Tilburn, can Mummy stay with us?" Aaron's hazel eyes were wide, pleading.

Tilburn's stern frown quickly melted. "Of course, Prince Aaron. Her Majesty is free for the day."

The children let out a delayed cheer, and Adelena grinned. "Thanks, Tilburn, I'll get back to work tonight. And please let the Queen's Guard know that they have the afternoon off too."

With a polite bow, Tilburn took his leave.

"Oi! What about me?" Charlie was working his way through a heaped plate of sandwiches and cakes. "Didn't I earn my time off as well?"

Adelena cocked an eyebrow at the teenager. "When I said a family afternoon, of course that included you too."

Charlie chuckled until he saw that she was sincere. Then his smile crumpled to a scowl. Rainere found it exasperating. Adelena couldn't be clearer that she considered Charlie another lost child needing her maternal care, but the boy was letting his hormones cloud their relationship in a way that he must have known she would never allow.

"Don't worry, Cheeky Charlie, we all love you," Natalie told the boy.

"Get off!" Charlie threw a bread roll at Natalie, missing her by a wide enough margin that she wasn't frightened. She giggled and tossed her own roll back at him.

What am I doing? Rainere felt jealousy itching at him like the healing burns on his torso. *There are a hundred more useful things I could be taking care of instead of sitting here like a fool and letting her ignore me.*

"All right, so what shall we do today?" Adelena asked everyone.

"We could fill the paddling pools, Your Majesty," Siobhan suggested. "The children could splash around here on the terrace."

"Great idea!" Adelena clapped her approval. "It'll be perfect on this hot day."

By the time lunch was finished, the large, leaf-shaped ponds on the outer area of the terrace were filled with water, soft mats laid at the bottom to protect little feet, and all the pool toys were brought out in wooden tubs. The three nannies, ever keen to prove why they were needed, quickly got the children changed into their bathing clothes. The ponds weren't deep enough to swim in, but the children were in water up to their thighs, and it was enough for them and their three large puppies.

Charlie was off under a potted tree at the very edge of the balcony looking, Rainere thought, like he wanted to be anywhere else but here. Adelena had tried to get him to join in, but he just shrugged off her advances.

Finally, *finally*, she turned her attention to Rainere and patted the seat next to hers on the wicker sofa. Planning on telling her that he would leave soon, he sat and watched her watching her children, laughing along with their antics. He wondered if he'd ever seen her so relaxed before. For all the love there was between them, with the intensity of their lives, they'd never actually spent much time together like this—with no mission to plan or hideous plot to uncover. A servant handed him a glass of icy cold water, and Adelena clinked their glasses.

"Cheers," she said and released a happy sigh. "Oh, darling! Isn't this perfect? Just us, all together again as a family."

Eyes narrowed, Rainere tried to see what Adelena saw. Their family appeared to be an infatuated teenage thug from the Slums, a terrified Marchant urchin clutching her security blanket, a toddler infected by strange magic laughing at nothing, Natalie, still anxious, screeching at the top of her lungs, and Aaron, a demon abomination talking to the animals with his *mind*. And the parents of this catastrophe? An infertile Marchant immortal and a clueless demon queen.

But his beautiful Adelena was beaming as she reached for the hand on his knee, squeezing it. "All our children—some I made, one we found and one who found us. This is our family, Rainere. Ours. And I couldn't be happier."

Is this what our family is? An imperfect rabble of accidents pushed together by fate? Rainere wondered and was surprised by an answering surge of warmth in his chest. *Yes, that's exactly what we are but it's Adelena at our heart. She's the one who makes us whole.* He squeezed her hand and immediately felt a bolt of electricity rush through the Mark, twisting his stomach. "Darling, we mustn't, not here," he murmured. Life might be mad but there were still rules in the Golden Palace.

But Adelena only pulled his hand into her lap. "Rainere, I haven't said thank you for watching over my children while I was tramping through the Ice Mountains to find a dragon. Thank you for rescuing them when Orestes had them kidnapped and thank you for being prepared to sacrifice your life to do it. Thank you for looking after Charlie and Leafy too. I will always, eternally, be grateful to you."

"I don't need your thanks, *cara mia*," Rainere said, embarrassed to feel emotion stain his cheeks. "I would do it a hundred times over without any hope of your gratitude."

Adelena laughed. "Every time I think I'm being too serious, you manage to get even more intense!" And then in front of everyone—the servants, the children, and Charlie—she leaned into his side and brushed her lips against his cheek. "I love it when you blush, darling," she whispered.

He turned his head at an angle. They weren't kissing, but he felt her breath on his lips, and if he moved even a fraction, then—

"Goddess, it's hot today!" Charlie threw himself down on a

wicker armchair next to Adelena and stretched his legs out. "I'm bloody parched!"

Their intimate moment broken, Adelena relaxed back on the couch with a sweet sigh. But Rainere had to struggle to douse the flash of murderous rage at the boy.

"Charlie, I've got a present for you," she announced and waved over a servant carrying a wrapped box on a silver tray. "It's just a little thing to say thank you for all you've done for the children and me. I hope you like it."

"I don't need a box," Charlie said, determined to be a smartarse.

Adelena's smile was radiant. "Open it and pretend you like it."

Charlie pulled off the ribbon and lifted the lid. He narrowed his eyes at the gift inside. "This's too good for me," he protested. "What's a scruffy cat like me doing with an expensive bit of metal like this?" He lifted the pocket watch off its bed of velvet and let it swing by the chain, glinting in the sunlight. "That's solid white gold, new glass and gold numbering, ruby at the twelve, emerald at the six. This'll fetch at least six-fifty or seven hundred at a pawn shop."

"It doesn't matter what it'll fetch." Adelena gave Charlie a light punch on the arm. "It's yours to keep. Did you read the inscription on the back?"

Charlie looked like he was ignoring the question, but Rainere wondered what affection Adelena had shared to make the boy so emotional.

"And the next part of my present is your clothes, Charlie," Adelena said. "You've been stealing—"

"Borrowing," Charlie corrected her.

"—all of the Queen's Guards' civilian clothing, and they're really annoyed, so I'm sending you with Mrs. Ollenby to the palace tailors, and you're getting a whole new wardrobe made." She held up a finger to forestall any protest. "I won't have you looking like a scruffy cat when you're on business for me."

Charlie bit his lip to hide his grin. "If you insist, Your Maj."

"I do." She leaned over and grabbed his hand, giving it a squeeze. "And I'm very sorry about this morning, Charlie. It's this damn magic, you know."

"I know. It's all forgiven, Your Maj. Another hug?"

"Of course!" Adelena wrapped her arms around him.

Rainere caught the full force of the teenager's smug smile over her shoulder. Ready to do Charlie a serious injury, he instead got up and joined the children. Sitting in the water, Aaron was talking aloud to Hero Boy, these days looking like less of a puppy and more like the enormous hunting dog he was going to be.

Rainere wondered if anyone else remembered that these hounds had been originally bred to hunt Dark Entities and could sniff out magic from more than a mile away.

"And you have to be gentle—Leafy is our friend," Aaron was telling his dog as it sat in the paddling pool. Aaron looked animated, like he was hearing the other half of a conversation. "If she's sad, you need to hug her." He paused again, his little face scrunched in concern. "I know, Leafy is sad a lot. Oh, yes, I'll tell him too."

Rainere was surprised when both Aaron and Hero Boy turned to him. "I had another dream about your daddy," Aaron said. "He asked me to tell you that he wants to come home now." He hopped out of the pool, not seeing Rainere's shock.

But Natalie saw it. "Don't worry about him, Prince Rainere. He had the same dream yesterday night too. He's had it a lot since we stayed at your Gray Palace."

Aaron came back to the pool, and Rainere lifted him down off the slippery step into the water.

"Thanks, Daddy." Aaron gave him a pat on the shoulder before wading off to the other side of the pond, where the little toy boats were gathered. Rainere's gaze flickered to Adelena, but she was still engaged in conversation with Charlie and hadn't heard her son call a Marchant prince Daddy. *Maybe it's insane to think it,* he thought, *but I'm going to be a damn good father.*

Blinking away his emotions, he watched the sunbeams dance over the golden strands in Aaron's brown hair. "You're very welcome, son," he murmured.

CHAPTER NINE

"Moonlight Lovers"

The family day was almost over, and it was a beautiful, balmy evening. All the balcony doors of the royal apartment had been opened to let in the soft breezes and the scent of citrus candles perfumed the air. A group of servants moved discreetly about the apartment, tidying up the mess left by the royal family's dinner and after-bath games. Tucked away in their palatial nursery, the four children had begged Rainere for yet another bedtime story, so Adele had left him starting with, "When I was a young boy living alone in the Gray Palace," and retreated to the living room.

She stretched out on her favorite peacock-blue velvet couch, with the wide arms and poufy cushions, and couldn't remember the last time she had felt so truly relaxed. The afternoon on the terrace had been just what she needed. Spending time with her children, together with Rainere and Charlie, had been wonderful. Rainere was devoted to them all, and it made her heart sing to see how much Natalie, Aaron, and Stella all adored the man she loved. She was positive that Leafy would soon settle into such a loving environment too.

All the terror is over, and surely we deserve some calmer days now. Even the magics within her had seemed to come to an accord and lay quiet within their various parts of her body. Reaching for the jeweled flask on the coffee table, she poured herself a Firewhiskey and was surprised when the steward, Hollis, announced the arrival of her Queen's Guard.

"I thought I told you guys to take the day off," she said as the six men bowled into the room.

General Ohrig nodded at the open balcony doors behind her. "Yes, but it's night now," he said. "Who knows how much trouble you've managed to find in the few hours we've been apart? I thought it best if we check in and see what the plans are for tomorrow."

Adele grinned at the five men standing at attention in a line behind Ohrig, though no one smiled back at her. Returning to the Golden Palace meant returning to all the protocol that could usually be ignored when they were on the road together. Despite the evening hour, the QGs were all showered, shaved, and looking smart in their formal white-and-gold uniforms. They were ready to work again.

"How about you guys take the night off too?" she suggested. "And we can get together for breakfast tomorrow. But not too early, say midmorning?"

"Are you asking me or telling me, Your Majesty?"

Adele raised her eyebrows at Ohrig's terse tone. It wasn't unusual for him to be abrupt, but she'd thought he might be a little grateful for the continued holiday. *Surely he has a life that he wants to get back to,* she thought.

"I'm telling you to go away, Ohrig," she said. "I'm planning on spending the night with this glass of Firewhiskey, and I have a super fun meeting with Tilburn to argue about the birthday party thing Lord Orgustus is organizing. Not much chance of getting into trouble there."

Ohrig planted his feet wide and crossed his arms, the fabric of his white jacket straining over bulky muscles, his whole posture screaming "stubborn." Adele was annoyed. She wanted the Queen's Guard gone before Rainere came out of the nursery, and she had a nasty suspicion that Ohrig knew it. She stared up into his gaze, a pale, sunbleached blue that noticed way too much. "Right—I command you to go! You're all dismissed," she snapped.

Not a man moved, though with a quick glance at Captain Lucky, Adele could see that disobeying a direct order from her was causing him serious discomfort. Swallowing a sigh, she unfolded her legs from the couch, shook out the silk layers of her dress, and stood up, crossing her own arms. "Fine! Go on, Ohrig," she said. "Say what you're apparently desperate to say."

"It's actually impossible for you to dismiss your Queen's Guard as the regulations stipulate that while in the Golden Palace a corps of six men must remain with the queen's person at all times," Ohrig said, a frown beetling his gray brows. "We are only six, so at least two of us will be on duty at any time."

Adele took a pinch of gold magic from the back of her neck. It helped her jump through a dozen or more scenarios in her head to find a solution to the problem tonight. They were her own thoughts, of course, but the gold magic helped her get to an answer faster. "There are twelve bedrooms in your quarters, aren't there?" She raised her chin to look up at him. "Why don't you compile a list of six men that you would like to add to the ranks, and we can look at beefing up the Queen's Guard so that you can all work in proper shifts and not every day and night like you've been doing. Brilliant, yes? This is something that we can definitely talk about in the morning."

Ohrig didn't reply and Adele couldn't help herself—she glanced at the nursery door, where, right now, Rainere might be about to finish up with the children and walk through wearing his midnight-blue silk shirt, the top three buttons undone, ready to share a not-so-quiet moment with her.

Then Ohrig read her mind again, damn him. "Jordansson has yet to wake this evening, Your Majesty. The wizard said that he was in a stable condition but gave him something to keep him asleep. Said it was the best method of healing for the big lad."

"Ah, that's good, I guess." Adele felt guilty again. "Was it High Wizard Ohren?"

He shook his head, and his eyes almost disappeared under their brows. "I've looked, but I can't find the high wizard anywhere. I thought he would turn up for dinner here, but I see that isn't the case. Do you think we should be worried?"

"I don't like it," she admitted. "But my stewards said that they saw Ohren in the palace last night. Has someone checked his bedchamber?" She hated the sick feeling in her stomach at being reminded that no one was really safe in the Golden Palace. The three magics roused and began sending tendrils through her blood, trying to find the source of her stress.

"You want me to go look for him, Your Maj?" Charlie had appeared so suddenly at her elbow that she yelped, earning his cheeky grin.

"Yes, you can go and look for the high wizard, but do it tomorrow." She raised a hand. "Seriously, Ohrig, take the goddamn night off."

"But what if his brother has managed to catch him and he's being held against his will?" Ohrig protested.

"What if he is?" she snapped, poking him in his beefy chest. "Ohren is a centuries-old, incredibly powerful wizard. He can look after himself for a night. If Orestes has got him, then maybe a bit of prison will remind him what the rest of us have had to put up with. Now, off you go, and take Charlie with you."

"You don't have to tell me twice, Your Maj," Charlie said, clearly enjoying the tension between the general and his queen. "But just by the by, are all of the nannies on duty tonight, or can I take Siobhan out for a bit?"

"Of course, great idea!" Adele handed Charlie the bottle of Firewhiskey from the coffee table behind her. "Take Siobhan, Caitlin, and Seraphina, and go have a party. In fact, order as much wine as you like and have a great time. But"—her glare encompassed the whole Queen's Guard as well as Charlie—"far away from me. I'll see you all tomorrow."

"That's very kind of you, Your Majesty," Captain Lucky said and looked just as eager as the other men to be away for the evening.

Ohrig could see when he was beaten, but he wasn't happy about it. "I'll not be having any party, Your Majesty," he said. "Anything you need, any time of night, just send a messenger, and I'll be there."

"Not necessary, but thank you, Ohrig!" Adele started waving like she was on a ship ready to depart and watched her happy Queen's Guard leave the room, already discussing how to use their rare free evening. General Ohrig gave her one last dark look before he left, and she knew exactly what he was thinking. *So maybe we can read each other's minds?* she thought, rueful.

"What's the trouble, *cara mia?*" Rainere closed the nursery door and made his way across the room to her.

"Ohrig thinks I've forgotten how many people still want to depose me, and he thinks it's very important that I remember I've got a god wanting me knocked up, and poor Jordansson still injured after trying to help me today." She sighed heavily, sitting back down on the couch.

"Those things are all true, and he's right to worry about you." Rainere sat next to her, so close their knees were touching. She still missed the songs of her Chime Voices, but the new magic seemed just as excited to have her prince this close. To stop herself from jumping on him that instant, she took a sip of Firewhiskey.

"I'd like one of those," Rainere said. He looked for it, but she had given the flask away.

"I've got another bottle in my bedroom." She looked up at Rainere from beneath her dark lashes. "And I've dismissed all the servants tonight."

Rainere rose from the couch. "I'll fetch it for us."

But she caught his hand. "Rainere, I've dismissed everyone," she repeated. They both knew the stewards were too discreet to count as witnesses. "We're alone."

In a flash, Rainere had swung her up in his arms, holding her close to his chest as he walked through the balcony doors. "Outside," he said. "I want to see the moonlight on your skin."

"Oh, my prince, how scandalous!" Adele swept the back of her wrist against her forehead, trying to make him laugh, but he was too intent on finding a place directly under a moonbeam. He carried her to a grouping of large potted trees and several wicker armchairs and sofas. The paving stones glowed in the silvery light.

"Perfect," he whispered, and set her down.

She grabbed all the cushions from the furniture and arranged them in a heap on the ground while Rainere did a quick prowl to make sure there were no servants lingering in the shadows. The whole time, Adele was telling herself to calm down and take it slow. Green sparks were already dripping from her fingertips and singeing the sturdy cotton of the cushion covers. *I will not hurt him tonight,* she promised herself, but really, she was begging the dragon magic and Dahk'hani to pay attention. *He deserves more than me feeding on him, he deserves pleasure, he deserves it all.* Then she felt a shift within her chest, followed by a violent shiver throughout all her organs. For one awful moment, she thought she might throw up, but it was the dragon magic settling itself deep in her gut. There was no other way of describing the odd sensation as it lay in her lower abdomen and heated the already warm place between her legs. *Thank you, Magics. Just please stay there while we do this.*

Finally, she could return her attention to Rainere. He stood in front of her, his face in shadows but his eagerness plain in the set of his jaw and the hands that already reached for her.

"Darling," she whispered. "I know we have to talk. There's so much I haven't told you about the journey to find Sighmere, and I know you're keeping details from me about what the Boss has been up to in the Golden Palace, as well as in the city. There's so much we don't know about Dahk'hani—" Her breath caught when the dragon magic twitched, but it didn't do anything else, so she continued. "Or how we're going to stop him from forcing me to have his baby. I still haven't properly apologized for hurting you last night when we made love . . ."

"*Cara mia,* can we talk afterward?" Rainere sounded like he was smiling. He muttered the charm that undid all her ribbons and buttons, and her dress fell to the ground. Adele stepped out of the pile of silk and tulle, standing in her wispy, lace underwear.

Please let me touch him. Please let me love him, she begged, and felt an answering pulse of liquid heat between her legs. Pressing her hands to his chest, she traced them down his body as she dropped to her knees on a stack of pillows. She kept her gaze on his face as he shucked off his jacket and shirt and she undid the ties on his trousers, releasing his magnificent erection. "You are beautiful, Rainere," she said as she took him in her hands, delighting in the heat and his particular smoky scent. With an effort, she pushed out all the dark worries that fluttered around her head like so many bats—High Wizard Ohren's disappearance, her children's trauma, Jordansson and what his presence could mean to Dahk'hani, the strange new magic that made her behave so violently. All of it got pushed aside tonight for Rainere.

Parting her lips, she licked the top of his cock, and he groaned so deeply she grinned. She didn't need magic for this. Using her natural skills, she worked him with her tongue and lips and fingers. He let her get further along than he ever had before pushing her away with a pained moan. "*Cara mia,* no."

The next instant, Adele found herself on her back, his fists on either side of her shoulders to hold his weight as he settled between her legs. She whimpered with pleasure when Rainere whispered another charm and his pants and her underwear disintegrated in puffs of shredded fabric. He began to slide over her slick heat in a way that would lead to madness if he didn't do something else soon. She held his face between her hands, seeking a kiss, but his eyes were closed, and his lips were moving as he whispered to himself.

"The alloy created by the chemical combustion is equal to the result of seven . . ."

With a hand, Adele tried to smooth the frown from Rainere's forehead. "Darling?"

Rainere opened his eyes, his lips curled in a beautiful half smile. "You got me too close, *cara mia.*" He dropped his forehead to hers. "I want this to last all night."

"Oh, God, I've missed us," she said, punctuating every word with a kiss. "Just you and me without magic or pain. Rainere, I love you so much."

"*Cara mia*, you must know, I love it when you use me." His voice rasped with the passion that sent tingles over her heated skin. "I love that only I can do that for you. Let me give you a little magic."

"Not tonight." She pulled her hand back from the hot skin of his chest, fighting the hunger that flared at his offer. Thankfully, the dragon magic stayed where it was between her legs and began pulsing along with her racing heartbeat. She reached down between them and wrapped her fingers around him. "This is all I want."

Their kisses were deep and wild, tongues melding together as they learned each other all over again with their lips. Adele was gasping by the time Rainere slipped down and along her body, his tongue tracing the skin of her stomach. His broad shoulders pushed her thighs apart, and his kiss finally found her aching center. She didn't have his discipline, and her first orgasm was quick enough to make him chuckle as he arched back up over her.

"I'll have to teach you my trick of reciting the Finite Rules of Chemistry in Spell Lore," he said, brushing his lips over her nipple. He licked and then blew a little on the wet skin.

Adele writhed with pleasure, excited to feel the tension build within her again. "Nothing can help me resist your tongue. It's diabolical." She enjoyed the chance to prove her lack of control twice more before she slung herself over his hips and rode him hard, holding his wrists above his shoulders so she wouldn't be tempted to steal a sip of magic. Rainere came in an exquisite, lyrical moan that made Adele giggle as she draped herself over his chest.

"That's so much better than talking." She licked a drop of sweat from Rainere's collarbone and gave herself a quick mental scan, but the dragon magic didn't feel like it had moved. She rolled off him to her back, pleasantly exhausted.

Rainere groaned again, curling around her. His long fingers ran over her stomach and trailed down between her legs, resting there. "*Cara mia*, what bliss," he murmured. "Give me a moment to recover, and we can do all of that again."

Adele smiled up at the night sky. "Show-off." The sweat was already cooling on her skin, and the breeze felt divine. She inhaled the vanilla-scented air. The moon was only halfway full but bright enough that she could see the silvery trunks of the trees in their ceramic pots and the silver thread in the fabric of their nest of pillows. She guessed it was still before midnight, as the moon hadn't yet started its descent.

"Darling, was it better for you this time? I hope I didn't hurt you," she whispered and was rewarded with Rainere's soft snore. She smoothed a hand over his cheek. Relaxed in sleep, his face looked younger, belying the decades he'd lived in isolated misery, alone in the Gray Palace. Her heart was filled with so much love that it ached. *We won't ever be apart again,* she silently promised him. *Our love is fated by Serena herself, and you're all mine, Rainere.*

The dragon magic chose that moment to rouse itself from her pelvis and move into her chest again. She felt the acidic burn of hunger and, as reluctant as she was to leave her prince, she had to get away. She covered him with one of the silk throws from an outdoor couch, pulled on her dress, then arranged her messy hair into a bun. She went inside and closed the balcony doors so Rainere could sleep undisturbed.

Franks was standing in the center of the room, apparently happy to wait all night for his queen's tryst to finish. "Good evening, Your Majesty. Majordomo Tilburn is on his way to see you."

"Thanks," she said and took a seat on the peacock-blue couch again.

"Your Majesty!" Tilburn called brightly as he entered the room, rushing despite the late hour. His two tired scribes trailed in behind him. "You're looking relaxed and rosy-cheeked, which is good because we have much to discuss, and not all of it pleasant."

Adele waved Tilburn to sit. "I've got all night for you, my friend," she said. "Let's go."

Chapter Ten

"Dahk'hani Bound"

At dawn, Adele found Rainere still sleeping on their improvised bed out on the terrace. The birds had already begun their morning songs, and the sky was awash with soft pinks and blues, tinting the vanilla-scented air and turning his pale skin a shade of rose. Standing over him, she drank in his mouthwatering beauty, his skin stretched tight over defined muscles, the vines of his glorious tattoo curving around his ribs and down his hipbones. She was about to wake him when the hunger for magic tore through her and she felt Dahk'hani's hands descend upon her shoulders.

DO YOU LOVE HIM, MOTHER?

Shocked by the intrusion into her thoughts, Adele was pushed to her knees next to Rainere. Without her permission, her hands hovered over his chest, and his green magic was drawn out, gathering under her palms in a puff of green sparkles. "Stop," she whimpered. "Don't make me hurt him."

YOU LOVE HIM LIKE HE IS YOUR CHILD.

Adele shook her head and felt Dahk'hani's grip loosen. She cradled her hands against her chest in case he used them again. "I love him, and he is . . ." she whispered, searching for the words that an ancient deity might understand. "He has my heart and my love; I cannot live without him."

THEN HE IS MY FAMILY TOO.

Dahk'hani left her as suddenly as he had arrived. The instant his control released her she fell next to Rainere on the cushions. Dashing tears from her eyes, she felt her anger spark. *Stupid goddamn stalking god! I have to think of something before he gets his way and I'm having his baby.*

She curled into Rainere's side and sought his warmth, draping her arm over his chest and her leg over his thighs. His eyes were still closed when he rolled over her, settling between her legs and holding both her wrists overhead with one large hand. His lips tracked down her neck.

"Darling, we need to be careful," she murmured as Rainere began licking at the sensitive place under her ear. "My magic is feeling wild and Dah—"

Rainere chuckled and the vibrations shook them both. "That's good, I'm feeling wild too," he said, sliding further down her body, his tongue painting the curves on her chest above the neckline of her dress.

She groaned. *All right, it's time to stop being weak. I need to tell him that Dahk'hani is controlling me through the dragon magic, and if he thinks I'm too dangerous to touch, then that should be his decision.* But Rainere had shoved up her skirts and shouldered her thighs wide. *And I'll tell him right after this,* she promised, hating herself.

Then through the open terrace doors came the sound of chattering servants entering the apartment to ready it for the day.

Distracted, Rainere lifted his head from between her legs, and Adele took the opportunity to wriggle out of his grasp. "Come on, we can sneak into my bedchamber from here, before anyone catches us," she whispered, but he seemed to take an unnecessary amount of time to gather up the blanket to cover himself and follow her. She smacked him on his sculpted butt when he wandered into her room.

"Are you trying to get us caught?" she asked and climbed the high sides of the enormous Glass Bed, using one of the cut-glass pillars as a support.

Rainere slid much more easily onto the tall bed and under the counterpane she had opened for him. "I would say that the time for sneaking around has passed, *cara mia,*" he said, archly. "Everyone knows we spend our nights together."

Adele had to check his expression to see if he was serious. He was. A nasty feeling of unease squirmed in the bottom of her stomach. "I guess you're right," she admitted as he pulled her to sit astride him, her chest to his as he leaned back on a bank of pillows. She had nowhere else to look but his deep, forest-green gaze. Their love was pure, but a proper relationship had always felt like an impossible dream. Maybe Rainere wanted to make that dream a reality. *I must tell him about Dahk'hani now.*

"*Cara mia*, don't look so nervous, I'm not going to propose to you again," Rainere said, and his tone held a trace of bitterness that made her squirm again. "But I did want to talk to you while we have a moment of privacy. It's about something that's very important to me, and I need you to keep an open mind until I've finished."

"Darling," she cut him off before he could go any further. "Never doubt that I love you and that I want to spend my life with you too."

"No, but it's not—"

She leaned forward and let her kiss explain the rest. For a moment, Rainere resisted, then his arms slipped around her and no words were spoken.

It was so hard to gauge time while kissing her prince, but all too soon there was a loud knock, and Lady Olivia's head popped around the door. Adele was surprised by the vitriol in Rainere's curse, though she couldn't help feeling the same way.

"Your Majesty, my apologies." Lady Olivia bobbed a curtsy in the doorway. "I didn't know I would be interrupting you . . . both."

"Olivia!" Adele snatched up a handful of sheet to cover Rainere's lap. "Could you give us a minute?"

"It would be my great pleasure to help His Highness dress too," Olivia said. Adele thought it was probably nerves that made the girl lick her lips.

"Your queen said to get out, you stupid girl!" Rainere snapped.

"Yes, Your Highness." Lady Olivia flushed, curtsied again, and shut the door.

"You should fire that maid." He was still holding her tightly, though his erection had melted with the interruption. "She is . . . disrespectful."

"I do wonder how trustworthy she is." Adele reluctantly disengaged from Rainere's clinging hands and wriggled out of bed. "But Olivia is probably the only female friend I have, other than Mrs. Ollenby. Not to mention that if it wasn't for her talent with dressmaking, I'd have to wear Mrs. Ollenby's gowns with all the hot pink feathers and huge bustles!"

"That maid is not your friend." Rainere climbed off the bed, looking furious. "And I'm telling you to get rid of her."

Adele frowned over her shoulder at him as she walked to the bedchamber door. "Darling, what's the matter?" she asked. "Did she do something to you?"

Wrapping the silk blanket around his hips again, he stalked toward Adele and brushed a kiss across her forehead, holding his lips there for a moment. "She did nothing for me," he muttered and then disappeared into the secret passage beside the cupboard.

Sighing at her moody prince, Adele opened the chamber door. She attempted a smile for her beautiful nineteen-year-old head lady-in-waiting. "Come in. I've got a meeting with my Queen's Guard in a few hours, but I want to have breakfast with the children first, so I've not got a lot of time for the usual beauty regimen this morning."

"Oh, Your Majesty! Surely we have enough time for a face mask?" Lady Olivia was scandalized. "Your cheeks are still so red and chapped from your travels, and I can see the dilated pores on your nose from here."

Adele found that hard to believe, but she accepted that everyone in the Golden Palace had different priorities. Olivia's were to make the queen look as flawless as possible. Remembering her conversation with Lord Orgustus, she took her place on the couch in the bathroom and allowed Olivia to get to work with all the plucking, tweezing, and masking that she needed to do.

Olivia never stayed silent for long, and Adele could tell that the girl was desperate to ask about catching Rainere in the Glass Bed.

"My relationship is not a secret, Olivia," Adele said as she suffered cold goop being painted on her face. "But we are trying to be discreet, as you can imagine."

"Oh, of course, Your Majesty," Olivia gushed, all smiles. "I would never presume to ask your private business. But can I just offer congratulations, perhaps?" She giggled. "You know I think the Marchant prince is absolutely gorgeous!"

Adele's grin cracked the already-dry goop on her cheeks. "He's certainly something else," she said, but ended up giggling too.

"And such a brave choice for a St. Lucidis queen," Olivia added, smearing more gunk on her forehead. "I can only imagine how upset everyone in the court is with you. But you *are* the queen, even if you look nothing like us—no one can tell you who to keep in your bed."

Adele was used to Olivia's tactless and sometimes catty comments, but this time she was saved from having to respond by the rest of her team of dressiers—Piers, Julien, and Katie—entering the bathroom. Apparently Olivia hadn't informed them that the queen was awake, and they were all very annoyed, though they hid it behind fake smiles and barbed compliments about the low-cut gown that Olivia was wearing.

Don't mind me, Adele thought as her dressiers went on to argue about what to do with her hair, makeup, and wardrobe choices. She knew from experience that her opinion would be ignored. But the upside to listening to the bickering was that she also got to hear all the gossip that was floating around the court. For instance, she found out that her Queen's Guard had ended up having a big party in their quarters last night. They'd taken Adele's offer to order booze very seriously, and her beauty team had all sorts of stories about who had ended up in whose bed. Charlie and Siobhan were now an official couple after the nanny had publicly rejected Benjamin Belvoir for the younger man. Jordansson has also caused a scandal when he stripped off his clothes and danced all night in a provocative way.

After all the chatter, Adele ended up in a floor-length, peach-colored gown with a crystal-beaded bodice. Her dark hair was curled and stacked high, then stuck through with little diamond and pearl pins. Her makeup was kept light, her lipstick so glossy and transparent that her lips looked like glass. It was only when the matching elbow-length gloves came out that she decided she'd had enough.

"Thank you, everyone. You've done me proud, as always," she called to her team on her way out of the bathroom.

"Your Majesty, at least don't forget your perfume." Lady Olivia followed Adele out into the bedchamber and sprayed her neck and décolletage liberally. "I know how much a special someone likes this scent." She giggled.

By the time Adele made it to the breakfast table she was ravenous, and her children were already halfway through their toast and eggs. She kissed all of them and discovered they were in the middle of a heated argument.

"It's Stella's fault," Aaron shouted, tears pooling in his hazel eyes. "Mummy, she was trying to kill Bunny."

Natalie was furious with her little brother. "You're so mean, Aaron," she yelled. "Stella's just a baby."

"But she wanted to kill Bunny," Aaron said. "With her hands!"

Stella laughed and threw her food around. She was the only one not concerned by the accusations.

Adele took her chair, thanked Mrs. Ollenby for the cup of tea, and tried to smooth things over between her kids, but without any success.

"The children are still very much out of sorts, Your Majesty," Mrs. Ollenby murmured. "Aaron found Stella sitting on her dog in the bathroom this morning and thought the worst."

It was rare to see Aaron so upset. His cheeks were pale, and his hands were clenched into little fists on the table. "Sweetheart, Natalie is right," she soothed. "Stella is just a baby and she loves Bunny."

"Bunny told me everything!" Aaron pointed a finger at the laughing toddler. "Stella is bad now. There's a dragon in her."

"Aaron!" Adele was shocked, thinking, *But Stella only had a tiny taste of the dragon tear, there's no way she should be as affected as I am.*

Hollis announced the arrival of the Queen's Guard, and she left that frightening line of thought for another time. General Ohrig looked as sharp as ever, as did Captain Lucky in his pristine uniform, but they were the only ones.

"I heard about the party last night, lads. Well done!" Adele grinned to see Pepper, Leith, Owens, and Bear looking sorry for themselves. She had never seen any of them drunk or even close to it in all their time together, so they deserved teasing. She waved away their muttered thanks for the night off and told them to get a greasy breakfast with lots of bacon and as much tea as they liked. Pepper lost his color and made a quick exit to the closest powder room.

Before she could ask where he was, Jordansson entered the apartment. Thankfully, he was wearing a shirt with his trousers today, even if he'd only done up half the buttons and was trying to shake off Turner who followed on his heels. "Queen, this man says I cannot come to you without an *invitation*." Jordansson spat the word like it was something offensive. "I say that I go where you go, but he says you must call for me."

"It's all right, Turner," Adele assured her steward. "You can let Jordansson in any time. He's with the Queen's Guard."

"No, he's with you, Your Majesty," General Ohrig said quickly. "I'm not taking responsibility for this great galumphing lad walking half-naked around the Golden Palace."

"He's yours if I say he is." Adele sent Ohrig a sweet smile that made his eyes roll. "He's already staying in your quarters. I'm sure he'll be happy to get involved with whatever you do when you're not guarding me."

She could tell Ohrig was going to argue, but then Hollis announced the arrival of Lord Orgustus, and he was forced to stand with everyone except Adele and greet the young lord.

Orgustus was looking very dashing in a sky-blue three-piece suit with gold piping. A starched white shirt and a tightly knotted gold scarf completed the look. He'd only just taken his seat when Charlie dashed into the apartment, his jacket hanging off one shoulder as he dragged an embarrassed Siobhan in behind him. He let go of her hand as soon as he saw Adele staring at him, one eyebrow raised in amusement.

"I'm sorry, Your Majesty. I slept late, and Siobhan here also slept late, and so that's the only reason we are both coming in now, so late." Charlie was cute when he was flustered, but she didn't want to let him suffer too long.

"Come and get breakfast," she said. "You're excused after the night you've had."

"It really isn't appropriate to fraternize with a nanny of the royal family, Charlie," Captain Lucky admonished.

Adele threw a bread roll at Lucky's head and laughed when he caught it without even looking. Her captain had the reflexes of a cat.

"Leave Charlie alone," she said. "The Golden Palace employs hundreds of citizens, and if no one is allowed to meet someone at work, we wouldn't have any couples at all in the palace."

"Oh, we're not a couple," Charlie said, so quickly he choked on his tea. "It was just a party and a bit of fun, you know."

"Oh! So I'm just a bit of fun?" Siobhan had unfortunately returned to the table. She dropped the washcloths meant for the children and ran from the room.

"Smooth, kid, real smooth," QG Bear said, but he sounded approving. "You'll get no bother from that one now."

"Charlie!" Now Adele felt compelled to reprimand him on behalf of the nanny her children adored. "I know it might have been a casual thing for you, but please be respectful to Siobhan while you're both at work."

"And this is why we have rules," Captain Lucky said, staring hard at the teenager.

Charlie sank low in his chair, looking mortified.

"Your Majesty, what are the plans for the day?" Ohrig's voice carried down the table, returning the conversation to a more neutral topic.

"Your Majesty, if I may be so bold as to—"

"Orgustus, this is only my first cup of tea," Adele said. "Just get to the point, please."

"I want you to come into the city with me," he said. "I think it's about time you walked the streets and your citizens saw you doing the work I normally take care of. I've arranged a meeting with the Lady Mayor of Concordis, and I'd like to engage her services in helping us change your image among the people."

"I didn't know Concordis had a mayor," Adele said. "Where's she been all this time?"

"Our Lady Mayor works very hard, Your Majesty," Orgustus said, happy to correct her ignorance. "Not only with her official mayoral duties, but she runs several successful businesses too. Concordis would never have survived the tragedy of the Summer Influenza without her tireless efforts to financially support the hospices and businesses most heavily affected. I believe with my whole heart that our Lady Mayor will be instrumental in getting the people on your side."

"With your whole heart, you say." Adele quirked an eyebrow at Orgustus's hyperbole and considered his words. If it really was time for her to take on the mantle of queen in action instead of decree, then the former regent could make that happen. Though there was no doubt in her mind that he had an ulterior motive, for now, their interests aligned, and she would just have to go along with him. She looked down the table to gauge Ohrig's reaction to Orgustus's request. He met her gaze and gave a tiny nod.

"All right, I'll meet the Lady Mayor," she said, shifting in her chair so that Stella could climb onto her lap. She was immediately distracted by the kerfuffle Rainere's presence always brought, even before she saw him. He hadn't yet sat down when Aaron and Natalie began telling him about the incident with Stella and her dog, Bunny, and both demanded that he side with their own account of events.

"Good morning, Your Highness," Adele called to him over the children's shouting.

"Good morning, Your Majesty, I pray you slept well?" Rainere tone was crisp, and she knew he was still annoyed with her for suggesting they keep their relationship quiet. "If I may trouble you for a meeting?"

"I see the Marchant prince finds it too difficult to be informal with you at breakfast despite your request, Your Majesty." Directed at Rainere, the young lord's glare was pure poison.

"Prince Rainere can speak in any way he prefers," Adele said, giving Orgustus a glare of her own. "He's a Marchant prince, my lord. I have no jurisdiction over his speech." *And don't you forget it, jerk,* she wanted to add but didn't because the dragon magic rose with her anger, bringing a flush to her hands.

She looked down and focused intently on Stella's blonde curls to calm herself.

"Your Majesty, I believe that I have a potential solution for the problem that the dragon's magic is causing you," Rainere announced.

Adele felt a surge of excitement strong enough to eclipse the magic coursing through her. "Tell me!"

"Perhaps we should discuss this in private," he suggested.

"Rainere, if you have a solution, then spit it out." Adele heard Lord Orgustus gasp at the impropriety of her using the prince's first name, but ignored it.

"Of course, Your Majesty." Rainere raised his chin high, so his voice carried. "I would like to free my father, Prince Rainold, from his prison dimension. He is a very powerful immortal wizard, and I believe that reintroducing him to Evendaar would help in some way to redress the balance of magic here. But more importantly, Prince Rainold will have crucial information on demons and their powers, as he was married to your mother. I also believe that he will be able to help remove this foreign magic which overwhelms you."

The silence around the table was absolute.

"Rainere, when we met your father in his prison, we barely escaped with our lives," Adele said, shocked.

"I feel that might be a slight exaggeration," he replied. "Of course, there was that unpleasantness when he drugged me and then attacked you, but it was only because he was so curious about why we wanted the map to Sighmere's home in the Ice Mountains. He didn't cause us any lasting harm."

"But you'll agree that we thought he was unstable at best," she argued. "And probably insane at worst."

"Nevertheless, I will claim full responsibility for Prince Rainold and his actions once we have him safely back in Unisia," Rainere persisted. "He is my father, and it is only right that I should—"

"Your Majesty, if I may?" Lord Orgustus interrupted, already granting himself permission. "We're trying to improve your image and disassociate you from the Marchant element. Why in the name of the goddess Serena would you choose to bring a criminal Marchant prince into the Golden Palace now?"

Rainere's lip curled as he looked to Adele, but she could only raise her hands in a gesture of peace. "That's not as bad as it sounds," she said. "It's all just for show. I need to give the court and citizens what will make them happy."

"You're talking about politics, and I am talking about your safety, Your Majesty," Rainere snapped, his anger showing in the green sparks that were coalescing in a halo over his head.

"Still, we cannot risk causing any more trouble in the kingdom, and your father would be the worst kind of trouble," she said.

"I believe that Prince Rainold is a font of lost knowledge," Rainere repeated. "You need his help."

"Yes, but *would* he help me?" she countered. "It was pretty clear to both of us that Prince Rainold hates me."

"You must accept your queen's command, Your Highness," Lord Orgustus said, delighted to get a point over Rainere in such a public scene.

Rainere's expression froze, yet his stance relaxed as his fingertips started a staccato tapping on the tabletop. "Of course, if you're being advised to disassociate yourself from the Marchant element by your trusted servant, Lord Orgustus, then why would you want to free a wizard imprisoned for saving your life when you were a newborn and then giving you the map to find Sighmere?"

"Your Highness, my hands are tied on this." Adele tried to sound reasonable, but it felt more like she was begging. "I will not free the prince from prison. The risk that he'll do something terrible is too great."

"Can you think of someone else with his knowledge of demon magic?" he asked. "Because I can't."

Stop trying to badger me, Rainere, Adele thought, and felt a wave of magic race across her skin, making her shudder. Unable to continue without exploding, she swung her gaze around the table.

"Where in the hell is my high wizard?" She'd raised her voice but hadn't meant to shout quite so loud. "Somebody find Ohren, now!"

"No need—I'm here, Your Majesty." High Wizard Ohren was wearing his usual long, gray robe over a black suit and an unusual purple tie pinned by a sparkly gray rock. He made his way from the door, and Adele had never been so angry, or so relieved, to see the old wizard.

Ohren took a place at the table next to Lord Orgustus and locked eyes with her. "What did I miss?"

CHAPTER ELEVEN

"Burned by Dragon Flame"

Ohren will definitely want to help me! Rainere thought, standing up to draw the focus of the table. "High Wizard Ohren, I wish to release my father, Prince Rainold, from his interdimensional prison." He planted his fists on the table, leaning in. "He's the only one with any knowledge of demon magic and will be able to help the queen with the problems she is having."

"Wonderful idea!" Ohren said, clapping his hands. "Prince Rainold will be invaluable to our cause! And by that, I mean he will be invaluable to our queen. We should bring the Marchant prince to the Golden Palace immediately."

Rainere felt triumphant until a stab in the Mark on his side forced him to sit. Adelena's fury hurt like hell. "Your Majesty," he said through gritted teeth. "If you would listen to reason—"

But now Adelena was on her feet too, her eyes lit with a white-hot glow and magic pouring in a shower of sparks from her hands. "Rainere, you will obey me," she said in a voice that wasn't her own. "Leave your father where he is. My word is final."

All around him, men were rising from their seats and backing away from the table. It took all Rainere's strength just to stay upright. Her magic was hideously powerful, almost feral in its attack. Just like the violence in her tone, nothing about it felt familiar.

106

It's not her, he told himself. *It's the magic using her to fight me.*

The only other man who hadn't left the table was Jordan Jordansson. He took her little hand in his giant ones and spoke quietly. With the agony pounding through his system, Rainere couldn't hear what he said, but soon the white light dimmed in her hands and burned brightly in Jordansson's. Yet, all Rainere could think was, *No! That should be me, not him.*

Finally, the pain receded and he drew a long, rasping breath, wiping the sweat from his brow. His first thought was for Adelena and how terrible she would be feeling now that she had recovered. But she was already surrounded by her Queen's Guard. He slumped in his seat, feeling stupid and increasingly homicidal toward the tribesman.

"It's all right, Queen," Jordansson was saying, cradling his bright red hands against his chest as General Ohrig called for ice. "We know one way I can take a little from you." But he closed his eyes as the white light continued crawling up his arms. He swore colorfully in his own language, and Rainere was pleased someone was hurting as much as he was.

Intent on watching the drama play out, Rainere didn't notice Lord Orgustus until the man was at his shoulder. "Your Highness, if I may?"

Orgustus didn't take a seat but chose to loom over him. Rainere was still too sore to stand, so he feigned indifference.

"The queen and I have come to a most intimate understanding." Lord Orgustus was brazen, but Rainere noted that he kept his voice low. "She's finally listened to me and agreed to become the epitome of the St. Lucidis queen that we need in Unisia. She will dress the part, act the part, and go into the city to let the people know she isn't a Marchant whore but a woman worthy of taking the arm of their beloved former regent."

Rainere couldn't even begin to comprehend the gall of this young lord who would dare to challenge him in such a way. He began to plan the multitude of ways he could kill him.

Orgustus continued, "The queen will not want to hurt your feelings, but it would be best if you return to the Gray Palace and stop getting in her way. If we don't fix her image soon, there will be more rioting, and the mob will call for her death. With no high magistrar to govern the court, we are on the precipice of complete chaos. One wrong move, and we all go down." Orgustus looked over to Adelena. "And she'll be the first to fall."

Rainere didn't want to hear it, but the desperation behind Orgustus's pompous attitude was too thinly veiled. He himself had seen the degradation in the Slums and the hatred that the people of all quarters had for the alien queen. But Rainere would be damned to an eternity in Hell before he ever agreed with Orgustus St. Lucidis. He glared in response as the young lord finally moved away from him.

A pull in the Mark called Rainere's gaze back to Adelena. Makeup ran in dark streaks under her eyes, and her cheeks were flushed red. "Rainere, I'm so, so sorry." She gestured at the empty table, miserable. "But my command still stands—do not free your father. Can't you see I'm making enough trouble for everyone as it is?"

"My queen, you can't go on like this," Rainere said, but she was already leaving, Mrs. Ollenby supporting her with an arm around her shoulders. Through the Mark, Rainere felt her sorrow and her confusion, and it made him ache in sympathy. Yet he had a responsibility to make her see sense.

"Your Majesty, I assure you that I will create the strongest safeguards for the prince," he called out as she limped away from him. "It won't be like he's really free."

But the door to her bedchamber closed, and he was left fuming.

With no apparent sense of self-preservation, High Wizard Ohren slipped into the seat next to his and tapped him on the shoulder. "I think you're right, Your Highness."

Rainere narrowed his eyes. It was impossible to ever trust Ohren. The man lied and manipulated more than a logical mind could fathom, and Rainere had a very logical mind. "Why?"

"Because the queen is possessed by some primitive magic, and I've got no idea how to heal her," the high wizard replied. "If we leave her like this, she'll be an incomprehensible danger to herself and the rest of us. I knew your father well, and he understood the workings of demons like no one else—certainly more than anyone in our time. It was only a month ago that we thought of demons as mere creatures of legend, like the Dark Entities. Also, you said something about safeguards?"

Rainere nodded. "The interdimensional portal requires both colors of magic to open, but with the apex on Prince Rainold's door destroyed the last time Her Majesty and I broke in, it should be easier. Once he's free I'll take him home to the Gray Palace and contain him there."

"I know Prince Rainold can be reasonable if we bargain with him," Ohren added, confusing Rainere—*What prisoner wouldn't want to be free again?* "And of course he'll want to see his son."

"High Wizard, you have already revealed the full extent of your romantic relationship with my father." Rainere arched an eyebrow. "Please don't start being coy now."

"Oh, yes." Ohren's head twitched a little. "That's right, I told you everything about Rainold and me, didn't I?"

Rainere felt a little hand on his knee and looked down to see Stella. With a smile, he pulled her up to stand on his lap and indulged her with a dozen kisses on her sticky cheek. At any moment, he expected Ohren to snatch the baby out of his arms as he always did. His soft heart for the royal children was well known. But Ohren was looking around the room as if checking for anyone eavesdropping. "When should we go, Your Highness?"

Rainere stood, swinging Stella to his hip. "I need to discuss this with the queen again. I know she will understand when I explain it to her properly. It was the presence of Jordansson that set her off. That boy needs to stay well away from her."

Ohren's head flicked to the side again, the movement tiny but enough to make it clear how furious he was. "We have no time for your adolescent drama with the queen and her tribesman," he snarled. "She needs you to take charge and do the right thing for her now."

Rainere frowned, and Stella mirrored his expression. "I will not go behind Adelena's back with this," he said. "I have to make her understand."

"So be it." Ohren huffed in frustration. "But when she tries to kill you again, don't come crying to me."

Rainere felt his lip curl. "Adelena would never."

"Idiot!" Ohren spat and lurched to his feet. "Did you think those were kisses she was blowing you earlier? If that mountain boy hadn't been there to save you . . ." He left the suggestion hanging as he turned on his heel and stomped out of the royal apartment.

Stella babbled something incomprehensible, and Rainere took it as reassurance. "Your mummy wouldn't try to kill me," he said. "That old wizard is an imbecile." But the cold feeling didn't leave him, and Rainere decided to give Adelena a moment to recover. He headed out to join the rest of the children on the sunny terrace, suddenly feeling the need to give them another lesson in controlling their own magics.

Chapter Twelve

"The Lady Mayor"

In her bedchamber, it had only taken a few minutes for Adele's team to fix her makeup and hair after her magic-induced fit, but she requested a change of outfit to something more convenient for traveling into Concordis. With Pere Raven and Orestes still at large, there was the possibility of another assassination attempt, so she thought it best to be prepared to run or fight. Not to mention, she felt ridiculous wearing a sparkly ball gown outside the confines of the palace.

Lady Olivia had designed some gorgeous pant-and-jacket ensembles, and Adele felt much more herself as she dressed in the wine-colored, velvet leggings and matching knee-high suede boots. The jacket had bracelet-length sleeves and was nipped in at the waist but fluted out at the back, falling in soft folds over her behind. Jeweled double buttons fastened at the front, leaving a deep V that was filled with the ruffles of an almost-transparent white silk shirt. Several gem-strewn necklaces managed to cover any cleavage on display. Then, the moment she was ready, she insisted on leaving for Concordis. As she hurried down the front steps of the palace, she told herself it was to get this meeting out of the way and not because she wanted to avoid dealing with Rainere and his impossible request to free his father.

One of the huge royal carriages was waiting to carry her and Lord Orgustus, and two of his scribes, while the Queen's Guard would ride alongside on their matching chestnut steeds. Captain Lucky wasn't riding Redfire, as his favored horse had yet to fully recover from Ripenzo's journey from the Black Mountains to the Golden Palace— something he'd mentioned several times, causing Bear and Owens to question the true nature of Lucky's affection for his horse. Pepper and Leith weren't stupid enough to join in the teasing but barely stifled their laughter at their stiff-backed captain.

Adele had been told that the trip was going to take about forty minutes from the Golden Palace to the office of the Lady Mayor, but they'd only passed through the gates and she was already sweating in the stuffy carriage. She took off her pretty jacket and opened the shuttered windows to let in the dust-laden breeze. Orgustus was sitting on the padded seat opposite her reading a scroll, but he kept casting her glances every so often, making her feel very self-conscious. She took a sip of water from one of the glass flasks sitting in a rest between the carriage cushions and tried to think of something other than her magic-tantrum this morning.

"I would've arranged an open-top carriage for you, Your Majesty," Lord Orgustus broke their long silence. "But it's so hot today, I thought it might be too uncomfortable."

"This is fine," she said, "thank you."

The scribe sitting next to her began scratching at a scroll and then stopped, quill poised as he watched her intently.

"Wait. Are you writing down everything I say?" she asked. The scribe couldn't have been more than fourteen or fifteen, still fine-boned and lanky, with short, blond hair and sky-blue eyes. Blushing, he showed her the scroll.

"Nice handwriting." She raised an eyebrow at Lord Orgustus, demanding an explanation.

"We're going into a political meeting," Orgustus said. "The Lady Mayor is a formidable woman and a complete rogue when it comes to getting what she wants. I don't mind telling you that I have been bested in several disputes with her in the past, hence my insistence that every discussion is recorded."

Adele was impressed with his candor. "It takes a strong man to admit when he's wrong."

Lord Orgustus didn't accept the compliment but only glowered down at his scroll. "I'll be surprised if it's not the first thing she mentions," he muttered.

Adele stared out her window, thinking, *Maybe I'm going to like this Lady Mayor.*

As they traveled the wide, paved road of the King's Highway, Adele studied the country around her, watching as green fields became sprawling farms, farms became hamlets with cute wooden cottages, and hamlets became the densely populated, stone-walled suburbs of Concordis. The only blights on the picturesque landscape were the charred burial pyres and hastily constructed outdoor chapels for the mass funerals. Dark evidence of the pain the citizens had suffered when the Summer Influenza took hold of the kingdom just weeks ago.

Adele was somber as they entered the city. The main thoroughfare was accessed through a large gilt gate that had been erected for no practical purpose except to announce entry to the wealthiest quarter in Concordis—the Guild Quarter.

"What are the other two quarters called, my lord?" Adele asked. "I only know of the Lower Districts and the Guild Quarter."

Lord Orgustus's expression suggested that he thought she was making a joke, and a bad one at that. "There is the Guild Quarter, the Traders Quarter, the Artisans Quarter, and the Lower Districts. As you know, the Lower Districts are more commonly called the Slums." He didn't blink, as if determined that she should not look away while he imparted this lesson to her. "In fact, the city isn't divided into four mathematical quarters, you understand? It has always been the wealth and prosperity of a suburb that determines its size, not the geography of the city. A hundred years ago, the Guild Quarter spread over most of these blocks; now it's reduced to six wide streets and a few boundary avenues where the up-and-coming families live. The largest population in the city lives in the Traders Quarter, where most of the workshops are. The second biggest sector lives in the Slums. It's always seemed ridiculous to me that the Court of the Golden Palace insists on placating the whining minority in the Guild Quarter when the real balance of power resides in the rest of the city. Woe betide the day when the citizens themselves realize it."

Adele sat back on the velvet cushions of the royal carriage. As the adopted daughter of two university academics on Earth, she'd never been blessed with the burden of wealth. She'd had to work and earn her own way. Now she was the head of the monarchist government of the largest nation on an alien planet, and the time had come to find out just how the place was being managed while she'd been distracted by tragedy, adventure, and falling in love with the most hated man in Unisia.

"Does the Lady Mayor represent the citizens with no magical powers too?" she asked. She'd heard from General Ohrig's angry mutterings that there was a growing group of non-magical citizens with no representation in the Court of the Golden Palace.

Lord Orgustus was quiet for a long moment. His blue eyes shifted minutely from side to side as if he was trying to read something in her expression. "As you should already know, many of the commoners— or non-magical people, as you call them—were lost to the influenza," he said finally. "And they will be mourned with all the dignity befitting their lives."

"I'm glad to hear it," she said, but couldn't help but wonder what that meant for the population. "So magic levels are healthy in the people left?"

"It's too hard to say." Orgustus turned away, hiding his reaction from her. "We'll hold a census when the mourning period is over."

"Of course." At his words, she noted that many of the houses and buildings they were passing had long black banners hanging out of their windows or over the doors. Words had been embroidered across the front and she could only guess that they were the names of those family members lost.

"Did you have any success with Jordan Jordansson this morning, after he helped you at breakfast?"

Orgustus's abrupt change of topic wasn't lost on her. "You saw everything he did, but there wasn't time for more," she replied. "We'll have to investigate his effect on the magic later today."

"Is it true that you don't sleep at all, Your Majesty?" He had blurted out the question by accident, she was sure, but he didn't apologize for it.

Adele was determined not to reveal too much of herself until Orgustus proved he wouldn't use it against her. "There is always so much to learn as a queen and a demon," she said. "And I've always enjoyed being a night owl."

She turned back to watching the city outside her window, signaling that question time was over. They were leaving the wealthy houses and gardens of the Guild Quarter and entering the Artisans Quarter. Here the houses were a little narrower, with long public carriages and carts filling the road. The streets were crowded with people, and the restaurants with outdoor seating were full for the lunchtime rush. Most of the citizens were dressed in bright colors, but there were plenty wearing the dull blue or gray uniforms of manual workers.

In this quarter there were lots of beautiful shops and boutiques, and Adele saw a very pretty children's clothing store that she thought might be fun to visit, right before she spotted the portraits of two children in the window. The door was draped in black cloth. She felt tears sting her eyes. *That could so easily have been Stella,* she thought.

A moment later, the carriage stopped in front of a large two-story building painted a deep burgundy with black trim on the windows. The ground floor was split—one side housed a busy restaurant with tables under large umbrellas decorating the pavement, and on the other side, grand double doors led to the hotel portion of the building.

The floor upstairs had a wide, wraparound balcony, and a large sign on the roof proclaimed the place to be "Merrills's Great Hotel."

Lord Orgustus opened the carriage door and jumped down the steps, then held out his hand to help Adele. The scribes scrambled out behind them.

She was waiting on the cobblestone pavement when several stable hands wearing long, leather aprons appeared. Her Queen's Guard handed over their horses, Captain Lucky giving instructions for their care. When she approached the hotel entrance, two young women dressed in black suits held the doors open, and the Queen's Guard fell into position around her. The hotel lobby was richly appointed with lots of dark wood, bright artworks, and heavy carved furniture. The concierge was a tall gentleman wearing a three-piece black suit, who recognized Lord Orgustus and greeted him warmly. The two men chatted amicably for a moment, and Adele was interested to see several well-dressed patrons passing through the lobby call out jovial greetings to Orgustus, which he returned with good humor. The young lord was clearly popular here. After offering them the chance of refreshments in the restaurant next door, the concierge led their group up a carpeted staircase and took them down a short corridor to the last door—the office of the Lady Mayor.

Adele was surprised to be stopped as the concierge knocked softly and called out, "My Lady Mayor, I have Lord Orgustus and several guests to see you."

"Several guests?" Adele mouthed to Ohrig, her eyebrows sky high.

Ohrig rolled his eyes and shrugged.

The concierge heard a response that Adele didn't and opened the door to guide them into the room. "Lady Mayor, may I present Lord Orgustus and guests." The concierge bowed. "Shall I fetch refreshments for everyone?"

The Lady Mayor was sitting behind an enormous desk, bent over a sheet of parchment and writing with a rather extravagant quill. The desk was beautiful, the wood stained black and a sheet of red, antique leather embedded in the surface. Matching shelves lined the wall behind her, piled high with books, loose scrolls, and brass ornaments. The room was well lit and fresh, as the windows were open, but it was also crammed with chairs of all sizes and dimensions, making Adele feel squashed between her six muscular Queen's Guards, Lord Orgustus, and his two scribes. The dragon magic was twitching in her chest, and she had to resist scratching at the hot, itchy feeling between her breasts.

The mayor continued writing as the concierge left without receiving an answer on the refreshments question.

Personally, Adele had already received the message loud and clear: the Lady Mayor was angry and wanted her to know it. She smothered a smirk, admiring the courage it took to openly defy a queen, even if she was the queen in question.

Lord Orgustus shuffled his way around a tapestry-covered wingback to approach the desk. "Lady Mayor, as we discussed, I have brought Her Majesty, Queen Adelena Olivia St. Lucidis, before you to conduct discussions."

"That was today?" The Lady Mayor's voice was melodic, but she didn't stop writing on her parchment, nor did she deign to look up.

"Lady Mayor, the queen is a busy woman. Perhaps we should reconvene at the Golden Palace when it is more convenient for you? Though I cannot promise that Her Majesty will have an opening anytime soon," Orgustus said, and Adele could see by the bright red of his cheeks that he was embarrassed. She had more trouble smothering her smirk, and continued to be impressed by the mayor.

The Lady Mayor finally laid down her quill in an absentminded way, as if she had chosen herself to stop writing. When she sat back in her chair, Adele could see that she was quite tall, beautiful, and probably in her late forties or well-preserved early fifties. Dark hair was piled high on her head, with long, tight curls trailing down her neck and flowing over a voluptuous show of cleavage created by her bustier dress. *She looks like a high-class madam in an old Western movie,*

Adele thought as the dark brown eyes of the Lady Mayor took her full measure.

Lord Orgustus began twitching oddly, and Adele realized he was trying to signal the Lady Mayor to stand and curtsy to the queen as protocol dictated. While it was fun to see someone else irritate the pompous young lord, he'd been right about one thing—Adele was incredibly busy. If she wanted to spend the afternoon with her children, then she needed this meeting over with, even if that meant an unfortunate resolution. Without an invitation, she took a seat in a black-and-white-striped slipper chair near the front of the desk. She returned the Lady Mayor's intense gaze for a long moment and could feel a pointless battle of wills beginning between herself and this politician. She decided to cut it short. "Lady Mayor—actually, may I call you by your name?" she asked. "I feel like it will help us move forward in our friendship."

The mayor pressed her lips in a hard line, probably annoyed that Adele didn't already know it. "Certainly, Your Majesty. My name is Bethany Merrills."

"Bethany, thank you." Adele smiled. Bethany didn't. "Would you like to discuss why you've requested this meeting with me today?"

The mayor opened a drawer in her desk and pulled out a sheaf of papers. She handed them to Orgustus without watching whether he caught them or not. "Your Majesty, I have orphanages full to bursting in the wake of the influenza. I have welfare programs on the brink of collapse and no funds to feed the citizens who've been left bereft without families to support them. I have a city on the edge of panic with Marchant Eldars screaming through the sky above us. And here, I had simply thought you might be interested in how badly your people are doing."

Adele blinked. Only General Ohrig spoke to her with such bald honesty, and despite her surprise she appreciated it. "I saw the funeral pyres," she said. "And my own daughter almost died of the influenza too. Of course I care, Bethany."

"Well, forgive me, but it's a little hard to tell, Your Majesty," the mayor snapped back. "You've been queen of Unisia for how long? And yet this is the first time you've met with me—"

"Bethany, am I right in thinking that you were elected by some kind of popular ballot or vote?" Adele interrupted, for both their sakes. The dragon magic didn't appreciate Bethany's candor as much as Adele did and she could feel it igniting in her chest.

Bethany Merrills nodded. "I've been in office for more than fifteen years. I run a board of ever-changing members, but their votes are unanimous because the citizens know that I do what's best for the city."

Adele made a show of looking impressed. "So, I guess that you know everyone important in the city," she said. "You know how everything works and who does what?"

General Ohrig coughed quietly behind Adele, but she ignored the warning.

"Of course." The Lady Mayor didn't miss anything, her eyes flicking to Ohrig then back to Adele. "I support our hospices and orphanages out of my own pocket when the Crown chooses not to help. I've done well for myself but what I earn I put back into the city."

"I respect your commitment to our citizens," Adele said, watching the mayor's gaze flick over her shoulder again. This time she followed it. "Is Queen's Guard Leith of some interest to you, Bethany?"

"I should say so," Bethany answered, with a broad wink at QG Leith. "Oleitham is my son, Your Majesty."

Adele hung on to her smile, though the dragon's magic had harnessed her green magic and was telling her to rip this woman's head off. "Is that so?" she said.

"Well, I'm sure when you're off doing the goddess only knows what for weeks on end and your men return home looking thin and overworked, thinking about their families is your last priority," Bethany said, that melodic voice now grating on Adele's nerves.

The rage felt so hot and so good, covering every inch of her skin in a halo of power. She could hear the heavy echo of dragon magic in her voice when she said, "Bethany, you run this city. Correct?"

Bethany arched a single eyebrow, amused. "I think that's been made clear."

Adele shot to her feet and stalked to the window. *Stay calm*, she warned herself, *I need to use my head not magic.* Looking down on the bustling stable yard, she could see a group of young women wearing white aprons, smoking cigarettes and laughing together. She felt a moment of bitter envy for their simple lives.

"You see, Bethany, there is another person who I'm told ran this city too," she continued.

"I'm sure I don't know what you mean, Your Majesty." The mayor was getting frustrated, and that suited Adele just fine.

"But you know the Boss of the Underworld, don't you?" Adele turned back to the mayor to gauge her reaction. "He lived in the Golden Palace, as it turns out. He tried to have me killed, and he tried to have my children kidnapped. He tried to kill my friends, and he spread hideous propaganda to incite the citizens to have me usurped. But as mayor of Concordis for fifteen years, I'm sure you know all about this."

The mayor gaped. "The Boss runs the Underworld, Your Majesty. I have nothing to do with his operations," she said. "I run the Topworld, that's . . . that's how it's always been."

"No, that's how it was," Adele said, clasping her hands behind her back to hide the shower of green sparks forming at her fingertips. "The Boss is gone, and he has left his position vacant."

The mayor looked to Lord Orgustus, who nodded in agreement. "It's true, the Boss has been disposed of, Lady Mayor."

"But that means—" The mayor was too clever to finish her own sentence.

"That means that a criminal industry worth thousands of bars of gold is just floating about beneath our feet waiting for a new leader," Adele said. "And ready to be used to fund orphanages and support hospices."

"But the industries of the Underworld are immoral, not to mention my own personal hatred of the opiate blue tonic," Bethany said quickly, and Adele could see the canny intelligence in the mayor's eyes as she calculated the opportunities available to her now. "I would want official powers to clean up all those who won't adapt to any new Topworld regime."

"My strategy exactly, Bethany." She tried to soften her growling tone, but the mayor paled anyway. "I find 'cleaning up' those who don't adapt to my new regime most helpful too."

The mayor swallowed hard, and her gaze flew back to Lord Orgustus, the only one in the room who looked genuinely happy.

"Bethany, I want you to take apart every bad thing that the Boss built," Adele said, "and I want the Underworld dragged into the light of day."

The mayor opened her mouth as if she would protest, but something in Adele's expression made her think better of it.

"And one last thing," Adele said. "I imagine you're familiar with The Magician's Wand, the public house where the Boss ran his operation in the Slums."

Weakly, the mayor nodded.

"Well, I want it," she said. "It will be my new base in the city, where I can hold court for all those commoners who want to meet their queen. I understand it's very difficult to get an appointment with me in the palace. And after all"—she swung her hand, encompassing the crowded office and her Queen's Guard still standing at attention—"we cannot expect you to provide your queen and her guard with such warm hospitality every time I want to see you."

The mayor gathered herself together and stood up. "I'd like nothing more than to help, Your Majesty, but change will not come easily to a city that has already been through so much. We have a fight ahead of us."

We. Adele liked hearing that. She was relieved to offer her hand, free of glittering sparks, and Bethany shook it. "I look forward to reading your report on this grand new Topworld regime very soon, Bethany Merrills."

"I look forward to writing it for you, Your Majesty," Bethany answered, looking a little shell-shocked though she kept her composure.

"Now, if you'll excuse me, I have other matters to attend to today," Adele said, tipping her chin at the QGs to signal that she was ready to go.

Ohrig was at the door and opened it for Adele. His bushy gray eyebrows were beetled. "We need to talk," he muttered as she swept past him. Adele didn't wait for her general, but she did hear Bethany call out to Leith and nodded to let him know he could take a moment with his mother.

Adele wanted to be far away from the stifling tension of the Lady Mayor's office, so she hurried through the elegant lobby and pushed through the front doors of the hotel. Her QGs kept up on their long legs, surrounding her in a protective formation. Once outside, QG Bear peeled off to find the hotel stables and organize for the horses and carriage to be brought around again. Standing in the hot sunshine and fresh air, the dragon magic in her body settled immediately. She checked under her necklaces, expecting to see the skin on her chest inflamed, but she was fine. Breathing a sigh of relief, she finally noticed the scents from the restaurant next door wafting through the air—grilled cheese and barbecued meat.

"God, I'm starving," she said. Breakfast felt like a long time ago.

"Threatening the Lady Mayor give you an appetite, did it?" Ohrig asked. She could tell he was bursting with all he wanted to say but couldn't in public.

"Yes, as it happens." Adele tossed him a grin. She was still riding the high of not letting loose her magic in front of the mayor and thinking that maybe her control was getting better already. "Tell me,

Ohrig, is that the woman you did a favor for by taking Leith into the Queen's Guard?"

Ohrig's expression said this wasn't what he wanted to talk about. "Merrills thought he'd be safer with me than running around on the streets with the bad crowd he hung out with. We're right on the border of the Traders Quarter here, and not far from the Slums. There was a lot the boy could do to get into trouble. Now, how about we address the fact that you've—"

"Bethany's very beautiful, isn't she?" she remarked, too casually. "Do you have some history together?"

Ohrig looked away at the restaurant. "I'm sure I can get you a table for lunch," he muttered. "Your carriage won't be ready for another twenty minutes, at least."

"I'll take that as a yes, then." But she was talking to herself, as Ohrig had already turned on his heel and marched away.

"And now I know how deep his connections to Concordis politics go," she said to QG Pepper, who only looked confused.

"Well, I'm a country boy, Your Majesty. We don't go in much for politics in the Blue Hills," he said.

Ohrig returned and showed their group to a table at the front of the restaurant. The other tables around their large one had been moved away to give a narrow corridor of space in the crowded dining room. Adele smiled at the staring diners and was pleased when some of them waved back at her. Ohrig knew the menu without reading it and ordered for everyone as the QGs took off their heavy white-and-gold jackets, settling in.

A server with trembling hands placed a chilled glass of something pink in front of Adele. The girl couldn't have been older than her late teens and looked terrified. "What's this?" Adele asked her.

"It's our own cold cherry wine," answered another server as she deposited frosty glasses of beer in front of the men. This one was a little older, brown curls poking out from her white waitress's cap and a bright curiosity on her pretty face. "All right, Mr. Ohrig? Is this really Queen Adelena, or are you jokin' me?"

"Watch your manners, Dolly," Ohrig growled, but Adele hushed him with a pat on his arm.

"I really am Queen Adelena," she answered. "It's nice to meet you, Dolly."

Dolly grinned in a charming way that reminded Adele of someone else. "You got Leith with you? Or did you chuck him out of the QG for being cheeky?" Dolly asked.

"Sorry, we'll get your food right now." The other, shyer server dragged Dolly away by the arm.

QG Leith came into the restaurant and threw himself onto a chair. He ran a hand through his short, light brown hair and his cheeks were red.

"I'm sorry if I made trouble for you with your mum, Leith," Adele said. "Not that I was even aware she was your mum—or Ohrig's friend. That would've been nice to know before going into the meeting. I'm sure Lord Orgustus knew the family connection."

Leith stripped off his jacket, fiddling with the gold braid to avoid Adele's frown. "Your Majesty, I'm sorry I didn't say anything this morning to you," he said, and he sounded it. "But you know, my mum, she's—well, she's used to having things all her own way. And thanks for not losing your temper with her. Really, thank you." He stopped stammering and took a quick swig of Pepper's beer. Adele winced internally, knowing that he must've been terrified that she would hurt his mum like she had Charlie and Rainere yesterday. And then Jordansson this morning. Her shame burned away any pride she felt about the meeting.

"All right, Leith? You got a nice job sitting on your arse, I see." Dolly came over to deposit a glass of beer in front of him, then refilled everyone else's from a jug. Adele got another glass of the delicious cherry wine. "And you've brought the queen in today. Mum'll be proud of you."

"All right, Dolly?" Leith looked embarrassed all over again and changed his accent to a courtly one. "And yes, Her Majesty is pleased to make your acquaintance, I am sure."

"Oh, I am sure!" Dolly mimicked, letting out a peal of laughter. "So fancy, Mr. Leith, I am sure!" She left the table still giggling.

"Apologies again, Your Majesty, Dolly's my older sister," Leith mumbled. "She knows better than to be that rude. I'll tell my mum."

Adele only nodded, still feeling awful, when a well-dressed couple approached her to pay their "humble respects." She thanked them, and the couple moved off to immediately tell their friends at another table the few words she'd said to them. She noticed that they had started a trend as other diners got up from their tables, wiped their chins with the white linen napkins, and began to head toward her table.

"Damn it," Adele muttered just as Dolly placed a large platter of crispy roast chicken legs drizzled with cheese sauce in front of her.

"What? It's our specialty," Dolly said, misunderstanding. Adele tipped her head at the growing crowd.

"And I'm not going to get to enjoy it today. Thank you, but I think we'll be going—"

"Oh, no, you're not getting bothered here. Sod that!" Dolly climbed up on a chair and raised her arms in the air, her voice carrying to the far corners of the large restaurant. "Ladies and gentlemen, Queen Adelena is here to experience the true magic that are our Crispy Lady Legs with special sauce for the first time in her blessed life. I'm sure you will join me in taking back your chairs and raising a glass in cheers to the health of our good queen, Adelena!"

The crowd dispersed back to their tables, and there was a resounding cheer as everyone raised their voices for "Queen Adelena!" It was such a happy sound that Adele got over her self-consciousness and raised her own glass, drinking a sip to applause.

"Now eat, before it gets cold," Dolly ordered after she'd climbed down off her chair. "There's more coming for you."

"I like your sister," Adele told Leith as she helped herself to a chicken leg. It seemed the thing to do was eat it with a tiny pair of spiky tongs, which took a bit of wrangling. She looked up from her task at the sound of cheering and shouts of welcome. Lord Orgustus had entered the restaurant and was waving to the happy crowd, accepting their compliments with a wide smile. Disconcerted to see how admired Orgustus was, she accidentally dropped a chicken leg and splashed liquid cheese down the front of her blouse.

"I must say, well done with the Lady Mayor, Your Majesty." Orgustus was still waving to his fans when he grabbed a chair and pushed between QGs Owens and Pepper, who reluctantly shifted aside for him. "That was—well, we'll discuss it later, of course. But I'm very impressed with how you handled yourself."

General Ohrig frowned at the young lord. "I'm sure the queen is delighted to have ascended in your esteem, Lord Orgustus. But give it a rest while we eat lunch."

Orgustus nodded and thanked the server for his beer. "What a day, though! Is life always like this when you're around, Your Majesty?"

"My lord, you have no bloody idea," QG Owens grumbled.

Lord Orgustus looked bemused while Adele and her Queen's Guard burst out laughing.

Chapter Thirteen

"A Lord and His Lady"

After returning to the Golden Palace that afternoon, Lord Orgustus retired to his apartment. His small but luxurious three-room suite had been put back to rights after the drama of a few days ago, but the metallic odor of dark magic still hung in the air no matter how many scented candles he burned.

Stretched out on his couch, he was examining the day's events. Bethany Merrills was a very useful ally, and Orgustus had always respected her ruthlessness and business acumen as she ran the city of Concordis with a deft hand. But he had to admit that it had been satisfying seeing the mayor bested at her own game. In as little as ten minutes, Queen Adelena had manipulated Merrills into not only running the Underworld but making it pay for the welfare projects in the city.

Lord Orgustus had never had anything to do with the Boss or his opiate industry. Of course, High Magistrar Orestes wouldn't have wanted him involved in any of that business. He must've worked very hard to keep the Court of the Golden Palace ignorant of the Underworld and all his actions down there. *This meeting with the queen has definitely put me in good stead with her, but unless she demands that I share a report, I can claim all the credit for her actions with the Court and treasury.* He chuckled to himself. *Adelena really is a piss-poor politician, and with no one to guide her hand but me, it seems I control the Crown again.*

"Why is it so quiet in here? Where is everybody?" Lady Olivia's voice interrupted his musings as she glided into the room. She was dressed in a royal blue gown, white ruffles at her waist and sleeves—pretty, but not very provocative, which was disappointing.

"My sweet Olivia, so much has changed, hasn't it?" Orgustus took her hand and pulled her to sit next to him on a couch. "The mysteries that vexed us are solved. The queen is home, Princess Stella is well again, and the Marchant prince seems to be behaving as the queen's personal lapdog."

"Yes, and?" Olivia asked, glancing around the room rather than holding his gaze.

"And I have achieved the impossible and made a friend of Queen Adelena." Orgustus touched Olivia gently on the nose to get her attention. "Now that I have her ear, I can help you rise in the ranks."

"But I'm already head lady-in-waiting," Olivia said, pouting. "And I did that myself by asking the queen for the promotion and then using my authority to retire the others. The queen didn't even ask about Lady Cara or Lady Lisbeth once they'd gone, which actually shows just how unimportant we are."

"But she likes you, Olivia, I know she does." Orgustus pressed a little closer and laid his hand on her knee. "You're the only woman near the queen's age who has any kind of friendship with her."

"Today she did wear the new velvet trouser suit I made her." Olivia sounded like she was softening up, but in the last few days, Orgustus had learned not to underestimate this pretty blonde. He hadn't any idea that she'd been ruthless enough to try and seduce the Marchant prince, or clever enough to manipulate Orgustus himself so he got the blame for taking Princess Stella from the queen's quarters.

"But, my lord—"

"Sweetheart, you know you can call me Orgustus." He touched

the tip of her nose again. *Can she really fake a blush?* he wondered as he watched her cheeks turn pink.

"Orgustus, I would just die if the queen found out that Prince Rainere attacked me in her bedchamber the day Natalie and Aaron were kidnapped." Olivia dropped her eyes in an affectation of modesty but peeked up at him. "I was too terrified of him to say no, but she might not see it that way. Could you mention it to her for me please?" She took his hands. "Please? I'm sure I'll have the chance to put in a good word for you too, telling her how hard you work and how loyal you are."

Orgustus almost chuckled at Olivia's veiled threat. He'd always found intelligence a rare commodity in beautiful women, and Olivia showing her true colors was something of a turn-on.

"You keep telling me what the queen is doing behind my back, and I'll make sure she keeps thinking you're her friend," Orgustus said. "But I'll keep your secret until it serves us *both* to reveal it." He leaned forward, but before his lips could touch hers he felt a hand on his chest.

"I spent last night at the Queen's Guard party with Captain Lucky," Olivia said, a note of triumph in her voice. "It wouldn't do to have any rumors about a liaison between us while the captain is courting me."

Orgustus snorted at the formal use of the word. "I presume this *courting* happens with your clothes on."

Olivia giggled and rolled her eyes. "Lucky declared that he's in love with me and calls himself a serious suitor but won't do anything but kiss the back of my hand."

"How odd." Orgustus leaned back against the couch and considered how this could lead to an advantage for him. "Is his chastity a religious thing?"

"Oh, yes. The poor thing is obsessed with prayer and talks about the goddess like they're personal friends." Lady Olivia got up and smoothed her skirt down. "But he adores me, and I wouldn't be surprised if he offers me his hand in marriage before too long. It's very sweet actually—the adoring part, not the chastity thing. Now, if you'll excuse me, I must get back to work. I have a pile of new designs for the queen that Tilburn needs to sign off for me. I'm using actual, real diamonds on the collar of one gown—it'll be so expensive, but so beautiful!" Only when talking about the dress did Olivia's face soften and her smile become genuine.

Orgustus slapped her on the rump as she passed him, enjoying her yelp of surprise. "Let me know when you get tired of Captain Chaste," he said. "I'm having a small party with a group of select courtiers—Lord Pine, Lady Onidia and a few others. You're welcome anytime, my sweet."

Olivia didn't answer, only threw him an unreadable look over her shoulder as she reached the door and closed it behind her.

Orgustus lay back on the couch, hands behind his head, and stared up at the crystal chandelier tinkling in the soft breeze. Olivia had pleased him by being willing to remain his spy but had proved herself too clever by half. They had both been aware of his erection, and she hadn't shown any interest in climbing into his lap. *She might be trying to make me jealous?* he thought before his mind wandered to all he had to do for the queen's birthday celebration. It was such a pity that it couldn't be a wedding, both the court and the citizens loved "love." *Maybe it doesn't have to be the queen's wedding, any royal wedding would do really, and Olivia would make a particularly beautiful bride. I wonder . . .*

There was a knock on his apartment door, and thinking it was his impatient friends returning for an afternoon of drinking, he bellowed, "Come in!"

The tribesman, Jordan Jordansson, was the last person Orgustus expected to put his head around the door. "My lord, I've come to visit you."

Orgustus sat up and swung his boots to the carpet. "Of course, please come in, my good man. What can I do for you?"

Jordansson lurched his enormous frame into the room, looking around the apartment with a dawning comprehension. "I've been here before, to help the baby princess, yes?"

Orgustus got up to pour them each a glass of Firewhiskey, but when he handed it to Jordansson, the taller man flinched. "Do you have any cold drinks?" he asked. "It is so hot in Unisia. I feel like a coal in a fire about to explode." It was true that Jordansson was red-faced and sweating profusely. His white-blond hair was sticking up in short, wet spikes, and his blue shirt was plastered to his back.

As a former regent, Lord Orgustus wasn't entitled to more than a maid and part-time steward, but he could send for things by asking any servant passing by his door. He ordered a tray of sorbets and a large urn of ice water for his guest. That done, he invited Jordansson to sit out on the balcony with him, as it was cooler there than in his stuffy apartment.

Jordansson took a seat on a large wicker armchair and immediately undid the buttons of his shirt, flapping the tails to try and cool himself further. He began speaking in his own language, then apologized with a chuckle. "I'm almost too hot to think in the King's Tongue," he said.

"I understand that you came from a rather remote valley in the Ice Mountains, Mr. Jordansson. I would think it a rather fortunate coincidence that the queen managed to find you on her travels the way she did," Orgustus said. "How is it you come to speak the King's Tongue as well as you do?"

Jordansson paused for a long moment, frowning as he probably translated in his head. "You want to know how I learned to talk like you?"

Orgustus nodded.

"There was a traveling magician who came to our village in the Valley of the Three Sisters. I was very young then and was given the task of looking after him in the, uh, room with walls and guards for not escaping."

"A prison?" Orgustus was intrigued.

"Yes, a prison like that, but not protected with magic," Jordansson was keen to explain. "The man was a Marchant magician, not a wizard—he only did practical magic like crops and weather and these sorts of things. But the chieftess did not trust the wizard. She didn't like his dark hair and that he could control the clouds, so she put him in this prison."

There was a knock at the door, and Orgustus bellowed for entry again. He saw Jordansson's face light up as the servants brought refreshments.

"Hello, ladies, I am Jordan Jordansson of the Valley of the Three Sisters in what you call the Ice Mountains!" The maids giggled but didn't answer the giant tribesman, only turned and fled when Orgustus dismissed them.

"Oh." Jordansson was crestfallen. "I was trying to be charming. Leith told me that I would have much success with the small women of Unisia, but they laugh at me every time."

"Are you not devoted to Queen Adelena?" Orgustus asked, prying shamelessly as he handed a bowl of fruit ice to the tribesman. "Didn't you announce that you would marry her and she would have your child?"

Jordansson took another moment to translate silently. "The queen is my partner in destiny," he said. "But no god would wish his people to smile only at one person."

Orgustus laughed. "If it's only smiles you want, well, then . . ."

Jordansson joined in when he realized his mistake. "I miss women," he admitted. "In my village, I am known for being very good at pleasure. A question for you: the women here like to laugh and run away. Am I meant to hunt them down to prove my attraction?"

"Jordansson, you've been in our beautiful kingdom for a few days now—has anyone taken you out of the Golden Palace?" Orgustus asked, already knowing the answer. "Would you like to see more of our country, maybe even the city of Concordis? I imagine it's very different from your village."

Jordansson looked as delighted as a child. "I would like that," he said. "Can we see the place where you keep these giant ponies, the horses? And the houses where you buy things—shops, they are called? Also where the silver sea meets the golden shore?"

Orgustus laughed again, but not unkindly. Jordansson's happiness was infectious. "The silver sea is in Sandar, which is a four-day ride from here, so no. But all the other things I can show you. Let's start with the stables here in the Golden Palace, then take a couple of horses and ride into town for dinner and drinks tonight. Would you mind if I bring some friends with me? We can certainly find some women who prefer to dance than run away."

"Yes, wonderful." Jordansson pronounced the word *vun-dah-fool*, and Orgustus knew that all the ladies would find that charming, so he didn't bother to correct his new friend.

"Well, let's go!" Orgustus wondered whom he was really doing a favor by befriending Jordansson: the queen for keeping him out of her way, or himself for gaining a potential ally who practically had a place in the queen's bedchamber. Either way, it was a win, and the giant seemed like he'd be a lot of fun.

Orgustus knew just where in Concordis to take Jordansson on his night out. It would do the Lady Mayor good to know how close an eye he was keeping on her again.

What a vun-dah-fool day, he thought with a grin as he ushered Jordansson out of the apartment.

Chapter Fourteen

"Magic Lessons for Life"

After her meeting with Bethany Merrills, Adele returned to the Golden Palace feeling pleased that she'd, hopefully, contributed to solving some of the problems suffered by the people in Concordis. She'd also learned a lot about Orgustus, especially how beloved he was. Like the former regent, the Lady Mayor was entrenched in a solid position of power in the city, but Adele had believed her when she denied having dealings with the Boss and his Underworld. While Adele knew she should remain vigilant for betrayal, that could be said for any aspect of her life as a queen. She'd really wanted to discuss the meeting with Ohrig, but there was no privacy with Orgustus in the carriage. Then, when they'd arrived back at the Golden Palace, she'd left everyone down in the stables and raced up to her apartment to see the children, hoping they weren't too angry with her for disappearing that morning.

In the royal apartment, Seraphina told Adele that Stella was already down for her after-lunch nap and Aaron, Natalie, and Leafy were with Prince Rainere in his laboratory having a magic lesson. The nanny was rather desperate to explain that both she and Caitlin had offered many times to assist the Marchant prince with the children, but he'd refused their help.

Adele tried to remember the way to the prince's lab. She knew it was in a quiet part of the palace with rather dowdy wall hangings and threadbare carpets.

"I don't think His Highness really likes us, Your Majesty," Seraphina continued, her freckled cheeks pink and her chestnut-brown eyes glassy with tears. "He never wants us helping him, except to do the littlest things. Even Siobhan can't say more than one word to him about our orders, and she's as bold as you like."

"I'm sure His Highness just feels it would be safest to keep away while the kids are throwing their magic around. Don't let it worry you, Sera," Adele reassured the young woman, as she suppressed her own exasperation. Suddenly, she could see a lifetime of having to explain Rainere's behavior to the people of the Golden Palace. Rainere had never had any patience for the many niceties and protocols here. "Is Mrs. Ollenby around?" she asked.

"Mrs. Ollenby said she needs a few hours of personal time and we're not to disturb her," Sera replied. "Shall I go back to arranging the children's toys, Your Majesty?"

With a nod, Adele let the young nanny escape to the nursery. The list of things that she should do with her afternoon was long: First, she should find High Wizard Ohren wherever he was hiding and seek his help in trying to track down Orestes, using that magic mirror. Then she should take another meeting with Tilburn and tell him about her meeting with the Lady Mayor. She should also find Jordan Jordansson and try again to siphon the dragon magic out of her blood. Or at least have a conversation with the man. Since his arrival, Adele had done nothing but use him for his magic, and she guessed he was feeling very neglected.

But she did none of those things.

Instead, she changed out of her cheese sauce–splattered shirt and into a pink silk blouse with butterflies embroidered around the collar and down the front. In her dressing room, there was a rack of brand new gowns that she'd never seen before, as well as a stack of shoe boxes. She cheered up when she found a pair of satin slippers that were encrusted with pink stones and matched her top perfectly.

On the long walk to find Rainere's laboratory, she had to stop and ask directions a few times but eventually found it in a deserted wing of the palace. The hallway was lined with wide doors, each with a tin-plate sign printed with fading ink. Wandering her way to the end, she ran her hand along the plaster wall, fingertips skipping over the various ugly tapestries and dusty displays of magic paraphernalia— brass crucibles, mechanical tools, and odd-shaped beakers stacked on tripods. At the far end was a door with a new tin sign stamped with *HRH Marchant*. Her knock went unanswered, but when Adele opened the door, she found all the children hard at work and Rainere shouting instructions over their noise.

"Hi guys! Wow . . ." There were clouds of green magic drifting on the ceiling, and her dragon magic growled awake. To distract it, she started chattering a mile a minute. "Wow, this is a nice lab. Very cool potion-making stuff, and those must be hundreds of books. Magic books always look different, like they've been covered in glitter, don't they?" She approached the long workbench and kissed her children on their heads as they worked. "I missed you guys this morning. I really have to take you all into Concordis one of these days."

"Darling, how did it go with the mayor?" Rainere asked when she stepped close and leaned into his side. She slid her hand into his and was pleased when he squeezed her fingers, hoping that meant he wasn't angry with her after their miserable morning.

"I left her unharmed, so I count that as a win," she joked, then thought it was probably too soon when Rainere didn't smile. "What're you all up to?"

"We are conducting basic experiments on physical displacement," Rainere said, squeezing her hand again. Unfortunately, a surge of lust awoke the magics, and sparks shot from her fingertips. She quickly let go before she could hurt him and focused on the children.

Aaron had his dog with him and was managing to turn Hero Boy in a circle. Natalie screeched that Aaron was cheating because he was using his mind, not his magic, to tell the dog how to move. Leafy could move a crystal goblet back and forth but was having trouble with up and down. Natalie was doing more whining than magic, and again Adele marveled at Rainere's patience with her eldest daughter. She asked Rainere to explain the spell to her so that she could have a try at helping Natalie.

"It's very simple." Rainere held Adele's, now non-sparking, hand over a cut-glass bowl sitting on the counter. The children gathered close to watch her work. "Just concentrate on the words I tell you."

She enjoyed his touch so much that she had to ask him to repeat himself before she could remember the instructions. She reached for the green serpentine power that rested below her heart, but at the first word, the dragon magic grabbed hold and forced the magic out in a dangerous rush. The children screamed as the glass bowl exploded with a screeching noise. It was sheer instinct that guided her to launch a magical net quick enough to catch all the shards. Then Rainere took over, using his own magic to pull the glass pieces back into a bowl shape. Adele's hands were shaking when she saw it was safe to collapse the net.

"Is everyone all right?" she asked, then saw a tiny streak of blood on Aaron's forehead, tears leaking down his pale cheeks. "Oh, honey! I'm so sorry!" She dabbed at the blood with her sleeve while Aaron cried in her arms.

"Prince Aaron is fine, darling." Rainere's gaze was analytical now as he studied her. "Are you sure that *you* are all right?"

"The poor kids have already been through so much and now I barge in and frighten everyone." Adele felt like the world's worst mother as she looked into the unhappy faces of the three children. "I'm so sorry." She squeezed Aaron tight when she felt another hand on her elbow. It was Leafy.

"Queen, I gotta bad one 'ere." The little girl showed Adele the palm of her hand, where there was an old scar. "But it got bedda. And anovver one 'ere." She showed her forearm, where three little pink stripes crossed the white skin.

"Leafy, I'm so sorry." Adele stroked the little girl's old scars and felt sick wondering how the injuries had been inflicted.

"Doesn't madder, it got bedda." Leafy handed a corner of her lavender blanket to Aaron where he was curled in Adele's arms. "Aaron, it's nuffink, no more blood. All right?"

"All right, Leafy," Aaron said and wiped his tears with the scrap of blanket. "I want to do it again. I want to be as strong as Mummy so I can hurt people too."

Alarmed, Adele exchanged a glance with Rainere as he pulled her son from her arms and set him on his feet. "Prince Aaron, first we must learn the rules before we break them, even your mother," he said. He handed her son a crystal goblet. "Now, let's all begin again."

"I guess it's probably better that I go," Adele said, knowing it was the right thing to do, but it still hurt when her children turned back to their work and Rainere simply nodded at her.

Closing the door to the lab, Adele decided to head back to the royal apartment. But she scuffed her feet along the faded carpet, walking very slowly and telling herself it wasn't because she was waiting for one of her kids or Rainere to call her back.

"Sweet Christ, I'm such an idiot!" she muttered in the deserted hallway. She hadn't even considered how dangerous it was to use her unfamiliar magic around the children. *I'll have to find time to spend with them later, but this kingdom isn't going to save itself if the Marchant Eldars decide to come back. Or what if Rip makes another attempt to steal the crown? Or what if Orestes tries to kidnap the kids again, or kill me?*

It was awful to admit, but Adele knew spending time with her children was a luxury she couldn't afford with so many enemies of the royal family still at large. *I'll make it up to them,* she reassured herself. *As soon as I can, I'll take them away on a holiday. Maybe we could go to Sandar—they loved the beach there. I should write to Empress Sundu'huni, see if she is missing her mage yet.* But thinking of Sandar brought her thoughts back to Rip and how he'd helped her escape the place after she'd murdered their mage. She returned to feeling like a monster.

Turning a corner, Adele was surprised to find herself in a much busier corridor. Here, the walls were lined with large oil paintings and the floor-to-ceiling gilt-framed mirrors that decorated every public area of the palace. Open doors revealed large, luxurious apartments decorated in the family colors of their permanent residents, the Carparell family. Maids and stewards rushed about on the business of the well-dressed courtiers who stood in small groups, gossiping and eating snacks from silver trays—more than a few of them obviously drunk.

To think that just a few months ago, I was intimidated by these beautiful people and their nasty cliques. But, seriously, does no one recognize me? Having to push through the crowd annoyed her so much that the dragon magic began heating her fingertips, and she was relieved to reach the more familiar hallways near her own apartment. On a whim, she changed direction to the QG quarters. The men were doing training exercises in the grounds, but Ohrig had said he was going to do paperwork this afternoon and that he'd come to her anytime she called. She had been making a lot of big decisions lately, and though she didn't need Ohrig's permission, she did need his counsel.

When she got there, she noted that the sign on the door was copper plate and very shiny: *Royal Queen's Guard Quarters.* Smiling, she imagined that Captain Lucky polished it every day. She knocked twice, but when there was no answer, she went in anyway, walking through the living area and calling out for Ohrig. She gave him a few moments to respond, hearing noises from the bedchamber that she knew was his.

"Ohrig, do you have a minute for me, or should I come back later?" Adele shouted through his door, but then had to add, "Of course, I won't have any time later as I'm going to try to have a magic lesson with Rainere and then dinner with the family. I guess maybe after dinner?"

"Don't go on about it, I'm here, Your Majesty." Ohrig came out of his room, closing the door quickly behind him. He was wearing his shirt untucked and his hair was all rumpled. Adele figured he'd been napping.

"I'm sorry to wake you," she said. "I was just hoping we could talk?"

Ohrig shrugged, looking grumpy, and headed to the kitchenette. He drank an entire glass of water before pouring himself another and then one for Adele. "I didn't think you'd want to make time for me today," he said as he handed her the glass. He took a seat on an armchair, glancing at his bedroom door again.

"Yeah, it's much easier to avoid your lectures when we don't sleep next to the same campfire." Adele grinned to soften her insult. "But I want to discuss all the decisions I've made and what to do next."

"Bit like closing the stable doors after the horse has bolted, Your Majesty," Ohrig said, eyes still skipping from her to his bedroom door again. "But I can't say I have any bloody idea of what you're trying to do."

"Ah, yes! A purpose would be good." Adele groaned as she threw herself down on a couch and kicked off her slippers, getting comfortable. "Then maybe you can help me work that out too."

Ohrig rubbed a hand over his face like he was trying to massage away the despair. "Why can't you ever tell me, 'Ohrig, I have the perfect plan to be a great queen and catch all the monsters in Unisia, and I know exactly what I'm doing'?"

"That's a terrible impression of me, far too high-pitched," Adele said. She sipped her water. "But I'm sure my bizarre actions are half the reason you love me."

Ohrig's expression was so severe she had to laugh. He'd never given her any cause to think he found her bizarre actions charming at all.

A small cough from the doorway of Ohrig's room made Adele jump in surprise. "Mrs. Ollenby, what are you doing here?" She looked at Ohrig and then back at Mrs. Ollenby. "Oh."

Mrs. Ollenby's usually pink cheeks were even pinker, and her dress was a little off-kilter, as if it had been put back on in a hurry. Her curly blonde hair, normally worn up in a bun, was draped over her shoulders.

"I'm sorry, Dolores, I'm afraid the queen—" Ohrig gestured to Adele, his frustration clear in that small movement.

"No, I'm the one who should be sorry," Adele protested and leaped off the couch. Her mind was reeling. "I'll leave you two to get back to . . . whatever. I shouldn't have interrupted. I just . . . didn't know."

Ohrig sent Adele a dark look, so she stopped blathering and let Mrs. Ollenby speak.

"Your Majesty, please don't worry at all," she said, and managed to look calm about the whole thing. "Our duties to you always come first. I'll have refreshments sent for afternoon tea, as the goddess knows our dear general won't remember to feed you."

"You can stay if you like," Adele offered. "I mean, you're privy to all my dark secrets anyway, and I need sensible advice right now."

But Mrs. Ollenby shook her head, her expression stubborn. "No, thank you, Your Majesty. I have no interest in sharing the political burden on your shoulders," she said. "It is not for me, and I'm grateful for it."

Adele was disappointed. She respected Mrs. Ollenby and had hoped she'd gain another trusted advisor with her.

"Dolores, when can I see you again?" Ohrig asked as he took Mrs. Ollenby's elbow and led her to the door.

"Oh, I'm always around." Mrs. Ollenby let out one of her tinkly laughs. "But perhaps it's all for the best, Ohrig. Trying to rekindle old flames probably isn't wise."

"Dolores, no. It's not like it was before." But Mrs. Ollenby slipped out the door and was gone.

Ohrig took a moment, his head bowed, pressing the closed door with his fist. Adele sat down on the couch and sipped her water, feeling very awkward. But Ohrig soon gathered himself again, coming back to the living area. He chose an armchair close enough that she could smell Mrs. Ollenby's sweet, peachy perfume on him. His usually stern face was soft, his gaze unfocused.

"I'm really sorry, Ohrig," Adele said. "Next time I'll send a messenger."

Ohrig resumed his usual stoic expression. "It's fine."

"No, it's not." Then she couldn't smother her giggle any longer. "But seriously, Dolores Ollenby! Isn't she a bit above your pay grade?"

Ohrig smirked and suddenly looked thirty years younger. "She still is, thanks to your divine intervention, Your Majesty."

They both chuckled.

"And now tell me," he said, leaning forward, elbows on his knees. "What the hell are you doing messing with Concordis politics? The dramas of the Golden Palace not enough for you?"

Adele slapped a hand to her forehead. "Politics is the least of my worries!" she said. "Don't you want to talk about how I keep exploding with hideous magic every time I lose my temper?"

"Go on, then." Ohrig gestured at Adele with his glass of water. "Can you also tell me why you've practically announced Prince Rainere Marchant as your consort?"

Adele didn't take offense to Ohrig's bold question, and, thankfully, neither did the dragon magic. She described all the magical changes wreaking havoc in her body and her guilt over killing the three Eldars; her worries about Stella and the dragon magic that was making her daughter act so oddly; and her anxiety about hurting Rainere when she magically fed from him. It was a lot but, as he always did, Ohrig listened without comment or judgment.

"I want Rainere to teach me to control the magic better," she said. "Honestly, if I hadn't had a glimmer of gold magic in the office with the mayor today, I'd never have come up with any strategy at all. If the green magic had come first, then I'm afraid of what I would've done to Bethany when she annoyed me."

Ohrig frowned. "Why do I feel like you aren't telling me something important?"

Adele sighed. He knew her too well. "I think all this magic in me has to do with a certain plan of a certain god trying to push me to get pregnant and give him that baby he wants."

Ohrig considered this. "But you aren't on Dahk'hani's land anymore. Does he really have any effect on you here?"

"Oh, yes, Ohrig, he's very close," she admitted, she tapped her temple. "Sometimes, I can even hear him."

"You think you can hear him? Or he's actually speaking to you?" Before she could answer, there was a knock at the door, and he went to answer it. Two servants bustled in, each pushing a silver trolley laden with food, tea, and chilled drinks. Relieved for the interruption, Adele watched as they dressed the dining table with white linen and vases of fresh flowers before setting the food out on fine porcelain plates.

"Where is Jordansson, by the way?" Adele asked the general.

"He went off with the rest of the Queen's Guard to the training yards," Ohrig answered. "I presume he's still there unless he cried off because of the heat. Captain Lucky was keen to put the men through their paces and no doubt had a few competitions devised to challenge Jordansson too."

The servants finally finished their setup, accepted Adele's thanks, and left. They sat down at the table, Ohrig at the head and she at his right side.

"Does Lucky still have a problem with Jordansson? I thought everyone was getting along well," she said, filling a plate with an assortment of delicacies.

"Lucky's very jealous of anyone who gets near you," Ohrig said, pouring them both cups of tea. "He doesn't like the idea of Jordansson worming his way into your life like he has, or all the foreign god business, or his foreign magic, or the fact that Jordansson mistook Lucky for a woman when they first met. Personally, I think that our captain might be a little prejudiced. He was brought up as a proper aristocratic lad in the palace, and the pride of St. Lucidis blood runs thick in his veins. I had thought he might wobble in his loyalty when we found out you were actually a demon, but it was too late for him—he'd already fallen in love."

"Wait! What?" Adele froze, holding a tiny sandwich halfway to her mouth. "Not Captain Lucky, he's too proper to love someone . . . like me."

"The lad isn't stupid," Ohrig continued. "He knows he hasn't got a charm's hope in hell of ever seeing his love requited, but it's just the way he likes it. The kid is twenty-five and still a virgin, for goddess' sake! Do you know how much willpower it would take for a handsome kid with his sort of family money to stay virginal?" He shook his head, incredulous. "Nope, unrequited love with his demon queen is just another leaf on his tree."

Adele chewed her sandwich slowly. "Well, as long as it doesn't get in the way of his job, I guess."

"Oh, it's in the way of his job," Ohrig said. "But it's definitely working in your favor."

"You know, on Earth, I always felt like I had to beg men to notice me," Adele mused aloud. "Hardly anyone ever asked me out, even when I worked as a bartender. It must be all this magic making me seem so attractive."

Ohrig snorted. "And a queen's wealth and power don't hurt, either."

Adele threw a tiny scone at his head. "You're meant to say my sweet personality and scintillating wit, Ohrig."

"Go to your courtiers if you want flattery, my queen." He grinned at her. "Do you mind if I go outside for a smoke?"

Adele made them both fresh cups of tea and followed Ohrig out onto the small terrace, which overlooked a corner of a hedge maze in the palace's western gardens. Up on the third floor of the palace, the breeze was warm but pleasant, and statuesque laurel trees provided shade. They sat at the little wrought iron table and chairs.

Ohrig opened a silver case of pale yellow cigarettes, and after offering one to Adele, who shook her head, he lit up and took the first puff, letting out the sweet-scented smoke with a long sigh. She sipped her tea, determined to enjoy this quiet moment with her general. Times like these were so rare.

"What did you make of High Wizard Ohren's sudden reappearance this morning?" she asked, finally. "And why has he been hiding?"

"Don't go looking for trouble if you don't need it, Your Majesty. Ohren was only out of the royal apartment for two days, but he was in the palace, because I heard lots of different reports that he was keeping busy," he said. "I did think it was odd that he sided with the Marchant prince over the issue of breaking Prince Rainold out of prison, though. That seems reckless, even for Ohren."

"God, and I behaved like an animal," she said, groaning. "Rainere was only trying to make a suggestion, and I went insane, spitting and frothing at the mouth with magic."

"But still?" Ohrig raised his eyebrows.

"But still, we can't let Prince Rainold out of prison," she agreed. "I mean, the man is a maniac. I understand Rainere's idea to bring more magic back into Evendaar, but there has to be a limit on how we do that."

"Though His Highness did make a point about his father being familiar with demons," Ohrig said, apparently deciding to play devil's advocate.

"What do you think I should do?" Adele asked, feeling desperate for some concrete guidance from her general.

Ohrig took a long drag on his cigarette and blew the smoke out of his nose in two long tendrils. "I think you were right to deny Prince Rainere. But watch him. I've seen that look on his face before. He won't give this up easily, and he'll be trying to seduce you into agreeing with him." He pointed his cigarette at her. "And I know when it comes to the Marchant prince, you always let what's between your legs do the thinking for you, so he'll probably get what he wants."

Adele squirmed. It was embarrassing but true. One orgasm and she had agreed to marry the prince, only to go back on her word and lose his trust, which led to him stealing Natalie, and then . . . She shook her head, not wanting to go further down that rabbit hole.

"All right, enough honesty, Ohrig," she said.

He grinned at her through a cloud of smoke. "I'm glad you didn't try and deny it."

"On another topic," Adele said with false cheer, "have you got any ideas for adding to the ranks of our Queen's Guard? I was thinking Charlie would be an obvious choice, though he's still young. Maybe he could be a cadet? Like a junior guard?"

"Sure." Ohrig nodded. "But no need to make him a junior anything. The kid's got a hard head and has proved himself loyal and clever. I'll run him through his paces, but it should work. I'll keep my eyes peeled for any others, but what about that Benjamin lad, from Belvoir? He lacks discipline and training, but he's fit and would be a pretty addition to the ranks."

"No, Benjamin is a different kind of trouble," Adele said. "Why don't we just hold trials or something? But don't give me too many aristocrats. Those pompous twits really get on my nerves."

"We could hold one in the Golden Palace and one in Concordis." Ohrig sat forward and stubbed out his cigarette, warming to the idea. "We could even hold one out in Templeton for the Carparell family, and one at Belvoir Estate for those kids too."

"But make it tough—we only want the best," Adele said, "to compensate for their subpar queen, of course."

She was joking, but Ohrig didn't think it was funny. "Of course we only want the best! And we've got a very tight team now. It'll be hard for anyone else to find their place with us."

The chiming of a clock inside reminded her that she was late for her lesson with Rainere. "Well, I'm off." She finished her tea in a gulp. "Will I see you tonight at dinner?"

"Remember what I said about the prince, Your Majesty," Ohrig warned. "And I'll skip dinner, if it's all the same to you. A couple of QGs will be posted outside the apartment though, in case you need them."

"Hopefully, we can all have a quiet night in." She stood up.

"No new crises?" Ohrig feigned shock, a hand over his heart. "What will I do with myself?"

"Whatever you were trying to do to Mrs. Ollenby, I guess." Laughing, she left the terrace before Ohrig could get out of his chair.

Chapter Fifteen

"The Fluorescent Glare"

Adele was so distracted by her conversation with Ohrig that when she left the Queen's Guard's apartment, she got lost on the way back to Rainere's laboratory. She retraced her steps through the Carparell family's hallway and discovered that the gathering in the corridor from earlier had degenerated into a raucous party. There was even a four-piece band playing jaunty music in the juncture of the halls. She had to fight through the crowd and was annoyed to be knocked into by a couple of drunken dancers.

Unfortunately, by the time she got to the lab, the door was locked and the lurid green runes of a protection spell flashed at her knock. Still wrestling with her irritation at the Carparell courtiers, she tried to find another way to get around their apartments. By chance, she took a wrong turn and ended up in a deserted hallway of unused guest suites. She stopped outside the door of the old royal Marchant suite, surprised she'd found it. Rainere had stayed here during her coronation, and then again when he'd returned the Fire Orchid stamens to her. Though, of course, there was no reason he would be here now.

With a sigh, she changed direction to head back to the royal apartment. Her new slippers had a pointy toe, and they were starting to pinch. But just as she was turning to leave, the door opened and

Rainere's manservant, Grottonski, stood glowering at her with his creepy, fluorescent-green eyes. "Your Majesty?"

Adele felt the usual horror at being alone with Grotto, but he wasn't pleased to see her either. "Mr. Grottonski, I didn't think—I mean, I thought you'd be back at the Gray Palace by now."

"The Gray Palace is yours, Your Majesty." Grotto enunciated every word as if he were speaking to an imbecile. "I only remain here at the pleasure of my master, but it seems he has no use for me. Perhaps you would wish that I return to prison?"

It was on the tip of Adele's tongue to say, "Yes, go to Hell, Grotto!" Then she noticed his ancient, threadbare suit, the white shirt stained and missing two buttons above the cummerbund. The greasy black strands of his hair looked even thinner stretched across his shiny, white pate. Grotto was pathetic in his despair. Without the support of Rainere, his years of service were over, and his care for the prince obsolete. But that didn't change the fact that he was a despicable creature, and he would have been delighted to see her dead, her children cast aside in an alien world.

No, it's too hard to feel sorry for him, but I should never have taken the Gray Palace, she thought. Rainere had given her his ancestral home in a desperate gesture of reparation after stealing Natalie and giving her to the empress of the Spider People. The dragon magic stirred as she remembered the moment when she'd discovered his hideous betrayal. She said she'd forgiven him. *But should a mother ever forgive such a crime?* She still wasn't sure. What she did know was that she felt safer having Rainere in the Golden Palace, sleeping next to her in the Glass Bed, and she wasn't ready to examine that conflict in her heart with so much already on her plate.

In the moments that Adele took to consider all this, Grotto had been waiting, his glare so hot she could almost feel it crisping her skin.

"All right, well, I'll go find Prince Rainere," she said.

"Have you lost him?" Grotto asked. "Is he in any danger? What have you done to him?"

Adele ignored the stupid questions and spun on her heel. She'd just made her way out of the guest wing when she realized that Grotto was following her. He kept well behind, but he wasn't hiding. She picked up the pace and nearly jogged along the hallways in her pinching slippers, somehow ending up back in her own part of the palace, though she hadn't passed through the Carparell hall again. She burst into the living area of the royal apartment only moments before Grotto reached the door.

His back resting against a couch, Rainere was sitting on the floor with the children gathered around him, reading to them from a large book of magic. In an instant, it struck her how perfectly happy he looked, then he raised his eyes to hers, and his joy became radiant. The moment he spotted Grotto, his smile died.

"Grotto?" Rainere's tone dripped icicles.

"Master, Her Majesty gave me reason to think that you were missing." Grotto bowed from his waist. "I was compelled to help her come and find you."

"Darling, I just need a private word with you," Adele said, but she wasn't prepared for the loud protests that erupted from the children.

The dogs started barking, and Stella screeched, touching one of them on the ear. Natalie's dog, Princess Lala, yelped in pain and bounded away.

"Stella did it again!" Aaron shouted at his sister, his little fists flailing at her. "Bad Stella! Bad baby!"

Leafy stood up and shouted louder than the other children, "You can't hurt dogs, nasty witch!"

Shocked, Adele tried to grab little Leafy, whose pointing finger was showering green sparks at Stella, but the toddler just laughed, not frightened at all.

"Silence!" Rainere's voice boomed, and the children stopped yelling, frozen. But Adele didn't listen to what he said afterward because she was focused on Stella. Her daughter's eyes were glowing with white-hot magic, and her rosebud lips were twisted in a cruel smile. She was laughing even as she reached, fingers blazing, to hurt another dog.

Grotto stepped up to her shoulder. "There's something wrong with that child," he said. "She's possessed by evil."

"No!" Adele felt her hand fly high, but she hadn't meant to hit Grotto. She'd just wanted him to stop speaking before anyone else heard.

Grotto dropped to a knee with the force of her blow, his hand holding his jaw, and his fluorescent-green eyes flared with hatred. Stella laughed, the sound hollow, and clapped her little hands.

"Grotto, what did you do?" Rainere had leaped to Adele's side, as if to protect her from his old servant.

Grotto looked up at his master, contrite. "I do not know," he said. "But you have my sincerest apologies for any transgression, Your Majesty."

Rainere caught Adele's face in his hands, forcing her to look at him. "*Cara mia*, tell me what he did and I will make it right."

But Adele was distracted again by the three older children. Their dogs were corralled behind them, and Stella was standing up on her chubby legs, still laughing her strange laugh.

"Rainere, you and I have to talk. Now." Adele waved at the balcony, calling the nannies back in. Seraphina had a bandage on her wrist that Adele hadn't seen earlier.

"Sera, what happened to you?" she asked, but it was Natalie who answered.

"Stella bit Sera." Natalie glared at the giggling toddler. "Only Prince Rainere could get her off."

Adele swung Stella up onto her hip and looked deeply into her toddler's eyes. The iridescent rings of power spun around the irises, but the weird glow had died down. "Poor Sera is your friend, and we don't bite friends," she said.

Stella gnashed her teeth. "Bite," she said, clearly enough to make Adele study her harder. Stella's speech development seemed to have sped up in the last couple of days.

"Oh, never mind, Your Majesty, it's just the age," Seraphina rushed to say. "My little brother was the same, and it only took a few months for him to grow out of it."

Natalie interrupted again. "Mummy, Stella burned Sera when she touched her with her hand, just like she did to Princess Lala."

Adele looked to the nanny for confirmation, but Sera just hung her head, as if ashamed. "It was an accident, Your Majesty. No harm done."

"You were crying, Sera!" Natalie shouted, her eyes glistening with angry tears. "Stella hurt you a lot."

"Natalie, calm down." Adele felt sick to her stomach, and Natalie's screeching was getting on her last nerve. "Stella was sick for a long time, and maybe the magic I gave her is making her act a bit funny."

"But she wasn't kidnapped and put in the dark!" Natalie screamed, as her tears fell. "Stella didn't have mean men put knives on her. Nothing happened to Stella—she was just *asleep*!"

"Oh, my sweet girl!" Adele reached for Natalie, but her daughter turned away and threw herself into Leafy's arms, crying great sobs on the other little girl's shoulder. Leafy wrapped her lavender blanket around Natalie and glared at Stella.

Rainere moved in and scooped Natalie up, the little girl looking even smaller in his big arms as she sobbed into his neck. "Hush, darling," he soothed her. "Charlie and I killed all the bad men. You're safe now."

"What is all this ruckus?" High Wizard Ohren had appeared in the doorway and was looking at the sobbing children with a bemused expression. Usually, Ohren hated to see the children upset and swooped in every time to comfort them, handing out sweets and doing magic tricks until they smiled again.

"It's a family thing, Ohren," Adele snapped. She swung Stella onto her other hip. "I'm sure the children will fill you in while I speak to His Highness."

With a flick of her chin, she asked Rainere to put Natalie down and join her in his bedchamber. It was smaller and more private than hers, and she knew he'd put charms on the door so that no one could hear what was spoken inside. Of course Natalie wanted to be transferred to Ohren's arms without her feet touching the ground. The wizard seemed to accept the little girl with bad grace, but Adele didn't have the time to wonder why.

Adele carried Stella to Rainere's room, pacing to the window. The heavy curtain tassels were threaded through with fine silver chains, and Stella soon became engrossed in picking them out with her little fingers while Adele studied the view outside. From this angle she could see straight down to the front steps of the Golden Palace. There were large groups of Household Guards marching through the gardens, trying to move in decorative formations. Adele thought that they must not practice much, because they looked terrible. *Let's hope no one comes to invade us,* she thought just as Rainere rushed in the room. He closed the door and didn't seem to notice that Grotto had followed him into the room.

"We need to speak alone." Adele looked pointedly at the manservant, who returned her glare.

"Adelena, there is something very wrong with Stella," Rainere said.

"You think I don't know that?" she hissed, then quickly faked a smile when Stella looked at her. "But I'm sure she's just adjusting to having this dragon magic inside of her, the same way I am. I'll have to teach her how to control the violent urges, that's all."

"I think that Prince Rainold could help you both now." Rainere sat on the side of the bed, Grotto still standing at attention by the door. "If I release him and keep him—"

"No!" Grotto's shriek made them both turn to him. "Master, you cannot free your father from his prison dimension. It is forbidden by the Eldars. Forbidden!"

"Shut up, Grotto," Rainere snapped. "My father knows more about demons and their magic than anyone else in Evendaar."

"He will not help you!" Grotto was shouting now. "He betrayed the Marchant family by marrying a demon, and he will do it again if you free him. Master, he is a cunning animal and has always been disloyal to his family."

In the next instant, Rainere's hand was around Grotto's throat. "I said, shut up," he growled.

The violence in the atmosphere made the hair on Adele's skin rise, and the magic in her blood soon followed, racing so fast it made her vision blur.

But Stella had started laughing, watching Grotto slowly turn red.

"Rainere, we have enough problems of our own without adding your father to the mix," she said. "Please, let go of Grotto. I can't have you hurt him with Stella watching." *I think she'd enjoy it too much,* Adele thought, and felt nauseous.

Rainere let go of his elderly servant, and Grotto dropped to his knees. "Master, my eternal thanks for your mercy."

With a powerful surge, the magic suddenly slipped her control and sent Adele staggering to the chaise. Rainere dived in and took Stella from her arms, setting her safely on the ground.

Rainere knelt in front of Adele. "Darling, this can't go on," he begged.

Adele focused hard, but it took a minute before she could extract the gold magic from behind the heat of the dragon magic. She took a deep breath and opened her eyes into his troubled gaze. "Don't fear me, please. I couldn't bear it," she whispered.

"*Cara mia.*" His kiss was soft on her forehead.

It almost tipped her over the edge again, but she grasped his hand and forced herself to change to a calming topic. "Darling, I want to give you back the Gray Palace," she said. "It's your home, and I should never have agreed to take it. I'll draw up the papers with Tilburn tonight to transfer it back to you."

"I refuse to accept it."

Grotto made a strangled protest at the prince's words.

"No, I want to do this," she insisted. "Then Grotto can go home and keep it ready for whenever you want to return."

"Return to what?" Rainere's expression said he was having doubts about her sanity. "The Gray Palace is a husk of what it once was, and with no staff, it will be uninhabitable. Surely you know this."

Adele shook her head, stubbornly trying to give Rainere what she thought was good for him. "Then you will have—what do you call it?—a stipend for palace upkeep and servants and things."

"Adelena, I said no."

"But I want you to have a choice," she said, and they both heard the dragon magic echo in her voice. "If I get too dangerous, or the Golden Palace isn't safe for you, I want you to have somewhere to go that they can't get to you. Somewhere away from St. Lucidis politics."

It was the wrong thing to say.

"I suppose this *gift* is coming from the former regent?" Rainere said, taking his arm off her shoulders and standing up. "You want to hide me away as part of your new campaign to be their perfect queen?"

"No, not at all!" She grabbed for Rainere's hand as he stepped away. "But with the Gray Palace back, you will be the king of your own castle again, and we'll be seen as equals, as we always used to be."

"So, without the Gray Palace, you don't consider me your *equal*, my love?" Rainere seemed determined to misunderstand her intentions.

"Darling, no, you're not *hearing* me!"

"Then what is it you're trying to say?" he snapped.

"Rainere, I want you to have your freedom," Adele growled. Her entire body was flushed from the heat of the magic, and she was struggling hard to form coherent sentences. "You can do anything you like in your own palace, without a hundred eyes watching you."

"Whatever I like . . ." Rainere murmured as he turned his attention to the window, his arms held behind his back and feet planted wide—the stance he took when he was thinking hard.

Stella had tottered back to the curtains and was singing to herself, pulling out the silver chains in the tassels. "Mum-my," she said. "Care-fool."

"I'll be careful, sweetheart," Adele reassured her baby, but her gaze was on Rainere who suddenly spun to face her, his smile radiant.

"Ah! Now I understand," Rainere said. In a few steps, he was at her side and his lips were touching hers when he whispered, "A brilliant idea, *cara mia*."

"Mum-my, care-fool," Stella repeated.

Rainere brushed the back of his hand over Adele's cheek. "I'll leave immediately." He swept out of the room before she could ask him what he meant or where he was going. When she hurried out to the living room, she found that he'd already left, with High Wizard Ohren in tow.

"Grotto, you will meet your prince at the Gray Palace," Adele ordered, gesturing to the two stewards closest to her. "Turner and Franks will escort you to the portal chamber."

Grotto sneered. "I know the way."

"But I want to make sure you get there," she hissed, tired of this horrible elf-man. "Don't ever return to the palace without Prince Rainere again."

The children were playing out on the terrace with their nannies, but they were out of sorts, bickering and crying. Stella was another mystery entirely. Though Adele wasn't sure it was the right thing, she brought them all together, hoping that her attention and time were the best medicine she could give them.

Chapter Sixteen

"A Father Returned"

Rainere was grateful for small mercies, and he couldn't quite believe that Ohren had joined him so easily when he had hooked the high wizard's arm and said, "Come with me, now." They went out the front door of the royal apartment, but Rainere soon turned in to the secret passages, finding a narrow entrance behind a gaudy red-and-green tapestry that hung at the end of the hallway, out of sight of any passing servants.

As they raced through the dark corridors, green protection spells lighting up as they passed, Rainere took High Wizard Ohren on the detour through Orestes's bedchamber and then into the portal chamber. He didn't check to see if Ohren followed but plunged straight through the shimmering portal, stepping out into a dingy alleyway in the Slums. Using the shadow-jumping spell, he raced through the gloomy, nearly deserted streets to the abandoned shop where the portal he needed was hidden. His steps crunched broken glass on the floorboards, and he could tell by the untouched layer of dust that no one had broken his protection spell in the weeks since he'd laid it. The basement was at the back of the shop, and the trapdoor was closed, just as he'd left it. He heard Ohren finally catch up to him and curse at having to descend a rickety ladder into an unlit basement.

"Wait, Your Highness." Ohren pulled up short just as they were about to enter the underground tunnel that led to Prince Rainold's portal entrance. "Do we need anything for the spell?"

"No, our magic will be sufficient," Rainere snapped, eager to be away. At least the wizard wasn't whining about being so far out of the Golden Palace, as he'd expected, but Rainere still wished Adelena were here with him.

"And the queen?" Ohren asked, as if he'd read Rainere's mind. "She agreed to this? You're allowed to free Prince Rainold and bring him back to the Golden Palace?"

Rainere looked ahead down the dark, dusty tunnel, focusing hard on what he had to do instead of Ohren's insulting question. The spell to break the apex had almost killed him last time, and if Adelena hadn't been there to heal him with her gold magic, he wouldn't have survived physically intact.

"The queen has suggested that I take the prince to the Gray Palace," he answered. "She'll attempt to transfer the palace into my name tonight, and the legal chaos will be enough to protect us should the court get involved. My father will be safe there, at any rate."

Oddly, Ohren seemed to accept this without the thousand questions Rainere had expected. "Well, let's go before she changes her mind," Ohren said. "The quicker we get Rainold free, the better for Evendaar."

"I'm not doing this for Evendaar, I'm doing this for her." Rainere narrowed his eyes at the high wizard. "Why aren't your disguise charms flickering like they did at The Magician's Wand? And why do—"

"So now you have time for stupid questions?" Ohren snapped. "I thought you wanted this. Let's go!"

He's right, Rainere warned himself, *I'm looking for trouble where none needs to be. Instead, I should be grateful that the wizard seems to have grown a pair of balls along with a brain.*

Without exchanging another glance, the two wizards entered the tunnel.

Chapter Seventeen

"Crown Land"

That evening, Adele put the children to bed without Rainere. They weren't happy with this arrangement, but eventually, after a dozen stories about Earth and singing all the nursery rhymes she could think of, she shut the door to their nursery, fairly certain that they would all stay in their beds.

She was really, really looking forward to a glass of cold cherry wine and a moment's peace, but Tilburn was early for their meeting and waited for her with several scrolls and one of his usual scribes perched on a couch close to the front door. They both stood to bow.

"You are looking radiant as ever this evening, Your Majesty," Tilburn said. "To what do I owe the pleasure of this meeting?"

Adele gave Tilburn a wry smile, shaking her head at the unjustified compliment. The pins had fallen out of her hair, her blouse was smeared with food from dinner, and her pants were sporting big damp patches after bathtime with the kids. She gestured for him to sit as she sank onto a plush armchair. "This shouldn't be too hard."

Tilburn looked expectant, knees pressed together, hands resting on his lap. With just a glance, he had his scribe poised to take notes.

Adele curled her feet up under herself and grabbed an overstuffed pillow to hug. "I want to give the Gray Palace back to the Marchant prince."

Tilburn sucked in a breath. "I see."

"It's a gift for him, but it also works for me," she explained. "As you know, I've agreed to go along with Orgustus's campaign to make me popular with the citizens of Concordis. But I thought it would be nice for Prince Rainere to have somewhere to escape from all the St. Lucidis fever that's going to hit the palace soon."

"Mm-hm." Tilburn nodded for Adele to continue, though his eyes were squinting in that way they did when he wasn't happy—not happy at all.

"I know," she agreed with his silent protest at the expense. "But if it helps you with the treasury, I had a meeting with the Lady Mayor yesterday."

Of course Tilburn knew about the meeting, but he was interested in Adele's version of events and listened closely to everything she had to say, even taking a few notes of his own.

"It's putting a lot of trust in a woman I hardly know, but what else am I going to do?" she asked when she'd finished her account. "It's not like I can take over the Underworld myself."

"I understand, Your Majesty. However, I don't think it's wise to assign more power to our former regent, in respect to city issues. With your permission, I would like to meet with the mayor myself and keep an eye on these financial affairs—from a polite distance, of course," he said.

"How about we say that Lord Orgustus represents the Court of the Golden Palace's interests and that you represent the queen's personal interests with the mayor?" she suggested.

Tilburn seemed happy with this and made a note in his agenda to follow it up. Adele was relieved to have his practical help with the Underworld issue. General Ohrig hadn't been able to offer anything but his doubts, and High Wizard Ohren wasn't interested enough to even have a conversation with her. The affairs of Concordis certainly wouldn't entertain Rainere—he'd probably just suggest burning half the city to the ground.

"And now back to the reason we're meeting—transferring ownership of the Gray Palace."

Tilburn took a moment to find a bottle of Firewhiskey, returning with two tiny crystal glasses of the golden liquor. "Quite honestly, Your Majesty, it is impossible to do as you wish."

"No, Tilburn, don't say that!" She groaned. "I've already promised him."

Tilburn's eyes were entirely unsquinty now as he gave her the truth. "The Marchant prince not only gave you the Gray Palace, but he signed over the residence, the lands, and the township to you. The entire area is now Crown Land, and there is no law that allows even a St. Lucidis queen to give away Crown Land. I'm sure I explained all this to you at the time."

"So the prince could give it to me, by Marchant law," she clarified, "but now I'm not allowed to give it *back*?"

"I suppose he meant for it to be a very grand gesture of his desire to be forgiven," he said.

She took a sip of her Firewhiskey. "As if you can buy forgiveness," she murmured.

"Your Majesty, while I have your ear for a moment." Tilburn unrolled a scroll. "The gray crystal mines at Mount Ecrusius have been closed, and the children and adult workers who consented to it are being brought to Concordis. The journey shouldn't take more than a few days, but I was wondering if you had any idea of where we should put these predominantly Marchant refugees and orphans. As we both know, the orphanages and hostels in Concordis are full to bursting already."

"Could we bring them to the Golden Palace?" Adele asked.

Tilburn breathed in sharply and seemed reluctant to exhale again.

"Oh, right." She rubbed her forehead. "I'm meant to be pretending that Marchants don't exist."

"If only we could hide them away in the Gray Palace," Tilburn said with a chuckle. "It's much closer to Mount Ecrusius, so the journey would be shorter, saving us transport costs."

"We could turn the Gray Palace into an orphanage. Grotto would love that. Lots of children to torture and—wait just a minute!" Adele slapped her forehead. "That could work, you know, Tilburn."

"Letting Grottonski torture children?" He was confused.

"If I turned the Gray Palace into a refuge with a school." She tossed the cushion away and got up to start pacing. "The adults from the mines could work as staff, and the children could attend school or train in magic. That would fix the practical problem of having so many refugees floating around."

Tilburn was squinting again, but Adele was delighted with her solution. "Send a message to the refugee caravans to change direction for the Gray Palace," she said. "Then send food, clothing, and all the necessary medical supplies. The palace is a beautiful building, but it'll be no more than a roof over their heads until we can get it fixed up. Grotto can certainly oversee the renovations—that should keep him out of my sight."

"Would you like to run any of this by the Marchant prince, Your Majesty?" Tilburn asked, his tone so dry it crisped at the edges. "Perhaps he will have an opinion."

She shook her head, resolute. "Rainere will be happy to see it helping his people, I'm sure."

Tilburn didn't look as positive of this as Adele felt, but she decided he was probably tired. She didn't need sleep with all this magic coursing through her body, and sometimes she found it hard to remember that the people around her still did. She dismissed him with the promise of another meeting tomorrow.

Retiring to her bedchamber, Adele was just wondering where Rainere had got to when she found Lady Olivia sleeping on a narrow couch at the foot of the Glass Bed. The poor lady had clearly been on duty waiting for Adele to dismiss her for the night. She was tempted to let Olivia sleep, but the couch was very uncomfortable, covered in a beaded fabric and heaped with needlepoint pillows.

"Olivia." Adele gently shook her shoulder. "You can go now."

Lady Olivia woke with a start despite Adele's whisper. "Your Majesty, my apologies. I, ah—" She yawned hugely. "Can I help you with your bath?"

"I'll do it myself, Olivia," she said. "I'm sure I'll see you first thing in the morning, anyway."

"Is His Highness joining you tonight, Your Majesty?" Lady Olivia asked, blinking sleepily. "I'm sure I saw him earlier. I had just closed my eyes when I heard him come in, or maybe I dreamed it." She laughed. "I often dream of the Marchant prince and when we had our little moment."

Adele felt her smile drip right off her face.

"Oh, Your Majesty, forgive me." Lady Olivia dropped her eyes to the carpet, then peeked up again. "I didn't mean any disrespect by mentioning it. After all, what is a dalliance with a lady-in-waiting compared to an affair with a queen?"

Shocked beyond words, Adele suddenly remembered every time Olivia had tried to make her look small or stupid in front of Rainere, and all the times Olivia had flirted with him. And just this morning, Rainere had wanted her fired for no apparent reason. It all added up now. A "dalliance"—of course. What did that mean? Sex? Or kissing? Or a full-blown affair while Adele was out of the palace trying to find a dragon?

Olivia looked up at Adele through her long, dark eyelashes. "If you are quite sure you don't need me further tonight, Your Majesty?"

Adele should've known it was a mistake to think the dragon magic was asleep because she'd had a calm evening. Her hand flew up, and then Olivia was on the floor. Adele watched as the beautiful young woman gasped and writhed on the carpet. She couldn't have said how she was causing Olivia pain, but she had felt a tendril of dragon magic leap from her chest into Olivia's.

"I know you think I'm stupid." Adele's voice echoed with magic. "And it's true that sometimes I can be blind to a friend's faults."

Olivia made a little mewing noise as saliva dripped out of the corner of her mouth.

"But let me be perfectly clear. From now on, you do not drink my Firewhiskey, flirt with my Queen's Guard . . ." She smiled as Olivia's eyes widened in shock. She really thought Adele hadn't noticed. "Or *fuck* with my prince. Do you understand me?"

Gagging, Olivia couldn't answer.

"Keep your hands to yourself, or you will lose them." For one terrifying moment, Adele wasn't sure she could turn off the magic. There were no Chime Voices to whisper words of Command, so she had to guess, taking hold and giving it a savage pull. Olivia screamed as the magic was ripped out of her.

"Your Majesty?" Turner was on duty, and he peeked his head around the door from the front entry. "Everything all right?" His gaze fell to Olivia, who lay whimpering on the floor, and he ducked out again without a word.

Adele grimaced at how easily a queen could get away with torture. "Now go away and pray you heal quickly. I'll need you tomorrow."

Olivia rolled over, tearing the hem of her gown as she tried to get to her feet. She shuffled to the door of the bedchamber and left.

Adele went to the nightstand and poured herself a tiny glass of Firewhiskey from the jeweled bottle that was usually empty whenever Olivia was on night duty. Ducking through the gauzy curtains of the double doors, she made her way to the balcony's edge. She braced for the guilt and self-recriminations that would be flooding in to swamp her conscience any moment now.

I was prepared to kill that girl. I acted like a monster, Adele thought, testing herself. An image of Olivia and her large breasts pressed up against a naked Rainere made the dragon magic ignite again, but the gold magic flared on its own. *And if Olivia is punished, doesn't Rainere deserve to be punished for his faithlessness too?* She closed her eyes and pulled harder on the gold magic, letting it fill her mind. *And if Rainere is punished, then shouldn't I be punished for letting Jordansson touch me to get to the magic? Letting him kiss me, letting him run his hands over my body. It wasn't sex but it was intimate.*

But try as she might, she just couldn't seem to feel bad about hurting Olivia, nor about her own betrayal. *Maybe my conscience left with the Chime Voices?* She felt a chill despite the heat still coursing through her veins. *I have to get rid of this damned dragon magic so I can be me again.*

But who can help? Her problems were always unique, even in this alien world. *I can't ask Rainere—he'll just suggest his insane father again.* She shivered, remembering Prince Rainold's arms around her, squeezing tight, his emerald-green gaze filled with madness. He hated her for the Mark she'd put on his son and for being a demon.

The twinkling lights of Concordis spread like a map of stars before her. The streets were lit with tall lamps, and there were still bonfires kept in the squares in a hopeless gesture to discourage a return of the Marchant Eldars. She looked beyond the lights and thought she saw something flash bright green over the city, but she blinked and it was gone.

The breeze was cool, and on it she could hear the distant strains of music being played on one of the lower levels. The Golden Palace wasn't a home—it was more like a city apartment block. She thought about the drunken courtiers she'd seen today. *Clearly none of them work for a living, yet no one has bothered to meet the queen who finances their luxurious lifestyle. How stupid and lazy and very annoying.*

A small, dark creature jumped up onto the balustrade next to Adele and rubbed against her elbow.

"Hello, little one." She stroked Gorrik's black cat, and its purr went squeaky with pleasure. "I hope your day was better than mine?" The cat rubbed her elbow again, seeking more ear scratches. "Do you know where Rainere is? It's the first night since I got back that we haven't been together. I'm trying not to read too much into it, but it's so hard to know what he's thinking."

The cat only purred louder as it blinked very slowly in a cat smile. Adele reluctantly returned to her bedchamber, preparing to wait out the long night alone.

Chapter Eighteen

"A Woman Scorned"

Lady Olivia didn't even glance at Turner when she passed him. She'd always thought the stewards were arrogant asses, thinking themselves better than the other servants, and certainly better than a lady-in-waiting. Thankfully, whatever the queen had done to her seemed to recede the further she got from the royal apartment, and soon she could walk straight again.

"Well, well, Queen Adelena, what a surprise you are," Olivia muttered as she began striding the quiet hallways toward her dormitory. *I only wanted payback for Rainere humiliating me and her never saying a word in my defense. She's usually so giggly and pathetic, I honestly thought she'd just cry and be all heartbroken, not fight back with bloody dark magic. I bet all the rumors are true—she is a demon!*

Rage burned inside Olivia's young heart. This was just like that time her mother had locked her in the basement for playing with the boys next door . . . and the time that Lord Pine had decided that if Orgustus wasn't around, he could take her and not even say thank you . . . and the time her sister stole all her clothes and left her with her poorest, plainest gown to wear for weeks. Oh, Olivia had rage to burn! A wicked pile of wrongs heaped up against her, and Adelena had just lit the match.

Everyone thinks the queen is so sweet. But Adelena was a woman, and like any woman, she inflicted the worst injuries without marks. A bruise lasted for a week, but the pain of humiliation was forever. *She thinks she can scare me!* Olivia came to a junction in the corridor. *She thought she could punish me for what her man wanted to do with me. Well, I can—* Olivia looked down one corridor, then in the other direction. "Yes, what can I do?" she muttered. "What will hurt her the most?" She had been made to gag and drool on the floor, and that required vengeance.

Prince Rainere was probably out of the question now—he only had eyes for his bitch queen with her stringy brunette hair. The children would be an obvious choice, but she was no monster who could harm a child beyond a nasty pinch or a quick slap. She remembered too well what it was like to be surrounded by cruel adults, and she couldn't bring herself to do any lasting damage. *The queen has no friends to speak of, only servants and her Queen's Guard. Well... imagine if her QGs were in disarray, or at each other's throats.*

And as if the goddess Serena herself had blessed Olivia's plan, she spotted one of them walking down the hallway right toward her. Leith was holding hands with the nanny, Caitlin, and Charlie had his arm around Siobhan. Olivia tossed her hair over her shoulder and stepped to the middle of the hallway so no one could avoid her. Charlie's eyes narrowed, but she ignored him. It was Leith she wanted.

"Hello, Lady Oh-livia," Siobhan said. Her country accent was even stronger when she'd had a bit to drink, but Olivia was careful not to sneer.

"I'm so glad I caught you, Caitlin." Olivia looked down her nose at the petite nanny hovering behind Leith. "Her Majesty has called you back to the nursery. Seraphina's wrist is really hurting, and you have to replace her. The queen sent me to find you in your dorm, but you weren't where you were supposed to be." She let the suggestion hang while the younger girl paled in fright. "You're very lucky I found you first." Olivia winked. "And don't worry, I won't tell Mrs. Ollenby."

"Oh, thank you so much, Lady Olivia!" Caitlin even bobbed a

little curtsy, which Olivia thought was just precious. "I'm so sorry, Leith, I really have to go. Maybe we could do this another time?"

Not making any promises, Leith kissed Caitlin's cheek before she dashed away. In an instant, his disappointed expression morphed to a bright smile. "Looks like you owe me a date for the party, Lady Olivia," he said.

"C'mon, Leith, that's Lucky's girl," Charlie muttered.

"I'm not anyone's girl, Charles!" Olivia said, outraged.

"It's Charlie, not Charles, darlin'," he snapped back, and his glare reminded her of Prince Rainere for some reason.

How is this thug even allowed to live in the palace with the rest of us? she wondered. Olivia couldn't stand Charlie. He was always hanging around looking shifty, like he was about to pocket the silver cutlery. He also flirted constantly with the nannies but had only ever snarled at her.

"You go on, Charlie," Leith said, his eyebrows communicating how much he wanted this. "I'm going to walk Lady Olivia back to her dorm, then I'll join you later."

"I think you should leave her to find her own way, mate," Charlie said, his dark eyebrows signaling the strength of this belief back to Leith.

"Charlie!" Siobhan tugged at his hand. "I've got an early shift tomorrow, and it's already nearly midnight. If you want any more time with me, then hurry up."

Charlie gave Leith a last warning glance before Siobhan dragged him off down the corridor in the direction of the QG's quarters.

Olivia almost crowed with victory. The most handsome of all the guards after Captain Lucky, QG Leith was always quick with a flirt, but not nearly as pushy as some other young men she knew with a little bit of power and position in the palace. She was still trying to forget the memory of Lord Pine bouncing away like he was riding a horse with very poor technique. *If Leith's reputation is anything to go by, he'll be much better than that,* she reassured herself.

"So, Lady Olivia." Leith leaned his back against the wall, his gaze speculative. "What are you in the mood for tonight?"

"You know, it really annoys me that people think I'm attached to Captain Lucky," Olivia burst out like she just couldn't keep it in a minute longer. "I think the world of Lucky, but he and I are just friends. He really isn't interested in being more than that, and neither am I." She pushed at Leith's broad shoulder, but it turned into a caress. "Even you're spreading rumors that I'm attached to the captain."

Leith shrugged. "I thought he said you two were getting serious. But it doesn't matter, I guess."

"Not tonight," Olivia agreed.

He held his arm out, and she linked her elbow in his. "Shall we go somewhere a little more private, my lady?"

Olivia pressed close. *Lucky will forgive me anything,* she thought, smiling up at Leith as they made their way to a quiet linen closet she knew at the end of the hall. *But he'll probably try to kill Leith, and won't that be something to see?*

Chapter Nineteen

"A Prince for Breakfast"

It was the next morning when Rainere raced from the Gray Palace and burst into the deserted portal chamber of the Golden Palace with Ohren right on his heels. His heart was thumping out of his chest. *How could I have been so stupid? I should never have let him out of my sight,* he thought, cursing himself again.

Prince Rainold had seemed completely disoriented by his arrival in Unisia, falling in and out of consciousness and talking nonsense. They'd left him sleeping in his old marital bedroom, the one he'd shared with Princess Rainestra, when Rainere took Ohren to the Great Library, intending to research the destruction of interdimensional portals. Then Grotto had appeared at the door, bleeding from a wound to his head and shouting that Prince Rainold had escaped to the portal chamber.

Goddess Serena, if Adelena finds him, she'll kill him! The thought made him hurry through the secret passageways to the royal apartment, his progress only slowed by the narrow sections between walls and rickety ceiling struts. Behind him, he heard Ohren ask, "What're you going to do when you catch the prince?"

"I'll lock him up in the Gray Palace, properly this time," he said, looking back over his shoulder at the wizard. "The queen and I had an arrangement."

"So you said earlier." Ohren was wearing his elderly man disguise but leaped nimbly over the gaps in the floor planks. "I wonder what she'll do when she sees that you don't have a hope in hell of controlling him."

Rainere stopped and spun to face the wizard. "Ohren, you're with me in this. You helped me to free my father from his prison, and the queen will know that."

"There are far more important things in Evendaar than the threat of Adelena's temper," Ohren said, sneering.

Rainere narrowed his eyes at the high wizard, stunned he could be so cavalier about a demon queen infused with dragon magic she barely had any control over. But, yet again, he shouldered aside his doubts about Ohren. The path before them was a little confusing in the dark, and he had to concentrate hard to find the door to Adelena's bedchamber. When he found it, he cautioned Ohren to be silent. It was early morning, and Adelena might be still getting dressed. Hearing nothing, he stepped out, and Ohren followed him. There were voices out in the living room.

Rainere brushed the dust from his jacket and adjusted his silk cravat. "I think the family is sitting down for breakfast. I will tell the queen what has transpired."

Ohren nodded, and Rainere opened the door to the living room of the royal apartment. He heard the steward, Franks, call out, "Prince Rainere, Your Majesty." The stewards were getting used to his sudden entrances, and he appreciated it.

Rainere moved around the dining table, kissing each child on the head. He didn't presume to kiss his lover but instead dragged a finger along the back of Adelena's bare shoulders, enjoying the burst of her pleasure through the Mark that shot straight to his groin. She looked beautiful, dressed in a strapless gown of pale green silk, her hair draped in long waves down her back. Rainere decided that he would take more than just a moment alone with her this morning. He took his usual place at the far end of the table, pleased that the

Queen's Guard hadn't arrived for breakfast yet. "Everyone is up very early today," he remarked.

"I had bad dreams, didn't I?" Aaron replied, far too morose for a four-year-old. "Stella gave me them."

Stella laughed at hearing her name, but the three older children exchanged dark looks.

"Where were you last night, Prince Rainere?" Adelena called down to him. "I missed you."

"Darling—Your Majesty, I wonder if I might have a word with you in private?" Rainere asked. "It's about a very important matter we were discussing yesterday."

"Your Highness, I'm in such a good mood this morning, let's not—" Adelena stopped when she was approached by Franks, who whispered something in her ear. "What? But that's impossible!"

"Impossible is for fools!" A voice sang out from the door, and a young man strolled across the living room to join them in the dining area. He wasn't quite as tall as Rainere, perhaps just over six feet. His silky black hair hung to shoulders, framing a handsome face. No older than his early twenties, he had fine features—his cheekbones sharp, lips full and pink, his nose neat. He was dressed in a suit of black silk with a velvet waistcoat and very shiny shoes.

Rainere felt his stomach plummet. *Goddess damn the man!* He should've known Rainold would need to create chaos in his first act of freedom.

"Your Majesty, may I present the formerly late Prince Rainold Marchant." Franks didn't even blink when Prince Rainold burst out laughing, the sound so happy and infectious that it started the children giggling.

"Formerly late!" the prince said. "That's too perfect. Once considered dead, but not dead anymore!" He clapped his hands in delight.

Rainere rushed to his father, moving to stand between him and the dining table. "Prince Rainold, I told you that you shouldn't come to the Golden Palace."

But Rainold was already craning around his shoulder. "Hello, I'm alive!" He beamed at the children, who were all staring at him, faces alight with curiosity. "I'm Prince Rainold, your Prince Rainere's daddy."

"Are you our grandfather now?" Natalie asked, making her own connections.

Prince Rainold laughed gaily again. "Why, yes, call me Grandfather, poppet!"

Aaron waved at Prince Rainold. "Do you remember me, Grandfather? From our dreams together?"

"Yes, of course." Rainold waved back at Aaron. "You're a very good boy, helping me talk to my son. Now we can be together, finally."

"Why are you here?" Adelena asked, hysteria giving each word a funny lilt. "And how were you in my son's dreams?" Rainere didn't like the white magic that was flashing in her eyes.

"My dear, ever since the first night you slept in the Gray Palace, Aaron has been communicating with me in my prison dimension," Rainold said, his hands waving like birds taking flight. "He is such a special boy and has such intriguing powers. You'd better be careful that the demons don't get hold of him."

"What?" Adelena gasped but didn't seem capable of much more.

"My sincere apologies, Your Majesty." Rainere took his father's arm. "I will remove Prince Rainold to the Gray Palace immediately, as we discussed."

"We—what?" Adelena repeated, frowning in what looked like genuine confusion. She skipped a little way from the table and waved at him to follow. He joined her and she lowered her voice to whisper, "Rainere, what in the holy *fuck* are you talking about? We decided that you shouldn't free your father." She threw Rainold a cautious glance, but the prince had wandered to the dining table and taken a seat.

"Adelena, what are *you* talking about?" Rainere felt his insides chill as he wondered, *Could she have forgotten our conversation? Was*

173

she overwhelmed by the dragon's magic again? "We both understood that you couldn't be seen to give me permission to free my father after you refused me so publicly at breakfast. But if I keep him on Marchant sovereign soil no one in the court will have to know. You were very clear!"

"Are you serious? That's not at all what we discussed!" Adelena had white and green sparks flashing above her head. "Rainere, I told you releasing your father was a bad idea. I said, *don't* do it!"

Mrs. Ollenby entered the room and was making her way to the dining table. Though the lady's discretion could be trusted, Rainere had to get his father out of there before anyone else arrived. "Adelena, I didn't misunderstand you," he growled. "We were discussing releasing my father, and then you suddenly changed the topic to ownership of the Gray Palace. You said, 'You can do anything you like there without a hundred eyes watching you.'"

"And you—wait. What?" Adelena controlled herself with a visible effort. "Rainere, I need you to understand that I was trying to give you back the Gray Palace so you wouldn't be angry with me for denying you permission to free your father. I wasn't speaking in some kind of code. I was being very literal, in fact."

"But how could you possibly give the Gray Palace back to me?" Rainere was getting impatient while his father was chatting with the children. "I thought you understood that I'd signed it over as Crown Land. The Crown never releases property."

"I actually didn't know that," Adelena said through clenched teeth. "Now can you tell me what the hell you think you're doing bringing your insane father into the Golden Palace?"

"Well, you see, Prince Rainold was very disoriented when we rescued him, so I thought it was safe to leave Grotto guarding him, but he regained his senses enough to attack Grotto and get himself down to the portal chamber. And then . . . you know, I'm not sure why he wanted to come here, specifically."

"You said 'we' freed him," Adelena snapped. "Who's we?"

"Ohren, though I'm not sure where he is now. I thought he was following me," Rainere replied, embarrassed to be in a new habit of losing wizards. "Darling, we really should return to the table—the prince just introduced himself to Mrs. Ollenby. Let me get him back to the Gray Palace, and then we can discuss what I need to do with him later."

He ushered her to the dining table with a hand on the naked skin of her back, though he didn't feel the flush of pleasure that his touch had elicited earlier. Mrs. Ollenby was laughing at something the prince had said, but when she looked up at Rainere, he could tell that she knew something was dreadfully amiss with their guest. Aaron was sitting on Prince Rainold's knee and telling him all about his ability to talk to animals, and Natalie was buttering the prince a pile of toast to go with his eggs.

"Oh, it's so nice to be back in the real world!" Prince Rainold cried when Rainere and Adelena returned to the table. "You have no idea how lonely I've been. So very horribly and indescribably lonely!"

"But we're your family now, Grandfather." Natalie handed over the stack of toast to the prince. "You can live with us."

Rainere watched Adelena flinch when Rainold planted a kiss on Natalie's forehead.

"Your Highness, perhaps it would be wise for you to rest a little before meeting anyone else this morning," Rainere announced. "You've had a very long journey and must be tired."

"Yet the truth is I have never felt more energized, my darling boy." Green tears sparkled in Prince Rainold's emerald-green eyes, making it look like his irises were melting. "I feel like I've slept for a hundred years, and now I'm finally awake."

"Were you in a sleeping spell?" Natalie asked, interested. "Our sister, Stella, was in a sleeping spell, you know? But she came back a bad girl."

"I've heard about this Princess Stella," Prince Rainold said. "Which one is she?"

Sitting in her highchair next to Adelena, Stella waved at hearing her name. "Me! Me!"

Prince Rainold squinted and then moved his head like he was trying to focus on something in the distance. "Oh, my goddess!" he said. "I didn't realize how little she was."

"She's mean to animals, and she hurt Sera, burned her," Aaron told him.

"It'll be the dragon's fire she has lodged in her heart," Rainold told them. "You should get it out of there, or she'll stay like that forever."

"Prince Rainold, I believe—"

"Hello! Who is this lady?" Prince Rainold interrupted Adelena, making all the children laugh at his theatrical shock. "I wonder who she could be? I know she never said, 'Good morning, Your Highness' to me when I joined you all."

Adelena clenched her jaw, and Rainere saw a new flurry of green sparks join the halo above her head. "Good morning, Your Highness," she said. "Thank you for joining us. However, I must insist that you leave with His Highness right now."

The children all protested, and Rainold ducked behind Aaron as if using the little boy as a shield. "Oh, please don't make me leave, Your Majesty. I'll be ever so good, I promise!" he begged, and the children echoed his cry.

Adelena glared down the table at Rainere, making a gesture with her hand, palm up, that he should do something.

Rainere didn't like Adelena being so close to the edge of her control with the children nearby. *She's not even trying to calm herself,* he thought, his own anger growing at her disrespectful display. *I suppose she thinks that's my job now?*

"Actually, I'm staying in the Golden Palace," Prince Rainold said through a mouthful of toast. "Oh, goddess, this is so good! Seriously, listen to that crunch." He took another bite of toast, making a meal of chewing it. "You know, in my dimension I had to invent everything myself, and I never could get the sound of a proper crunch right."

The children all giggled, falling out of their chairs and jumping around with their barking puppies, shouting, "Crunchy! Crunchy! Crunchy toast!"

Smiling at their antics, Prince Rainold tossed his long hair over a shoulder and said, "Anyway, I'm staying because not only would I like to spend time getting to know my adopted grandchildren and this sweet little urchin, Leafy, but this one"—he nodded at Adelena—"is going to do something dreadful very soon. It's best I keep an eye on her."

"Who told you that?" Rainere barked.

"The goddess Serena herself came to me in a vision," Prince Rainold said.

"Was the goddess very pretty?" Natalie asked, climbing back on her chair.

"Not as beautiful as you," he answered, charming the little girl into giggles again. "But she was very serious, and she said that Mummy will be responsible for the destruction of the world as we know it. So, I'm here to save you all!"

Adelena dropped her face into her hands, and Rainere felt her fear through the Mark with such force that he couldn't catch a breath.

"I can't take much more of this." Her voice was muffled by her hands, but Rainere thought she might be crying. "I really can't."

Mrs. Ollenby moved to hug Adelena's shoulders. "I'm sure it's all nonsense, Your Majesty."

"I bet it isn't." Adelena dropped her hands, misery etched on her pale face. "I'm right on schedule for another catastrophe. I had one night off, and now it's back to being the cursed Hidden Child of the End of the World Prophecy. I bet Rip is laughing his arse off wherever he is."

At that very moment, Tilburn burst into the royal apartment, running so fast that the coattails of his dove-gray jacket were flying out behind him. He was very nearly tackled by Franks, who was on high alert after the surprise arrival of two Marchant princes, but got past with a shriek to, "Clear the way!"

"Your Majesty, forgive me," Tilburn said as he panted by Adelena's elbow. "It's the Sandarian empress and her warriors, Your Majesty. They're at the palace gates and have demanded you receive this."

He handed Adelena a scroll of coconut fiber paper. At the opposite end of the table, Rainere read her face as she scanned the scroll, and his stomach twisted itself into knots.

"It's a declaration of hostilities." Adelena sat back in her chair, stunned. "Sandar wants to go to war with Unisia."

Chapter Twenty

"The Unheard-of War"

Adele stood in the great entry hall of the Golden Palace. The front doors were open and she looked out across the manicured gardens to the twenty-foot-high golden gates. Beyond them was a long line of Sandarian warriors standing at attention. A group of brightly colored Sandarian tents had already been erected for the Empress Sanda'hani and her royal entourage. Adele could see dozens of skinny white horses and a few open-topped carriages too. If this was a war party, it certainly looked more party than war, though she knew better than to underestimate the Sandarian empress.

Normally open for all to pass through, the gates were now closed, and a fifty-person contingent of the Unisian Ordinary Army stood along the line. The men and women wore uniforms of gray and blue with white piping and epaulets. Inside the palace, the Household Guard lined the entry hall in their own garish purple-and-gold uniforms, entirely unsuited to battle with far too many tassels for a soldier.

"You made sure that the Marchant princes left the palace?" Adele murmured to Tilburn, who was standing at her shoulder. "The Sandarians hate Marchant royals even more than Unisians do. I've sent Charlie into Concordis to speak to the Lady Mayor for me. We'll hear if there are any rumors spreading about this war. Did you tell anyone that this is more than just an official visit?"

"Your Majesty, please." They'd already been over this and Tilburn had also mentioned that he'd organized an impromptu party in the gardens on the other side of the palace to distract any courtiers curious about the arrival of their foreign guests.

War! Adele couldn't believe she now had to fight with an empress she'd once betrayed and still admired. The letter trembled in her grasp, fingertips already lit with magic. Sparks singed the delicate paper, releasing the scent of roasted coconut.

"Empress Sanda'hani says she wants Rip back," Adele muttered. "Perhaps I can spell someone to look like him? But that person would forfeit their life for sure. Dammit, I have to think of something!"

Adele ignored Tilburn's shocked gasp. He'd had no better ideas, except to tell her that a declaration of war from Sandar was unheard of. "Completely and utterly unheard of! Upon my life, this is utterly unheard of, Your Majesty!" Just like that, over and over.

She was grateful when General Ohrig and the Queen's Guard arrived dressed in their active-duty uniforms, hardened leather breastplates over gray short-sleeved shirts and pale gray denim trousers with gold piping down the sides. They all carried a ceremonial helmet under their arm, the purple feathers limp, and a sword at their hip.

"All right, Your Majesty, what's the situation?"

"War, Ohrig."

"Go on."

"Sanda'hani wants to know where her mage is, she wants Ripenzo back, and she thinks I've been sending Marchant Eldars to harass them. She's heard I'm a demon and a false queen." She handed Ohrig the letter.

Ohrig read it quickly, then passed it to Captain Lucky. "This is unheard of, Your Majesty," he said.

"Yes, that's been brought to my attention already," she said softly, trying not to agitate the angry magic in her system. "What am I going to do?"

"Tell me what you think is going to happen," Ohrig said.

"I think the empress is going to say something horrible, and I'm going to lose my temper, and the dragon magic inside me is going to explode, and I'll accidentally kill everybody," Adele admitted.

They both ignored Tilburn's gasp.

Ohrig reached to clasp her shoulder, like he did with the QGs when they needed comfort. "Well, how can we help you hold on to your temper, then?"

There was an odd sensation in her chest, like the dragon magic took a deep breath. It receded a little. "Your touch helps." Adele glanced at his large hand with its scars and threads of white hair on the knuckles. "Maybe it calms the magic to have nothing to challenge it."

Ohrig turned his frown on her. "We can't go out there like this," he said. "But who could hold your hand and make it look convincing?"

A loud bellow of "Your Majesty!" echoed through the vast entry hall. His shoulder cape flying as he sprinted, Lord Orgustus dramatically skidded to a stop at her side. "Your Majesty, I just got your message!"

Adele felt Ohrig's hand drop away, and instantly the dragon magic fired through her blood, dragging the green and gold magics behind it.

"Tell me it isn't true, Your Majesty," Orgustus demanded. Thin rings of gold encircled his sky-blue irises. "War with Sandar? It's unheard of!"

"My Lord Orgustus, it's true." She grasped his hands experimentally. The dragon magic paused—it didn't recede, but it didn't get worse either. "I'm so glad you're here to help me, I have no idea what to do."

She knew right away that she'd overplayed it when Orgustus narrowed his eyes and stepped backward. "Your Majesty, I have no experience with Unisia in a state of war. It's—well, it's un—"

"Unheard of, yes, I know," Adele snapped. She yanked him closer so she could whisper. "But you're going to stand right by my side, and we're going to present a united front to the Sandarians. Empress Sanda'hani is smarter than you and I put together. Logically, she knows we could crush them with our military, but she won't fight like that. She'll use darker tactics—poison, kidnapping, assassinations. Sanda'hani will hit us where it hurts and where we are most unprepared for her to be."

Lord Orgustus was horrified. "How do you know that?"

Adele looked out at the milling Sandarians. "Because in her place, that's what I would do."

"May the goddess protect us," he whispered. He tried to yank his hands free again. "Our army is not prepared. *We* are not prepared. What if we fail?"

"But we can't fail." Adele hooked his arm in hers and saw a flurry of emotions cross Lord Orgustus's face—fear, excitement, a flicker of lust—then settle into a calm mask.

She glanced back at Ohrig. The general gave her a tiny nod that said he had her back, no matter what happened now.

The walk to the front gates felt interminable, the sun beating down on their heads. Adele sweated while mentally calculating a dozen ways of opening the conversation with Empress Sanda'hani and then discarding each one as a bad choice. The empress wanted something that she couldn't give her, but perhaps she could convince Sanda'hani to want something else instead. But what could equal both a mage and a lover?

When they arrived at the gates, she still wasn't ready.

A general of the Ordinary Army shouted a command, and the huge golden gates were opened before the queen and her company. Adele squinted in the sunshine and scanned the row of Sandarian warriors before her. They were all six and a half feet tall, heads shaved bare, their skin a deep, burnished brown glistening with sweat and coconut oil. They were dressed in short sarongs, toughened leather straps crossing their broad, muscled chests. Every warrior carried a short-handled trident in each hand and knives tucked into their belts. Adele knew from seeing a few training skirmishes on her visit to the beachside court of Sandar that they were poised for battle. She gulped in fear even as the dragon magic urged her to strike them all down.

If it were me, I would have an assassin kill me now before I could begin all the pomp and ceremony that St. Lucidians are so famous for. One quick blade through the heart would do it, Adele thought. *So I suppose that if I survive this first encounter, it's diplomacy that Sanda'hani really wants, not war, after all.*

She spotted the empress. Sanda'hani was sitting under a small, brightly colored canopy, surrounded by her four sisters. The empress rose to her feet and gestured imperiously for Adele to come and join her behind the line of armed warriors. *Like I'm stupid enough to separate myself from my own guard,* she thought. Yet there was no way to refuse the gesture without causing insult, so Adele pretended that she hadn't seen it. She shaded her eyes with a hand while holding on to Orgustus's arm.

"I am Queen Adelena St. Lucidis," she called out. "I have come to speak with Empress Sanda'hani."

The gambit worked. The empress conferred with her sisters for only a moment before she stepped into the sunlight, threading her way through the line of warriors to stand in front of Adele. Four warriors broke ranks to box the empress in.

Empress Sanda'hani was as tall as Adele remembered, almost six feet of voluptuous curves dressed in flowing, pink silk chiffon, her robe cinched at the waist with a wide, shiny leather brace holding two jeweled knives. Her waist-length black hair was caught back with a rope of gold chain. Her dark complexion was shiny with sweat. The fragrance of coconut and flowers hung about her in an almost intoxicating cloud.

"Queen Adelena." Empress Sanda'hani looked down her nose. "I come to wage war on the queen who would defile our great god Dahk'hani, kill his mage, and steal his son. At his behest, we—his people—are here for justice."

The empress pulsed with magic. Power danced in her aura, and the dragon magic in Adele's blood called to it, firing with excitement. She gripped Orgustus's elbow, but it wasn't helping anymore.

"Sweet Christ, Sanda'hani—war?" Adele hissed. She could feel the magic blazing in her eyes. "Are you saying Dahk'hani sent you here? You know I would never seek to cause you or your nation any harm, and I certainly wouldn't defile your god. He and I have had a complicated interaction, but it wasn't negative."

"Queen Adelena, I have written missive after missive to you, all of which have gone unanswered. You cannot ignore me any longer. I need to know if the fate of my people is at stake. I will do what is necessary to protect my empire." She began to sway on her feet, but her expression was resolute as she lowered her voice to say, "You should have told me you were a demon, Your Majesty. I am not Unisian and I do not regard the first tribe of Serena as evil. You should have trusted me."

Adele took a step toward the empress, and so did the four Sandarian warriors surrounding her. "Call your men off, Your Grace, and let's discuss this matter like civilized women," she begged.

"It's never too late for Unisia and her queen to make amends," Empress Sanda'hani conceded. "But the way will not be easy. You will have to . . ." She paused again, taking a deep breath, and swallowing heavily. "The pride of our god will have to be satisfied." The empress's four sisters approached and gathered around her. One held a flask of water, and another held a small package of fresh fruit wrapped in a banana leaf. Sanda'hani raised her hand to her mouth, closing her eyes. In that instant, Adele understood one reason why the empress was here now.

"Have your men drop their weapons, Sanda'hani," Adele suggested. "I know your warriors don't need steel to cause a great deal of harm, but it will stop them frightening my Household Guard. My men aren't warriors, and they will make mistakes if there is any question of violence."

Empress Sanda'hani nodded. She turned to her warriors and spoke at length in the tongue of the Sandarian people. It was the same language as Jordansson's people in the Ice Mountains, which made sense as they considered themselves the same tribe, created by Dahk'hani.

While the empress was distracted, Lord Orgustus took the chance to bend low and whisper in Adele's ear, "Should we take the empress prisoner when her soldiers are unarmed, Your Majesty?"

Adele understood the lord's duplicity, but she couldn't condone it. "I wasn't lying, Orgustus—her warriors are brutal fighters, while our own Household Guards are merely decorations. No, we'll try diplomacy before bloodshed, for our own sake as much as theirs."

"The empress seems quite fragile," Orgustus remarked, his lips on her ear. "What do you make of it?"

"Not sure. The long journey, perhaps?" Adele whispered back. She didn't want to share her theory with him just yet.

Sanda'hani had finished addressing her troops and Adele pinched Orgustus's arm to get him to shut up.

"Your Majesty, we are willing to accept your offer of open-hearted hospitality to Sandar and her empress," Empress Sanda'hani said, and swayed on her feet. "We should really get out of this sun."

"Your Grace, my sincere apologies! Of course, you must be exhausted after your voyage." Adele stepped forward to take Sanda'hani's arm and gestured for Lord Orgustus to take her other side.

"Your Grace, my name is Lord Orgustus St. Lucidis, former regent of the Crown of Unisia and chief advisor to Queen Adelena." Lord Orgustus wore his most charming smile. The empress was a woman in the grip of serious nausea, but she was still a woman and smiled back at him. Adele filed that flicker of interest away in her mind.

Calling Tilburn to her side, Adele gave him instructions to find accommodation for the Sandarian party and a place where they could conduct negotiations. The majordomo sprinted off, and Adele hoped she wasn't asking for too much.

A large crowd of St. Lucidis courtiers had gathered in the entry hall to stare and whisper at the odd sight of the barely dressed Sandarian warriors marching in formation as Queen Adelena walked behind, arm in arm with the Sandarian empress. Adele remembered vividly how it felt to be gawked at by these very same people when Lord Orgustus had marched her through the Golden Palace wearing manacles and headed for the prison below the palace called Hell.

I will see Orgustus dead for that humiliation, she thought, hot with sudden hatred, but caught herself just before the dragon magic took hold and made her do something stupid. She stepped away from the empress's side. *Lord Orgustus has a lot to answer for, but at least he's working for me now.*

As they crossed the entry hall, a young steward approached Adele and leaned into her side, whispering, "Your Majesty, the majordomo told me to take yer to the Garden Wing. It's where all yer guests will stay."

Adele nodded. The young man had red hair and freckles and reminded her of QG Pepper. "Lead on," she told him, having no idea where the Garden Wing was.

Luckily, it was easily found on the ground floor and accessed by a long, narrow, glass-walled corridor that branched out into the surrounds of the Lily Pond Gardens. The entire wing was shaped like an enormous hexagon, the outer walls made up of framed glass panels. A hallway traveled around all six sides. The suites were situated within the central space, and the ceiling was a clever system of louvers that let in the blue Unisian sky. There were also canvas shades that could be pulled across if the sun got too hot.

In the short time between Adele's command and their arrival in the Garden Wing, Tilburn had had an army of servants cleaning and removing white dust sheets from the furniture. With the doors and louvered windows open, the rooms were beautifully fresh and cool—the perfect accommodation for the outdoor-living Sandarians. Beds were still being made up, but Tilburn had already organized a cold buffet for their guests, and servers carrying trays of sweet juices and chilled wine began circling the crowd. Outside, by the collection of ponds filled with lily flowers, chefs were assembling outdoor ovens and shoveling hot coals to cook an array of freshwater fish and slabs of red meat.

Impressed, Adele caught hold of Tilburn by the arm as he made to dash past her. "You've done an incredible job, thank you," she said.

He looked at her askance. "There are problems with the plumbing in the fifth bathroom, and the lamps aren't working in the second suite," he muttered. "I'm getting straight on it now, Your Majesty."

Adele returned her attention to Sanda'hani, stepping in as close as she dared with her hold on the dragon magic feeling tenuous. "Your Grace, I hope you find the accommodations comfortable. Please rest and refresh yourselves. When you're ready to take a meeting with me, I will join you here in the Lily Pond Gardens."

Sanda'hani lowered herself onto a chair. Sweat streaked down her temple, but she spoke calmly. "Your Majesty has been most gracious. I will call for you as soon as I see to the needs of my people."

Adele didn't miss the slight but decided to ignore it. She wasted no time getting out of the Garden Wing, grabbing the red-haired steward as she went through the door.

"Right, kid, what's your name?" she asked. Standing in the glassed-in corridor, she could feel herself burning as the sun beat against her bare skin.

"I'm Brien Pepper, Your Maj." The young steward's accent was thick and familiar.

"Are you from the Blue Hills?" Adele received a wide-eyed nod in response.

"Blue Hills boys are more polite than that," QG Pepper snapped, glaring hard at the young man. "I'm a Pepper too, and I'll thank you to address the queen by her proper title."

"So sorry, Your Maj-esty," Brien stammered, his cheeks going strawberry red in an unattractive contrast with his bright orange hair. "S'just me nerves—I've never chatted with yer before, like."

"You used to have that accent too," QG Leith teased Pepper. "Why d'you think we wanted to beat it out of you?"

"Brien, I'd like to you to remain here in the Garden Wing as a messenger for the Sandarian empress when she's ready to take a meeting," Adele said.

Brien nodded, Adam's apple bobbing in his skinny throat. "Yes, Your Maj-esty."

"They probably won't be speaking the King's Tongue around you, but nevertheless . . ." She trailed off as a Sandarian warrior took up a post near them.

"Spy for yer?" Brien whispered, breathless.

Pepper made a noise of disgust. "Your Majesty, please let me recover some Blue Hills pride and give this kid a lesson on manners."

Ignoring Pepper, Adele asked, "Can you do that for me, Brien?"

Brien gave a firm nod. "I'm at yer service, Your Maj-esty."

"Now, someone go and fetch Lord Orgustus away from the ladies," Adele said. "We need to get out of here."

Captain Lucky went to Orgustus as the former regent tried to converse with a clearly fading Empress Sanda'hani. He took the message from Lucky and then waved him away.

"He's getting himself involved," General Ohrig warned her quietly. "It could be dangerous for you if he ingratiates himself with your enemy."

"He's getting in right over his head," Adele whispered back. "And what he doesn't realize is that he's swimming with sharks. We all know it only takes a drop of blood to send them into a frenzy."

"I've no idea what a shark is, Your Majesty," Ohrig whispered. She gave him a grin.

"My dear Lord Orgustus!" Adele called out, twinkling her fingers in a wave. "Your queen has need of you."

Lord Orgustus almost frowned, but he caught himself just in time. Politely excusing himself from the company of the Sandarian royals, he joined Adele and her Queen's Guard by the door.

"Take my arm," she instructed him quietly. "And then kind of give me an affectionate look or touch. Like you don't want me to be jealous."

Orgustus did as he was told, barely touching his lips to Adele's cheek before offering his arm to lead her down the glass corridor and back to the main palace. "Do you mind telling me what this is all about, Your Majesty?" he asked, his eyebrow arched as he looked down on her from his superior height. Adele was getting very tired of people doing that today.

"It's important that the empress knows how important you are to me," she said. "It needs to be clear that she can't touch you without serious political repercussions."

Orgustus smirked. "Your Majesty, I didn't know you cared."

Adele fought rolling her eyes and continued, "We need to have all the important players in these war talks. I want Tilburn, Mrs. Ollenby, and Jordan Jordansson for this too. If Charlie hasn't left for Concordis yet, I'll need him to go and fetch Prince Rainere for me from the Gray Palace. We'll all meet in the Lavender Room."

"I know where Jordansson is, I'll go and fetch him for you," Orgustus said, releasing Adele's arm so quickly that she stumbled.

"Just send a messenger," she said. "I really need to speak to you alone, my lord."

"It's no trouble. I won't be long." He dashed away.

"Apparently, your dear Lord Orgustus had Jordansson out at Merrills's last night for a raucous evening of booze and dancing," Ohrig said. "By some accounts, a few dancers returned to the palace with them."

Adele considered this. "That suits me just fine," she said. "Because right now, I need to tell you guys what I want to do and have you try to talk me out of it."

"It'll be my pleasure, Your Majesty." Ohrig beetled his gray brows. "Lavender Room it is."

CHAPTER TWENTY-ONE

"Translations"

Rainere checked the hallway outside the Marchant guest suite. Seeing no one lurking, he shut the door and applied a powerful spell of protection around the frame. He was getting frustrated with all the running he'd had to do today. After the terrible news at breakfast, he'd hurried Prince Rainold down to the portal chamber of the Golden Palace, but High Wizard Ohren had been waiting for them, hidden in the shadows. Ohren told them there was no time to explain, and then the three of them had made a mad dash through the secret passages to the only safe place Rainere could think of quickly.

"Tell me again why we aren't in the Gray Palace, as the queen demanded?" Rainere asked his father.

"I've already told you everything, my handsome boy." Prince Rainold was stretched out on the four-poster bed, hands behind his head, his boots leaving dusty tracks on the damask bedspread. "The queen is going to do something terrible, and I must be here to stop her. I'm not going to be any help if I'm all the way over in the Gray Palace, now am I?"

"But you don't have any idea what she'll do?" Rainere asked. He thought his father looked ridiculously calm for someone who'd just escaped prison and was now on a holy mission to save Evendaar.

"Unfortunately, the goddess wasn't very specific. She just told us

190

that Queen Adelena will destroy Evendaar, and we can't stop her, but we must stop her—or something like that."

Rainere couldn't believe that High Wizard Ohren was just going along with this madness. Ohren was sitting in a chair by the window and didn't even appear to be listening to the conversation. "High Wizard, did you share this vision?" Rainere asked.

Ohren jumped at the question. "Sorry, what? No—I mean, yes, I shared the vision with His Highness. It's why I was so keen to help you get him out of prison."

"Then why didn't you tell me that?" Rainere asked through gritted teeth.

But Ohren only turned back to the window, silent.

Rainere narrowed his eyes at the two men. "And why aren't you happier to see each other? Ohren, you have always spoken of my father with such affection, and now you won't look at each other."

Prince Rainold raised himself up on his elbows, grinning. "Should Ohren and I make love in front of you, darling?" he asked. "Would that convince you?"

Rainere crossed his arms over his chest. "I want proof of something," he said.

Rainold let out a peal of laughter at that, but Ohren rounded on them both. "Would you be quiet!" he hissed, then jabbed a finger in Rainere's direction. "And you, stop asking stupid questions. We need to come up with a plan to protect the whole world from Queen Adelena. For goddess' sake, focus, Your Highnesses!"

"She's going to destroy everything, darling," Rainold said. He sat upright on the bed, folding his legs. "Now, how about we start with you telling me what you think could make Adelena dangerous, and then we can work out what might happen from there. For instance, has she happened to have killed any Marchant Eldars recently?"

"Yes, three of them," Ohren barked.

"Ah, that's not good." Rainold pouted at the news. "Anything else?"

Rainere took a beat, wondering what he should tell his father.

As it was, the facts painted a rather grim picture of Adelena, and he didn't want his father to think less of her for it. Though why he should care so much about his father's opinion puzzled him.

"I never made the journey to the Ice Mountains with Adelena— she asked me to stay behind and guard her children," Rainere began. "But as soon as she reached the edge of the Black Mountains, she started dreaming of the god Dahk'hani. He said her step on his land had woken him. She continued to dream of him as she made her way to find Sighmere in his underground lair high up in the Ice Mountains. She claims that Dahk'hani saved her life by feeding her magic from the sky." Rainere paused. He knew this story sounded ridiculous. "She called it the Gottessteppen and says it was like a river of magic filled with portals, which opened all over Evendaar—even one to the Realm of the Gods. After she spoke with Sighmere, she sent the dragon back to the realm to be reunited with Serena."

Rainold fluttered his fingers in the air. "Stop, my darling! The goddess told me this bit about Sighmere keeping her captive in the Realm of the Gods. She said blah, blah, Dahk'hani has chosen Adelena to be his mother, blah, blah, he wants to walk the world and destroy Evendaar. Something about returning to dust?"

Rainere held on to his temper with a supreme effort and continued, "According to the savage tribesman, Jordansson, Dahk'hani has chosen him to father that child. But it was the dragon Sighmere who forced Adelena to bring him to Unisia with her."

"A-ha!" Rainold raised a finger in the air. "With Sighmere in the Realm of the Gods, Dahk'hani no longer has any enemies here. He could very possibly be born as a fragile child and skip around as he pleases."

"Why would Sighmere want to help Dahk'hani, his rival?" Rainere thought he was asking the obvious question, but both men seemed to disregard it.

Prince Rainold wriggled off the end of the bed to stand in front of Rainere and brushed a gentle hand over his cheek. "What else can you tell me about Adelena, dear boy?"

Rainere stepped away from his father's affection. *I won't betray her confidence, but may the goddess forgive me, this man is the only one who can help her,* he thought, and chose his words with care. "After drinking Sighmere's tear, Adelena has changed so much. She can no longer hear what she calls the Chime Voices in her head, nor can she control the dragon's magic within her. Anytime her magic is activated, she says it feels like the dragon's magic grabs hold and multiplies the strength of her reaction a hundred times over. She's already tried to siphon it back to Jordansson but says nothing has worked so far. My fear is that she will become so desperate to be separated from the dragon magic—" *She'll do something stupid,* he stopped himself from saying. "She'll hurt herself."

"So, what do you make of it?" Ohren asked Rainold. "You're the only wizard who has ever studied demons and their magic before. What do you think makes Adelena so dangerous?"

Rainold chewed his bottom lip and began to pace the room again. "We all know that when it's concentrated under the right conditions, dragon tear converts to dragon flame," he muttered. "That must be how Adelena killed our Eldars."

"And where is the goddess Serena in all this mess?" Rainere asked both men. "She came to me in a vision while I was in Hell and begged me to save Adelena from Dahk'hani. Now Adelena has returned to Unisia under some sort of contract to the god, and maybe it's only the dragon's magic that is protecting her from his visions. But then why would Serena come to you both, but not me again?"

"No one can truly know the ways of the gods," Ohren said, his pompous tone grating.

"But Serena clearly wants us to know something about their ways," Rainere growled. "If not, then why would she suddenly be laying out visions to wizards left and right after a thousand years of silence?"

"Not quite a thousand. She gave us the Prophecy of the End of the World only a few hundred years ago," Ohren corrected him. "And look at the mess that got us into."

"I really want to have a closer look at Adelena," Rainold said. "Do you think she would let me examine her?"

Rainere couldn't believe his father had forgotten what had happened at breakfast already. "Not now, she's dealing with a crisis," he snapped. "Remember the war?"

"Yes, the Sandarian empress has declared war on Unisia," Ohren said with a dry chuckle. "It's unheard of, of course. Sandar cannot think to go against the military might of Unisia. I'm sure the gesture was only meant to gain Adelena's attention after I destroyed all their letters. They were being harassed by the Eldars and wanted Unisian aid to get rid of them."

"And what if the dragon magic overwhelms the queen and she publicly kills the empress of Sandar?" Rainere asked, while thinking, *By the goddess, I'm dealing with idiots.*

"You know, the gods love blood being spilled in their honor," Rainold said, his hands fluttering in a complicated dance. "Blood is a wonderful conductor of power, and sacrificial blood is just the best. Oh! I bet those Sandarians are all here to die!"

Ohren got up from his chair and shook out his dark gray robes. His face twisted and then untwisted itself, oddly. "You make a good point—perhaps I'd better join the queen for these negotiations," he said, and raced out of the room.

Rainere and Rainold sat in silence for a long moment, staring at each other.

"Dar-ling," Rainold sang. His eyebrows were arched, and a smile played across his lips. "I'll give you three guesses who Ohren really is under his ugly disguise."

All the doubts in his mind coalesced into one answer and Rainere felt his blood turn to ice. "Ohren is Orestes? Shit! How many of our secrets have I told him? You know, he kidnapped Adelena's children and tried to have her killed, and I'm sure he'll do it again."

"You kidnapped one of Adelena's children, and she forgave you," Rainold said. "Maybe she'll forgive him too?"

Rainere hated that his father could mention his deepest shame in such a casual manner. "Perhaps he engineered this war so that the Sandarians will kill Adelena for him," he suggested.

"Actually, it's almost like Orestes is working for Dahk'hani," Rainold mused, not listening to him anymore. "First, he allows her to kill the three Eldars, which I'm pretty sure Serena specifically asked us *not* to allow. Then he hand-delivers her a hundred sacrifices from Dahk'hani's own tribes so the god can rise on a tide of blood—"

"Stop!" Rainere snarled. "Adelena cannot be forced to be a plaything of Dahk'hani. She is mine. *Mine!*"

"Oh, darling." Rainold surprised Rainere by patting his stiff shoulders and smiling at his fury. "There is a reason Serena granted the Marchant kings the most potent magic of all the families, as well as the gift of immortality. We are her Chosen, and we can play the game of gods and win. We've done it before, and we'll do it again."

What the hell is he talking about? Rainere wondered, but he felt strangely comforted by his father's words. "What do you want to do?"

"What do you want to do, my honey cake?" Rainold repeated, as if it were a game.

"I want to kill Orestes," Rainere answered. "Painfully."

"Then that's what I want to do too, darling." Rainold laughed, the sound a little manic. "Our first project together as father and son. How exciting!"

There was a soft knock, and Charlie poked his head around the door. His eyes widened to see the two Marchant princes standing face-to-face.

Rainold waved at Charlie. "Can we help you, sweetheart?"

"How the fuck did you get past the ward I put on the door?" Rainere snapped.

Charlie came in and shut the door behind himself. "You always use the same one, so I've had plenty of time to figure a way around it. Anyway, the queen sent me to the Gray Palace to fetch you back, but Grotto told me you never got there. I had instructions that your, uh . . . that Prince Rainold was to remain at the Gray Palace."

"Sorry, we come together or not at all," Rainold said firmly. "I'm Prince Rainere's father, you know."

Charlie looked skeptical. "If you say so."

"When and where does the queen want me?" Rainere asked.

"Her Majesty said that you should go to the garret above her dressing room where you hid Princess Stella that time," Charlie replied. "She's left instructions for you explaining everything."

Rainere had heard enough. He pushed open the door to the secret passage that was hidden behind a panel. "Charlie, entertain His Highness for me," he said. "I'll be back when I can." Then he ran to answer his queen's call.

Chapter Twenty-Two

"Kissing in the Stables"

The secret door closed with a quiet click and Charlie turned back to the room to see Prince Rainold bouncing on the end of the bed.

"How are you going to entertain me, handsome?" He smiled in a way Charlie really didn't like and patted the bedspread. "You know, I haven't been kissed in a very long time. Over a hundred years, in fact."

Charlie raised his chin, his mouth twisting in a snarl. "Sorry, Your Highness, I don't play for your team."

Rainold pouted. "You know, in my day, there weren't any teams— we all played the same side. It was so much fun."

"I should go."

"I'll come with you then, Charlie," Rainold said, brightening. "Where're we going?"

"I'm going to the stables," he replied. "I've got work to do for the queen so I'm too busy to stay with you."

"You're too busy!" Rainold got off the bed and prowled across the room. He only stopped when Charlie had to either look up at him or back up against the wall. "Listen, sweetheart, you would do well to remember that I'm an immortal Marchant prince. If you don't watch your manners, I might not let you refuse me again."

Charlie blinked. "And you should know I'll fight to the death to stop you touching my arse."

It was Rainold's turn to blink. The madness in his emerald-green eyes dissolved, and he laughed gaily. "Oh, I like you, Charlie!" he said. "You're just the sweetest thing."

Charlie moved to leave, but Rainold moved quicker and caught his hand, yanking him over to the hidden door with surprising strength. He pushed the panel open. "Let me show you how to get to the stables by the secret passages," he said. "It'll be much quicker."

Charlie eyed the dark passageway that Rainere had gone down. "And who's to believe that you won't lose me in there?" he asked.

"Oh, so cynical for one so young!" Rainold chuckled and pulled Charlie in behind him. "Darling, if I wanted to kill you, you'd be dead already."

Reluctantly, Charlie followed. But he didn't like holding hands with Prince Rainold, nor tripping on his own feet as the floor in the corridors changed from wooden planks to tiles to mismatched stepping-stones. Fortunately, the prince did seem to know his way well enough in the dimly lit passageways, only backtracking once with a flustered apology.

Charlie distracted himself by thinking of his mission. Queen Adelena had asked him to go to the mayor, because she was terrified that rumors about the possible war might already have traveled to the city. Charlie was bursting with pride that she had chosen him for such an important meeting. He even carried a letter written in Adelena's own hand allowing him to speak on her behalf. But it was nerves that made Charlie jiggle the knife holstered up his right sleeve. There was another one up a trouser leg. *No sense in going into this meeting like an idiot,* he'd already decided. *Merrills might not like what I have to say, and I can't have her taking advantage of me on my own.*

The prince pushed a door open, even the dim light making Charlie blink as they exited the passages via an old storage closet in the armory attached to the back of the palace. Charlie was dusty and out of breath, but it had been a much quicker journey to the sprawling Great Stables. He wasted no time, loping along the paved path between outbuildings, and couldn't help but glance into the trotting paddock where the children had been kidnapped only days ago, but the broken fence had been replaced and there was really nothing to see.

Prince Rainold was still close on his heels when he passed under the enormous beech trees framing the stable doors. A couple of squires were lounging on white picnic benches in the shade, and he asked them where Benjamin Belvoir was. One lad pointed the way, and he took off in that direction.

He found the stables in absolute chaos because the Sandarians had brought fifty Tree Horses with them. Charlie had never seen a Tree Horse up close before, and he marveled at their pale green pelts and pearl-colored eyes. They couldn't be put in stalls like normal horses—their skinny legs were articulated, so they could climb out or hurt themselves trying, so they were left to roam the wide corridor of the stables under the watch of a dozen stable hands.

"Oh, aren't they gorgeous!" Prince Rainold stopped to pet one, and Charlie took the chance to ditch the prince as he wove his way between horses and grooms. He followed the bellows and screams of a very pissed-off Marchant stallion to find Benjamin cooing at the furious Titor locked in his stall.

"I promise these tree ponies aren't getting near your girls, sweetie," Benjamin said as Titor reared and crashed against the metal-reinforced stall door. "Calm down and I'll give you your treat." He waggled the piece of carrot through the bars.

"Why'd you lock him up like that?" Charlie asked. "He doesn't look happy."

Benjamin sighed and pulled his hand away from Titor's gnashing jaws with no real sense of urgency. "The poor guy is just annoyed that there are so many newcomers here," he said. "If I left him in a normal stall, he'd get out in no time and kill 'em all."

Charlie winced as Titor scraped his iron-shod hooves against the metal door. Then his screams were suddenly cut short.

"Well, aren't you a beauty!" Prince Rainold walked straight up to the bars where the stallion now stood as meek as a mouse. "What's his name?"

"Titor. He's Prince Rainere's steed," Benjamin answered. He raised an eyebrow at Charlie to ask, "Who's this guy?" but Charlie felt it wise to let the prince introduce himself.

Prince Rainold looked over his shoulder at the tall, dark, and handsome Benjamin, and Charlie saw his interest spark immediately. "And who might you be?"

"Benjamin Belvoir, sir." He took off his cap and pushed his black curls off his forehead. His pale green eyes were framed by long, black lashes that were famous throughout the Golden Palace, but his smile had a reputation all its own. He was smiling now. "I'm head stable hand for Prince Rainere, and for the queen too. Not that she rides much."

"She's not a horsewoman, then?" Prince Rainold asked, but Charlie sensed he was more interested in keeping Benjamin talking than in what he was saying.

"The queen does well for herself," Benjamin said, moving closer to the prince. "But her style's more practical than sophisticated."

"Yeah, like all of us city dwellers who prefer to walk," Charlie interrupted. "Look, Benjamin, I have an urgent mission, and I'll need a guide into the city." He frowned at him, but the prince made no show of leaving to give them privacy. "It's important we take the back way, and I was told you'd know it."

"If you want to be discreet, then let's take a couple of the Belvoir racers that Prince Bertrand sent over for training," Benjamin said over his shoulder. "Can you handle a spirited animal?"

"I can!" Prince Rainold said, coquettish in a way that made Charlie's skin crawl. "Would you like me to help you saddle up the horses?"

"I don't know about that. You haven't told me your name yet," Benjamin said. "Let me guess though, from the way Titor is making eyes at you, it's something La-di-dah Marchant."

"That's a very good guess." Prince Rainold leaned in to touch Benjamin's arm and ran his hand along his well-toned biceps.

"Yeah, excuse me, gents. But I'm in quite a hurry here, on the *queen's* business," Charlie interrupted again.

"Calm down, Charlie, I've got to tack the horses first," Benjamin said. He took Prince Rainold's hand. "You want to come and see where I keep the tack, Mr. Marchant?"

"Yes, please," Prince Rainold said. He pressed himself against Benjamin's side. "Is it very quiet there?"

Benjamin nodded and pulled him away. "Give us twenty minutes, eh, Charlie? I'll be right back."

"He means thirty minutes," Prince Rainold said, and both men laughed as Benjamin led them between bales of straw and barrels of feed to the back of the stables, where the offices were.

"You have got to be fucking kidding me," Charlie muttered. "Now I have to wait here like a fucking idiot while they dip their wicks and I'm—" He stopped talking to himself when he noticed he'd caught the attention of a couple of young stable hands.

"Oi! You two! Stop gawking and saddle up two of those racing horses that Prince Bertrand sent over for training," Charlie demanded. He expected the lads to give him a rude gesture, but they only touched their caps at him and raced off to do as they were told. It was then he remembered that he was dressed as nicely as a courtier courtesy of Mrs. Ollenby. He looked down at the shine on his new brown riding boots. "The power of a good costume, eh? That's the real magic," he whispered to himself.

Feeling mollified, Charlie flicked dust off his expensive suit and prepared to wait for the horses and his soon-to-be-satiated guide to the city.

CHAPTER TWENTY-THREE

"The Council of War"

Adele and her Queen's Guard were the first ones in the Lavender Room, so she'd had a chance to explain her hastily thought-up plan and now waited for the men to give her their opinions.

Dust motes danced in the sunbeams shining through the two sets of balcony doors. The lavender silk fabric on the walls sparkled, and the unlit chandeliers gleamed, throwing shards of light on the polished surface of the huge meeting table. She hadn't always liked this room, as it had been the site of many uncomfortable meetings, but it was a practical choice, being thoroughly protected with enchantments to prevent anyone overhearing what was spoken within its walls.

Adele finished her glass of water and looked around for the jug, but Captain Lucky already had it in his hand, ready to pour her another glass. She felt uncomfortable remembering General Ohrig's words about Lucky's being in love with her in his own warped, yet special, kind of way.

"Any arguments?" she prompted her men. "Anyone think what I'm doing is incredibly stupid? Or generally any ideas on how this is going to backfire?"

General Ohrig rubbed his chin, his hand rasping against the five o'clock shadow that always appeared by midday. "I don't even know where to begin," he said.

"But?"

"I think it's quite diabolical, Your Majesty," Captain Lucky answered. "I also think it's rather perfect. Many problems solved even before they occur."

"I just hope you aren't underestimating Jordansson," Ohrig mused. "Yes, I agree the kid is ambitious, but that doesn't mean he is ruthless enough to betray you, even to gain a pregnant empress. If she really is pregnant, which hasn't been confirmed, I'll add. But Lord Orgustus couldn't be trusted to hold your hand, let alone if you offered him a chance at the big prize."

"Will it work, though?"

"We can't know the future, Your Majesty," QG Bear piped up. "Let's just give it a go."

Adele smiled at Bear in thanks. Though the entire Queen's Guard were always present for her briefings, it was only ever General Ohrig and Captain Lucky who joined in the discussion; Owens, Bear, Pepper, and Leith usually listened without comment.

There was a knock at the door, and Adele stood up. "Right, lads, that's the end of our privacy. Game faces on," she said, then called out, "Come in!"

Mrs. Ollenby, Lord Orgustus, High Wizard Ohren, and Jordansson entered, followed by a train of servants pushing trolleys laden with a selection of hot and cold dishes.

"Please, everyone, take a seat," Adele said. "And thank you for remembering lunch, Mrs. Ollenby. I'm starving!" And she was. Normally in a time of crisis, her stomach would be tied up in knots, but she felt like the dragon magic was burning up her energy and she needed to replace it quickly.

Tilburn entered when everyone had taken a plate and found a chair. He informed Adele that he'd been told by the steward, Brien, that the empress was taking a nap and wouldn't rise until the early evening.

There was another knock at the door, and a tall, blond gentleman entered. He was dressed like any modern young courtier—a violet brocade jacket, and velvet trousers tucked into knee-high boots. His shirt buttons were gold and done up to the neck, where he wore a chiffon cravat in a fashionable knot. Radiant blue eyes were cast to the ground as he took a seat next to Tilburn. The young man raised his chin as everyone fell silent, staring at him. *Oh, yes, he's gorgeous,* Adele thought as she nodded a greeting at the courtier and bit her bottom lip to keep from smiling.

"Your Majesty, would you care to introduce your guest to us?" Lord Orgustus asked. "I was led to believe that this was a private meeting."

"Hi-ho, I'm Jordan Jordansson of what Unisians call the Ice Mountains." Jordansson leaned over the table and held out his hand to the stranger. "I greet you in the ways of your people."

The young man stood and shook Jordansson's hand. "A pleasure to meet you, Mr. Jordansson," he said.

"And, sir, you are?" Lord Orgustus asked, his tone equal parts curious and dismissive.

The stranger was probably in his late twenties. With his chiseled jaw and high forehead, he looked like an older version of Captain Lucky. In fact, the likeness was so close that Orgustus was staring from one man to the other, his eyes narrowed in suspicion. It gave Adele a wonderful idea.

"Ladies and gentlemen, this is, uh, Odin St. Lucidis, and he comes highly recommended by my own Captain Lucky. Odin is Lucky's cousin from . . . abroad." Adele worked hard not to grin when Odin's eyebrows climbed his forehead. "He speaks many languages and is fluent in Sandarian."

"Far be it from me to doubt any of your advisors, Your Majesty," Orgustus said, clearly doing just that. "But have you had this man's background verified? How do we know that he hasn't come to us as a spy for the Sandarians?"

Adele leaned forward in her chair. "Odin knows the price for betraying the queen of Unisia."

Boldly, Orgustus held her gaze, and she wondered why his bravado suddenly felt so cute, when normally he irritated her. She blamed the change on her magics and returned to the topic at hand.

"We have to discuss what must be done about the Sandarians' demands and this issue of war." Adele didn't like the silence that followed, so she added, "You're my counselors, so please counsel me. What should we do?"

Mrs. Ollenby was the first one to break the heavy silence. "Your Majesty, I have no experience in matters of politics. But I do know people, and Empress Sanda'hani is like any other woman, overworked and under pressure. She wants her lover back, and she wants to know what really happened to her mage. My advice is that honesty is the best remedy for this situation."

"Why is the Royal Housekeeper here?" Orgustus whispered loudly to Adele.

"The same reason you are, Lord Orgustus," she answered at a normal volume. "Because Mrs. Ollenby gives good advice. Now stop interrupting her."

Mrs. Ollenby was blushing. "His lordship has a point, Your Majesty."

"No, he doesn't," Adele snapped, feeling a fizz of irritation that Mrs. Ollenby wouldn't stand up for herself. "Apparently it's unheard of for Sandar to declare war on Unisia, so it's anyone's guess how we fix this." She turned to her majordomo. "Tilburn, when you were getting the Sandarians settled in the Garden Wing, did you see anyone who might look like a mage? I'm wondering if they have a new one who is stirring up as much trouble for us as the old one did."

The majordomo was chewing on a manicured nail. "I presume any new mage would look like the last—feathers in the hair, terrible teeth, filthy clothes? I didn't see anyone who looked like that."

"How do we know the old mage is really dead?" Orgustus asked. "The Sandarians could be tricking us."

"I know he's dead," Adele said. She decided not to sugarcoat it. "Because I killed him."

To his credit, Orgustus barely paused to digest his shock. "How is Dahk'hani involved with this, exactly?" he asked. "I mean, can we even believe that the empress is really in such close contact with her god? She could be lying."

"Dahk'hani doesn't seem to move in very mysterious ways," Adele said, her stomach clenching at saying the god's name. "And now that he is awake, we have no idea what he is capable of, including manipulating his own tribe to start a war with us."

The expressions around the table ranged from doubtful to horrified.

"Queen Adelena, please tell me, why do the empress of Sandar and Dahk'hani want war with the queen of Unisia?" Jordansson asked. He was clearly confused by how fast the conversation was flowing round the table and the complex tangle of issues. "They are a tiny empire, and Unisia is mighty."

"The empress said we've insulted Dahk'hani," Adele said, "and that she has written to me many times but never gotten a response. Yet Tilburn can verify that no letters ever arrived, because anything that important would have gone straight to him."

"Or Orestes read those letters and understood the empress's increasing fear of the Marchant Eldars too," General Ohrig added. "Perhaps he made a deal with the Eldars to devour the Sandarian children instead of the children of Concordis?"

"If I may?" Odin raised a hand like a child in school. "Sandarian magic works very differently than other magics. There is no possible way that a Sandarian child could perform the same tasks with the gray crystal in the mines. It's more likely that the high magistrar facilitated a war so that the empress of Sandar would be tempted to kill the queen and he could claim back his position at court."

Adele sighed and rubbed her eyes. "I'm sure if Orestes is trying to organize an assassination, this one will fail like all the others."

"I wouldn't underestimate him, Your Majesty," Ohren piped up to caution her. "My brother is very determined when he's pushed. I hate to be the one to point out that, with all your power and resources, you—I mean, we—haven't managed to catch him. I keep waiting for him to get in touch with me, but so far, nothing."

"Not helpful, Ohren," Adele replied, irritated with the high wizard and too worried to hide it. "All right, we're done for the moment. However, I'd like everyone available during dinner with the empress tonight. I'm going to suggest an outdoor party, so you should all be able to attend in some capacity. You, Lord Orgustus, will sit at my right hand. I'll need your eyes on the empress in case I get distracted."

"You mean, in case your magic overreacts again?" Orgustus leaned forward to touch the back of Adele's hand in a familiar way. "Your Majesty, I wouldn't advise bringing in this Odin St. Lucidis to the dinner—instead, Jordansson would be much more useful. He speaks Sandarian and might garner some sympathy as a foreigner in the court, much as our guests are."

Adele pretended to consider Orgustus's suggestion as if she hadn't already decided to do just that. "I think that would be wise. Of course, there is no doubt that our friend Jordansson is loyal to me."

Jordansson grinned at the compliment. "Queen Adelena, you are the queen who would bear my child. We are destiny together. I will fight the Sandarians for you, if you ask me to, but I share a god with them—it will not be easy for me."

Adele glanced at Orgustus, checking that he got all that. He bared his teeth in a forced smile. "I'll make sure Jordansson keeps the topic of destiny to a minimum, Your Majesty."

"Thanks, everyone." Adele waved at the door. She still didn't have the hang of dismissing people. "You can go about your business again."

When the room had mostly emptied and they wouldn't be overhead, Adele turned to her general. "Ohrig, tonight get all the lads into their most formal uniforms, and make sure everyone is shaved and looking very handsome. I need to distract the empress's sisters. They're her support and trying to help cover up the pregnancy. The empress may be more susceptible to me if their attention is elsewhere."

Ohrig nodded and half-stood, but Adele grabbed his forearm. "And if you could work your own charms on Mrs. Ollenby, I would appreciate it," she said. "I need her to step up. She'll be a great help to me if she can just get over her confidence problem."

The general frowned. "I'll do as you ask, this time," he said, "But you have to know, Dolores loves you, but she hates politics, always has. You can't use her like that."

"Do your best for me," Adele insisted.

Ohrig huffed and stomped out of the room. He had no patience when she got bossy with him.

Captain Lucky lingered after the rest of the Queen's Guard had left. "Your Majesty, I know that now isn't a good time, but I was hoping to have a private word with you about something important. Only it's not a matter of national interest."

Adele glanced at Odin as he walked out with Tilburn, the major-domo peppering him with questions as to his pedigree and education.

"This is as private as it gets, Lucky. Fire away."

Captain Lucky fiddled with his collar, something he only did when he was very nervous. Adele sat back down in her chair and encouraged him to sit opposite her. She could see this was difficult for him, and that made her very curious. "Captain Lancelot St. Lucidis, I imagine someone is going to walk in that door in about thirty seconds with another crisis for me to handle, so whatever you have to say, say it now, please!" she begged.

Lucky coughed into his fist. "Your Majesty, what I ask, I do not ask lightly," he began. "But I would like your permission to marry." He let it all out in a rush, and Adele took a moment to understand.

"A woman?" she asked.

Lucky's smile drooped a little. "Yes, Your Majesty, to marry a woman." He brightened again. "I have been courting a lady of pedigree, somewhat discreetly, for months now, and I think the time has come to ask her to be my wife. She's from a good family, though not of the established aristocracy, and I think it's a sensible match. As a captain in the Queen's Guard, I will provide well enough for both of us when it comes time to have children."

"Forget all of that, Lucky," she said. "Do you love the lady?"

Lucky smiled down at his lap. "Yes, I love her."

"Then you have my blessing." Adele was delighted that someone among her dearest friends was finding happiness, and she couldn't wait to gloat that Ohrig had been wrong about Lucky being in love with her. "I'd prefer it if you have the wedding after all this war business is cleared up. Then I promise that I'll release you to take a nice, long honeymoon."

Captain Lucky nodded. "Of course, Your Majesty, we'll be married whenever you wish—and time for a honeymoon would be a wonderful gift."

"You can go and tell her now, if you like," she said. "But then I'll need you to get ready for tonight."

Lucky bowed, then dashed out of the room in a way that reminded Adele of her own son rushing somewhere with good news. The door hadn't closed before another head popped around it.

"Your Majesty, I was hoping to have a private word with you about something important," Odin said, his tone humble as he echoed Captain Lucky's request.

Adele sighed and waved him in. "What is it, Odin? Are you nervous about tonight? Don't be. Just stand around looking beautiful, keep your mouth shut, and you'll do fine."

Odin crossed the room and offered Adele his hand. "You think I'm beautiful, Your Majesty?" he asked, his eyes round with wonder.

Adele gasped when he swung her to sit on the table and pressed himself between her legs. "Odin, how dare you!"

But Odin had slid his hand up under her skirt and along the inside of her thigh, and she gasped for a very different reason. "Stop," she protested with a giggle. "I feel like I'm cheating on you, I can't do this."

Odin buried his face in Adele's neck, and she felt his tongue trace the pulse racing there.

"Seriously, Rainere, take it off," she said. The dragon magic was excited, and it was getting hard to focus. They needed to be talking about the threat of war, not behaving like teenagers.

Odin raised his head. "Your letter said to look like a St. Lucidis courtier," he said, and his were fingers merciless in their exquisite rhythm between her legs. "I thought maybe you wanted to try a little role-playing."

"No, I love you, not this stupid, gorgeous Odin." Adele heard the desperation in her own voice as she pulled at Rainere's shirt. "Do that spell thing with all the buttons."

Rainere muttered, and a moment later, his shirt and trousers were hanging open. Adele thanked all the gods that he never wore under-wear as her gaze roamed his new body. Her own gown fell off her shoulders, the ribbons untied.

"Oh, but you don't even have your tattoo," she complained, then groaned when he pushed closer to her. She yanked the jacket and shirt off his shoulders, sliding her hands over his chest. "Even your skin feels different. Rainere, come on, take it off now."

"You said I was gorgeous," he insisted, strange blue eyes smiling as he wove his fingers through her hair, pulling her head back and exposing her neck to his kisses.

"But I want to see your face," she demanded, though she was almost blinded by pleasure, her hands pressed against his chest, the magic waiting to take over.

"Not till I've finished with you," he growled.

In a moment, Adele found herself spun round and bent over the table. She cried out as Rainere yanked her dress the rest of the way down and used his thigh to part her legs. He slammed straight into her, beginning a rhythm that was aggressive and tender all at once. The sensation of pleasure was overwhelming as Adele allowed herself to be pinned on the tabletop, his hand on her hip and one on her shoulder. She tried to hold it off but her climax came with the force of a hurricane, wringing her out until she collapsed panting. Then she felt Rainere's own release, and his shudders and groans caused another orgasm to wash through her. This time, they collapsed together. She loved the heaviness of him, his tongue tracing the sweat on her neck. "*Cara mia*," he breathed. "My beloved."

"I know." She couldn't resist giggling. "Dragon magic is definitely good for this."

On shaking arms, Adele pushed herself up from the tabletop. In front of her was a maze of scorched lines marring the glossy wood. Rainere placed his hand over hers as she traced them with a fingertip still fizzing with green sparks.

"Is that what you used my tears to heal on your stomach?" she asked quietly, although she didn't really want an answer. *That would've hurt him so much,* she thought, and felt tears pricking in her eyes.

Rainere gently withdrew and turned her around. His naked body felt unfamiliar pressed against hers, as he studied her with strange blue eyes. "*Cara mia*, Prince Rainold thinks that the dragon magic inside you is converting to dragon flame," he said. "That's why it carries your other magics, exacerbating their power. Dragon flame is a conduit, or a conductor of magic, not a source of magic itself."

"It's also one of the few things that can kill an immortal," she whispered, remembering when he had given her the gift of a single dragon flame in a little glass globe, along with a choice: kill him or use the magic flame to kill the Spiders who held Natalie prisoner. Adele had chosen to use the flame for genocide. Ruthless and relentless, the dragon flame was infused with the spell to kill every Spider it touched. It continued to burn in the Nest beneath the ground, now and for eternity.

"But what will the flame do to Stella?" She felt her heart squeezed in a vise, and Rainere-as-Odin didn't look reassuring.

"Let's not find out," he answered. "I'll work on a way to get it out of her. Hopefully, my father can help." He leaned down and kissed her, offering the only comfort he could when the future was still so uncertain. She melted into the kiss, then pulled away.

"Where is your father now?" she asked, breathless.

Rainere trailed his lips along her jaw, murmuring, "I left him with Charlie in my old suite of rooms in the guest wing."

Adele groaned when he nipped at her earlobe. "Sweet Christ, that was hours ago. He could be anywhere by now."

"I know." He stopped kissing her and sighed as if it were a huge effort. "I'll go and find him."

"Find him and hide him." She was starting to think that Rainere wasn't taking the risk that Prince Rainold posed very seriously. "And I don't want him anywhere near the children."

She picked her gown up off the floor and turned for Rainere to mumble the spell that did up all her ribbons again. As Odin he looked too pretty and not at all imposing when he frowned. "*Cara mia*, my father might be insane, but he isn't stupid. He seems very keen to help us."

"Even if I believe you, I don't believe him." With two hands on his naked chest, Adele reached up for a last kiss.

This time, it was Rainere who pulled away. "I knew you were partial to blonds," he said, looking comically vindicated.

But Adele remembered a certain confession from another blonde, and a shadow of that fury fell over her good mood. "Yes, well, I've heard we both are, Your Highness," she said, finding it suddenly very easy to slip out of his arms and make her way to the door. "Find your father," she commanded, without looking back. "Bring him to me when you have a solution to help Stella."

"Adelena?" But Odin's voice didn't even sound like Rainere, and it took no effort to shut the door on him.

Chapter Twenty-Four

"Premonitions and Ammunitions"

It was late afternoon, but Adele's bedchamber was a hive of activity as she began the hours-long process of getting ready for the evening's event with the Sandarians. Her children ran around the room with their dogs, getting underfoot and making their nannies chase them. Servants streamed in and out carrying hot curling tongs, armfuls of petticoats for different gowns, trays of jewelry, trays of makeup, and everything else required to make the queen beautiful for the important dinner.

Adele was bored and feeling increasingly edgy sitting at her dressing table, still wearing a velvet robe, while her team of dressiers argued with each other behind tight smiles. Their intense debate revolved around whether Adele should wear one of the silk dresses that she'd been gifted by the empress on her trip to Sandar, to honor Sandarian culture, or if she should wear a more traditional gown befitting the queen of Unisia. Julien was doing her hair, and Katie was doing her makeup, and Piers was not doing much of anything as Lady Olivia brought forth gown after gown from the dressing room, only to have the other three ridicule each choice.

So Adele was very pleased when Charlie entered the room, knocking loudly and calling out, "Hello, Your Maj, d'you have a minute?"

Benjamin Belvoir came in behind Charlie. Even dressed in simple denim trousers and a blue shirt with a black waistcoat, he was so handsome that every woman in the room stopped talking and started giggling when he smiled.

"Good evening, Your Majesty." Benjamin bowed from the waist while keeping his gaze on her, those infamous pale green eyes gleaming in a way that made her feel naked despite her belted robe. "I hope you don't mind the intrusion?"

"No, it's fine," she said and almost got poked in the eye with a mascara wand as Katie ogled Benjamin. "Do you have good news for me, Charlie?"

But Charlie couldn't answer, as he'd been instantly accosted by the children and was swinging Natalie, then Leafy, around in a circle by their hands. Both little girls were shouting, begging him for more. From long experience, Adele knew they would get to a hysterical pitch in about ten seconds.

Before she could get Charlie's attention, the Queen's Guard entered with a loud round of calls at the door, and suddenly her bedchamber felt overcrowded as the big men moved around greeting everyone and trying to find a place to sit down. They were wearing spotless white-and-gold uniforms with very tight shirts underneath, the top few buttons undone to show off their muscular chests. Only Lucky had his shirt and jacket buttoned appropriately.

Adele breathed in as Leith wafted past her in a cloud of cologne. "Oh, my God, you all smell amazing! What is that?"

"Told you she'd like it, lads." QG Leith was very proud of himself. "It's a secret recipe of my mum's, Your Majesty. Brings in the ladies like bees to flowers."

Adele closed her eyes and only then could detect a trace of honey-scented magic in the perfume. Bethany definitely knew her potions. "You'll be the perfect distraction!"

"Give it here, QG." Charlie was already grinning as he held out his hand to Leith. "I could do with a bit of that action."

Leith opened a tiny glass bottle and dripped a little on his hand, warning him of its power, and then whispered something else that made Charlie laugh uproariously. Leith offered the bottle to Benjamin, who declined it with a humble, "I'd be dangerous if I used that, mate."

"Speaking of dangerous, where's Jordan Jordansson?" Adele asked. "I thought he was with you guys."

"He's getting ready with Lord Orgustus," QG Pepper answered. "Those two are getting to be good friends, looks like."

"As long as he's not late to the party." She frowned, worried what could go wrong if those two bonded too closely. "It's crucial that the Sandarians get to enjoy his company tonight."

The front door to her chamber opened, and Adele waved in a train of maids pushing trolleys piled with snacks and drinks. She knew Mrs. Ollenby wouldn't be far behind. Though the lady had agreed with good grace to come to the party, Adele was still anxious about her. She didn't want to push her only confidante too hard out of her comfort zone, but she felt she needed every magically powerful supporter by her side going into negotiations with Empress Sanda'hani. Not that Her Grace would be discussing war tonight. Adele suspected the real talks would begin tomorrow.

Distracted, her gaze fell on Benjamin as he meandered across the bedroom toward her, laying out winks and compliments to the giggling maids. *Sweet Christ, he's handsome. I wonder how it feels to run your fingers through those black curls?*

Adele shook herself and called out, "Charlie, come here!" Charlie swung Aaron to the ground and threw himself into the armchair next to her moments before Benjamin could claim it. He grinned smugly at the tall stable hand, but Benjamin only leaned against the wall behind Adele, seeming happy to loiter.

"Tell me what happened today," she said, poking Charlie in the ribs to get his attention, which had now strayed to Siobhan, who was flirting with him from across the room.

Charlie raised an eyebrow in a quick gesture at the dressiers still working on her hair and makeup. "Long story or short story, Your Maj?"

"Short story," Adele answered. "For now."

"I got into town with Benjamin just after lunchtime, saw the person who you requested I see." Charlie leaned back in the chair, stretching out his legs. "All good."

She rolled her eyes at his cheekiness. "How about a slightly longer story than that?"

She waved away her dressiers to join Lady Olivia, still in the wardrobe. When they were as alone as they could get, Charlie rested his elbows on his knees. Adele automatically leaned closer to him.

"The Lady Mayor only heard rumors of Sandarians on the road," Charlie whispered. "Herself, she thought it was something to do with your upcoming birthday festival and wasn't delighted when I mentioned that should she hear whispers of war, she should continue to support the birthday party idea."

Adele swallowed a curse—this was trouble. She couldn't afford to get the Lady Mayor offside when she'd just got her into an uneasy alliance. "Do you think she'll support me?"

Charlie narrowed his eyes, considering this. "You want to know what my gut tells me? Even if you don't like it?"

She grabbed his hand and shook it, frustrated. "Come on, Charlie, we're on the same team. Tell me what you think."

"Concordis is a mess," Charlie whispered, so close and quiet that his lips were on her hair. "You've got the Underworld in chaos, and you've got drugs that used to be expensive flooding the streets cheap as water now that the Boss no longer controls distribution. The mayor runs the Topworld, Your Majesty. She might've taken a cut to look the other way on certain issues, but she had to pay for protection from the Boss like everyone else. It all came out even, I guess. But now the cats are running, and the mayor is still trying to feed orphans and old people. She isn't in any position to try anything against you. She just wants her quiet life back. Well, quieter life, at least."

Adele's head was spinning, and it made her realize that she should be breathing. "Sweet Christ, that cologne is strong, Charlie." She let go of his hand and shifted away. "Don't stand by any open flames, will you?"

Charlie looked inordinately pleased at her reaction. "I thought it might've been the new suit you liked, Your Majesty. Mrs. Ollenby took good care of me at the tailor's, I thought."

"Did I hear my name?" Mrs. Ollenby wafted into the room wearing a gown that could barely fit through the doorway. White, sparkling tulle puffed out in dozens of layers from her waist, and the bodice was decorated with overlapping white feathers, her bust pushed up and out as far as it was possible to be pushed. There was a giant bow fastened at her hip, and the ribbons had tiny satin bows sewn to them like confetti. Her golden curls had been piled high and dotted with multicolored gems and more of the tiny satin bows. Mrs. Ollenby's usually pink cheeks had been powdered white and a little constellation of gems stuck down one side of her face. On her lips she wore very red lipstick.

"Mrs. Ollenby!" Adele covered her gasp with an effort. "You look, ah—"

"Mrs. Ollenby, you look like a real-life fairy princess!" Natalie shouted, and all the children cheered for their favorite lady.

"Oh, thank you, Your Highnesses." Pleased, Mrs. Ollenby blushed under her caked-on makeup. "I thought I might have overdone the bows a little."

Coming out of the wardrobe holding yet another gown in her arms, Lady Olivia shrieked, "Mrs. Ollenby, for the love of the goddess, what is that *thing* you're wearing?"

Mrs. Ollenby's smile wilted, and Adele couldn't bear to see her disappointed when she had done her best to look good tonight.

"Olivia is just upset because they finally decided on me wearing white," Adele said, giving Olivia a warning glance behind Mrs. Ollenby's back. "But there is no chance my dress will be equal to yours, so we'll just go with another one. Right, Olivia?"

"I can change, Your Majesty," Mrs. Ollenby protested. "I shouldn't go, anyway. There's no reason for me to be at the dinner tonight."

"No!" Adele jumped up and dashed to the dressing room, dragging Olivia with her. "I wanted to wear red, anyway. Won't be long!"

Adele wasn't sure how to approach an intimate chat with her lady-in-waiting after the violence of their last encounter, but she needn't have worried.

"Forgive me, but I need a minute, Your Majesty." Olivia bent over with a hand at her mouth like she was going to throw up. "That dress is just appalling. I mean—I have no words."

Adele pinched her palm to kill her own smile because she refused to laugh at Mrs. Ollenby with a traitor like Olivia. Julien and Katie peeked out the door of the dressing room giggling, and Adele decided they could control themselves and get her dressed finally.

"Right, I choose that one." She pointed at a pretty gold dress that was quite comfortable to wear.

"You took that one to Sandar and wore it at the Gray Palace, and then at Belvoir Estate," Lady Olivia reminded her. "Anyway, didn't you just say you wanted red, Your Majesty?"

Olivia dug into the racks stuffed with never-worn dresses and pulled out a gown with a full-length scarlet organza skirt, a strapless ruby-jeweled bodice, and a long silk sash flowing down the back of the skirt. There were even two hidden pockets on the waist. It was so beautiful and deceptively simple and utterly perfect that Adele felt a movement in her chest as if the dragon magic itself approved.

"Yes, that's the one," she whispered, dashing the tear from her eye. *Get a grip,* she warned herself, *why would the magic like a dress? Do dragons like red?* And that answer felt so right she immediately pushed the dangerous thought away.

After the hours of arguments, it only took a few minutes to finally get dressed. She reentered her busy bedchamber and saw that servants were circulating with fresh drinks. She took a sparkling plum wine and sat back at her dressing table for jewelry and touch-ups.

Natalie was disappointed with Adele's simple gown and told her so, but Adele received the usual number of polite compliments that she imagined every queen got just for wearing anything at all.

"Your Majesty." Benjamin was suddenly leaning over the back of her chair and placing a ruby pendant necklace around her neck, handed to him by a giggling Piers. "You look completely ravishable."

Adele waited until the titters of her dressiers died down. "I don't think 'ravishable' is actually a word."

"It is the way I do it," Benjamin whispered. He brushed the back of his hand across her shoulders, making her shiver and then hate herself for it. He slipped into the seat Charlie had just vacated and threw his arm around the back of her chair.

Don't giggle and don't look at him! But she almost broke into a sweat from the effort it took not to run her gaze over the gorgeous stable hand. Benjamin was an incorrigible flirt. Ever since the horse carnival at Belvoir Estate when he had been assigned guard duty at her chamber, he had been trying to get in her bed and didn't seem deterred by her constant rejection of him.

The atmosphere in her bedchamber was festive and relaxed, but dread was curdling in the pit of Adele's stomach. The dragon magic shifted in response, the sensation like sharp knives raking her lungs. *For God's sake, I'm about to drag my people into a dinner with an empress who might want us all dead for my betrayals. Let them have a drink and laugh a bit first.* But the feeling in her gut only mounted, and soon her hands were shaking. *I need Rainere,* she thought as panic rushed in with the pain. *I need him, I need him, I need him.* For the first time ever, Adele tried to use the Mark to call Rainere to her. *Darling, I can't do this without you. I feel like I'm dying.*

"Hey, are you all right, Your Majesty?" Benjamin gently stroked her back, but before she could answer him, Captain Lucky had stepped to the middle of the room and called for quiet.

Still struggling with the weird mix of lust and dread, Adele was surprised when Lucky raised his chin and cleared his throat.

"Your Majesty, peers of the Queen's Guard, friends, I would like to announce that a very special lady has agreed to be my wife." He held out his arm, and Olivia stepped in, clinging to his side, and looking up at him. "Lady Olivia and I are to be married."

Adele felt her jaw drop, shock distracting her from the pain of the magic. Of course, she'd heard the men tease Lucky about his infatuation with Olivia, but she had thought it was an unrequited affection. QG Leith seemed to be in the grip of a severe coughing fit, and Adele could see that her shock was mirrored on the faces of the other QGs.

"Aw, that's a shame for the rest of us," Benjamin said, with a wry shake of his head. "Olivia is always game for a good night."

"Shut your mouth, Ben!" Charlie reappeared at Adele's side. "Never tell Lucky you had a thing with his lady. You get me?"

"*Had* a thing with her?" Benjamin grinned. "I *have* a running thing with her midweek after work. She went sour on Lord Orgustus and all his crew, so I've been filling in."

Adele didn't want to hear any of this. She rose from her chair and plastered a big smile on her face. "Congratulations to the both of you," she said, approaching the happy couple. "I wish you all the very best."

Over her bright smile, Olivia's eyes were wary, but Lucky couldn't have been happier, getting slapped on the back by his fellow QGs and even accepting their ribald jokes with good grace. Not one of them mentioned his lack of experience with women in an off-color way, and Adele was pleased for him. She stepped away to allow Mrs. Ollenby and others to embrace the couple and went to stand by Ohrig's side.

"Did you know about this?" she asked him, still wearing her fake smile in case Lucky looked over at them.

"I knew last night when he asked my permission to ask your permission to marry the girl, but I was sure you'd say no." Ohrig's voice held a heavy note of accusation. "She's not right for him. Not at all."

"I didn't know it was her when he asked me," Adele said. "God, if I had, I would definitely have given some excuse for him not to do it. Why does Leith look like he's about to choke again?"

Ohrig's expression said it all.

"Him too." Adele turned her back on the room and groaned. "But that'll actually kill Lucky if he ever finds out."

"And Lucky won't find out from any of us," Ohrig said. "But if that girl says anything to him about every one of his mates that she's been with, Lucky might just try to kill them all to defend her honor, or some such noble catshit."

"You know, Olivia confessed to me that she and Rainere had a *dalliance* when I was off hunting Sighmere."

Ohrig shot her a sideways glance. "Why's she still alive, then?"

"Don't joke." Adele flicked green sparks from her fingertips and heard the crackle as they singed the gold-patterned carpet by her slippers. "I'm not a monster, Ohrig," she whispered.

Still in the middle of the room, proud as Adele had ever seen him, Lucky even smiled at Benjamin as he shook hands with him, offering his congratulations. But Lucky didn't see Benjamin lean in to kiss Olivia on the cheek or whisper in her ear. *If she tells Lucky about Leith and breaks his heart, then my whole guard is going to be a mess. I should've done as Rainere asked and fired her,* Adele thought.

"Your Majesty, don't we have a Sandarian empress waiting for us?" Ohrig interrupted Adele's brooding. "Put all this drama out of your mind and focus. You need to be on your game tonight."

Adele was about to reply that Lucky was just as important to her as the empress when Charlie approached.

"I reckon all of that is a bad idea." Charlie nodded at the happy couple. "Still, Captain Handsome deserves a bit of fun, so I hope she gives it to him."

"Charlie, shut up for a second." Adele grabbed his elbow, pulling him in so quickly he fell against her. Instantly she knew she should have resisted the urge to touch him when she saw the circles of silver turn in Charlie's eyes and the magic responded with a greedy lurch. "Find Rainere, tell him to send Odin to me, then you babysit Prince Rainold."

Charlie flicked his hair off his forehead and looked worried. "That's no easy job, Your Majesty," he said. "The prince has already tried to put his hands on me."

"He did what?" Adele hissed and fury engulfed her, her vision turning red.

Charlie flinched but tried to pass the movement off as another hair flick. "Calm down, Your Maj," he said, which only make her grip him tighter. "He never got close to doing anything."

"I'll kill him!" she snarled. Charlie was her responsibility, and she had already put him in danger on too many other occasions. She couldn't bear it if he came to harm here in the palace.

"Er, General? She's got magic coming out of her fingers." Charlie turned his body to shield Adele from the room.

"Easy, Your Majesty." Ohrig's usually gruff voice was soothing. "Charlie's not in any trouble."

Adele took a deep breath but her hold on the magic felt tenuous. "I'm sorry, Charlie. I wasn't thinking." She unclenched her hand from his elbow. "You don't have to watch the prince if you feel unsafe."

"No, it's fine, Your Maj," he said quickly. "I can handle a Marchant prince, no worries at all. You just stay calm tonight, and I'll come find you at the party, all right?"

"I don't want you to get hurt," Adele said, but Charlie was already shuffling away from her and then slipped out the main door of the bedchamber.

"Do you think he'll be all right?" Adele asked as nausea churned her stomach, and her head felt hot. "All I can think about is seeing Empress Sanda'hani and . . ."

"And what, Your Majesty?" Ohrig's gray brows were beetled down over his eyes. "You don't look so good. Can I find the high wizard to check you over?"

"I think it's that love potion you're all wearing, General," she said. "It's very strong, and I'm sensitive to any kind of magic right now."

Ohrig frowned. "Queen Adelena, don't lie to me. Not now, not ever. Tell me what you're thinking."

Adele felt her skin prickle painfully as tingles shivered up and down her spine. "It feels like a dreadful premonition," she whispered. "And the magic is chewing at me—here, on the inside."

Ohrig took her cold hands in his big, rough ones, his warmth leaching into her. "I'll be right by your side all night," he promised. "You hold on to me whenever you think you need it."

Adele shuddered with one of those awful spinal tremors again. "You're so brave," she murmured. "I know something bad is coming for me, and I don't want it to get you too."

Ohrig leaned down close, his pale blue eyes boring into hers. "Nothing is going to get you while I'm alive," he said. "You stick with me, and we'll face this together."

"Your Majesty? We've just gotten word the festivities are to commence soon," Captain Lucky called out.

Ohrig let her go and she wiped her sweating hands on the back of her gown, hoping the marks wouldn't show. *Rainere, come and find me soon.* The dragon magic untwisted a little in her gut. Able to speak again, she lifted her chin. "Right, gather the troops, and let's go show this Sandarian empress that we mean business."

CHAPTER TWENTY-FIVE

"Chalky Curses"

After the meeting with Adelena and her council in the Lavender Room, Rainere spent hours looking for his father, finally meeting up with him in the secret passageways heading back to the Marchant guest suite.

Prince Rainold greeted Rainere like they hadn't seen each other in years, instead of an afternoon. "Sweetheart, you look different. What's wrong?" Rainold stroked Rainere's cheek, studying his face as if trying to read something written there. "Tell Daddy what's happened."

Rainere yanked himself out of his father's affectionate embrace. "Your Highness, please. I'm wearing several charms to change my appearance, that's all." He pulled off the two thin bracelets and changed the rest of the way from Odin to Rainere again.

Prince Rainold smiled but looked uncertain, like he had suddenly lost his mental footing. "Oh, of course, forgive me, darling. You changed. I didn't notice, or maybe did I?"

If he doesn't stop acting like a lunatic, then Adelena will never trust him, he thought. And for a reason he couldn't explain, Rainere really wanted the woman he loved to accept his father as her family too. "I have questions for you," he said. "Come with me to the laboratory, Your Highness."

"Ask me nicely, and I'll think about it, *Your Highness*," Rainold said, and something in his tone warned Rainere not to push the prince too far.

Looking frantic, Charlie appeared around a dusty corner. He was checking up and down the corridor when he spotted Rainold and Rainere in the gloom. "There you are," he said, but casually, as if he hadn't been lost at all. "The queen wants Odin to join her at the garden party. She seemed very keen that he get there soon."

So Adelena's sending the boy to call me to heel regularly now? "She can wait," Rainere snapped. His pride was still smarting from the way she'd left him with his pants down this afternoon. He continued along the narrow corridor and heard Prince Rainold asking about the success of Charlie's mission in Concordis that afternoon. Charlie only gave one-word answers, but it didn't stop Rainold chatting away as if the two were old friends, or as if they weren't traveling the *secret* paths between walls and under the floors of the Golden Palace. Rainere wanted to tell his father to shut up but found it too difficult, so he just picked up the pace until they reached the tiny door that opened into his lab.

This lab wasn't as large or light as his laboratory in the Gray Palace, but Rainere was very pleased with the setup he had managed with Tilburn's help. There was a full pharmacy of herbs, powdered minerals, and other ingredients in uniform glass jars on the shelves against the back wall, as well as all the hardware he could need for distillations and potion-making. His basic library of magical books was stored on shelves under the windows. The walls had been freshly painted in a pale blue and the old floorboards waxed to a low sheen, but still showing the deep scratches and burn marks from when the lab had been used as a schoolroom.

"Oh, look, you have a terrace with a lovely garden!" Rainold was delighted as he toured the room, opening windows to release the metallic-scented air and letting in the evening breeze. With a wave of his hand, he lit the chandeliers and candelabras that were scattered over the three workbenches. "How far up the palace are we? Fifth floor?"

Rainere ignored his father's inane questions about the lab as he headed straight to the lab's blackboard and found a finger of chalk. He began sketching a diagram, filling the full height of the board and most of its width. It took him the best part of an hour and lots of erasing, but eventually he felt like he had a fair representation.

Charlie had jumped up to sit on a nearby workbench, and Prince Rainold was leaning next to him, chatting away as his hands waved in elegant gestures. Rainere wondered what those two could possibly have to talk about even as he interrupted them, "Your Highness?"

Rainold closed his eyes as if pained, and one hand fluttered to hold his throat. "Yes, my darling *son*, what is it?"

Rainere felt chastened but didn't correct himself. "Could you look at this diagram for me?"

Rainold wandered over to the chalkboard, already delighted with Rainere's efforts. "It's beautiful, *cara mio*," he said. "You have created something very complex and interesting here. I can see so many layers of enchantment it makes me quite dizzy." He clasped Rainere in a one-armed hug. "You are terribly clever!"

"It's not my design," Rainere said, stepping out of the embrace. "I saw this on Adelena's skin when the dragon magic was activated within her. It often changes size and moves rapidly all over her body. I don't think she knows it appears, and I have to presume the sensation of the dragon magic and this diagram are one and the same for her—"

He felt a sudden stabbing pain and pressed a hand to his side. Adelena's pull twisted the Mark on his skin, and his pride balked at yet another attempt to command him. *She must be feeling nervous about meeting the empress for dinner, that's all. I'll go to her later,* he reassured himself. The pain receded, and he noticed Rainold watching him, eyes narrowed.

Rainere dropped his hand, and his father returned his focus to the diagram, tracing it with his long fingers while muttering, "And this thing here?" Rainold pointed at a spiral inside a triangle. "Is this meant to be a little bit longer or wider at the apex?"

Rainere plumbed his memory. "Maybe," he said. "I don't see it for very long each time."

He shivered at a chill in the air and looked up to see that clouds had formed at the open windows and mist was drifting in. In his intense concentration, Rainold had changed the atmosphere in the room. All Marchant wizards studied weather magic, and Rainere prided himself on his expertise with storms and lightning. He wasn't as good with snowstorms but still took a lot of pleasure from remembering the blizzard he had created over the Dark Forest to trap Adelena at the Gray Palace when he was in the initial throes of obsession with her. *But to change the weather inside a room? Where does he even find the ambient humidity on such a warm evening?* Rainere wondered, impressed.

Less so Charlie, who pulled his thin jacket around his shoulders and crossed his arms. "Oi! Your Highness, just for your information, Her Majesty is supposed to be having a garden party right now," he said. "Does someone want to get rid of these clouds?"

Rainere had to shake the prince's shoulder to get his attention. "Your Highness, the weather."

Rainold dragged himself back into the moment with a great effort. "Hmmm? Weather, what?"

Charlie gestured to the clouds hovering on the ceiling of the laboratory, already cloaking the long arms of the chandeliers. With a single sweep of his hand and a distracted smile, Prince Rainold cleared them, impressing Rainere all over again.

"My sweet son, let's talk about this spell—or rather, in Marchant terms, we would call it a curse. I was right about the dragon magic containing an element of the flame, only it's been harnessed by another power and molded into something quite different. I'm relying on my knowledge from *Diagram Curses in Dahk'hanian Theorems*, by Rainstrom Marchant HRM, which I'm sure you've both read. I mean, its intent is clear. For instance, these glyphs, here and here"—he pointed to the side of the diagram—"and even down here on the bottom left corner. I mean, just look at it!"

"Pretend I have no idea what you're talking about," Charlie said, smirking. "How would I explain this diagram to a novice?"

Rainere was curious as well. He'd never heard of the book his father mentioned.

Rainold waved his hands like nervous birds and chewed his bottom lip, clearly trying to arrange his thoughts into words. "We know that Adelena drank a vast quantity of the dragon tear, yes? If you distill the tear under the right conditions, all the magic condenses into flame. You know this, Rainere, I gave you one in an unbreakable glass ball for your fifth birthday, remember?"

Rainere exchanged a glance with Charlie. They'd both been there when the tiny blue flame had been released from the glass and Charlie had thrown it into the heaving maw of Empress Ka-kik of the Spider People at Adelena's command. The violence of the blue fire was absolute. The screams of the dying Spider People had been horrific.

"Adelena was saturated with this magic," Rainold continued. "But, and here is the funny thing, it's not Sighmere's signature on this diagram. As I showed you, it's clearly a Dahk'hanian diagram. So, somehow, Dahk'hani has managed to use the dragon's magic to create his own curse within Adelena."

Rainere snapped his fingers. "When she entered Jordansson during the spell to heal Stella!"

"It's probably the only time the god would've had access to Adelena intimately," Rainold said, but his expression was doubtful. "Gods have relatively limited power in Evendaar when they aren't in corporeal form. They can visit and talk to us, but to function on this plane, they need to follow the regulations of this dimension, which means they need a body. I mean, this Jordansson person would have to have been infused with Dahk'hani's essence to be able to conduct the god's influence. And believe me when I say this dragon magic has been *influenced*. It's formed a kind of fluid curse on Adelena that is constantly adapting to her desires." Rainold's hands danced over the diagram, showing where the courses of power ran.

"The curse changes its properties with Adelena's mood?" Rainere asked, dumbfounded.

"No, her desires," Rainold replied. "Whatever she wants, the magic literally flies to obey her will, dragging her other two magics with it. They are just tools for the Dahk'hanian curse now. See, in this curly bit here, this is how it silenced her Sister Voices."

"Sister Voices?"

Rainold raised an eyebrow, as if Rainere's ignorance was very surprising. "My honey cake, Adelena is a demon, yes? So of course she has a connection to the Temple with her Sister Voices. They—what's the word?—'sing' to her if you will. It's the Sister Voices who hold the knowledge of all demon magic, and they sing it to her whenever she needs a Command or a spell. They allow the angels in the Temple to watch over Adelena, and they alert her to danger when it's close. Rainestra told me that it sounds like a hundred instruments playing exactly the same tune all at once. But now Adelena can't hear anything because this curse has cut her off from them. I imagine they're still talking, but now they've been muted."

Rainere felt the wonderful sensation of a dozen puzzle pieces all falling into place at once. "Prince Rainold, this is incredibly helpful, thank you." He couldn't wait to share this knowledge with Adelena. She would be so happy to find out more about her own very special nature and that her Chime Voices were the voices of her sister angels.

"It's just this squiggle that is confusing me." Rainold tapped a finger against an odd-looking snarl of lines. "Are you sure you drew it properly?"

Rainere stepped closer so he was shoulder to shoulder with his father as they both studied the diagram. Charlie stood to the other side of Rainold.

"It's correct," Rainere said. "It's the first part of the curse that appears when we—when the magic activates."

"It looks kind of like a cock," Charlie said. "I mean, if you say that bit there is the shaft and these two roses here are the balls."

"Goddess, you're right!" Rainold clapped Charlie on the back. "But why would there be a fertility symbol drawn into a Dahk'hanian curse on a demon's skin?"

"Dahk'hani wants Adelena to have his child," Rainere reminded his father.

"But Adelena is already fertile, unless this fertility device is for the male she partners with?" Rainold pinched his chin, thinking hard. "Looking at the lines, you can see the dangerous and potent power there. I pity the poor fool who gets caught up in that spell." He slid his arm around Rainere's shoulders and squeezed. "Thank the goddess you aren't still having sex with that demon, my darling. I'd have serious concerns that this fertility spell is actually strong enough to affect the sterility of our Immortality Curse."

Rainere heard Charlie's low chuckle, but the boy was too far away to punch.

"What's the worst thing that could happen if I did have sex with Adelena?" Rainere asked.

Rainold spun to face him and put a hand on Rainere's chest. "Don't even think of it, darling!" he said. "The demon is *alive* with dragon flame. According to this diagram, it literally courses through her blood and bones. If you put your fragile cock inside that body"— he shuddered theatrically—"the flame could travel through your cock into your body, and you would burn internally—to death!"

Rainere hesitated to speak his dream aloud but was compelled to ask the only man who might know. "Do you think, or is it possible, if I should manage to successfully overcome the difficulties of the dragon flame, that I could be the one to impregnate Adelena, and then she would be carrying my child—and Dahk'hani would have no recourse but to wait till our child was born?" He studied the diagram as if his life depended on it.

But Rainold stepped in front of Rainere, cupping his jaw and forcing him to look into his emerald-green gaze. "You stupid boy," he whispered. "You're still fucking her, aren't you? Even after I told you about the dragon flame this morning. How could you be so suicidal? Is this because of me? Because you hate me?"

Rainold's eyes became shiny waiting for an answer, and Rainere felt a wild surge of frustration with this insane, young-old wizard. Then a bright green tear trickled down Rainold's cheek, and his bottom lip wobbled like Aaron's did when he was upset. So instead of walking away, Rainere awkwardly patted Rainold's shoulder.

"I don't hate you," he said, trying to keep the anger out of his voice. "I'm really very grateful to have you here. It's why I rescued you."

Rainold lurched forward and buried his face in Rainere's chest. "Then why won't you call me Daddy?" he asked, his voice muffled.

Over Rainold's head, Rainere gave Charlie a desperate "What do I do?" look, but the boy just shrugged. He'd never had a daddy either.

"Fine—Father," Rainere said.

"And you'll stop having sex with that demon?" Rainold asked, raising his chin, his eyes lit with hope. "Because she *will* kill you, my darling."

"I'll discuss everything that you have told me with Adelena," Rainere said, refusing to promise. "And we'll make a decision together."

"Oh, yes, I'm sure you two do a lot of talking when you're alone." Rainold rolled his eyes, then his expression softened with something that looked a lot like pity. "You cannot befriend a demon, my darling, no matter how much you want to. She's a magical creature with a bottomless appetite for magic, and you're just her food."

Rainere stepped away. "Adelena and I have a deep connection. It's almost always—"

"Sexual," Rainold interrupted, then held up a hand to stave off any protest. "Honeypot, can you tell me how many times she's asked your opinion on something? Or asked your advice on anything? Can you tell me how this deep connection means you two can talk for hours, sharing common interests or hobbies? Do you know her favorite charm? Favorite color? Or does she know yours?"

Rainere shook his head. "You don't understand. Adelena is always dealing with so much chaos. We never get any quiet time together."

"She branded you!" Rainold shrieked, his mercurial mood swinging to rage. "She branded your body with her Mark and enslaved you. She doesn't love you; she needs you, and there's a bloody big difference between those two things, my son."

Rainere crossed his arms and returned his father's glare. "You're wrong," he said.

Rainold reached to caress Rainere's cheek. "I hope I am, darling," he whispered. "But I know I'm not."

Charlie waved his hand, looking impatient. "Your Highnesses, what are we gonna do about the high magistrar?"

"Oh, we're going to kill Orestes," Rainold said. "But first he has to tell us what he's done with Ohren."

"Do we really need Ohren?" Rainere asked. "What does the high wizard actually do, other than meddle where he isn't wanted?"

"I love Ohren," Rainold replied. "This is not negotiable, darling. The high wizard is mine."

"Orestes should be getting ready for dinner with the empress and the queen," Rainere said. "But if we set a trap, we can catch him after it finishes tonight."

"Why in the hell would Adelena let him anywhere near the Sandarians?" Charlie asked, shocked.

"I didn't get around to telling her that he was actually Orestes disguised as Ohren," Rainere said, trying to hide his embarrassment with a glower. "We only had a few minutes together after the meeting in the Lavender Room this afternoon."

Rainold cocked an eyebrow. "But you had time to memorize a complex diagram on her breasts?"

Charlie sniggered.

"Actually, it was on her lower back," Rainere said quickly. The Mark on his side began tingling, distracting him. "I should check if she's gone to the dinner yet. Then warn her about Orestes."

"Oh, your queen's got enough to worry about," Rainold said. "Don't you think she'll be happier if you can tell her that you've actually caught Orestes?"

Rainere thought about this for a moment. "Then we need to get him before he goes to the dinner," he said. "At least he won't be expecting us to try anything."

"You're right." Rainold nodded like Rainere had said something very profound. "Charlie, would you like to come too?"

Charlie checked his pocket watch, though Rainere was sure that the boy had nowhere else to be. "I could be willing to help you catch the Boss," he said. "But you have to promise me that it's going to get bloody."

Prince Rainold laughed gaily. "Charlie, you really are the sweetest thing," he said and clapped his hands. "Gentlemen, let's go catch a wizard!"

CHAPTER TWENTY-SIX

"The Unthwarted Will of a God"

What a waste of a night! Rainere thought, cursing. Orestes should have been easy to trap and Rainere found it humiliating that the wizard had managed to evade them. They had spent most of the night hovering around the Garden Wing and the Lily Pond Gardens in charmed disguises, waiting for him to show up at the dinner. But Orestes-as-Ohren had never arrived. Later, Rainere had tried to use the mirror in Orestes's chamber to reveal the wizard's location but it was no help, only showing a blurry mess of lines and green clouds, proof that Orestes was hiding behind magic.

Prince Rainold was very upset to have disappointed his son, and Rainere had spent too long placating his tearful father, although he really did blame him. He cursed himself for believing his father's confident assurances. Charlie blamed Rainere for believing them too. The boy was furious and had stormed back to the QG quarters when they'd finally given up the search.

It was close to midnight when Rainere decided to find Adelena. He heard the noise of a party before he even turned the corner into the royal wing. Courtiers still in their extravagant evening clothes spilled out of the royal apartment into the hallway, drinking, chatting, and eating. There was even a trio of musicians playing raucous tunes in the antechamber. Rainere presumed the dinner with the

Sandarians had gone well for his queen and there was a reason to celebrate. *At least one of us can,* he thought, jealous that he hadn't been by her side to share the success.

His bad mood only got worse as he stood in the doorway of the royal apartment and couldn't even get the attention of a steward to announce him. He pushed through the crowd, ignoring greetings from the partygoers. He'd stayed disguised as Odin all night to make it easier to get around the Golden Palace. Yet it had rankled just how much more pleasant life was as a blond, blue-eyed courtier instead of a superior Marchant prince. Scanning the room, he soon spotted Adelena sitting on the blue couch with several of her Queen's Guards, deep in conversation. She was still wearing the gorgeous red gown that he hoped he could take off her later, but Captain Lucky was absorbing all her attention, as usual.

Rainere felt the habitual surge of jealousy at seeing the handsome captain with Adelena. He'd always thought there was a certain tension between them, which he could only guess was a suppressed attraction. They looked so perfect together. A petite, feminine brunette with a tall, masculine blond. Out of pique, Rainere hid for a minute unobserved and eavesdropped on the chatter in the room.

Lord Orgustus was closest to him, leaning against the wall and drinking a glass of Firewhiskey while Jordansson slumped in a nearby armchair.

"So you think the queen is angry that I shared my bed with a woman last night?" Jordansson was looking so morose that Rainere almost laughed.

"I'm just saying that you did the wrong thing mentioning it at dinner," Orgustus said. "A queen doesn't share bed partners, you see. So when you proclaim that you are destined to be with her and give her a child, by Unisian standards, that equals a monogamous relationship."

"A mogo-what?"

"Don't shag anyone but the queen," Orgustus explained. "Not

ever. But if you do shag someone else, for goddess' sake, don't mention it."

"But the queen doesn't bed me," Jordansson complained. "Why should I not bed other women while I wait for her?"

"Look, I'm not saying she's my type," Orgustus said, "but the way the queen was all over me tonight, and those little zaps of power in her touch. I definitely think that a roll with her would be worth waiting for."

Rainere couldn't hear any more without needing to do Orgustus an injury, so he moved away and passed by General Ohrig and Mrs. Ollenby huddled together on another couch.

"No, Riggy, stop your flirting. I really should go to bed," Mrs. Ollenby was protesting with a lot of giggles.

Ohrig was pressing Mrs. Ollenby with an insistence that surprised Rainere. "Come on, darlin', I've only got an hour before I'm on duty for the queen again."

"Ooh, a whole hour." She giggled. "What can you do for me in an hour, Riggy?"

Rainere had heard enough and crossed the busy room to his queen. Adelena had curled up on the couch, hugging a cushion, and Captain Lucky was sitting too close. They were talking about something that made Adelena rub her temples and look frustrated. The rest of the Queen's Guard were perched on armchairs or the backs of couches, listening in without comment.

Rainere was almost in front of her when she finally noticed him, but it was gratifying when her face lit up. "Odin, what are you doing here?" she asked.

But Rainere wasn't in the mood to keep playing this game. "I was looking for the high wizard and presumed he would be with you after dinner," he replied in his own voice.

"I haven't seen Ohren all night." Adelena looked worried again. "It's very odd."

Lady Olivia had wandered over and tried to sit on Captain

Lucky's lap, but the captain deftly moved her to the place next to him before she sat down. Olivia pouted at the slight, and Rainere accidentally caught her eye.

"Good evening, sir." She looked up at him through her lashes. "I don't believe I've had the pleasure of your acquaintance."

"My lady." Rainere gave a shallow bow. "I am Odin St. Lucidis, Captain Lucky's cousin from abroad."

"Oh, you're the cousin of my intended?" Lady Olivia's gaze roamed Odin up and down. "Well, then, you must come to the wedding."

Rainere straightened with a jerk. "You're intended to marry Captain Lucky?"

"Yes, he proposed tonight." Lady Olivia clasped Lucky's arm to her chest. "Now I'm the lucky one!"

Captain Lucky gave his intended a chaste kiss on the cheek. "My lady, I must speak with the queen, and then I shall walk you back to your dormitory."

But Adelena waved him away. "You can go, Lucky, and take the rest of these damn courtiers with you," she said. "We'll debrief tomorrow when I've had a long think about everything that happened at dinner."

"Or didn't happen," Captain Lucky added. "I felt the empress was prevaricating intentionally, Your Majesty. It was as if she was just making small talk while waiting for something to happen. I don't like that we haven't discovered if she has a mage with her yet."

"I know," Adelena agreed. "But we can't fix anything tonight. You all need sleep, and we can discuss our plan of action tomorrow— hopefully I'll think of one."

Captain Lucky stood and took Lady Olivia's hand in his. "Good night, Your Majesty. Good night, ah, Odin." He gave Rainere a polite nod, but the other QGs ignored him as they took their leave.

Taking the cue, the stewards began discreetly ushering everyone else out of the apartment too. Only Lord Orgustus approached Odin, questioning his reason for lingering with the queen, and he clearly didn't believe the lies Rainere supplied. He made a comment about Odin needing to watch his back for Prince Rainere's knife and flounced away. Frankly, Rainere found it amusing to have the young lord acting jealous. Someone else should know how he felt all the damn time.

The apartment emptied quickly and Rainere peeked into the nursery and saw Adelena cuddling Leafy back to sleep. "All the children are coming back from the mines," she was saying. "If your brother, Carl, is with them, we'll find out straightaway. Sleep now, sweet girl."

Rainere had to stop himself from going in and kissing the children as they slept. It was two nights now that he'd missed telling them their bedtime stories, and he knew their nannies had paid hell for it. The children loved the stories of his terrible childhood in the Gray Palace and hearing about the horrors Grotto had inflicted on him.

He was waiting by the dining table when Adelena came out from the nursery, crossed the room, and didn't stop until she'd wrapped her arms around him. Holding her tight, he felt suddenly sad that he could only add to her problems tonight. As excited as he'd been to learn so much about her demon traits, she might be disappointed to have it proved that she was even more dangerous than they'd previously thought. He also didn't want to tell her the truth about Orestes-as-Ohren when he didn't have the Boss in hand already.

"Are you hungry, darling?" she asked, smiling up at him, her chin resting on his chest. "I can hear your stomach rumbling. I'll sit down with you so we can talk."

Though he was reluctant to let her go, Rainere took the seat next to hers at the dining table. There were still platters of fresh food left from the post-dinner supper, and he filled a plate with cold cuts, buttered bread, and pickled vegetables. Adelena poured him a large glass of sparkling amber liquid.

"Beer?" Rainere was surprised to see it on the queen's table.

"I remembered how much you liked it at The Magician's Wand

and asked Charlie to order some from Merrills today." She clinked his glass with hers. "Cheers, darling."

"Cheers, *cara mia*." He felt Adelena's reaction to his words as if molten metal poured through the Mark. He winced at the heat of her passion and then covered it with a smile. *My father is wrong—she does know me,* he thought, *and now we are going to have dinner together and talk for hours.* He drank deeply before he put his glass down.

Adelena was already reaching for him, but Rainere didn't want to risk touching the white magic he saw lighting her fingertips. "Let me just take off this disguise." He made a fuss of removing the few bits of charmed jewelry.

"There you are, my prince!" Adelena rested her chin in her hand and gazed at him as he began eating. "Odin is gorgeous, but I'll take you over him every time."

"You said Odin's skin felt different," he said between mouthfuls of food. "Is it unnatural? Should I adjust the spell?"

Adelena sighed and traced a finger over the whorls in the polished table. "It's not unnatural, but very soft and too supple. Your normal skin feels—" She paused, and Rainere felt her lust tingle through the Mark up his spine, then shoot straight back down between his legs. "Like silk over steel. Your muscles are so hard, and the skin is stretched tight over every curve. It's hot too."

"I think that might be you, *cara mia*." While Adelena was speaking, he spotted the curse floating across her collarbone. "Quick, look at this!"

But it was too hard for her to see the diagram. "What is it?" she asked, picking up on his anxiety. "What's on me?" But it had disappeared, and she was left fretting, trying to look down at her own chest.

A clock chimed the first hour of the morning, and Rainere realized how exhausted he was. The beer and food made him lethargic, and it took him time to gather his thoughts. "*Cara mia*, you know I spoke with my father this afternoon," he began. "Well, I told him that when we make love, a special diagram appears on your skin, like a light—"

"When we *make love*? Rainere, why would you tell him anything about us?" Adelena whispered and looked around for the stewards who waited in every doorway.

Why does she still care what they think of us? "Yes, the last few times we have *made love*," he repeated loudly. "There has been a diagram that appears on your skin."

He revealed everything that Prince Rainold had told him about the effect of dragon tear and his theory about the god Dahk'hani but couched it in much gentler terms. He certainly didn't mention that Rainold thought she might incinerate his cock.

Adelena was silent for a long time after Rainere had finished. He drank the rest of his beer and instantly craved another, but the jug was empty. He wondered whether he could take Adelena's glass, as it was still half full, but one look at her expression made him think twice. Then caution flipped to anger in a heartbeat. *We're lovers and share everything, including her children, so why don't I have the right to share her drink?*

"Adelena, there is something else," he said, willing himself to reach for the cold glass but not doing it. His tongue felt furry and thick when he tried to speak. "It seems that Orestes has tricked us once again. He is—"

"Show me this diagram made of light," she interrupted him. "I want to see it myself."

Magic had coalesced in halo above her head, but he leaned forward into it, feeling the little grazes on his face as the sparks fell over him. "It only happens when you're in the mood, darling," he said, his words slurring. "And you don't appear to be in the mood just now."

"That's very convenient for you and your father," she snapped.

Rainere narrowed his gaze. "Look at you, *cara mia*," he said. "You're raining fire on me, and I'm simply trying to talk to you." He held out his hand and caught a spark of white magic in his palm, where it fizzed and left a tiny red mark on the skin. "That fucking hurts, you know."

He finally took Adelena's cold glass of beer and wrapped his hand around it. "You're saturated with dragon flame, and because of that, Dahk'hani has manipulated the magic of Sighmere and made you his tool. We must be careful."

"And your father, who hates me, is the one who told you all this," Adelena said, eyes narrowed at him. "Prince Rainold told you that I'm dangerous, and you believe him."

"I thought you might focus on the fact that you have an incredibly powerful fertility enchantment inside you now." Rainere was trying to sound reasonable, but anger made his whole body tremble. "An enchantment that might be able to change my Immortality Curse and would mean we could have a child together."

"A child!" Adelena slammed her hands on the table, and the varnish blistered and bubbled beneath them. "Rainere, you cannot be serious! How can you even think of having a child together when my baby is still in danger? Did your amazing father have any advice on how to get the dragon flame out of Stella? Or did he spend all his time trying to convince you to leave me?"

"No, it wasn't like that," he protested. *Why is Adelena taking this all wrong? It's like she isn't even trying to understand,* he thought, but now his head was feeling heavy, and his vision wavered alarmingly.

Adelena rose out of her seat, looking down at him. "How about we focus on what's actually important and save my child?"

He forced himself to drink the rest of her beer instead of speaking. Unfortunately, the alcohol buzzed straight to his brain, short-circuiting his self-control. "Why don't you focus on Stella?" he growled. "If she's your child. You fix her."

Adelena threw her hands in the air. "Sweet Christ, I can't do everything! I only ask you to do this one thing to help—"

"Adelena, all I do is help you!" On his feet, the power of Rainere's shout rocked the chandeliers above the table. "You think I *need* this catshit? You think I *like* having to run around fixing the whole fucking world for you? Stella is in danger again because of you, Adelena—no one else." He jabbed his finger in the air, dripping green sparks over the table. "She was safe in that beautiful death spell I constructed, and you had all the time in the world to actually do some proper research before using the dragon tear on her. But did you wait? Did you ask any advice from a wizard? No! Not you! Adelena wanted her daughter awake, so she bloody well woke her up!"

Rainere's arm swung through the air, knocking his chair to the ground behind him. "If you'd just been patient and searched for the right spell, or read a fucking book for once, instead of guessing all the time, maybe Stella wouldn't have a dragon flame burning her alive."

"Is that what you think of me?" Adelena's fury had abated, and she looked shocked. "You think I'm impulsive when my children are in danger? You think I risk their lives on purpose?"

Rainere picked up his chair from the floor but almost fell on his face. *No doubt the entire bloody palace is listening to us argue, and her Queen's Guard will come racing to her rescue and take her away from me.* The thought stoked his fury. "You need to realize what you are capable of!" he shouted. "You need to stop fucking around and expecting everyone else to fix your mistakes."

Adelena stared at Rainere with an intensity that sent shivers down his spine. He could see her magics flashing in her eyes. He was losing her to their thrall, and instead of fear, Rainere felt jealousy. *She's mine, not some acolyte of Dahk'hani. Mine!*

He sat back in the chair, sliding his hands to his thighs. "Come here," he demanded. In her eyes, anger changed to hunger and through the Mark, he felt her eagerness to consume him. *Let's see Captain Lucky do this for her,* he thought, gleeful. *She needs me and only me.* He watched her move to stand between his knees, her expression so sullen and impatient he could have laughed. Instead, he bent over to take the hem of her silky scarlet skirt. He smoothed it up over the back of her calves, then her thighs. Cupping her behind beneath the lace of her underwear, he pulled her to sit astride his lap.

"Kiss me," he whispered.

"I don't want to hurt you." Adelena turned her face away, but Rainere knew what he was doing. *She cannot protect me. I want this too badly.*

He moved so fast that her hair was still swinging when he set her on the table and pressed his lips to hers, devouring her reluctance with a kiss. He freed himself from his trousers and gathered her skirt up and out of the way. He tore the flimsy lace of her underwear and clasped the back of her neck, pulling her upright and forcing her to look down. "Watch me enter you, *cara mia*," he said as he positioned himself then slid inside her wet heat. "Watch me take you and see what the magic does."

Eyelids halfway closed as she gave herself over to pleasure, her first lust-drenched moan almost tipped Rainere over the edge. The carnal sound of their bodies coming together and the burn as she braced her fingertips against his chest combined in such overwhelming sensations that it was Rainere who closed his eyes. He prayed the diagram would appear before he orgasmed.

"Rainere, there is it!" Adelena gaped at the glowing lines dancing across her abdomen, just above where he was pounding into her. "God, it's beautiful." She grabbed his shirt front with both hands and tore it open. "I need you to come right now!"

At her words, the orgasm swirled up from deep within and claimed Rainere as Adelena sucked the magic from his body. Exquisite pain electrified his spine, though his pelvis kept moving of its own accord and he spent himself inside her. He was still shuddering with pleasure when she abruptly pushed him aside and slid off the table.

"*Cara mia?*" His first thought was that she wanted to change positions, but Adelena was muttering as she stepped away from him. He reached for her but quickly recoiled. Her face was suffused with magic, her eyes white glowing balls in a hollow skull.

"My goddess, what've we done?" he whispered. She began chanting a song of hideous Commands, words that gripped him and held on tight.

Adelena's hands clamped into fists at her sides as a dense halo of white, gold, green, red, blue, and other magics coalesced into a portal above her head. Beneath her bare feet, the silk carpet was smoking, and blue flames were running up the folds of her red silk gown.

Horrified, Rainere smelled the metallic tang of dark magic. There was a hideous, wracking pain in his chest, and he saw his magic leaching out of him in long, green vines that flew through the air and joined the portal above Adelena's head. He tried to get away, but the edge of the table pressed against the back of his thighs. *She's going to kill me for Dahk'hani,* he thought, but his anger was a weak and feeble thing compared to a god's power.

Arms raised above her head, Adelena floated upward into the bizarre, rainbow-colored portal.

"Your Majesty, stop!"

Rainere saw the blurry figure of Jordansson leap and wrap his arms around her legs before she could disappear. General Ohrig, Charlie, and Prince Rainold appeared as if from nowhere and worked together to try to pull her down to the ground, shouting in panic as their clothes started burning.

"Don't let her go!" Rainere felt useless tears coursing down his cheeks. "Fucking hell, she can't leave me here by myself." The floor met his face with a nasty slap, and then everything went dark.

Chapter Twenty-Seven

"As the Children Wept"

Rainere woke before he opened his eyes. He knew he was in his bedroom next to the royal nursery because of the scent of the children's dogs, who sometimes slept under his bed. There were two male voices in the room speaking quietly, and he strained to listen.

"The queen will remain contained. The enchantment I've put over her cannot be broken by ordinary means," Orestes said, sounding smug.

"I could give a cat's tit for the queen—it's my son I need to protect," Rainold answered, and perhaps because he couldn't see his face, Rainere heard the profound fear in his father's voice.

"The toxin in Merrills's beer was a distillation of blue tonic," Orestes snapped back. "If your son wasn't so compromised by his past addiction he wouldn't have been affected by it."

"My poor boy," Rainold whispered.

"Don't cry, man," Orestes said. "The goddess's work was done today. The queen is disabled and she certainly can't get pregnant while under enchantment."

"How can you be so certain?" Rainold said. "Surely Dahk'hani . . ."

"Rainold, enough!" Orestes interrupted. "The next thing we have to do is get rid of these damned Sandarians. That savage empress has hidden a mage in her entourage, I know it. I spent last night casting revealing spells over every warrior I could find but perhaps she's hidden him in plain sight."

"Orestes." Rainold's voice was a purr. "Can you tell me where Ohren is, please? I'd love to see him."

"As soon as I've got Concordis back in hand and the palace set to rights, you two can be together again, I promise," Orestes said. There was a moment of hesitation before he asked, "You haven't told anyone about me, have you?"

"No, of course not," Rainold said. "But surely Ohren could help . . ."

Rainere heard the door close with a soft click.

"Damn you, Orestes," Rainold whispered. "I'll kill you if you've hurt him."

There was a rustling noise, and then Rainere felt a hand dab the sweat from his brow with a lemon-scented cloth. "How long have you been awake, my sweet boy?" Rainold asked. "You often did that when you were little too, scrunching your eyes closed, pretending to be asleep."

Rainere looked up into his father's loving gaze.

"There he is," Rainold whispered. "*Light of my heart,* how're you feeling?"

Rainere pushed himself up onto his elbows and winced at the headache that pounded his temples. "Worried," he croaked. "How could you let that madman go near Adelena?"

"She's fine, my sweet." Rainold stroked the cloth against Rainere's brow and tried to push him back on the pillows. "She has her guards with her and that Jordansson boy to protect her from him now."

Rainere frowned. "Why did Orestes say she was contained?"

"Well, after ingesting the poison in the beer, she was susceptible to the course of the curse on her and I think maybe . . ." He waved his hands like wounded birds, too reluctant to continue.

"Tell me," Rainere insisted.

"I think maybe the god Dahk'hani was trying to bring her to him."

Rainold looked down at the white sheets covering Rainere's chest, teasing the black silk piping straight. "That portal was like nothing I've ever seen. I'm not sure if its destination was in the mortal realm or the realm of the gods. When I looked through it, I could only see a dark place with lots of rocks and a lake of lava."

"It's like the vision Adelena had," Rainere said. "A couple of months ago, she murdered a Sandarian mage who brought her to Dahk'hani's home beneath the mountains."

"That woman!" Rainold was horrified. "My darling, how can you lie with such a beast? You know, not all demons are so wicked. Why, even Rainestra was more reluctant to kill humans than your queen."

"She's not wicked, she's . . . misunderstood," Rainere croaked. "Tell me what Orestes has done to her?"

"Well, my precious, Orestes is an ass, but he is also a bit clever when it comes to constructing containment spells." Rainold's smile looked guilty. "It should be harmless, so there's no need to worry. I'm sure she can breathe quite well. Probably."

Rainere swung his legs over the side of the bed. He was thankful to find he was still wearing his trousers, though his chest and feet were bare. "So it was Orestes who poisoned the beer?" he asked as he tried to stand.

"Honey cake, you live in the Golden Snake Pit." Rainold waved his hands, encompassing the room. "It could've been anyone. It could've even been Adelena herself. The poison weakened your defenses against her, letting her take your magic more easily for her horrible portal."

"No, I heard him admit it, I'm sure I did." Rainere's head swam, and he fell back on the bed again. "Fuck. This hurts."

"Well, Adelena took a lot of magic from you when she built that disgusting portal." Rainold tucked the sheets around him. "You aren't very resistant to blue tonic, *cara mio*, and that could only be because you've already had quite a lot of it. I only ask because I know some immortals try to replace the Gift of Life with blue tonic, and the results of the addiction can be hideous."

Rainere closed his eyes, waiting for the spinning in his head to slow down. He tried not to gag on the metallic taste in his mouth. "I know about the blue tonic," he rasped.

Rainold was blessedly silent for a moment, and that was when Rainere finally heard what his father's chattering had been hiding from him—Stella's screams.

*

Adele woke with a gasp. She could only see the blurry figures of her Queen's Guard as if they stood behind a wall of glass. She knew it had to be magic keeping her trapped like this. Animal panic flashed through her and she tried to scream, but her lungs squeezed too tight. In the breaks between her gasps, she could hear voices talking about her.

"You're telling me she's asleep? I still don't like this," Ohrig said.

"You'd like it even less if the queen attacked the Sandarian empress." Ohren's face, contorted by the magic, was peering down at her. "You saw her after the portal incident, General, her demon nature has taken over completely now. At least like this, we are safe and she can rest."

They aren't coming, Adele realized with frightened certainty. *No one's going to help me.* She felt the dragon magic explode and was blinded by a lightning flash—everything around her was on fire, and it burned up the rest of her oxygen.

It was then she heard the booming voice of the god Dahk'hani. *BE CALM, MY ANGEL.* His power surrounded her, battering against her like the wings of a thousand butterflies. *I CAME THROUGH YOUR PORTAL, LITTLE MOTHER. OPEN, SO I MAY ENTER YOUR VESSEL AND BE MADE ANEW.*

With every ounce of her strength, Adele fought the urge to submit.

Dahk'hani smothered her even tighter. *BREATHE ME IN, ANGEL. OPEN TO ME.*

With no air and no choice, Adele opened her mouth and breathed the god inside her.

*

Rainere waited until Prince Rainold went to the bathroom to get him a fresh cloth before he pushed back the sheets and staggered from his bed. He passed through the nursery, where the three nannies were trying to comfort the hysterical children.

"She's dying!" Aaron shouted when he saw the prince. "Save her, Prince Rainere!"

Natalie was sobbing in Leafy's arms. "They're killing her."

Helpless to comfort them, Rainere limped on through the living room. The door to the queen's bedchamber was open, two stewards standing guard. Behind them Rainere could hear General Ohrig shouting for High Wizard Ohren to "Come back and fix her!"

He was grateful that the stewards parted for him, because he could hardly put one foot in front of the other to make his way to Adelena's side. She had been laid out on the Glass Bed, her beautiful red gown in charred ruins. Raising a hand above her face, Rainere watched the gold-and-green magics of the containment spell light up. It was intricate and, in his drained condition, impenetrable. He touched the Mark at his side, and it felt cold. He was totally cut off from her. A wave of hopelessness swamped him.

Adelena's eyes were open to the ceiling, her lips pursed as if waiting for a kiss. Yet she looked anything but peaceful. In the containment field, her long hair floated around her shoulders as if moved by an otherworldly breeze.

"Darling!" Prince Rainold dashed to Rainere's side. "You should be in bed. Let's leave the queen for now. You can visit her later."

"No, she's not well," Rainere managed to say, exhaustion making him sway on his feet.

"Well, she seems all right to me." But Prince Rainold didn't look at Adelena—he was looking at Rainere. "If you're going to walk around, then I'll have to give you the antidote, *cara mio*. I didn't want to, as it's more of the blue tonic, and it would be so much better for you if you could just rest."

"Give it to me." Rainere held out a trembling hand.

Rainold dropped a tiny vial of a bright blue liquid into his palm. "I mixed it with Ohren's Firewhiskey and another little secret ingredient of mine," he said. "Drink it slowly, sweetheart, it's very powerful."

Rainere knocked the fizzing liquid back and closed his eyes. The effect was instantaneous and, if he was honest, a little frightening. Energy poured into his weak limbs, and he felt magic thumping through every vein in his body. His mind, suddenly clear and sharp, focused on Adelena and saw that her eyes were marginally wider and her lips had parted. "She's not breathing," he said, then more loudly, "She's not breathing! Father, do something—Adelena isn't breathing!"

Charlie was there in an instant, and so was General Ohrig. "I knew it!" the general growled. "Just before he put her under, she screamed, and it was awful."

"Father, help me," Rainere shouted, panic warring with his control. "We must break the containment spell or she'll die."

"Now, just calm down, sweetheart." Prince Rainold held his hands in a gesture of peace. "This is for the best. You didn't see the queen after we saved her from the portal, but she was bleeding dragon flames and magic everywhere. Demons are terribly dangerous creatures, but one under the influence of a god could kill us all in a blink. I refuse to put you in that kind of danger."

"Then I'll do it," Rainere snapped. He held his hands over Adelena's chest and the magic in the containment spell lit up again. He studied it and swore colorfully. "He's locked it so we need a blood key to open it."

"Oh, that's clever. Whose blood?" Rainold asked, curious.

"Stella's."

Rainold's calm façade dissolved to fury. "He's bleeding a baby for dark magic? No! I have to save . . ."

"Prince Rainere, help!" Mrs. Ollenby came running into the room holding a screaming, struggling Stella. The lady's hair was smoking in patches, and her dress had scorches all down the front. "The princess has gone mad, Your Highness. She's burning everyone and everything."

The normally unflappable Dolores Ollenby almost dropped the child when Stella slapped her face, leaving a small, red handprint. Stella was shouting bizarre words, and it was Prince Rainold who took her from Mrs. Ollenby. He spoke similar words, and Stella immediately calmed.

With deft hands, Rainere felt for Stella's pulse and examined her strangely blank eyes. "What's wrong with her?" he asked his father.

"Oh, you bastard, Orestes." Rainold was staring at Stella, horrified. "It's not just her blood, he's used the living soul of her own child to chain Adelena to the spell. Stella's losing her mind as the dragon magic takes over her little body."

"No!" Rainere said, refusing to let panic overwhelm him again. "No, I can fix this. Father, you keep her dragon magic out of the way and I'll reattach Stella's soul when I break the enchantment."

"Rainere, it's too dangerous. If I don't catch the dragon flame in time, we both die. If you manage to free Adelena she could sit up and kill us all." Rainold grabbed Rainere's arm. "Please, darling, I won't risk your life."

"I won't have a life if Adelena dies," Rainere snapped. "Nor will she forgive me for allowing Stella to die. We save them both."

"But it's—" Rainere whimpered.

"It's not impossible," Rainere said, grimly. "It's just very fucking difficult." He turned back to Adelena and activated the spell over her body. "Give me Stella."

Rainere felt grateful that his father handed him the chattering little girl. "Somebody get me an unbreakable glass bottle or flask, quickly now. Ohren usually puts his Firewhiskey in one," Rainold requested of no one in particular, his gaze on Adelena.

"I feel like I should understand her but I don't," Rainere muttered as Stella's chatter became shouts.

"It's an ancient dialect of the Old Tongue," Rainold told him. "I can't understand a lot of it, but it sounds like she's saying the queen has been placed in a doorway between two dimensions. A single knock, and we could send her into oblivion if we aren't careful."

"Then we'll be careful." Rainere held the little girl under her arms, dangling her over Adelena. Stella kicked her feet, wanting to be put down.

"Surely she'll disrupt the spell and get caught in it," Rainold protested.

Rainere shook his head. "She has to physically touch the spell for me to have a chance to knit her soul back." Concentrating, he lowered Stella down to her mother's chest. The enchantment lit up and strands of magic came loose, only to wrap themselves around her tiny bare feet.

"Rainere, careful," Rainold begged as he edged closer, holding the flask.

Rainere heard Charlie and the rest of the Queen's Guard begin chanting prayers to the goddess Serena. Then he shut them all out and let the magic flow through him. His mind racing with the power of the blue tonic, he invented and spoke a spell strong enough to break a live soul from an enchantment. Reaching to his father, he raised Rainold's hand holding the flask. Rainere felt the vibrations of his father's incredible power as Rainold called the dragon flame forth. In a single heartbeat, the toddler's soul detached from the containment spell and the dragon flame melted out of her chest. In a second heartbeat, Rainere slammed the soul back into Stella while Rainold dived for the floating dragon flame. Stella's tiny hands lit up with a sizzling white light and then cast it down over Adelena's face.

All at once, there was an almighty crack. Stella was flung backward as the spell shattered, and Adelena sat up screaming. Rainere caught the child as she fell, clasping her to his chest. When the clouds of smoke and magic had dissipated, Adelena had collapsed back onto the bed.

"Ha! I knew I could do it!" Rainold crowed, now wearing a broad grin and waving the whiskey flask. "One dragon flame plucked fresh from the little princess. Oh, and your queen is free too, darling."

Rainere was too stunned to do more than assess the child. He curled Stella into his arms and looked down into her perfectly normal, beautiful blue eyes. There was no longer an iridescent circle of magic. She was common once more. He kissed her sweaty forehead and handed her off to Mrs. Ollenby.

Leaning down over Adelena, he whispered, "Darling, are you all right?" He checked the pulse at her wrist and throat. With gentle fingers he pulled open her eyelids. The circles of magic around her irises were the odd coppery color they usually were, but there was a flash of iridescent black in the pupils, as if something winked back at him within her eyes. Rainere released the delicate tissue and straightened, wondering at this new mystery.

"She's in a natural sleep," he told the waiting crowd and was rewarded with their filthy curses of relief and profuse thanks that their queen had survived. Rainere didn't want to see it, not really, but the emotions of her Queen's Guard were sincere—they loved her too.

"Prince Rainere, I have no idea what Ohren intended for the queen, or why he'd do this to her," General Ohrig said. "Tell me what you know."

"General Ohrig, you have my promise that I will deal with the high wizard personally." Keeping secrets was second nature to Rainere, just as protecting Adelena was, so he wouldn't say a word until he had fixed what needed to be fixed. He lay a sheet over her, covering the ruined dress. "I suggest you remain close to the queen's person now, and not let anyone but me near her." Rainere thought for a moment about how easily disguises could be made. "Actually, not even me unless I give you a code that only you and I know."

"How about 'sweet Christ'?" Ohrig suggested. "I'm sure the queen would approve—she says it often enough."

He nodded. "Find Jordansson. It's imperative that we keep the tribesman away from Empress Sanda'hani until I understand what's occurred here. We were poisoned, and Adelena used my magic to open a portal to Dahk'hani's world. I have no idea if he came through before I passed out."

"Well, I didn't see any god, Your Highness." Rainere could tell it grated on Ohrig to trust a Marchant prince on his word alone. "How can you be sure?"

"I will reveal everything I know to you later, General," he said. "But for now, I need both Charlie and Prince Rainold to come with me."

Rainere didn't miss that Charlie looked to Ohrig for approval to follow the prince. He saw the general nod, then quickly point to his eyes and ears. He was almost amused. Ohrig had no idea how Marchants worked at all.

Rainere led his father and Charlie to the secret doorway in Adelena's bedchamber, and the three of them slipped into the passageway.

"Where are we going?" Charlie asked Rainere. "To find the high magistrar, I hope."

"Find him and kill him," Rainere confirmed.

"How do we know where he'll be?" Charlie asked.

"Oh, I know! I put a tracer spell on him while he was doctoring Rainere," Prince Rainold said. "He never even saw when I attached it to his hideous purple tie."

"So, where's he going?" Rainere asked.

Rainold pointed down the dark path between the walls. "I'm not sure, but he went this way."

Chapter Twenty-Eight

"An Evening in Concordis"

It was the post-work rush hour in Concordis when Rainere, his father, and Charlie stepped out the front door of The Magician's Wand public house. At this time of night, the street lamps were already lit and the roads were filled with public carriages. The huge vehicles lumbered alongside the smaller, fleeter private carriages and single riders jostling for space on the road. The sidewalks were heaving with citizens all wearing the focused expressions of people eager to escape the bustle and get home. Rainere also noted the small groups of poorly dressed young men and women hanging around on the street corners, watching the passing crowds with sharp eyes, nimble fingers at the ready. *Thieves, and so ridiculously obvious as to what they're about,* he thought, disgusted.

But it was the smell of the Slums that bothered Rainere most. The stench of fresh horse manure mixed with a sharp sourness that came from the workshops using poor-quality magic, and it hung in an invisible fog over everything.

Rainere glared at every smiling street magician and any young person daring enough to look over his rich clothing and see a potential victim. Most of the citizens here in the Slums had black hair and dark eyes, showing traces of their Marchant blood—his blood. Yet he felt nothing but shame for the people who would let themselves be corralled into such poverty and misfortune. Green Bloods, they were called by those in the Golden Palace—green like the slime on the crust of this once-beautiful city.

As they passed out of the dirty streets of the Slums and into the pretty avenues of the Artisans Quarter, Rainere found himself admiring his father's ingenuity in thinking of a tracer spell for the high magistrar. Though Rainold was having a bit of trouble holding his focus as they wove through the busy streets, luckily Charlie knew his way through the city and spotted the little ball of light of the tracer outside Merrills's Great Hotel.

"He's visiting the Lady Mayor." Charlie was surprised. "I wouldn't have thought she'd scheme to kill the queen."

"Perhaps Orestes is tying up a loose end?" Rainold suggested, his fingers miming tying a knot.

"I'm just as happy to kill two of Adelena's enemies tonight," Rainere growled.

"Uh, darling, can we talk about all this killing, please?" Rainold tried to grab his arm but Rainere shook him off as he stalked through the entrance to Merrills's Great Hotel. He had feared causing a scene, but oddly, no one was at the door nor the concierge desk, and no patrons lingered in the well-appointed lobby.

"This isn't right," Charlie said, palming the blade from his sleeve. "This place should be jumping with people."

They hurried up the carpeted staircase and turned left, but paused when they saw what waited for them at the end of the hallway. Four large, muscular men dressed in black denim trousers and sleeveless shirts filled the space in front of the mayor's closed office door. The thugs were leaning on the walls, weapons held by their sides, and one was even smoking a cigarette as they chatted among themselves.

Charlie flicked his hair off his forehead with a sharp toss. "All right, lads?"

"You fellas going somewhere?" one of the thugs asked, tapping a long hardwood baton in his palm, indicating that he didn't think they were.

"The Lady Mayor is busy tonight, so clear off, eh?" another said, his insolent tone grating on Rainere's last nerve.

"You guys don't work here." Charlie stepped forward, gesturing to their dirty clothes. "No way the Lady Mayor would let your ugly mugs in her fine establishment."

The largest thug, probably the leader, heaved himself off the wall, dropped the butt of his cigarette, and strolled forward to meet Charlie, his hands behind his back. He was just over six feet tall and completely bald, his face marked by half a dozen cuts, one of them still bleeding. Small, dark eyes took in Charlie's much slighter frame, and Rainere could see that the boy was going to die very quickly at the hands of this killer if he didn't do something. "All right, lads, have at it," the leader growled.

The thugs fought as a team, barreling down the hallway and parting around their leader like water around a boulder. Rainere felt an incredible rush as the blue tonic activated his magic, and then time seemed to pass in disjointed increments as the leader of the thugs raised two glowing balls of green magic in his hands, aiming one at Charlie. Charlie was quick, but Rainere could jump through shadows, so he spun around and shoved the boy against a wall, protecting them both with a shield. Dropping the shield in an instant, he released a violent killing spell at the leader, but it met with another spell in the air and was amplified to hit all four thugs at once, spraying the corridor with blood and entrails. Instinctively, Rainere threw up an umbrella charm to protect himself. The fight was over in moments.

"I'm so sorry, my darlings, I should've said that I could take care of those nasty men for you." Just like Rainere, Prince Rainold was immaculate despite the gore on the walls and floor.

Charlie was swearing a blue streak as he stood dripping on the carpet, spitting out blood that wasn't his. "Fuck, you could have warned me!"

"You're welcome," Rainere snapped.

"I'm welcome!" Charlie spluttered. "My new suit is ruined, and you properly smashed my head against the wall, Your Highness."

Rainere looked around. He always forgot exactly how far blood could spread when a body was exploded from the inside. "Yes, but now that I saved your life *again*, we're even for the closet thing."

Charlie's jaw clenched. "The night you damaged my brain because you thought I was Ripenzo Shale? *That* closet thing?"

Rainere snarled. "Don't be so dramatic, boy. If I wanted to kill you, you'd be—"

"Oh dear, Charlie's got someone's brain on his head!" Rainold laughed as he flicked off the gray matter with his long fingers. "Never mind, I'm sure your mother always wanted you to have a few more."

Charlie paled under his blood-spattered cheeks. Frowning, Rainere muttered a spell that dragged all the blood from Charlie's clothes with a wet, squelching noise as well as collecting up all the body parts on the floor, regrouping them into a steaming pile in a corner of the corridor. "We're wasting time. Let's go kill Orestes."

"No, no." Rainold hastened to follow behind Rainere. "We need to capture Orestes, not kill him just yet. He still needs to tell us where Ohren is."

"Yes, of course." But Rainere's heart was already racing with dark joy at the idea of getting his hands on the high magistrar and being the one to end his life.

The first part of the plan worked perfectly. He burst through the door into the mayor's office and found the high magistrar in the flesh. Without his enchantments, Orestes was young and beautiful again, his blue eyes sparkling as he held the Lady Mayor by the throat across her desk, a knife raised high in his other hand.

Orestes looked up at them and actually smiled. "Excellent, Adelena must be dead," he said. "Merrills here thought to take my Underworld, now she'll die too."

Rainere felt the rage smother him like a heavy blanket, suffocating all reason. He opened his mouth to utter the most malignant spell he knew, but—too quick—his father was in front of Orestes, a shield protecting them both from Rainere's attack. Then Rainold struck his own blow against Orestes, knocking him backward into the bookcase behind the mayor's desk, where he fell unconscious. Furious at being thwarted, Rainere leaped around the desk and raised a hand, green sparks bursting from his fingertips and showering his enemy.

"Rainere, no!" Rainold's voice thundered. "We need to know where Ohren is."

"Do we?" Charlie was leaning against the window frame, arms crossed, as if he witnessed murder every day.

"Yes, we do." Rainold's voice was firm as he reached for Rainere's raised fist and pulled it to his chest. "Sweetheart, use your head. What would your queen want?"

"He's right," Rainere agreed with a grunt, still loath to admit it. "Adelena would want us to find Ohren. I overreacted. It's all the, uh, blue tonic."

"You're forgiven, darling, think nothing of it." Rainold released Rainere's fist and gestured at a limp Orestes. "Now help me drag this wizard back to the palace."

"Wait. I demand an explanation," the Lady Mayor croaked, rubbing at the red marks that would soon be nasty bruises on her neck. "Who are these men, Charlie? And how did you know the Boss would be here tonight?"

"Mayor Merrills." Charlie gave her a shallow bow that seemed to only convey disrespect. "We believe the Boss came to kill you tonight because he'd bribed you to poison the beer delivered to the royal apartment and couldn't leave you alive to tell the tale. But I have to ask—why'd you do it?"

"Was the Boss doing Queen Adelena's bidding?" The mayor sank back into her chair, stricken.

"No, the Boss was doing his own bidding," Charlie corrected her. "If Queen Adelena wanted to kill you, she'd do it herself."

Rainere couldn't disagree. Adelena's temper was awful to behold. He would always remember lying in the dirt of the Dark Forest as she walked away from him after he'd sacrificed so much to help her rescue Natalie from the Spider People. "Leave him," she'd said. "We're done here." He blinked away the memory and returned his attention to the room.

"May the goddess protect me!" The mayor covered her face with her hands, hiding tears.

"If you're quite done?" Charlie asked, unimpressed. "You still haven't answered my question. Did you poison the queen?"

"No, never!" The mayor raised her shocked gaze to Charlie's.

"And why should I believe you?" he asked.

"The queen lied to *me*!" Bethany protested, wringing her hands. "She told me that the Boss was dead. How many of my own guards died trying to protect me? What price have I already paid for trusting that woman?"

Charlie ran a hand through his blood-crusted hair, trying to smooth it. "I'll admit death's been a little contagious tonight, but that's the fault of the Boss, not your queen."

"Sorry, my sweet lady, but I missed your name?" Prince Rainold interrupted. He handed the mayor a handkerchief from his own pocket, patting her shoulder while she blew her nose.

"Bethany Merrills," the Lady Mayor said, her voice wobbling as she tried to regain her composure. "And you are?"

"My name is Prince Rainold Marchant," Rainold said. "And I'll start by apologizing for the mess we've left out in your hallway."

Rainere groaned at his father's lack of discretion, and Charlie threw his hands in the air as if to say, "Well, that's done it!"

"That handsome man is my son, and the lovely Charlie is a very good friend of ours," Rainold continued. "Now, dear Bethany, we'd appreciate it if you didn't mention us saving your life tonight, and we'll just quietly steal away with Orestes and not bother you again."

Bethany wiped her eyes. "When you find who actually poisoned the beer we sent to the palace, you must tell me."

"No, that'll be your job," Charlie replied. "After all, how could anyone have known that I'd ordered beer for the queen's table from you today? I didn't even tell my colleagues that I'd asked for it."

Rainere couldn't help but be a little proud of how Charlie was handling the situation. Gone was the boy shaking in his boots to stand next to a Marchant prince. Gone was the immature thug who tried to smartarse his way out of every problem. Charlie looked good in his dark blue suit, his shoulders back and his hazel gaze sharp as he probed the Lady Mayor for guilt.

"I promise on my children's lives that it wasn't me who poisoned the beer." Bethany climbed to her feet, shaky but determined to face the accusation. "But you tell Her Majesty that I will find the culprit, and they will be dealt with accordingly. What about the Boss?"

"You have my word, Lady Mayor, the Boss's life will end tonight," Charlie promised her.

"It was delightful to make your acquaintance, Bethany," Prince Rainold said, hands fluttering elegantly. "I do hope we shall see each other again under better circumstances."

"Prince Rainold, a pleasure." Bethany attempted a wan smile to go with her curtsy, then directed another at Rainere. "Sir, I suppose you can only be the infamous Prince Rainere? A pleasure to meet you."

Rainere studied the Lady Mayor. Her dark hair was matted with sweat and disheveled from the tussle with the Boss. There was makeup running in dark streaks beneath her eyes, yet she was anything but cowed, even staring down two powerful Marchant wizards and a cold-faced boy after an attempt on her life. "My Lady Mayor, the queen will honor any loyalty shown her in this matter," he replied. "But she will also expect your retribution to be swift and severe."

"I understand," Bethany answered, and he could see in her expression that she did. Completely.

"Then we'll be off, my lady." Rainold gave a little clap. "Now, darlings, yes?"

Rainold picked up Orestes by his shoulders, and Rainere took his feet. Weaving through the many chairs in the room, they made their way to the corridor and laid the wizard out flat. Then Prince Rainold whispered a spell and the high magistrar rose upright off the floor, his feet floating a mere inch off the ground. Rainere was impressed and made a note to ask his father for the charm that could carry an unconscious body so easily and have it move in such a lifelike manner.

They commandeered one of the hotel carriages and returned to The Magician's Wand through the less-busy streets that Charlie recommended. Once back in the pub, they headed straight for the portal to the Golden Palace and then sprinted through the secret passages to Rainere's laboratory. Rainere was grateful yet again that Tilburn had chosen a lab in a deserted part of the palace, as he planned to test the quality of his soundproofing spells tonight.

Rainold tied Orestes to a chair with enchanted ropes and set up a spell around him, but it was Rainere who had the satisfaction of slapping the unconscious high magistrar across his face.

"Darling, stop it," Rainold admonished. "I'll wake him with this Truth Telling potion. He'll have to talk once he gets a whiff of this." He waved a tiny bottle under Orestes's nose, and the wizard came to with a loud gasp. His gaze was wild as he took in the darkened laboratory, with the two Marchant princes and Charlie standing in a semicircle, staring at him with varying degrees of murder in their eyes.

"You can't kill me!" he shrieked. "If you kill me, then my brother dies too because of the Immortality Curse."

"I'm not going to kill you now, Orestes," Rainold scoffed. "I need you to tell me where you hid Ohren, then I'm going to flay the Immortality Curse off your skin, *then* I'm going to kill you."

"Orestes, you are accused of attempting to assassinate the queen three times," Rainere said, pleased he managed to keep his tone even.

"Attempting?" Orestes's mad gaze flickered, and his head snapped to the side in a tic. "You mean she's not dead?"

"You have failed again," Rainere assured the wizard and allowed himself a grin.

"I couldn't have her demon blood touch me," Orestes snarled, his head twitched to the side. "The goddess Serena will not take demon killers into her Garden in the Beyond."

This time it was Charlie who stepped forward and backhanded Orestes across the cheek, snapping his head to the side. "You ordered the death of every child in the mines of Mount Ecrusius. Serena will see the blood of innocents on your hands, and she will turn away from you," he promised.

"This idiot will never tell us where his brother is," Rainere said, impatient to make Orestes bleed. "I say we kill him now."

Orestes turned his feral, wide-eyed focus to Rainold. "Remember that Serena brought us back here together, Rainold." He spoke slowly, as if he were talking to a child. "We have a *mission*. Let us fulfill our promise to the goddess. We must save Unisia and kill the demon queen."

"But that's not what Serena meant us to do," Rainold protested. "She said Dahk'hani would—"

Orestes continued without pause. "I have a potion in my room— God Dust. It's the foundation element for the Summer Influenza. If we give it to Adelena and then drain her blood, her magic will travel out with the blood. Then we chop her up and burn her bones." He smiled as if he could already see the smoking body of Adelena before him. "Unisia will be safe, and the goddess will love me."

Rainere barely resisted the urge to strike Orestes again. "Where is Ohren?" he asked.

"I hid him somewhere you'll never find him, even if you look for one hundred years." Orestes bared his teeth in an animal grimace.

"Ah! A riddle!" Rainold was delighted.

"It's not a fucking riddle," Charlie muttered, kicking a leg of

Orestes's chair. "He's just trying to get around your potion by telling us a bunch of catshit. Orestes, *when* did you catch Ohren?"

"I hid and returned to my office at the pub." Orestes's teeth were clinking as they ground together. "I knew he'd be vulnerable outside the palace. He's not protected out there."

"Why?" Rainere asked out of curiosity.

"The time traveling hurt him badly." Blood dribbled down Orestes's chin and he looked a little vacant as he tried to fight the Truth potion. "He must stay in one place, protected by the wards on the palace now. He can't leave."

"Time traveling?" Rainere and Charlie echoed one another.

"And where're you keeping him?" Rainold repeated.

"Did he say *time traveling*?" Charlie was still grappling with that one.

"Yes, Ohren was very naughty." Rainold shook his finger at him. "He played with time, and the consequences were severe. He thought if he could bind himself with the Immortality Curse, then he'd be safe. He asked me to break into the Eeyrie to find the dragon's blood we'd need to do it. I really wanted to impress him, and he'd said he loved me so I did it. But unfortunately, Orestes was caught up in the curse too, and now they're connected by it."

While listening to his father chatter on, Rainere felt the effects of the blue tonic suddenly wear off. He fell against one of the workbenches, and a stabbing sensation in the Mark on his side stole his breath. He folded in half with the pain.

"Your Highness?" Charlie was the only one to notice his moan.

"It's her." He whispered and felt the pain release him for long enough that he could stand again. "She needs me."

He headed for the entrance to the secret passages and didn't stop when he felt another stabbing pain in the Mark. He just managed to shut the door before the pain forced him to collapse on his knees. Adelena's pain and despair nearly overwhelmed him as he crawled in the dark, trying to find his way to her.

*

Charlie watched Rainere go and knew he was heading for the queen. He decided that he would take command of this interrogation now. Rainold was looking very vague, like he wasn't quite in the room anymore, while Orestes was smiling.

Charlie kicked the leg of Orestes's chair again. "Why're you feeling so chipper? We've still got you tied up."

"You know, Ohren never loved you," Orestes said, his mocking gaze on Rainold. "It was a dare, sending you to the Eeyrie, idiot! When he told me about it, we laughed and laughed."

"No, the Truth potion has worn off and you're lying," Rainold said, but he didn't look sure. "We were in love, and we *are* in love. It was you who stopped him from rescuing me from prison, I know it. He would've come for me."

Orestes laughed as he struck his next poisonous blow. "He wanted you locked up! And who do you think was feeding your son blue tonic for all those years—the last Marchant prince kept as feeble as a drug-addled kitten?"

"No!" Prince Rainold gasped and covered his mouth with his hand. "No, he wouldn't."

Charlie drew fast and felt the magic ball in his hand make solid contact with Orestes's jaw. He saw the Boss's head whip around, and he heard the crunch of bones grinding over other bones. Still panting with the effort of pulling that much magic out so quickly, he flicked his hair off his forehead and readied another ball in his hand.

"Charlie, your mother was a two-bit prostitute who died of some disgusting venereal disease, and your father was a blue tonic junkie who sold you to me for a single dose," Orestes said, hatred burning in his eyes. "You had a sister, but she was put on the window too young, and a drunk killed her when she wouldn't suck his—"

Charlie stepped in close and punched Orestes in the gut with a fist hardened by a green-magic glove. It felt so good that he did it again, and again, until the world faded away to just him and the wet thud of flesh on flesh. His chest ached from the dry sobs that wrenched his lungs. "I want the Boss dead," he said, gasping. "And I never want to remember what he did to me, ever again."

Then Rainold's arms went around him, pulling him away from Orestes. Charlie was so tired that he lay his head on the prince's shoulder and let the tears leak out. He noticed the prince smelled like flowers and dark magic. "There, there, sweet boy," Rainold murmured. "Did you know about your sister before tonight?"

Charlie closed his eyes and remembered standing at a countertop, looking up at a jeering madam of the house, her painted face ugly with malice. "I heard a rumor, but I never found her."

"There, there." Rainold stroked Charlie's back, moving his hand in circles that felt wonderful. "All Marchants are used and abused in this world. They want our magic, blood, and bodies and give nothing in return. Don't worry, honeypot, you have a family now."

Nope, that's too weird, Charlie thought and pulled out of Rainold's tender embrace. "I don't need you," he said, wiping his nose on his sleeve. "I've got my own family. Queen Adelena is my friend, and the Queen's Guard are my brothers."

"Are they really, darling?" Rainold's emerald-green gaze was filled with sympathy. "Then why did she send you away?"

"Ohrig said I could go," Charlie protested, then stopped himself with an effort. "I don't have to explain anything to you. Queen Adelena understands me."

"Queen Adelena is a demon, and you are probably running a decent strain of royal blood," the prince said, like that explained everything.

"It's not just about magic," Charlie said. "We're friends, me and her."

Rainold sighed. "Darling, how can I explain this without breaking your heart?"

"Don't bother," Charlie snapped, but he still watched as Rainold picked up a black feather from the workbench nearest to him.

"See this feather, Charlie?" Rainold dropped it from head height. "Now, in this metaphor, you are the feather, Adelena is the floor and gravity is her demon magic. The floor doesn't need to fall in love with the feather to know that the feather will join her soon. But the feather can decide that he is in love with the floor as he gets closer. Yet without gravity, he might just float away and never look back. He isn't choosing to fall down, he *has* to."

"I'm not a fucking feather." Charlie shook his head. "Honestly, I should've never got involved with you Marchant princes. I should've taken Ohrig's offer of a place in the Queen's Guard and put on their uniform. Then I'd be standing by the queen's side right now, instead of in this room with two of the craziest men in Unisia."

"That's hurtful." Rainold pouted. "Charlie, you can't pretend to be St. Lucidis any more than I could. We're Marchant, and we need to be sharp, or they'll break us all."

"I'm done." Abruptly, Charlie made his way to the laboratory door. "Keep Orestes secure. I'm going to search his rooms for the God Dust he was just talking about, and then I'm going to try and find the high wizard myself using that mirror again." He glanced over his shoulder to make sure Prince Rainold was listening to him, but Rainold had wrapped his arms around himself, softly weeping as he watched over an unconscious Orestes.

Swallowing a curse, Charlie closed the door.

Chapter Twenty-Nine

"Mettle of a Queen"

Adele awoke with a start, hearing someone shout her name. Her heart was pounding, and her head was filled with jumbled thoughts. *I have to go and get . . .* But she couldn't quite remember what she was meant to do.

It was early evening, and her bedchamber was filled with the warm light of a setting sun. Fading sunbeams streaked across the faces of the QGs surrounding her and sparkled on the glass columns of her bed. She knew instinctively that she'd been asleep too long. "I have to go!"

"Easy there, Your Majesty." General Ohrig was sitting on the edge of the bed, with Mrs. Ollenby standing next to him holding a smiling Stella.

"Mummy!" Stella crowed and broke into giggles.

"Stella," Adele wheezed, her lungs aching. "Thank God, she's all right. I remember . . . was there an explosion?"

"Stella broke the containment spell that Ohren put you under," Ohrig explained. Adele frowned in confusion and didn't like the slow, gentle way he spoke to her. "Prince Rainere has taken Charlie and his father to go find him. The high wizard has turned."

"Into what?" Adele tried to sit up, but Ohrig's hand was heavy on her shoulder.

There was a snort of laughter. "It's not funny, Owens," Captain Lucky admonished. "The high wizard committed dire treason. He nearly killed the queen."

"Oh, she's tougher than that," Bear scoffed. "And it looks like Princess Stella inherited Mama's balls too."

Adele smiled despite not understanding, and Captain Lucky muttered something at the QGs too low for her to hear.

"Stella was possessed by magic," Ohrig said. Then, still speaking in that odd, calm voice, he told Adele about Rainere and his father breaking her out of the spell.

Ohrig's calloused palm felt rough on her cheek, and she realized he was wiping her tears away. "Stella is normal again?" she whispered.

"Yes, Your Majesty, Stella is back to common." Mrs. Ollenby tried to smile, but her chin was wobbling hard. "She survived some very powerful, very terrifying magic."

"Prince Rainold put the dragon flame in a Firewhiskey bottle," QG Pepper piped up. "Apparently, the high wizard always puts his brew in unbreakable glass bottles."

Adele took Ohrig's hand from her cheek and gave it a squeeze. "At least Stella is all right."

Ohrig's pale blue eyes studied her. "Are *you* all right?"

Adele shuddered, remembering the sensation of Dahk'hani's magic sliding into every orifice of her body. *He came inside and he never left.* She wanted to collapse back on the bed and hide under the covers. *Sweet Christ, what has he done to me?*

"Mummy." Stella giggled again. "Care-fool."

Adele felt another wave of panic engulf her. *Sweet Christ, I'm so late! I have to go and get . . . it's waiting . . .* Rolling herself out of bed, she dropped her feet to the floor, then caught the front of her ruined dress before it fell away completely. "I need to get dressed then we have to go."

"I don't think it's right for you to be walking around just yet," Ohrig said, wrapping a shawl over her naked shoulders.

"Ohrig, stop talking to me like that—it's weird." Adele tried to put some strength into her wispy voice. "I'm a bit sore, but it's already nightfall, and we've got a meeting with Empress Sanda'hani. She probably thinks I'm purposely ignoring her just to be arrogant. We've got to get down to her as quick as we can." *Yes, that feels right.* She enjoyed the wave of panic receding. *Sanda'hani is waiting for me, and everything is ready. I can't be late.*

Mrs. Ollenby held Adele's arm as she minced slowly across her bedchamber. Her entire body ached, and between her legs it felt swollen and hot. The QGs gathered outside the open door of her dressing room and turned their backs to give her privacy, but Ohrig didn't let her out of his sight.

Mrs. Ollenby set Adele on a chair and put Stella down in the corner with a pile of new shoes to play with and went to work. With constant apologies for causing her more pain, Mrs. Ollenby slipped a fresh gown over Adele's head and tied all the stays and ribbons as loosely as she could. The dress was a lurid kind of green, painted with pink flowers, with a large white organza bow at the waist.

"It's not the grandest gown I've designed, Your Majesty," Mrs. Ollenby said. "But it's the lightest I could find, and the boning shouldn't press too hard on your sore ribs."

"It's great, thank you." Adele winced as pain cramped in her abdomen.

"We're going to need lots of powder for these burns on your cheeks," Mrs. Ollenby warned and picked up the pot of makeup, but Adele might have fallen asleep as the next thing she was aware of was Mrs. Ollenby dabbing perfume on her neck, saying, "Well, I think you look beautiful, Your Majesty. Certainly no one will ever know what you've just been through." She held up a round hand mirror.

When Adele looked at herself in the glass someone else was in her eyes, looking back at her. "Oh, no!" she whispered. "Please, God, no." She batted the mirror away from her face. *I need my knife,* she thought for no coherent reason, and staggered to the chest of drawers at the back of her closet. She opened the drawer that held her collection of lace underwear and dug to the back to find the obsidian knife. *Thank God, I have it.* Clutching it to her chest, she fell back into a seat, unable to stand under the weight of her relief.

"Your Majesty?" Mrs. Ollenby knelt beside the armchair, enveloping her in a cloud of peachy perfume and concern. "Is there something else you need? Anything I can do?"

She's so powerful, but not strong enough to wield her magic. Adele didn't know how she knew it, but in that moment, she gave up on ever getting Dolores Ollenby's help. *Dahk'hani got to me just like he said he would. I've got to keep going on alone.* Staggering from the dressing room, she made it to where her QGs were standing then tripped on the carpet and fell straight into Ohrig's arms.

"You look nice, Your Majesty," QG Leith said. "Mrs. Ollenby did a good job on all the burns." The rest of the men murmured the sort of superficial compliments that Adele had come to accept as part of their job description.

"We've got to go," she said, trying and failing to push herself out of Ohrig's embrace. "Someone tell the empress that I'm on my way to her now."

"Oh, Your Majesty, don't worry," Mrs. Ollenby reassured her. "Lord Orgustus knew that you were indisposed, so he has spent the afternoon with Empress Sanda'hani. By all accounts, it's going very well. He is charming her right out of any thoughts of war." She laughed a tinkly laugh that Adele didn't understand. *Who laughs at the idea of a war?*

"Orgustus is going to fuck this up," she muttered. "Let me just kiss my children, then I've got to get down there now. I must see Sanda'hani—it's vitally important."

Ohrig put his arm around her waist, helping her limp out of her bedroom and across the living room. Mrs. Ollenby ran ahead to get the children assembled. "What's so vital?" he asked.

Adele gasped as all the air went out of her. Frozen in place, stars filled her vision. She held onto Ohrig's biceps for dear life, and felt his hand on her back, stroking her rigid spine. The rest of the Queen's Guard crowded around in a huddle as if to protect her from spying eyes in the empty apartment.

"Ohrig, I can't do this. I can't," Adele whispered into his chest. "I don't belong here. This isn't my home. Everyone hates me. I ruin everything..."

Ohrig raised Adele's chin with a finger, and his pale blue eyes locked with hers. "If it's any consolation, I'm doing a shit job too. My queen, you were just poisoned, then locked in a fatal spell and had to be rescued by your two-year-old daughter and a team of bloody Marchant princes. And all this while you're in the Golden Palace under the watchful eye of your general of the Queen's Guard. Fuckacat, man!"

Adele had never heard Ohrig berate himself like this. Her general was always a bastion of grim stoicism, and she relied on that. She needed it when her own had faded. "Fuck ... a cat?" She felt a smile twitch her sore lips.

Ohrig grimaced. "Apologies, Your Majesty, it's a new curse Owens invented."

Adele raised an eyebrow at Owens where he towered lankily over her shoulder, grinning his slow grin. "It's a hobby of mine—between chasing you across Evendaar, killing mythical creatures, and beating everyone at cards, Your Majesty."

"Well, it's good to have hobbies," she agreed and was rewarded with Owens's rumbling chuckle.

"What're we going to do with you?" Ohrig asked. The despair had returned to his voice. "How can we protect our queen when this world seems determined to kill her?"

Adele gasped as a shooting pain lanced her between the legs again. "Ohrig, I've got no idea," she said. *I should say goodbye to the men. I really need to be going* ... The thoughts crept through Adele's mind like thieves, stealing her focus. *I can't* ... *I need* ... *Dahk'hani wants* ...

But Ohrig was hunched beneath the shame of his failure to protect her. She couldn't lose his love or support or his grumpiness. Seeing Ohrig's pain made Adele's battered courage click into gear. *Tell them what Dahk'hani did, and they'll help.* Deep in her gut, Adele felt the pull to the Garden Wing and wondered if it was Dahk'hani who called her there tonight. *Well, fuck him!*

"So, do you want the good news or the bad news first?" Adele glanced around at the men. "But properly brace yourselves, because this is really going to shock you."

Her QGs started chuckling, and even Ohrig's face softened a little.

"Is it going to be worse than walking through a dark tunnel under a mountain to the sweaty lair of a living dragon? Because that was some pretty hard shit for me," QG Leith said.

"Is it going to be worse than crossing a melting ice bridge? With you smiling at me the whole fucking time like it was nothing?" QG Bear asked.

"Is it going to be worse than watching you walking into the arms of an ice bear? Because I almost died of shock that day," Captain Lucky added. It was so unlike him to be cheeky it made the men laugh louder.

"Is it going to be worse than the Spider Nest?" QG Pepper asked, shuddering. "Because I refuse to believe anything could be more horrible than that."

"You know nothing much spooks me, Your Majesty," QG Owens said, earning himself a cuff over the head and a few choice words from the other QGs.

Adele leaned against Ohrig for support. The men crowded closer, heads bent down. "Dahk'hani came to me while I was trapped in Ohren's spell. He told me he'd come through the portal," she whispered. "I couldn't breathe, and it felt like I was dying. Dahk'hani kind of pushed inside the spell and protected me from setting myself on fire. He was in there with me and he . . ." Adele worked to take a deep breath. "He entered me."

It took a moment to sink in. "The god raped you?" Ohrig whispered.

"And now I'm probably, I mean I think, maybe, that I'm carrying his . . . him." Adele swallowed hard. "I think I'm pregnant with a god."

Ohrig dug out a handkerchief from his pocket and dabbed at Adele's tears. "Gods don't break their promises."

"And the weirdest thing?" she continued.

"Fuckacat, there's something weirder than that?" Bear muttered.

"The weirdest thing is that Rainere is the biological father," Adele said.

"And how?" Ohrig asked, gray brows beetling low over his eyes.

Adele quickly explained what Rainere had told her about Dahk'hani manipulating the magic of the dragon tear in her blood, the spell diagram that appeared, and the fertility spell that was power-ful enough to override the sterility of an Immortality Curse when she had made love to Rainere just before the poison released her magic.

"Prince Rainere got you pregnant, and now Dahk'hani has pos-sessed the baby," Captain Lucky clarified.

"Maybe, but let's not call it a baby just yet." Adele sucked on her bottom lip. "We don't know what sort of monster has been made between a demon, an immortal Marchant, and a nasty, lava-dwell-ing god."

Silence fell over the group as everyone pondered the new crisis.

"So," Bear said finally. "Nothing for us to kill, as yet."

Adele felt a real smile stretch her lips. Ohrig frowned at her. "What're you thinking, Your Majesty?"

"I'm not properly thinking yet—I'm still too sore," she said. She rolled her shoulders as the muscles cramped. "But I am wondering where Jordansson fits into all this. Then my brain keeps reminding me to wonder why the Sandarians didn't bring a mage with them to Unisia. Why would they risk coming here without their wizard?"

"They wouldn't," Lucky answered.

"Which means we just haven't found the mage yet," Adele said. "Prince Rainold doesn't think a god would have any power here in

Evendaar except through visions, especially for people who aren't his own tribe. But the Sandarians are Dahk'hani's tribe, so?" Her mind blanked as a wave of pain flooded her abdomen.

"So maybe it's their mage who has lent their power to focus Dahk'hani onto you here in Unisia." Lucky put it all together for them. "Maybe the power of the empress and Jordansson's bizarre magic is all that's needed?" He gasped in sudden realization. "Your Majesty, the call to war was a ruse—they're here at the behest of Dahk'hani. The empress knew that you would invite her into the Golden Palace and try diplomacy, which would take all the time the mage needed to allow Dahk'hani to find the perfect conditions to invade you."

"I've been a fool," Adele whispered.

"Oh, come on, Your Majesty." Ohrig spoke at a normal volume again and broke their tight-knit circle. "So you couldn't outsmart a god. Don't beat yourself up about that, for fuck's sake."

"The goddess Serena will protect you, Your Majesty," Lucky promised. "You're her Favored daughter."

"Be that as it may, I'm going to find out how much Sanda'hani knows about what her god's been doing to me, and then find the new Sandarian mage and kill him," Adele said, more firmly than she felt.

"Well, you've got that knife Rip gave you to do it." Ohrig beetled his brows again. "Funny old coincidence, that—him giving you the very tool you'd need to kill the mage of the empress he's in love with. Could almost make you think he set this whole thing up."

Adele was shocked, or maybe in shock, but the pain was making it very hard to calculate risks right now. "Maybe."

"But could Rip have known about the poisoned beer from Merrills?" Pepper asked. "That almost killed you today too. There are so many things all piled up together. Some of them have to be coincidence, right?"

"That one has the hand of the high magistrar written all over it," Ohrig growled. "I can promise you that Bethany would no sooner poison you than she would her own child, and Leith could've drunk that beer too. It was a foolish and messy attempt on your life, and Orestes is to blame. Goddess damn him! I wish they'd caught that man when they rescued the children."

"Orestes could be to blame for Ohren trying to kill you with that spell too," Captain Lucky suggested. "The high wizard has been acting very odd lately. He's not himself at all."

Adele and Lucky came to the same conclusion at the same moment. "Twins!"

Ohrig caught on a fraction later. "Fuckacat," he spat. "Twins."

"Mummy!"

Adele stepped away from her men and dropped to her knees as three children came running across the living room to embrace her. Leafy hung back a little, clutching her blanket tightly, but Adele pulled her into the mess of limbs and tears.

"I thought you died." Natalie sobbed into her neck. "I thought Prince Rainere died too."

"Mummy, the puppies said you couldn't breathe," Aaron told her. "Then Ohren didn't listen when I told him what they said. Only Stella heard me. She went crazy."

Adele gripped Leafy's hand in her own and took Natalie's in her other. Aaron had linked his arms around her neck. "Stella did a very brave thing, and the magic that made her burn people has gone."

"She's just a baby now?" Aaron asked.

"Yes, and now she needs us to protect her," Adele said. "I'm going to talk to some people and find out why bad things keep happening to us. You all need to stay together with Mrs. Ollenby while I do this."

"Are you leaving the Golden Palace again?" Natalie asked in a small voice.

"No, tonight I can fix the trouble from home." She managed to smile despite the pain wracking her body. "I must ask you to be brave, and I'll be back by the morning." She kissed all the children and then rose to her feet with help from Ohrig's steady hand.

Mrs. Ollenby entered with Stella, now dressed in a frilly

nightgown, leaning sleepily against her. Adele kissed her toddler's cheek. "Your Majesty, you should be in bed," Mrs. Ollenby said, her lavender-blue eyes filled with concern.

"There's no rest for the wicked," Adele said. She was answered with a shocked silence and almost grinned. "No, I didn't—you know what, never mind." She kissed her kids again. "I'll be back by morning, but if I'm not, take the children to the hiding place where you had them after they were kidnapped. I'll find a way to contact you."

Adele made her way to the door and gave Hollis a nod of thanks when he opened it for her. "Oh, Mrs. Ollenby, if you see High Wizard Ohren before I do, please tell him the queen is coming for him."

Chapter Thirty

"Old Enemies and New Allies"

Adele and her Queen's Guard made their way to the Garden Wing at a statelier pace than she intended because of the pain wracking her entire body. When they finally reached the doors of the long glass corridor, she was surprised to hear loud music and saw there was a party in full swing.

"Well, I know I didn't sanction this shindig," Adele said, frowning. She leaned against Captain Lucky's rock-hard shoulder for a moment to gather her strength. "Anyone got any Firewhiskey?" she asked. "I need a shot for the pain."

Bear proffered a small silver flask with his initials carved on it in a calligraphic script. "It's not as strong as the high wizard's brew," he warned. "So it won't get you dancing."

Adele took a long slug but Bear was right, this brew barely fizzed on the way down her throat. She handed back the flask.

"Feeling better, Your Majesty?" Captain Lucky gently pulled Adele off his arm, setting her on her own two feet.

"Right as rain," she lied. "Game faces on, lads."

There were at least a dozen Sandarian guards lining the hallway, standing at attention, but Adele was irritated to see so many St. Lucidis courtiers and palace servants running to and from the Garden Wing. Clearly, the Sandarians were keeping their suit for war

278

very quiet if the entire court was enjoying a party. The great double doors to the central room were flung open just as they approached, and a group of disheveled courtiers fell out, screaming with laughter and waving half-empty glasses.

"Oh! This rum is amazing!" a young woman shouted. She drank down the rest of her glass before blearily squinting at Adele. "My goddess, look at that poor woman! What a perfectly hideous dress!" Her friends agreed as they swung past heading back to the palace proper.

Just inside the doorway, a familiar and very flustered steward ran up to Adele. "Yer Maj, you'll wanna avoid all'a this great cahoo and kerfuffle in 'ere, or you'll get jammed in a barney," Brien Pepper said, his whole face flushed and his orange hair sticking up in tufts. His starched collar was askew, and his shirt had come untucked at the back. "I'm sorry, Yer Maj, but the whole lot of 'em is gone straight skippin' barmy. Mr. Tilburn and I are the only ones not drunk as cows eatin' brown mash."

Adele cast her gaze wide. The interior of the hexagonal Garden Wing had been cleared of all furniture. The carpets were rolled away, and a hastily made dance floor was already heaving with drunken revelers—Sandarians and courtiers alike. The louvers in the ceiling had been opened, but the air still felt humid and sticky with the cloying scents of too many perfumes. Adele had never seen anything so hedonistic in all her time at Golden Palace balls.

"What did Brien say about Tilburn?" she asked Pepper over the noise of the orchestra and raucous crowd.

"He said that only him and Tilburn are sober," Pepper translated, close to her ear. "But he also said the party is getting violent, so we'd best be careful."

As if to illustrate his point, a couple of male courtiers fell to the ground wrestling at Adele's feet, arms flailing with ineffectual punches. Pepper rolled them away with his boot.

"It'll be the coconut rum." She remembered her own night in Sandar drinking too much of the sweet liquor. "Or maybe it's been poisoned with some sort of opiate. Pepper, ask Brien where Tilburn is."

"Och, I speak the King's Tongue an' all," Brien said, offended, but soon calmed down when he saw Pepper's severe expression. "My apologies, Your Maj-esty, Mr. Tilburn is trying to sit in on a, uh, conversation of sorts between his lordship, Orgustus, and the Sandarian empress."

"Take us to his lordship now," she ordered him.

As Adele followed the steward through the party, weaving between drunken dancers, she finally remembered to pull on her power, sending surges of green magic down her aching legs and to her lower back. Unfortunately, she had no idea what to do about the thudding cramps in her abdomen.

"Your Majesty, if you could just prepare yourself a wee bit." Brien had taken them down a well-lit corridor off the central room and stopped in front of a set of double doors, his hand on the doorknob. "This is a bedroom, if you catch me meaning."

Oh, please let Orgustus be doing something really stupid with Sanda'hani so I can be angry with him! Adele thought and sent another surge of green magic throughout her body, lifting her spine and pushing the pain to the back of her mind.

Brien opened the door and stepped away, allowing Adele to enter first. Peering through the gloom, she could already smell coconut oil and sex in the air. Half a dozen candelabras were lit, but it was still dim enough that she had to search for Orgustus. "My lord, is that you?" She made her voice quaver, which wasn't difficult with the state she was in.

The rhythmic movement under the covers of the large bed in the center of the room stopped, and Orgustus's blond head appeared from beneath a sheet. "Who's asking?" he slurred, swinging his head toward the door.

Adele could've laughed with relief. *Brilliant! Now I can legally toss Orgustus from the Court after he's betrayed me with a monarch at war*

*with Unisia. Tilburn was very clear that this is treason. He'll owe me big
time if he wants to stay.*

"Oh, my love, how could you?" She faked a sob, glad of the dim
light to hide her probably terrible acting. Trying to cross the floor
to attempt some sort of pull-the-covers-back-and-wail drama, she
tripped on the leg of another body lying in a nest of pillows on the
floor and almost fell over.

It was Benjamin Belvoir, lying in the arms of two of Sanda'hani's
sisters. "Hey, look who it is," he said. His curly hair was all disheveled,
and he reeked of rum. "Come and join us, beautiful."

Adele ignored him and made her way to the bed.

Lord Orgustus had finally managed to register that something
strange was going on. Sitting up, he leaned back on a bank of pillows.
Sanda'hani was sprawled across his chest, and a bleary-eyed Lady
Olivia appeared on the other side of the empress. She waved at the
Queen's Guard and Adele, then ducked back behind a pillow.

"Your Majesty, what is the meaning of this?" Even drunk,
Orgustus was still an arrogant jerk, and he made it very easy for Adele
to get angry.

"What? Now I'm 'Your Majesty' when I find you in the arms
of two women?" Adele tried to shout, though it ripped at her sore
throat. "But when you're in my bed, it's 'my darling queen.' Orgustus,
I thought we were committed to each other!"

"What? Orgustus never shagged you," Benjamin's slurred protest was cut off by a dull thump that one of the QGs must have
administered.

"Your Majesty, I had no idea when I asked your handsome lord
and lady to join me in bed that it would upset you," Sanda'hani
purred, running her hand down Orgustus's naked chest and across
his flat stomach before she slipped it under the covers. "He never said
anything about you."

"No, none of that is—not true." Orgustus's survival instincts
started kicking in despite his stupor, and it was amusing to watch

the usually articulate lord trying to form a sentence. He caught the empress's hand playing in his crotch and pulled it back outside the covers. "I have to . . . my queen is upset, so I'll just . . ." He slid his legs out of the bed and stood up long enough for Adele to get an eyeful of why he was so popular with the ladies of the court, before he sat back down.

"Orgustus, did I mean *nothing* to you, that you would fall into the bed of the empress?" Adele pressed her hands together in a prayer gesture. "Is it because she's taller than me?" Behind her, she heard one of her QGs snort with laughter and then quickly smother it with a cough. She worked hard not to break character.

"Your Majesty, I'm sho . . . shorry." Lord Orgustus leaned over his knees, and a belch ripped from deep within his belly. "I'm really very—"

Adele only had a moment to step back before Lord Orgustus lost a long stream of coconut rum onto the carpet at her feet. *The only thing that would've made it better is catching Jordansson in this love nest too.* But something wasn't right. Simply thinking Jordansson's name made Adele's stomach drop, and she remembered that she had urgent business to attend to. *But I had to see Sanda'hani, and she's right here. Why do I still feel like something is coming? What else could it be?*

"Orgustus, you dog!" Adele feigned another sob and then turned to flee just as Tilburn arrived in the doorway, Brien hovering behind him.

"Queen Adelena, I promise that I had no idea things had degenerated into this—this orgy!" Tilburn was more furious than she had ever seen him before. "When I left them, they had their clothes on, I swear on the life of our goddess."

"Yeah, that's great, Tilburn." Adele grabbed the majordomo's arm to pull him into the hallway and lowered her voice. "There are two of Sanda'hani's sisters missing. Two are with Benjamin on the floor, but where are the others? And where's Jordansson?"

Saying the tribesman's name aloud gave her another sharp jab of pain in her abdomen. She stumbled backward into Ohrig, who caught her in his arms, but his gaze was directed to Lucky.

"Are you with us, Captain?" Ohrig asked.

Belatedly, Adele thought to check in with Lucky. Even in the midst of of this new crisis she had the energy to hate Olivia for what she'd done to her captain, and could tell from their expressions the rest of the Queen's Guard felt the same.

Lucky's face could've been carved from stone but he nodded. "My queen comes first." He jerked his chin at the bedroom. "*That* will never come close."

Brien waved a hand to regain Adele's attention. "Your Maj-esty, the other two sisters wanted a quiet room with Mr. Jordansson, so I put them in the back of the wing. They had a maid bring them all their bits and bobs."

"What bits and bobs?"

"They needed a few bowls and a bit of a cooking setup," Brien replied. "I was quick about seeing them sorted, Your Maj-esty. They've been quiet for a few hours now, so they must be happy. They weren't as drunk as the others."

General Ohrig and Adele exchanged a knowing glance. Then, through her pain and distraction, she felt it. *Dark magic. Shit. The new Sandarian mage is finally showing himself.*

"A blood ceremony." Lucky knew it too after the one he and Adele had shared with the chieftess of the Three Sisters tribe.

Adele nodded and reached into her sash, touching the obsidian knife hooked there. *Sweet Christ, I hope I don't have to kill another mage tonight.*

Brien led them through the long corridor around the hexagon. The further they walked, the lower the lights burned. Ahead of her, she spotted a door illuminated in an eerie green glow, the surface covered in untidy glyphs scrawled in chalk. *It's here.* Adele felt the magic move through her body like the vibrations of a gong. *This is where I need to be.*

"Why are these lanterns not lit, for goodness' sake?" Tilburn *tsked*, but Adele raised her finger for silence, and her majordomo understood that stranger things were afoot.

"That's the room I put them in," Brien whispered, pointing to the glowing door.

Adele grasped her green and gold magics and spread them in a suit of magical armor over her skin. She felt the pain still pulsing between her legs but managed to lock the rest of it behind the wall of her own willpower.

"Right, Tilburn and Brien, fall back," she whispered. She waited for the two men to do her bidding, but they both stared at her.

"I'm a queen's man to the end, Your Majesty," Tilburn whispered, fiercely. "If there is danger in there, I won't let you go in without all the help you can get."

Brien's blue eyes were huge. "I'm up for a caper, Yer Maj."

Adele didn't have time to make either man leave; instead she focused on her QGs and saw that they were grim but ready, swords gripped tightly in their hands. "Lads, I have a nasty feeling that inside that room are Sanda'hani's two sisters, Jordansson, and a sacred fire working some terrible dark magic. I can feel the mage. I swear I can almost smell him."

"Priorities, Your Majesty?" Ohrig asked.

"First, we'll pray the door isn't protected by spells too compli-cated for me to break. Second, depending on what he's doing, I might need to kill the mage and disable the sisters if they are the ones creat-ing this spell. You guys destroy the sacred fire. Take down Jordansson if he's in on this—save him if he isn't. If anyone else is in that room, keep them away from me. All clear?"

Her men grunted in agreement.

"That's a kill order, my queen?" Ohrig confirmed.

Adele thought very hard for a moment. "I want those women alive, if possible. But if anyone else fights you, they die. Including Jordansson."

Captain Lucky touched her shoulder. "How will you kill the mage?"

"Last time, I had my Chime Voices to tell me the Commands." She felt her courage take a hit. "Now I have you guys and this knife." She slid Rip's obsidian knife from her sash, gripping the stone handle in her sweaty hand. "Let's hope it's enough."

"We'll pray to Serena," Captain Lucky said. "She'll protect us."

"Sure, Lucky, but walk and pray. Something is telling me that I need to get in there now," Adele replied. She didn't know any words that Serena might care for, but she did know a spell that broke through doors to interdimensional portals. She tasted the metallic flavor of dark magic on her tongue as she whispered the charm and the door exploded. At her shout, QGs Bear and Owens went in and then fell to the side to let Adele enter.

She thought she had known what to expect. She really hadn't.

All the furniture in the room had been shoved against the walls in splintered heaps, and in the center of the carpet, a sacred fire was burning underneath a large tripod holding three bowls. The air smelled of burned herbs and sulfur so thick she wanted to gag. There were tall, dark shadows that might've been the figures of men standing evenly spaced at the edges of the room. Strings of magic ran from the center of their chests to a man-sized portal hovering just above the floor in a glittering green-and-gold haze. Empress Sanda'hani's two sisters were both nude and squatting on either side of the sacred fire. Next to them, the huge, naked figure of Jordansson was lying unconscious, one hand still curled around the neck of a bottle of coconut rum. His wrists and chest had been slashed in long, neat strokes, blood staining his snowy-white skin as it dripped down to soak the carpet under his broad back.

They've killed him! Adele experienced a flash of fury that dissolved her fear.

"Welcome, vessel." One of the sisters looked up from the fire and her eyes blazed with an unholy red light, her dark skin bleached by the magic flowing in her veins. Her voice was little more than a hiss. "Follow the path to bring us Dahk'hani."

On the ground, Adele saw tiny bowls of sacred fire lining a narrow path from the door to the larger fire where the sisters were. Between each bowl were messily drawn streaks. *Jordansson's blood! This is what Dahk'hani wanted him for. This is our destiny,* Adele thought, and knew she was meant to be here. The hideous dread that had claimed her before was now shrouding her completely and she didn't register her men shuffling into the room behind her.

Both sisters rose to their feet, hands filled with balls of white light. "Only the vessel may enter," they intoned in unison and raised their hands.

Adele managed to scream "Get down!" before the nasty spells flashed around the room, ricocheting off walls. She heard the shouts of her men, but she couldn't tell who was hurt.

"Damn you, Dahk'hani!" Adele shouted, and felt a sensation like a rope of magic wrapping around her middle, dragging her in toward the naked sisters. Her feet were crumpling the carpet into swells, but nothing slowed her movement toward the sacred fire and the bowl of smoking blood.

"She's here! My angel's here!" In that horrible, dark room filled with fire and smoke, the dead mage of Sandar appeared within the glittering portal. His eyes were black, and his angular face with its hideous, broken-toothed smile looked out at her.

Adele vividly recalled the Holy Caves of Sandar, where she had killed this same mage after he had bled her and then tried to stab her in the heart. *But he's already dead!* Panic and desperation swamped her reason. *Dahk'hani, help me! Show me how to kill a dead man.*

She was pulled to stand between the sisters, her feet nearly touching the flames of the large sacred fire, when the mage clawed at the curtain of green and gold magic separating them. His hand pushed through a small slit in the fabric of the portal, his taloned fingers almost scratching Adele's cheek as she turned away with a scream. The Sandarian sisters were possessed by the enchantments that poured from their lips in a constant stream and did nothing but stare with glowing eyes, even when Adele crashed into one of them trying to get out of the mage's reach.

"Come here," the mage hissed. "You have my god within you. I will be with him. He promised me!" With a violent jab, his hand tore a bigger hole in the curtain of magic. He shrieked in excitement and his second hand began trying to open another hole for his head.

USE THE KNIFE. FREE MY SERVANT FROM HIS PRISON, ANGEL. HE WILL TAKE YOU HOME. The words boomed through her head, and Adele screamed in agony. The stench, the blood, the pain that rolled through her body in hideous waves were too much to bear. *I have to get away. I won't go to him.* Struggling against the pull of the enchantments, she clasped the obsidian knife with numb fingers, only to watch it tumble to the ground by her feet. *I'm too stupid and weak. I can't fight him.*

"Yes, mine!" The mage knelt on his side of the portal and reached through the gap to scrabble with one filthy hand for his knife, but it was just out of reach.

MOTHER, JOIN MY SERVANT! Adele's body crumpled with the impact of Dahk'hani's Command, her knees pressing into the carpet soaked with Jordansson's blood. She scooped up the knife with a slack hand and tried to slice the rope of magic restraining her, but her fingers were wet with blood and the blade was slippery stone. Instead she nicked the curtain of magic, making one of the holes bigger.

"Blessed angel and mother of Dahk'hani!" the mage screeched. He said something in the Sandarian tongue that made the two sisters reach for Adele, taking her by each arm and shoving her against the portal curtain. Green and gold sparkles filled her vision. She had no breath to scream when she felt his broken teeth against her cheek, his diseased tongue stroking her flesh.

Is this the end, Dahk'hani? Adele spoke to the deity inside her, horrified by what was about to happen. *Taken by the mage I killed and leaving everyone I love behind? You wanted me, and gods don't lose. But if you take me—I'm leaving my soul and my heart here, with my children and Rainere.*

"Mother, come now," the mage said, and his will was so strong that she knew he'd already won.

There was a burning pain in her abdomen and she couldn't feel anything except a profound need to escape the agony she was in. The last shred of her leonine gold magic was extinguished, and with it she felt her hope die. *Dahk'hani, you've destroyed me.*

The mage laved her cheek with his tongue again. "I can taste your despair," he hissed. "The god is burning inside you, and you will be cleansed—a perfect vessel to carry him to life. His mother and my lover."

Adele whimpered because she knew what was coming. She could see her future clearly—under the mountain, and under the mage's control. She felt the Sandarian sisters let go of her arms. Dread bound her now, and there was nowhere to escape to. On her knees, she stared at the knife held loosely in her hand.

"Cut the portal open and come to me," the mage instructed, his talon running down the curtain of magic in a line. "Come, angel. Do it now."

Adele raised the knife. There was only one way out for her. "If you love me at all, you'll let me die," she whispered to the god she didn't see. *Dahk'hani, you have to know I don't want to live if it's with your evil mage. That's not a life I would give my child.*

The blade was hot when she touched the tip of it to her chest and pierced the skin over her heart.

"I can't go with him," she whispered. She felt the blade drinking the droplets of blood beading from her parted flesh. "I won't do that to you, Dahk'hani."

The mage screamed, the sound inhuman and ferocious. He jammed his head through the gap in the curtain, his hand reaching through the other hole he'd made. Adele pressed the blade deeper into her skin.

I DON'T WANT THIS!

"Your Majesty, no! Stop!"

Adele didn't even recognize Captain Lucky's bloodstained face— or General Ohrig, who was holding one of the enchanted sisters to his chest, his knife at her throat.

I WANT YOUR LOVE, MOTHER!

"I have to die," Adele told these strange, ghostly men who pierced her with their cries of grief. She heard the screaming of the mage and the roar of the boiling lava world. *This is the best way.*

FATHER, SAVE HER!

Thunderous and loud, ancient Commands were bellowed into the room. It was the Old Tongue, the language of magic, spoken by the man she'd once traveled the stars to find. But tonight he also had the power of a god behind him. "Adelena, strike him!" Rainere shouted.

The power of the Commands guided her hands and Adele yanked the blade from her chest and slashed down hard. The obsidian sliced through the mage's skin, flesh, and bone. His head rolled to her, and she slashed again to see the hand fall next to it.

There was a great, crashing silence. Then:

"Your Majesty, are you all right?"

"What's happened? Is it over?"

"Fuckacat!"

And she was surrounded by her Queen's Guard, bloody and battered, but all six of them were whole.

"Queen Adelena!" Ohrig had his arms around her. "Talk to me, woman. Are you all right?"

"Right as rain," she said, her voice hoarse. "Sweet Christ, I almost got sucked through that portal to the lava pit beneath the world."

Ohrig stroked a tendril of hair off her sweaty forehead. "You gave us a scare, Your Majesty."

"Still killed the mage by yourself. Again," QG Bear noted.

"S'just a bit selfish, Your Majesty," QG Owens added, and Adele noticed that he was dripping with gore. All her men were. "Still, we got our own back on those warriors. They didn't go down easy."

The QGs parted to reveal the room strewn with a dozen bodies of dead Sandarian warriors. Adele felt a tremble in the ground under her feet, and her head swam. "Oh, lads, those poor men."

"They were possessed," Ohrig said. "Must've been. I mean, their eyes were glowing. There was no saving them, but we left the sisters alive because they didn't put up any fight."

The two sisters were weeping in a huddle on the floor next to a groaning Jordan Jordansson. Tilburn was wrapping his bleeding wounds with strips of cloth ripped from his own shirt. Dazed, Brien was still holding a bloody sword and listening to Tilburn's instructions as they prepared to move the enormous tribesman.

"The sisters were possessed too and didn't do anything on purpose," Adele said. "Can someone please check that the mage is really dead? Again."

The mage's head and hand had blackened and shriveled on the bloody carpet, but the green-and-gold curtain of magic still hung in the air like a large window into a volcano, showing his headless corpse. No one wanted to go near it.

"Maybe ask Prince Rainere?" Ohrig said.

"Yes, good idea," Adele answered, amazed that she felt so little of anything except the tremors that kept shaking her. *Tremors I can take,* she told herself. "Right, lads, let's get out of here."

But leaning in the doorway, looking exhausted, was Rainere. He straightened when he saw her and crossed the room, his arms opened wide. Adele felt the ground beneath her shake so violently that she stumbled. He caught her up and held her tightly to his chest. With his everlasting heart thudding against her cheek, the horror of what she'd almost done swamped her. "Rainere, I was going to kill myself," she wailed.

Her knees buckled, but he lifted her feet off the ground and gripped her even tighter, keeping her from flying to pieces as the sobs wracked her body. "*Cara mia*, my sweetest heart's song, my darling," he crooned in her ear, "you're safe. You're safe."

She wanted to stay in that place forever, with her nose buried in his shirt and his strong arms holding her, but there was so much to be done, and there were those affected by the poisoned coconut rum to help. So she lifted her head and opened her eyes on the world. "My love, I have work to do," she murmured, and Rainere released her. She wiped the tears off her cheeks with the back of a blood-covered hand. "General Ohrig, we don't know if the empress had a part in this, but I want all the Sandarians contained. I will speak with her when she sobers up."

General Ohrig grimaced and ran a hand through his hair, the gray now rusty red with blood. "I'll put a hundred men on it, Your Majesty, but these Sandarian warriors can outfight any of the Household Guard. I'm worried that I'll just be subjecting our men to a quick death."

Adele didn't hesitate. "Then we'll take these sisters here as hostages," she said. "Take the two drunk ones sleeping with Benjamin too. That should control the violence of Sanda'hani's reaction."

"Royal hostages, Your Majesty?" Ohrig asked. "That's more grounds for war."

"An attack on the queen of Unisia is grounds for complete Sandarian annihilation, as far as I'm concerned, General Ohrig," she snapped. "Do as I say."

Ohrig nodded, his expression blank, but his eyes on her were wary. "It's done."

The QGs gathered themselves, and Tilburn joined them. His vest had blood on it, and his wig was askew, but he held his dignity firmly. "Your Majesty, I will call the Household Guard to order," he said. "Will you return to the royal apartment now?"

Adele didn't know how to respond to such a simple question because all she could think was, *I was just there with the children, then*

I was almost taken by the mage to be his slave and live underground with him in the lava and . . .

"Yes, the queen needs to rest, and so do her Queen's Guard," Rainere replied to the majordomo. "Tilburn, see that the Sandarian sisters are taken somewhere comfortable but secure, as befits royal prisoners, and have a medical crew take Jordansson to the hospital wing. He'll need a blood replacement. When that's done, come and report to me."

"Your Highness." Tilburn's gaze darted to Adele for her nod of approval before he dashed from the room.

Adele felt the ground move again and this time realized that it wasn't in her mind. Large cracks appeared on the walls, and a huge piece of ceiling glass fell to the floor, smashing to pieces. Her stomach dropped away when Rainere scooped her up and carried her out into the long, dark corridor, now filled with screaming partygoers trying to escape the destruction as the earthquake continued. With the Queen's Guard pushing people out of the way, Rainere made it to the central space, and she saw that the entire Garden Wing lay in ruins. The glass walls were shattered and gaping, the beautiful columns rubble on the ground. Picking their way through the mess, they followed the crowd down the long glass corridor.

Adele was relieved to see that the structural damage stopped at the doorway to the palace proper. Nearby, Tilburn was standing on a large chair, arms flying as he directed servants to search for anyone trapped in the rubble and shouting for medical teams to help the wounded who were milling around the hallway, covered in dust and crying. *I'm sure I can live without Orgustus, but I couldn't survive without my majordomo,* she thought.

There was nothing more she could do, so Adele relaxed in Rainere's arms, her cheek pressed to the warmth of his chest, his thudding heart the only sound she wanted to hear. The world became blurry, then faded away.

*

When next she woke, she was naked and being held in a warm bath. Rainere was in the water with her, still wearing his trousers because her three children and Leafy were hovering at the side of the bath asking him if she was dead.

"I'm not that easy to kill, my darlings," Adele croaked. She found she had the strength to smile for her children.

"Mummy!" Natalie reached for Adele's hand but recoiled. "Is that your blood?"

"Nope." Adele snuggled back between Rainere's legs, letting his arms anchor her under the sweet-scented bubbles. "It's a nasty mage's blood, but he's gone now. Forever, I hope."

"Dead?" Aaron asked, his little-boy face somber.

"Yes, sweetheart, dead." She didn't have the energy to consider the new trauma that her children had been exposed to that day.

"Children, your mother needs to get to bed, as do all of you," Rainere said. "You can see her in the morning at breakfast and hear all about her adventures to save Unisia once again. It will be a wonderful story."

"With a happy ending?" Natalie asked, her expression anxious.

"A very happy ending," Adele said, her eyes closing when she felt their little kisses on her wet cheek. "Sweet dreams, my darlings."

The children's nannies had been waiting by the door and moved to gather the children together. After they left, the only sounds were the prickling of bubbles popping and Rainere's breathing. Adele felt his hands moving a muslin cloth over her arms, her neck and shoulders, then down to her torso. He scrubbed every trace of blood off her skin and then washed it out of her long, dark hair. Her insides ached, and the sensitive skin between her legs stung in the hot water. *I should tell him what Dahk'hani did to me,* she thought, but in her misery and exhaustion, she didn't have the heart to face it.

"Adelena, I know you have a secret for me because you were talking in your sleep," he whispered, lips on her ear. "But leave it for tomorrow. Nothing matters tonight except that you survived."

The tears streaked down her cheeks, and Rainere lapped them up, his sweet touch erasing the crawling feel of the mage's tongue that had gotten stuck under her skin.

"Take me to bed," she pleaded, and Rainere got them both out of the bath, wrapped them in warm towels, and carried her to the great Glass Bed. Still damp and smelling like sweet soap, Adele buried her nose in Rainere's chest and, for the first time in weeks, fell deeply asleep.

CHAPTER THIRTY-ONE

"Love in Other Languages"

Rainere woke the next morning to Mrs. Ollenby softly calling Adelena's name. He was lying on his back in the Glass Bed with his queen burrowed into his side. She kept shaking off the lady's hand and was trying to bury herself further underneath him.

"Mrs. Ollenby, allow me to wake the queen."

Mrs. Ollenby looked pale and unhappy, but she spared a smile for him. "I'd love to let her sleep all day, Your Highness," she said. "Our goddess only knows the poor dear needs it. But I'd appreciate it if you'd call me when I can make her presentable for the court."

He spied General Ohrig at the bedchamber doorway frowning at him, and behind Ohrig, there was an entire room full of people who Adelena would have to deal with today. She had killed Sandarian warriors and taken royal hostages, and she would need to bear the consequences, whatever they were. He waited for Mrs. Ollenby to leave the room, then scooped Adelena into his arms, drawing her up onto the pillows. Eyes still closed, she turned on her side, muttering something that sounded suspiciously like "Please, fuck off."

He stroked the hair off her neck and began kissing her, slow and wet. By the time he reached her breasts, she was writhing under him, groaning.

"Rainere." She dragged out his name for a dozen syllables.

"I heard something about 'fuck,'" he said.

Adelena ran her fingers through his short, spiky hair. "Don't make me wake up," she begged. "I don't want to face the world just yet."

"Then we won't, not just yet." He began sliding down her body, kissing every inch of skin under his lips.

Nothing made him happier than to hear his lover's weak protests and feel the thrill of her anticipation through the Mark. Dropping lower, he shouldered her thighs apart and prepared to go to work with his tongue, beginning softly as the wings of a butterfly, just how she liked it. But this morning, there was something different about her beautiful sex. Adelena was red and swollen where she should only be pink and soft. Her taste was different too, smokier and sort of . . . *Metallic*, he thought, and dread curdled in his gut. He kissed the inside of her thigh and noticed the rapid diminishing of her lust through the Mark. Eyes open now, Rainere moved up to kiss her stomach, and his lips grazed the lines of the Dahk'hanian diagram. It stretched from the dark curls of her pubis to fill the entire area under her belly button, from hip point to hip point.

"Darling, the god's magic has tattooed itself, and it looks permanent now." He traced the complex lines with a fingertip, watching the silver etchings glint as he passed over them. "Did it hurt?"

Adelena had covered her eyes with the back of a forearm. "Yep, it hurt," she said, choking on tears.

Rainere took her in his arms again, heart aching for his beautiful lover who was always in so much turmoil. He wove the silken tresses of her hair through his fingers. "Tell me what happened," he murmured.

Adelena's tears dripped down his chest, healing his new burns, as she took a shaky breath then described everything that had happened after she'd woken up inside the containment spell, right until she saw him standing in the bloody bedroom in the Garden Wing.

Rainere listened without comment, his excitement mounting in a way he'd never felt before.

"Dahk'hani said, 'You are my mother and Rainere my father.'" Adele took another shuddering breath. "I'm so sorry, but I don't know how to fix this, sweetheart."

"Adelena?" Rainere sat up, his heart beating so fast that he could hardly gather his thoughts or say the words that she hadn't. "Are you telling me that you're pregnant? Pregnant with our child?"

She dropped her gaze. "Rainere, if it's a baby, then it's not a normal one. I have no idea what will happen now."

"I'm going to be a father," he said, just to taste the delicious words. "*Cara mia,* you are carrying *my* child."

Adelena looked up at him again, and he was puzzled by the fear in her eyes. *Is she frightened of my reaction? But why? There is no betrayal if a god himself forced this divine conception. Perhaps it would mean something very different on Earth if she told her lover that she carried the child of a god? I must be gentle with her.*

"*Cara mia,* you have made me the happiest man in Evendaar," he said, flipping Adelena onto her back and kissing her lips, her cheeks, her forehead, and her throat. Yet she put her hands on his chest and pushed him back.

"But this *thing* was made against my will," she said, her voice still soaked with tears.

Rainere wanted to put his own pleasure aside and consider Adelena's hesitation to have this miracle child, but it was simply too intoxicating. *I'm going to be a father. God or no god, nothing can dim this joy!* "Darling, I beg your forgiveness." He moved them both so she was cradled against his chest, her legs draped over his lap. He pressed his still-smiling lips to the top of her head. "It was a terrifying ordeal for you, and I understand that it will take you time to recover from the conception."

Adelena tilted her head back to look up at him. Her smile was wry, but it was still a smile, and his heart leaped to see it. "You seem happy that I was taken advantage of by a god you haven't even met."

See, she's joking already. It couldn't have been all bad for her, he told himself. "If it helps you, my love, why don't you think of Dahk'hani as simply an assistant in creating our precious child," he suggested, careful to tamp down his excitement. "After all, it was my essence and your egg that we brought together with lovemaking. He just gave it . . . a little tap."

Adelena's eyes went wide, the shiny rings of power around her irises spinning. Rainere felt another surge of happiness. Foolish with ecstasy, he lay a hand on her stomach and imagined it swollen with his child.

"You're right, my prince," she said, as if she'd decided to be sensible and listen to him. She even slipped her hand down to stroke his proud erection, then lower to cup his tight, swollen balls. "I guess it felt just like a little tap."

Rainere leaned down to kiss Adelena, and she moved her face to his. He groaned into her mouth as her hand on his balls gripped him more firmly. But Adelena suddenly squeezed far too hard, and all the air raced out of his lungs. He leaned back on the headboard, stars clouding his vision.

"Does that feel like a little tap, darling?" Adelena hissed as she let go. Her eyes were flashing dangerously now. "How about I rip these off and then shove a living god inside of you? It'll only take a little tap, won't it? God damn it, Rainere, what a stupid thing to say!"

"Forgive me, *cara mia*." He wiped his watering eyes but was still disappointed to see Adelena already out of bed and slipping on a robe, tying it while glaring at him. "I am a fool and a beast. Of course I understand your pain. Forgive me, *please*."

"Get out of my bed," Adelena said and then shouted for Mrs. Ollenby to come in.

Rainere only had time to cover his lap before the team of dressiers and a half dozen maids came streaming into the room, headed by Mrs. Ollenby. The lady had remembered to bring his suit with her, and she waited while he got out of bed, wrapped one of Adelena's shawls around his waist and limped across the room to meet her.

"Mrs. Ollenby, thank you," he said, taking his clothing.

"You're welcome, Your Highness, but I'll thank you to stop distracting Her Majesty's maids." Mrs. Ollenby nodded at the group of servants behind him.

He looked over his shoulder to see every young woman in the room gazing at him, mouths open and eyes wide, drinking in the sight of his muscular frame and the jet-black immortality tattoo that covered his back. The shawl was transparent and hid nothing of his still-firm erection. Rainere grinned, and one of the maids lost her balance and collapsed onto a chair.

"Stop showing off, Rainere," Adelena snapped as she brushed past him. "You're not that cute." She slammed the bathroom door in his face.

Rainere laughed loudly, surprising even Mrs. Ollenby. No one else had seen it, but Adelena had pinched him as she'd passed. That meant he should ignore her words and beg for forgiveness. He could only hope it would be on his knees.

"Your Majesty?" Rainere knocked on the bathroom door. "It is I, Prince Rainere. May I come in?"

"Fuck off!"

"I'm so sorry, but I think Her Majesty might want to be alone, Your Highness." Mrs. Ollenby's expression creased with sympathy.

"No, that's the last thing Her Majesty wants." Rainere winked and was rewarded with Mrs. Ollenby's flustered giggle.

He didn't wait for Adelena to give him permission but opened the door, calling out, "Darling, you still haven't let me apologize properly."

Adelena had turned the shower on and was waiting for him. Her eyes were still flashing, but this time it was dangerous in a different way.

Rainere locked the door behind him. "*Cara mia.*" When he smiled, he felt the lust flowing hot and strong through the Mark and knew he was right.

"Oh, so you've recovered from my attack, have you?" Adelena's tone was arch, but she crossed her arms under her breasts, lifting them for him.

Rainere leaped the room in a few long strides. "I have recovered enough to ravish you," he promised, and dropped to his knees on the warm tiles. "After all, it was only a little tap."

CHAPTER THIRTY-TWO

"Sore Heads"

Usually a steward pulled her chair out at the dining table, but this morning, Rainere was hovering at her shoulder, and he held the chair and set her back in again. "My darling, can I get you another cushion if you're feeling a little sore?"

"*You* aren't sore, are you?" she murmured with a glance at his dark, forest-green eyes, studying the circles of magic for tarnish. "I hope I didn't take too much from you in the shower just now."

"*Cara mia*, I've never felt more vibrant." He grinned as he took her wrist, pressing his fingers against the inside and counting her pulse. "More to the point, how are you feeling after my ravishing?"

"All right, lower your voice, Rainere, we don't need the whole table to know," she complained. But he was clearly determined to give the game away about her condition—she could see it in his smug, gleeful expression. He even gave her a kiss on the cheek as he took the seat next to her instead of at the opposite end of the long table.

Well, all right, public displays of affection I really don't mind. Though she knew he was only being bold because things had changed, she still loved that he was finally dropping the stiff formality he used with her.

This morning, the breakfast table was laid for twenty, and every chair was filled. Her Queen's Guard sat in the chairs nearest to hers. Next came Charlie and Prince Rainold, then Lord Orgustus, Tilburn,

Jordan Jordansson, Mrs. Ollenby, the four children—with Stella in her baby seat—then Seraphina and Siobhan.

There's no room for another baby chair. Adele felt sad about that before remembering she wasn't being logical. *Sweet Christ, the hormones shouldn't have started already. I can't fall into the trap of thinking this is a normal pregnancy. Dahk'hani is probably more like a parasite.* The idea of some freakish god-seed-leech growing within her was nauseating.

"Your Majesty, how're you feeling today?" Ohrig asked. He had a pile of scone crumbs on his plate and a sprinkling of them on his unshaven bristles. She handed him a napkin.

"I'm as good as can be expected," she replied. "Prince Rainere gave me what I needed to recover after last night."

"Right." Ohrig's mouth snapped shut on that subject, but Rainere threw his head back and laughed very loudly in his husky, wicked way. Everyone stopped talking and stared at the Marchant prince as if he'd grown two heads.

"What has made you so happy, my sweet boy?" Prince Rainold was looking fresh and handsome this morning in a dark green coat and vest that played up the bright emerald-green of his eyes. Adele felt a tingle between her legs and was immediately disgusted with herself. She refused to let herself be attracted to Rainold.

Rainere was looking hopefully at her, but she shook her head. Now was not the time for announcements. The children jumped up, deciding their breakfast was finished, and ran down to their mother's end of the table, chased by their nannies. Both Rainere and Adele cuddled them before they dashed off to get ready for a morning in the pools out on the terrace.

Charlie got up from the table and approached Adele. "Your Majesty, I need a private word with you," he said. "It concerns the high wizard."

"The queen is far too busy to worry about Ohren just now, Charlie," Rainere interrupted, and Adele saw the two of them have a conversation with their eyes that she clearly wasn't supposed to be a part of. "Why don't you ask my father to help you find him?"

"Ohren is still missing?" Adele was surprised to be just catching up on this. "Does he know that his brother is back in the palace? I thought when General Ohrig said that Ohren had 'turned,' that meant he was involved in some stupid plan of his own devising, not betraying me to Orestes. Do you think they might have been working together to hurt me?"

"No, of course not," Rainere said, a touch too quickly.

"I was asking Charlie." She threw Rainere a sharp glance. "You'd been poisoned too and were in no condition to know what was happening at the time."

Charlie winked at the prince, which Adele thought was both very foolish and brave of the kid. "Your Maj, I'd prefer to speak about this in private," he said. "It's about what happened while you were—"

"Getting intimate with a containment spell," she said, but Charlie didn't take it as a joke. In fact, he looked weary, like something was weighing heavily on his shoulders. "I'll make time for you, Charlie. Just let me deal with the war with Sandar right now."

"I'd like to hear what Charlie has to say too, Your Majesty," Ohrig said at the same time he caught little Aaron trying to crawl under the table. "I don't like to have both the high wizard and the high magistrar unaccounted for."

"You're right." She chewed her bottom lip and tried to find a positive spin. "But Sandarians hate St. Lucidis wizards anyway, so let's count our blessings that Ohren has chosen now to continue his low profile. It's almost impossible to catch Orestes if he's got another disguise on, but we should stay alert in case he tries to kill me again."

She decided to deal with a problem much closer to home and looked down the table to where Orgustus was sitting next to Jordansson. She knew that they must have both been feeling terrible—Orgustus from humiliation and poor Jordansson from blood loss and disappointment.

"Lord Orgustus!" Adele called out. His shoulders rose to his ears before he plastered on a smile. Despite how petty it was, she enjoyed having this effect on the man who had plagued her first few months in Evendaar.

"Your Majesty, I understand that you have taken the empress's four sisters hostage after the events of last night," he began. "I would beg an explanation of you."

"Only because you were so drunk you don't remember anything, my lord," Tilburn snapped. "I've already given you an account of your own treasonous behavior as well as Lady Olivia's. That should suffice."

"Oh, exciting! What happened at the party?" Prince Rainold asked, smiling at all the serious faces lining the table. "Captain Lucky, were you and your pretty lady the most handsome couple at the ball?"

Even in his fury, Lucky was too polite to ignore a prince. "Unfortunately, we were not," he replied, but his fists clenched on the table as he sent an icy glare to Orgustus.

"Tilburn, why don't you fill us in on the activities of our former regent last night," Adele suggested, accepting the cup of tea that Rainere had made her, as well as another kiss on her cheek.

Tilburn stood, pulling his vest down with a sharp tug. "Your Majesty, the empress demanded entertainment with her dinner, and I was asked to invite all the aristocratic members of the court who cared to join them."

"Tilburn, jump to the part where Orgustus got so drunk he fell into bed with the empress and then threw up on my shoes."

Orgustus winced and dropped his chin. "Your Majesty, my humiliation is complete," he said. "No apology will ever be enough in recompense."

"No, it won't," Adele agreed.

"I made a grave mistake, Your Majesty," Orgustus said. "The only defense I'll muster is that I believe the coconut rum must have contained a narcotic. Being drugged is the only reason I would have bedded a dangerous monarch and availed myself of her request to involve others."

"That's the oldest story in the book," Adele muttered, exchanging a glance with Rainere, who chuckled.

"Why do you care who Orgustus beds, my queen?" Jordansson asked, a puzzled frown marring his bruised forehead. "You don't shag him, and you only pretend to like him."

"Jordansson, stay out of this," Adele said, but gently.

"The queen is right," Orgustus said. "I failed to do my duty, and I acted like an imbecile. If my actions have compromised our queen in any way, then this war will be as much my fault as that of the high magistrar who destroyed the empress's letters to begin with."

Jordansson clapped his friend on the shoulder. "I got drained of half my blood, but blood grows back," he said. "Your pride will grow back too."

Orgustus managed a grimace for his friend then turned back to Adele. "The empress is distraught, Your Majesty," he said. "Sanda'hani blames the Crown and St. Lucidis magic for her sisters' actions. She claims . . . a setup."

Adele let her breath hiss out through her teeth. "What?"

"No single Sandarian who was in that room with you survived the incident," Orgustus continued, his pompous tone diminished to a whine. "Because her sisters were not sober witnesses, the empress believes the worst of you—that you interrupted them in a dalliance with Jordansson, and when her warriors came to protect the women, you had your Queen's Guard attack Jordansson and kill the warriors. I believe this is the reason that she took a hostage this morning."

"Who'd she take as a hostage?" Adele hadn't expected the empress to have the gall to retaliate while still in the Golden Palace.

"The empress has taken the steward Brien Pepper, Your Majesty," Tilburn said, tugging at the bottom of his vest again as though he couldn't get it neat enough. "The poor lad was still in shock from last night and let the warriors hold him without a fight. He had no idea what he was agreeing to. He was just trying to organize their break-fast." A button popped off his vest as he gave it a hard yank.

Adele sat back in her chair and tapped her fingernails on the shiny tabletop in a staccato of irritation. A red haze clouded the edges of her vision, and green magic glowed at her fingertips. "Ohrig," she snapped.

"I know, Your Majesty."

Adele looked into her general's pale blue eyes, seeking, and find-ing calm there. "Ready?" he asked.

She took another moment to get her temper back under control. "Let's go sort this out." She stood up and Rainere rose with her. "I want Lord Orgustus with me, and Jordansson, if you are feeling up to it, I'd like you to sit in as a witness and translator. Tilburn, you come too." Of course her QGs didn't need an invitation.

"What about Odin, Your Majesty? I think he should be there for your protection." Rainere was looking annoyed, but Adele thought a Marchant prince in the mix with his newly pregnant lover was never going to be a good idea when dealing with angry Sandarians.

"Odin can wait for me," she said, then softened her tone when she saw his panic. "I'll be fine."

"Adelena, at the very least I can translate reliably for you," he said. "I insist I be there."

It's cute how he's so worried now that I'm carrying— She shook her-self. "I said no."

"You can't be serious!" he exclaimed, but she only had time to give his hand a last squeeze of reassurance and headed out.

It was normal for the steward, Franks, to open the door for her, but he had never put himself directly in her path before.

"Your Majesty, it's one of our own being held by the Sandarians," Franks said. Hollis and Turner stepped out of their own doorways, anxiously looking her way. "If it please you, Your Majesty, Brien is a good kid, and he'll be a great steward one day."

Adele took Franks's hand but shared her words with all three stewards. "Don't worry, I'll get Brien back from the empress," she said. "He'll be on duty by dinnertime."

Franks retrieved his hand and bowed from the waist. "Thank you, Your Majesty."

"Franks, really. Her Majesty must go." Even in all the turmoil, Tilburn was embarrassed at the lack of etiquette from the head steward.

Adele felt her heart clench in her chest and suddenly wondered, *Why the hell do I keep making people these sorts of promises?* She was grateful for Ohrig's quiet cough, which told her to hurry up and get on with it. Raising her chin high, she swept out of the royal apartment to conduct her first-ever war negotiations.

CHAPTER THIRTY-THREE

"To Catch a Wizard"

Charlie was slumped in his chair as he watched the Queen's Guard, Tilburn, Lord Orgustus, and Jordansson march out after the queen. The royal apartment seemed to echo with quiet after she'd taken all the noise and action with her. Looking around for his girlfriend, he noticed that Siobhan had disappeared, probably to play with the little kids out on the sunny terrace. Adelena was still nervous about letting the children go anywhere with a party of hostile Sandarians in the palace. Charlie didn't blame her for being overprotective, but he did wonder how they were ever going to have anything like a normal life when they were always coddled in their gold-plated apartment. No matter how grand it was, a prison was still a prison.

That got him thinking about Ohren and where he could be hidden in the Golden Palace. No doubt Orestes had used all sorts of spells and enchantments to hide his twin from their sight. They hadn't even been able to find him with Orestes's magic mirror. Charlie took a slurp of his cold tea and wondered how to keep himself busy now that he'd talked himself out of looking for the high wizard. *It just seems so bloody impossible.*

"Impossible is for fools," he murmured aloud and then was annoyed with himself. Despite his mistrust, Prince Rainold was getting under Charlie's skin.

Franks opened the main door to the apartment and let in a long train of servants to clear the breakfast dishes off the table. Charlie was about to get out of their way when a wet nose snuffled his hand. He gave Hero Boy a pat and spotted a small leather shoe peeking out from beneath the table linens. Lifting a handful of fabric, he found Prince Aaron under the table, looking up at him with big eyes. *That little fella is straight-up weird,* Charlie thought. *I wonder if anyone's checked if he reads human minds as well as animals'?* "Whatcha doin', kid?" he asked the prince.

"You want to know a secret, Cheeky Charlie?" Aaron's big eyes got wider.

He grinned. "Always."

Aaron motioned for Charlie to join him under the table and crawled away. After checking that no one was watching him, he slid under the dining table and found Aaron sitting cross-legged, surrounded by the three giant puppies. Only the smaller Princess Lala thumped her tail in greeting.

"What's the deal, kid?" Charlie whispered.

Aaron rested a hand on Hero Boy's head, and the dog whined. "Hero Boy says that you smell like bad magic and blood," he said. "But I told him that you're a friend."

Charlie felt a lurch of guilt. "I'm not trying to be bad," he said. "But sometimes a good guy has to do bad things to help good people."

"You help Mummy," Aaron said. "I told Hero Boy that too."

"Look, kidling, you're starting to creep me out." He really didn't like how the dogs were watching his every move. "Start telling secrets, or I'm gone."

"What does 'turned' mean?" Aaron asked.

"It means to go from one way to the other." Charlie frowned. "Aaron, I don't have time for games, I've got to go find someone."

"I know you do," Aaron said, and he began stroking Hero Boy's head. "Did Ohren turn, Charlie? General Ohrig said he did."

Charlie took a moment to catch up. "Look, I'm sorry that your mum got hurt, but it wasn't Ohren who did that nasty spell on her. As far as I know, Ohren is still a good guy."

"It was Orestes who hurt Mummy," Aaron said, and in the dim light under the table, his little eyes started to glow in a fluorescent way, a bit like an elf's. Charlie remembered that Rip had called Aaron a pure demon abomination. Right now, he could believe it.

"How did you know about Orestes?"

"The dogs told me, and Gorrik's cat agreed with them," Aaron said. His bottom lip trembled. "I was so scared, but no one believed me. Not even Mrs. Ollenby."

"Aw, kid, that's rough when no one believes you. I know how that feels." Charlie gave Aaron's knee a squeeze, but then Bunny nudged his hand off the prince's leg.

Aaron sniffled. "Hero Boy heard Ohren screaming."

"Did he?" The hair on the back of Charlie's neck stood up.

Aaron nodded. "Orestes hurt him a lot," he said, and tears dripped off his pointy little chin. "So much screaming, Charlie."

Charlie found it hard to believe that Aaron was a four-year-old prince of Unisia. If you didn't see his white silk shirt or the velvet pantaloons, he looked like any other terrified street kitten from the Slums, waiting for life to dish out the next beating. Charlie took Aaron's hand in his. "Tell me where Ohren is," he said. "I'll go rescue him, and nothing bad will happen, I promise."

"He's in Hell," Aaron whispered, his eyes glowing with that odd light. "He's deep down in Hell, Charlie."

"Right, then I'm off to save the high wizard," Charlie said, his voice at a normal volume. "You go back to your nannies, and don't tell anyone what you've told me. All right?"

Aaron nodded. Charlie gave the kid one of his new handkerchiefs and clambered out from under the table. He stood in the middle of the living room, hands on hips, determined to do something. *Should I go barreling down to Hell and try to free Ohren myself? Or should I ask Prince Rainere in case I need one of his killing spells?* Though no magic worked inside Hell, the outside door could still be protected by all sorts of deadly traps and he'd need help with that.

He was still wondering what to do when he noticed Prince Rainold sitting on the far side of the living area. The prince was hard to spot—his green velvet jacket blended into the green brocade upholstery of the sofa. He had tucked his legs up underneath him, watching as a dozen servants tidied the apartment and cleared the breakfast dishes.

As if he could feel his gaze, Rainold raised a hand and gestured for Charlie to join him. Reluctantly, he crossed the room but had no intention of asking the mad prince for help with rescuing Ohren because he was sure that he'd need Rainere's clear head for the mission. Prince Rainold was always flipping personalities on him, angry one minute and then fragile the next.

"There are so many people in the palace, aren't there, Charlie?" Rainold whispered when he got close enough. "I'd forgotten what it's like to be surrounded by humans who want to be invisible. Like those servants over there. They don't even look at me, but they know I'm watching. I *would* talk to them, though. I know what it's like to be forgotten and lonely."

Charlie coughed into his fist, trying to think of an excuse to leave.

"Shall we go and visit with the children on the terrace?" Rainold asked, but he still had a faraway look in his eye. "That'll be nice while their mother is out, don't you think?"

"I've got stuff to do," he said. "And unless you've asked the queen's permission, I wouldn't go out there, Your Highness. She's very strict about who gets to be with them."

There was the sound of a door slamming, and Rainere left the royal nursery with Natalie clinging to his leg. He was trying to extricate himself with gentle words, pulling off one of her little hands at a time. But when she started crying, he gave up and swung her up into his arms for a hug instead. He spoke quietly, handing her a handkerchief to dry her eyes.

"My son looks like such a good father," Rainold murmured. "I wonder if he remembers how many times I held him like that. My little Rainere was always having a tantrum about one thing or another. He would stamp his sweet little foot and wail so loudly. Only I could ever comfort him."

Charlie watched Rainere with Natalie. He'd made her giggle again. "I can imagine him being a little shit," he agreed.

"Can you, Charlie?" Rainold's curiosity was sincere. "Can you see Rainere as a little boy too?"

But Charlie didn't want to engage in these weird imaginary games with the prince. Instead, he tried to catch the gaze of the pretty nanny who'd been ignoring him all morning, though he had no idea why. Rainere finally managed to placate Natalie and hand her off to Siobhan, who was hovering by his side. Even from across the room, Charlie could see that Siobhan's cheeks were rosy from blushing. He frowned as he watched her try to engage the Marchant prince in conversation before she finally got the hint and took Natalie outside to the terrace.

Rainere strode over to Charlie and his father. "I don't trust those Sandarians, so I'm going to join Her Majesty at the meeting with the empress," he told them. He was jiggling his charmed jewelry in one hand so that the pieces all tinkled together. "Father, are you quite all right?"

The young-looking, yet very old prince was staring into the distance as if listening to a conversation no one else could hear. "The air smells like vanilla, doesn't it?" he murmured.

Charlie lifted his chin and silently asked Rainere to step away. He lowered his voice. "Prince Aaron told me where the high wizard is being kept."

Rainere frowned. "How does he know?"

"He said his dogs told him," Charlie said. "And I'm not sure I can get Ohren out by myself."

"Then wait for me," Rainere snapped, and Charlie could see that he was as distracted as his father. "I must go to Adelena. If anything happens to her, I'll have to kill them all." He flew out of the apartment, moving faster than Charlie could track.

"I need that running spell craft too," Charlie muttered. He'd love to be able to move like that.

"I can teach you that, Charlie," Rainold said, his expression dreamy. "I can teach you lots of things, if you like."

"In return for what?" Charlie could guess the deal Rainold wanted.

But the prince only shrugged. "I'm a very good teacher," he said, "and I'd love to train you. It'd be so easy, as you've already got a handle on your power."

"Can you teach me that killing spell you used the other night on the thugs at the Lady Mayor's house?" Charlie asked.

"Oh, no!" Rainold shook his head. "That one's very tricky. Often it can backfire and explode you instead of your enemies. No, we should start with something easier. Like freeing Ohren."

Charlie stepped back. "Er, what?"

"Sweet boy, don't patronize me." Rainold had flipped again, suddenly very clear and focused. "You just told Rainere you knew where he was. Tell me, and I'll teach you the shadow-skipping spell." He moved two fingers in the air, like running feet.

"All right," Charlie agreed. "But you'd better keep your nastier spells close, Your Highness, because the Boss's only gone and put his brother in Hell."

Rainold jumped off the couch. "How funny!" he crowed. "Why didn't we think of that?"

Still suffering from serious misgivings, Charlie nevertheless let Rainold take the lead as they made their way to Adelena's bedchamber and through the narrow door into the secret passages, then down into the bowels of the palace. Finally stepping out from behind an old tapestry into a hallway that was lit by a few green-flamed lanterns, Charlie checked no one was on guard. They both crept along the stone floor, keeping close to the gray plaster walls, and trying not to knock against any of the ancient shields and crossed swords that hung on rusty hooks. At the very end of the hall was a large metal door covered in a map of engravings and odd runes that glowed blue. There was a keyhole cut into the middle of the door, and the handle was a solid branch that you needed to pull outward.

"How do we open it?" Rainold asked in a whisper that sounded like a shout in the quiet hall.

"The key should be close by," Charlie whispered back. "Let's check if there's a hook or something."

As they approached, a tall figure dressed in the Household Guard uniform of purple and gold stepped out of the shadows and stood in front of the huge metal door. He held two swords crossed over his chest and wore the key to Hell around his neck.

"The word?" The guard's voice was hollow and cold. It was clear from the gray film on his eyes that he'd been hypnotized. This sentinel wouldn't have the capacity to report who came to the door and who went in.

Charlie stayed well out of the way of the sword's reach. "Right, time to play a guessing game," he whispered to Rainold. "It's Orestes, so it'll be nasty."

Rainold frowned. "I presume if we get the word wrong, then that guard will impale us with those swords."

"Oh, they're not for decoration?" Charlie was nervous, and that always turned him into a smartarse.

Rainold didn't seem to mind, though. "What's most likely?" he whispered. "It could be the St. Lucidis family motto? Or it could be their mother's full name? Or it could be their father's full name? Or it could be—"

"Probably more like 'Marchant scum,'" Charlie suggested, his voice at a normal volume. He only realized what he'd done when Rainold gasped in horror.

Charlie and the prince both froze, watching as the young guard with gray eyes slowly uncrossed his swords and dropped the points to the ground.

Rainold jabbed Charlie in the ribs, then backed up a couple of steps. "See if he'll let you take it."

Charlie threw Rainold a dark look, then held his breath as he moved in and reached to take the key from around the tall guard's neck. He closed his hand around the heavy key and saw that it could be detached from its chain. He unclipped it with shaking fingers and pulled back quickly.

Now that the danger had passed, Rainold was being helpful again. He snatched the key from Charlie's sweaty grip and opened the door to Hell. "Ohren, darling?" he called into the darkness. "Darling, I'm here to rescue you!"

With a huff of impatience, Charlie pushed past the prince and strode down the hallway between the two rows of cells—open cages on one side of the stone path, the solid walls of isolation cells on the other. Green-flamed lanterns flickered as he passed them, illuminating the prison in a sickly light. Ohren wasn't in any of the cages, so he began kicking open the doors of the isolation cells and found the high wizard in the last one. Without his disguise charms, High Wizard Ohren looked like a very young man lying on the narrow cot against the wall. His face was bloody and bruised, and there was vomit pooled on the floor beneath his bed. Rainold let out a shocked sob that roused the high wizard. He groaned and waved a hand weakly. "Don't torment me, brother," he croaked. "Let me sleep."

"Darling, it's me." Rainold flew to Ohren's side and grasped his bloody hand. "It's really me."

Charlie watched as Ohren slowly came back to his senses, struggling to raise himself on an elbow. "Rainold, my love? But that's impossible."

"Impossible is for fools." Rainold was already crying. "Ohren, my darling!"

Charlie turned his back as the two men fell into each other's arms. He gave them a moment, but no more than that. "We should head back upstairs now. We've drugged Orestes, but he still might pull a quick escape somehow. Your brother's wreaked havoc while you've been lying around down here, you know?"

"Charlie's right, darling, we should go," the prince said, stroking Ohren's bloody cheek with a handkerchief. With Rainold helping him up, Ohren shuffled out of his cell and along the stone path but stopped at the main doorway, staring at the prince.

"What is it, darling?" Rainold asked.

"I'm afraid that I'm still hallucinating from the blue tonic Orestes gave me," Ohren said, his voice trembling. "And if I walk out that door, you'll disappear again."

"Oh, my poor darling."

Ohren lowered his bruised lips to touch Rainold's forehead in a gentle kiss. "You even smell like Rainold," he whispered.

"Yes, that's because he is Prince Rainold." Charlie was well past impatient now. "You really think if you were dreaming of your man, you'd put me in the dream too, High Wizard?"

Ohren raised an eyebrow. "No, never," he said, and Charlie liked the clarity that came into the wizard's eyes. "I just can't believe it's true."

"Well, congratulations!" Charlie gestured at the open door of Hell and plastered on a smile. "Any day now, gentlemen."

The prince and wizard made their way to the tapestry that hid the secret passage while Charlie carefully returned the key to the neck of the guard. He jumped a mile when the guard swept up the two swords to cross them at his chest again. Standing on his tiptoes, Charlie chanced leaning in close to the guard's face and decided that he sort of looked like QG Leith. Charlie liked Leith, even considered him a brother. *For certain this poor cat never volunteered to be a hypnotized guard at the door to Hell.*

"Charlie, I need your help," Rainold called out.

Charlie went to Ohren, who was now slumped against the doorway of the secret passage, and helped Rainold lug him inside.

The Marchant guest suite was closer than Ohren's bedchamber, so they headed there. Tumbling out the narrow doorway, Charlie immediately opened the two tall windows of the suite, pushing back the full-length, black damask curtains to let sunshine and fresh air into the stuffy room—and also to help with Ohren's smell. After a few days in Hell, his odor was very ripe.

Rainold put the high wizard in bed and pulled the silk sheets up to his chin. "I'm going to get you some medical supplies from Rainere's lab, darling," he told Ohren and kissed his nose. "Then we'll get you cleaned up."

"You're all the medicine I need, my love, but it does hurt so much." Ohren groaned in pain and let Rainold fuss over him.

Charlie stood by the window, looking out over the manicured gardens of the Golden Palace. There were people everywhere, walking in pairs or groups, laughing, picnicking. *No one knows that right now the queen is fighting to keep Unisia safe from war with Sandar. No one knows that I just saved the life of the high wizard himself.* But Charlie couldn't help wondering why it all felt like such an anticlimax. He needed something else to do. Something worse or more dangerous than he'd already done.

"I'll ask him, shall I?" Rainold called out, "Oh, Charlie?" He was now lying on the bed next to Ohren, his jacket on the floor and his shirt undone. "Charlie, be a dear and take our sleeping Orestes down to Hell for me. I'll give you the spell to carry him, and I'm sure you remember the way through the secret passages, yes?"

Charlie tensed, careful not to betray his excitement. "Yes," he said. "What's the spell?"

"Rainold, you better go too," Ohren said. "What if Charlie can't cope?"

"Oh, Ohren, you always underestimate people," Rainold scoffed. "Charlie is stronger than he looks and the spell is quite simple."

The spell was actually very complex, but Charlie memorized it word by exacting word, as well as the gestures needed to guide the body suspended in midair.

"Now, be careful at the door, because the spell will fail—no magic can be used in Hell," Rainold reminded him. "You'll have to drag Orestes into a cell yourself."

Charlie allowed himself a grin. "I've moved bodies before," he said. "I know what to do."

"See, Ohren, Charlie knows what to do." Rainold snuggled down next to the wizard. "He'll take care of Orestes while you and I catch up."

Ohren groaned, and this time it didn't sound like pain. Charlie didn't look back. He dashed out of the room and made his way to Rainere's laboratory. He broke the protective charm on the door and pushed it open so hard that it slammed against the wall. Orestes was still tied to the chair, head slumped on his chest as he snored.

"Boss," Charlie called out softly. "You and me get to have some alone time now."

Orestes didn't move, and Charlie didn't have to control his dark appetite any longer.

CHAPTER THIRTY-FOUR

"Beneath the Willow Trees"

The Garden Wing was a catastrophe. In the light of day, Adele could see just what destruction the evil mage and his magic had wrought. The entire building was filled with rubble, the glass ceiling now open to the sky. The beautiful marble floors were cracked and buckled, leaving great slabs sticking up at odd angles.

Instead of moving to another wing, the Sandarians had set up camp within the Lily Pond Gardens. Adele spotted the empress was sitting under a colorful silk canopy with a fringed border. It reminded her uncomfortably of the first time she had met the empress, under a tent on a beautiful beach in Sandar. She'd been so nervous about disappointing this imposing woman that she'd made a total fool of herself.

And what's really changed? she wondered. *This goddamn empress is still running rings around me.* She couldn't help but admire how adroitly Sanda'hani had managed a volatile situation. Her charge for war had forced Adele to offer hospitality in the hope of a diplomatic resolution but had only opened her home to the real danger of the mage. Then Sanda'hani's vile accusations of a setup had forced Adele, as the opposing queen, to come to meet Sanda'hani's terms instead of the other way around. All the while, Sanda'hani had the courage to risk the wrath of Unisia, a far more powerful kingdom, playing the odds that her empire's small Fire Orchid industry was worth the trouble.

At the edge of a lily pond, Adele paused. She felt sweaty in her heavy dress of pale pink satin, but also hungry and a little nauseous as she contemplated what was at risk if she failed in negotiations with Sanda'hani today. *But I think I'd rather face down a dragon than an angry pregnant woman.* She dropped the hand that had gravitated to her belly. It was far too early to feel anything, but that didn't stop her from imagining there was a flutter where the baby would be.

"Are you all right, Your Majesty?" Ohrig asked. "You've got that dragon temper of yours held tight?"

"The magic hasn't bothered me all morning," she answered. "But my instincts tell me that's because of what happened yesterday."

Ohrig grunted. "Just as well, you can keep your head now when you need it most."

"Look at what the empress has done." Captain Lucky sounded impressed. "We have to walk through this little bridge of land between the ponds to reach her, essentially crossing a bottleneck. When we get to that island, there'll be hardly room for us to draw our swords, but her warriors with their hand tridents will be very comfortable."

"She's very practical," Adele admitted, thankful she had Lucky to see what she hadn't recognized as a danger. "But I suppose when you're a small empire, you need to use all your skills just to pull equal to a big, arrogant one like Unisia."

"Speaking of arrogant." Ohrig huffed as Lord Orgustus inserted himself between them.

"Your Majesty, may I ask what the holdup is?" Orgustus gestured at the Household Guard, who had gathered in bright, untidy ranks at the entrance of the land bridge to the little island. "We should join the Sandarians before any offense can be inferred by our just standing here staring at them."

"So keen to join your lover?" Adele said, and was glad to see Orgustus flinch. "As my captain just pointed out, walking into a bottleneck and sitting on an island surrounded by deep ponds is probably not the best idea for our safety. So I'm changing the playing field, if that pleases you, Lord Orgustus?"

As he had proved time and again, Orgustus was pompous, but he wasn't stupid. Surveying the tactical position of the Sandarians and their still-hefty group of warriors, he quickly concurred that she was right. To make up for his lack of judgment, the young lord even volunteered to accompany the empress's sisters as they were brought from the palatial suite where they had been interned.

Adele gave her new instructions to Tilburn, who set to work and within minutes had dozens of servants setting up an elegant garden party, complete with long tables, chairs with silk-covered cushions, and white tablecloths. While the teams were working, Adele wandered around the flowerbeds and ponds, keeping her distance from the Sandarians but staying where they could track her movements. She needed to appear unhurried and calm, hoping it would translate to the coming talks.

She found a carved wooden bench in the shade and sat. Ohrig leaned against a tree next to her. "So?"

She looked up at her general. "So?"

"His Highness was pleased with the news of your condition, I take it?" Ohrig muttered, too low for anyone but her milling QGs to hear.

"I don't think he understands what it means yet." Adele fiddled with the beading on her sash. "Sure, he's overjoyed to potentially be a father but then completely glossed over the part when I said the baby will be the living incarnation of Dahk'hani."

Ohrig considered this. "You can bet it's going to be a shitload of trouble."

"And probably the biggest yet." Adele squinted across the ponds at the Sandarians, who had started to pick up on the fact that their hosts wouldn't be joining them on their little island. "I just don't know how I'm going to deal with the kingdom, the children, and the

Marchant Eldar problem along with a new god-baby. But mostly I'm worried that this thing might kill me."

"I'm worried about that too," Ohrig said.

And seeing her own fear reflected in his face made Adele feel like crying. "I get really fat when I'm pregnant," she joked, hoping to dispel the tears she really didn't have time for. "Like, really huge."

"Yeah?" Ohrig's lips twitched but didn't quite make a smile. "I'll look forward to seeing that."

"Your Majesty, Lord Orgustus is back and the Sandarians are on the move," Captain Lucky announced.

Adele's stomach was twisted in knots when, finally, Lord Orgustus made his appearance with the empress's four sisters, dressed in St. Lucidis court gowns of velvet and lace, glittering jewels in their hair. They weren't weeping, but all four looked terrified. Adele hoped she could capitalize on that, as their fear would be Sanda'hani's primary motivator. Exhausted by the hideous events of the previous day and the responsibility on her shoulders now, she held on to the coils of her green magic tightly and instead called the leonine gold to fill her mind.

"Let's get this over with," she told her men, and moved to join the party.

The meeting table had been set under a canopy and draped in white tulle and wreaths of flowers, looking festive and very pretty. Adele instructed the four sisters to sit side by side at the end of the table and took her own place in the middle of one long side but didn't sit down. Empress Sanda'hani and her entourage moved at a sedate pace, and she had to wait so they, as the two monarchs, could sit at the same moment. The Queen's Guard ranged themselves behind her, and she heard Lucky muttering for all to be alert for trouble.

"Empress Sanda'hani, welcome," Adele said when the empress finally sat before her. "I hope you are well recovered from last night?"

Sanda'hani didn't return her courtesy. Her eyes were like chips of pale green glass, but when she spoke, her voice was thin and reedy. Adele guessed that nausea was holding sway over her, and with the stress and heat of the day, it was no wonder. "Queen Adelena, I demand an explanation!"

"You will demand nothing, Your Grace," she replied, ignoring the muttering that broke out among the Sandarians. "You brought an evil mage into the Golden Palace, and last night, two of your sisters tried to kill my guest and then me." She spread her arms to encompass Jordansson, covered in bandages, sitting at her right hand. "As you can see, they failed. I cannot be destroyed by Dahk'hani's servants, nor can those under my protection."

Empress Sanda'hani raised her chin. "I cannot believe my sisters would attempt such sacrilege," she said.

Adele flicked her wrist in a signal for Tilburn to help the two accused sisters to their feet and bring them forward. The two women looked as ill as Jordansson, their lips white and their eyes bloodshot. At a word from Sanda'hani, the sisters started speaking in Sandarian, launching into a lengthy description of the previous night's events.

Adele poked Jordansson in the thigh. "What're they saying?"

But Jordansson was wrapped up in the story and didn't even hear her. Suddenly, with his lips on her ear, Rainere-as-Odin began translating the sisters' tale of vision quests, haunted dreams, and murder. They had both personally poisoned the coconut rum which was served to their St. Lucidian guests at the party. They said that Jordansson had been chosen by Dahk'hani at the time of his birth and it was destined that his blood be the conduit for the god to transcend his world beneath Evendaar and fuse with the magic within the queen so she could carry him in his new incarnation, allowing him to walk the world.

Adele felt ill hearing all this and could only be grateful that no one else present from her court could understand what the sisters were saying.

"She says everything was perfect in the eyes of the god Dahk'hani," Rainere whispered. His smoke-and-spice cologne wafted over Adele, and she felt a spike of lust despite the horror she was listening to.

"Your Majesty, if you could focus on something other than me," he muttered with a feather-light kiss on her ear. "The sister with long hair said that the mage was to be your midwife, that he would cut the god out from your living body when the time was right." Rainere growled. "I'm so glad you killed that creature, *cara mia*, because I certainly would've."

Adele swallowed a sigh. "I can only hope he stays dead this time."

The morning was creeping toward midday as the sisters continued recounting their nightmarish tale of spirit possession. Adele's stomach growled with hunger and she wondered how much longer this was going to take. She tried to surreptitiously reach for a plate of cookies in front of Jordansson.

"*Cara mia*, are you not well?" Rainere-as-Odin asked, but she just shook her head because she needed him to concentrate. The empress's two sisters were winding up their story to the most crucial part of the retelling—her arrival with her Queen's Guard. According to Rainere's translation, the sisters were instructed to trigger the spell that allowed the mage to absorb Adele's willpower, thereby crippling her enough that he could drag her into the lava chamber, where he would keep her.

"My willpower?" Adele whispered to Rainere, thinking he might've mistranslated. "Why didn't he just have them tie me up with that magic rope?"

"Because he was afraid that you would still have the strength to fight," Rainere muttered. "The mage told them to bind the strongest part of you, your power of will. Now they're saying that the warriors were hypnotized by the mage through the two sisters. They'd been made—that's awful!" Rainere pulled up short in surprise. "The twelve warriors had been made wards of the spell. That means their souls were pulled into the spell—they were no longer men as such, but," he searched for an example, "like the unburned fuel in a sacred fire. They were only symbolic of men, or perhaps more—"

"I get it! They were dead inside," Ohrig growled at Rainere. "But we still had to kill what were twelve good men, all with families and lives of their own. Those deaths are on us."

Adele sipped more water, grateful that the Sandarians had finished their account. "Empress Sanda'hani, have you heard enough?" she asked. "I know I have."

"My sweet sisters do not lie," Sanda'hani said, her beautiful face crumpled with sadness. "Yet their actions were not their own because they were possessed by the spirit of the mage murdered by your hand, Your Majesty. The mage took my innocent sisters as his victims and was able to channel his hatred and lust through them because *you* had bewitched our most beloved god, Dahk'hani. Twelve of my precious warriors were killed because the mage used them as fuel to call *you*!" Sanda'hani raised both arms from her sides. "Look well, Queen of Unisia! Look at the devastation your arrogance has—"

But Adele pointed across the table, green sparks dripping over the linen tablecloth. "Don't say another word!"

Sanda'hani dropped her arms, and Adele saw the empress give up on a last attempt to save the pride of Sandar.

"I am a pawn of your god," Adele said, "and I have to live with the fact that he is using me to bring himself back into the world."

The empress pressed a hand against her abdomen, where life stirred within her too. "I know you're in pain, Queen Adelena," she whispered.

"You have no idea of what I'm dealing with, Empress Sanda'hani."

The empress stared, and Adele stared right back. There was too much to say in front of unfriendly eyes. Making a spontaneous decision, Adele stood up. "I think we need to talk elsewhere, woman to woman," she said.

The empress rose to her feet, nodding. "I think we've earned the privilege."

Adele snatched up the plate of cookies and followed Sanda'hani back to the little island among the lily ponds. It was peaceful beneath the willow trees and much cooler than sitting under a hot canopy in the sunshine. They settled themselves on heaped piles of silk cushions, and Adele kicked off her shoes. She offered Sanda'hani a cookie, and both women nibbled as they enjoyed the relief of the shade away from prying eyes.

"How far along are you?" Adele asked.

"Not more than a few blood cycles," Sanda'hani admitted. "I should be at home but I had to act when the Marchant Eldars flew over our court. You must believe, I had no knowledge of our god's plans for you to be his vessel or the visions Dahk'hani had sent my sisters. They hid this when they incited me to come here to declare war."

"Well, I'm sorry that I don't know why the Eldars and Dahk'hani appeared in Sandar and Unisia at the same time. I hate that he's planted himself inside me against my will. And I'm scared that my life might end when he chooses to be born," Adele replied, reminding the empress that she carried the greatest weight in this situation. "But I'm going to do everything in my power to survive this weird pregnancy and I am serious about wanting to make peace between your empire and my kingdom. What will it take for you to trust me again?"

"I want Ripenzo Shale back," Sanda'hani said quickly, like she couldn't help herself. "He wasn't just a lover—I love him. It's his child I carry."

"Did he ever take off his disguise and let you see his real face?" Adele asked, still feeling shame that she was the reason that Sanda'hani and Ripenzo had lost each other.

Sanda'hani nodded, and her gaze flickered with deep emotions. "Did you see his real face too, when you lay with him?"

Adele shook her head. "Rip and I were never lovers," she assured the empress. "It was for Serena's prophecy that he left you to come with me to Unisia. We share a family connection but I'm pretty sure Rip hates me with the passion of a thousand suns now."

"Oh, Unisians and their cursed prophecies." The empress reached for another cookie from Adele's plate. "Serena is a fickle bitch with her poetry and promises. At least Dahk'hani asks his people for what he wants with words we can understand."

Adele looked down to her midriff. "I'm not one of his people, and he didn't ask me."

Sanda'hani was surprised. "Dahk'hani is a fair and loving god—he would not take what was not offered to him freely. Did you not ask for a gift from him? Or his help in some matter?"

Adele remembered a vision of sitting in the palm of the god and swearing she would find the dragon for her child and he had given her magic to heal herself. "I suppose I got Stella back, and Dahk'hani took my body in recompense," she admitted. "But to be a pawn of the gods is some painful kind of luck, Your Grace. I would not wish it on anyone. Not even to save a—" She snapped her mouth shut before she could lie.

"Exactly, Adelena." Sanda'hani using her name wasn't lost on Adele. "We would do anything for our children."

She nodded. "Has Dahk'hani ever tried to be reborn before?"

Sanda'hani shook her head slowly. "I can't say that I have ever heard of this, but the mage would've known better than I," she said. "I only know that our god has slept peacefully for over a thousand years in his volcano home. Why he would choose to be born to a demon St. Lucidian queen now—these questions are not for mortals to answer."

"Personally, I'm very curious as to what Dahk'hani wants in this world, especially if he'll kill me to get here," Adele said. "My children deserve to keep their mother."

"As my own child deserves a father," Sanda'hani said. "We believe that if the father is not present when the baby enters the world, its spirit may wander free of the body. Sandarians would not accept my negligence in having my own child without her blond, blue-eyed father at the birth. The fathers of my four children all committed themselves to me before I conceived. Ripenzo also made that commitment."

Adele realized the time had come to bargain. It wouldn't assuage her own guilt, but at least she could help Sanda'hani in some small way. "I don't know where he is, so I can't give you Rip, but who else would you like to take?"

"I want your former regent, Lord Orgustus," Sanda'hani said, making it clear she'd planned for this eventuality. "He is clever and speaks proudly, just like Ripenzo. He's also very handsome in a similar way and is young, so he will have a lot of energy to be a father. Orgustus has a strong streak of magic, and it will not be strange when his child is born with power like him." She reached for another cookie. "He makes love like an overeager boy, but that I can teach."

Adele raised a cookie to her lips and nibbled. *This was my plan all along, but can I get rid of Orgustus so easily?* She felt a stab of guilty pleasure. *He is completely untrustworthy, and though our alliance works for him now, he is sure to turn on me any chance he gets.*

"I realize that the man is very important to you," Sanda'hani said, misreading her silence. "And you might even love him, as he does you. I don't want to cause you the same pain that I suffered when I sent Ripenzo away, but I must ask for the best man in your court. The prestige that he brings as your personal advisor and lover will repair the pride of my people. After such defeat at your hands, I must think of that too."

Adele thought she should probably put up a bit of protest so Sanda'hani didn't feel like the young lord was too easily given. She turned her gaze to the table, where the St. Lucidians were milling around with the Sandarians. Lunch had started while the monarchs discussed the future of their nations under the willow trees. "Yes, I do love Orgustus, and for that, he will not go easily with you," she warned. "He is devoted to me, doesn't speak Sandarian, and he hates leaving the Golden Palace."

"He will leave if his queen insists," Sanda'hani said.

"In Unisia we do not treat our citizens like slaves," Adele retorted. "I can *ask* Lord Orgustus to join you, but he will lose his rank in the court, and he'll hate that as much as leaving me."

"Former regent is not a rank," Sanda'hani scoffed. "It is a *former* rank. Give him a new one. Perhaps the royal Unisian ambassador to Sandar?"

Adele cast Sanda'hani a sharp glance. That was the reverse of the role Adele had offered Ripenzo. "He hates the ocean," she continued.

"He will learn to swim."

"He would want to be your equal and would never consent to sit at your feet, no matter how soft the cushion."

"He'll learn to like kneeling, then."

"Sanda'hani, please!"

"I swear on the life of my unborn child, I need a man exactly like him, Adelena."

Adele sighed as if she had given up the fight. "After my betrayal with Ripenzo Shale, I know I owe you this, so I will do as you ask. Orgustus will be furious with us both. He's going to be terrible company for you on your journey home."

"I have my ways of winning over a reluctant man." Sanda'hani smiled and, for just a moment, looked like a saucy young woman instead of an imposing empress.

Adele hoped after this that she could have Sanda'hani as a friend instead of an adversary, but knew nothing was so simple for monarchs. "All right," she agreed.

"And I'd like to keep that little steward Brien too. We can't understand a word he says, but he is very sweet."

"Out of the question." Adele was firm.

"Surely we can negotiate?"

"Nope."

"Very well, just Lord Orgustus."

"We're agreed." Adele offered her hand to Sanda'hani to help her up from the cushions, and the two women walked back to the negotiating table. Adele found she couldn't look at Orgustus as she took her seat next to him.

"Your Majesty?" Orgustus leaned close to her shoulder. "Did everything go well?"

Adele pressed her lips in a hard line, ignoring him. "If I may have the court's attention?" she called out. She darted a glance at General

Ohrig, who gave her a reassuring nod. "The Empress Sanda'hani and I have come to an agreement. In return for dropping her suit for war with Unisia, the empress will return peaceably to Sandar. To reward her remarkable comprehension of what has been a very unusual and complex situation, I have decided to build upon this relationship with Sandar and propose to open a new ambassadorial embassy in the Sandarian court."

Adele took a deep breath and let it out, sweating under the strain of having to stand by her word. "As a gesture of friendship, I have given the choice of first royal Unisian ambassador to Sandar to my fellow monarch. Empress Sanda'hani has bestowed that honor on the shoulders of our own beloved Lord Orgustus St. Lucidis. Lord Orgustus will accompany the empress and her entourage back to Sandar when they leave the court."

A horrified hush fell over the Unisian party.

"We will leave for our court in Sandar tomorrow at sunrise," Empress Sanda'hani announced, and the Sandarians broke out into loud, raucous cheers.

By mutual accord, Adele and Sanda'hani nodded and ended the meeting. Adele marched inside the palace as quickly as she could, with all her people hurrying to keep up. Of course, Lord Orgustus maintained pace next to her on his long legs. "Your Majesty, please!"

Adele held up her hand for silence. "Royal apartment. Now, my lord."

Tilburn streaked ahead of the party so that when they arrived, afternoon tea was set up on the dining table, fresh scented candles had been lit, and all the balcony doors were open to catch the afternoon breezes. With a sigh of relief, Adele took her seat at the head of the table and didn't much care where anyone else sat. She drank almost an entire jug of water and then shoved a tiny sandwich in her mouth, swallowing it before shouting, "Someone tell me where Brien is and if he's all right."

"I'm all good, Your Maj-esty," Brien called out from the main door. He approached Adele and bowed low. "I'd like to thank you for having me released, Your Majesty. The empress good as promised that she would take me back to Sandar with her, and I was ever so scared she'd get her way. I know I'm just a junior steward, but it means the world that you'd fight for me."

"Him! You negotiated for this *boy*, but you will let her take *me*?" Orgustus sounded furious, but Adele could see the man was terrified. She reached for his hand where it rested on the table and gave it a pat.

"My lord, the empress has fallen in love with you," she said. "It happened last night—apparently lying together is very serious to the Sandarians."

"No!" It was Jordansson who yelled this time. The tribesman jumped to his feet, his chair tipping to the carpet behind him. "To worship a woman is fine, but it means nothing for the future. You're lying to Orgustus, just like you lied to me and Dahk'hani lied to me. He only needed my blood and magic. He didn't want me to be the father of your child at all." Jordansson began ranting in his own tongue, gesticulating wildly and pointing at Adele a lot. She took the chance to shove a few more sandwiches in her mouth and chew them before he wanted an answer.

Rainere appeared, having removed his Odin disguise, and took a seat on her other side. He kissed her cheek and laughed quietly at Jordansson. "Calm down," he told the furious tribesman. "You've been played for a fool, as we all have. Gods toy with us, queens and savages alike. There is no blame here."

"But there is blame, and it's on my head," Orgustus said, crestfallen. "Your Majesty, I know I made a mistake falling into the empress's bed and telling her I had your heart when we both know I don't. But please, I beg you, don't let her take me to that goddess-forsaken desert with the water monsters."

Adele brushed the crumbs from her hands. "Actually, Sandar is very beautiful, my lord, and I think you might be surprised. I mean, yes, their court is made up of tents on the beach, and they sometimes sleep in tree houses, but there is no pomp and ceremony there. You can wear comfortable clothes and swim when it's hot. It's very relaxing."

Orgustus could only stare, aghast. Adele had just described his worst nightmare. "Anyway," she continued, "you should know that I did put up a fight for you, but you were cursed by your own success in charming the empress, something which I've never managed. Sanda'hani wants to take someone special in recompense for her dead soldiers and traumatized sisters. Our united front and your speeches—well, we played right into her hands. She told me that she wouldn't drop the suit for war without a man as important as you for her political hostage."

Orgustus gaped. "I'm to be imprisoned in Sandar?"

"No, no, of course not!" Adele worried she'd gone too far. "In fact, she would like you to sit, uh, beside her and teach her the ways of Unisian court politics, trade strategy, economics. You know, all the things that you're good at." Lying made her mouth dry, so she took a sip of water. "And then, in return for your supervised freedom, you would have the opportunity to become better acquainted with the empress in a romantic way."

"Never!" Orgustus shouted. "Should you release me to that cursed woman, I will never utter a word to her. I will be the worst ambassador in the history of Unisian ambassadors. She will come to hate me."

Adele barely stopped herself saying "Like I do." Because she didn't hate Orgustus anymore. The last few days had shown her that while the young lord was very much an arrogant jerk, he was also excellent at his job and loved the citizens of the kingdom of Unisia. Adele suddenly knew she shouldn't let him go.

Jordansson had taken his seat again, but his chin rested in both palms, and the poor guy looked utterly miserable at the mess that he found himself in. A flicker of gold magic lit her brain, and Adele knew it was time to move to the very shaky stage two of her plan. "My lord, I know you would never behave in such a terrible way. It would not only shame you but Unisia and her queen." She raised her voice to admonish Orgustus but her gaze darted to Jordansson to gauge if he was listening too. "If it is any consolation, the empress herself suggested that she would love to have a child with curly blond hair and blue eyes. Then you would get to be father to a prince or princess in Sandar."

"Never!" Orgustus roared and slammed his fist on the table.

"You didn't seem to have a problem with her last night, and the empress is very beautiful." Adele shrugged like there was no pleasing him. "Together you'll make beautiful babies."

"I'll be a *slave*, both political and sexual. If I had a child by her, it would tie me to Sandar for the rest of my life," Orgustus said, his voice choked with helpless fury.

Rainere was chuckling and started to say something to her, but Adele reached under the table and pinched his knee hard enough to shut him up. She held her breath, waiting for Jordan Jordansson to catch up with the conversation. With all the talk of babies, it didn't take long.

"Orgustus, my friend, are you sick in your head?" Jordansson slammed his own fist on the table. "You would give up a seat by the side of Empress Sanda'hani in her Sandar court just to keep your place here? I like you, Orgustus, but you have no friends in this palace! No woman loves you, and you are a grown man with no children of your own. Empress Sanda'hani is offering you paradise, and you give it up for secrets and lies and all these fucking clothes with buttons and buckles!" Jordansson pulled open his own sweaty shirt, buttons popping all over the table. "Just for being here, my god, Dahk'hani, has turned his back on me. Maybe he thinks I too want empty promises, but I do not. I want honesty and a strong woman to worship and carry my children. I want to go!"

"Jordansson, I'm so very sorry," Adele said, and she meant it. "But Empress Sanda'hani asked specifically for Lord Orgustus. She said she wants a baby with his powerful magic and beautiful blue eyes. She was very clear about needing a man who was intelligent and strong, who could fight for Sandar."

Lord Orgustus groaned and covered his face with his hands.

"No, Orgustus, don't cry," Jordansson said, suddenly determined. "I will go to the empress, and I will beg her to leave you here in this terrible place. Then I will beg her to take me to Sandar instead. Are we agreed, my friend?"

Orgustus slumped back in his chair. "Go and do your best," he said. "You have my thanks for trying anything."

Jordansson sprinted out of the room with Tilburn streaking behind him, shouting about protocol and begging him to dress properly first.

"I don't suppose he'll have any luck," Orgustus said. "So in that case I will pack and start my goodbyes, Your Majesty. My father is not well, and it might be the last time I see him alive."

"I'm so sorry, I didn't know." Adele felt awful. She remembered the withered old regent from her earliest meetings and could never quite understand how he had fathered such a young man as Orgustus. The lord bowed and left the room.

"And I understand now," Rainere murmured, leaning in to kiss her cheek. "You are a clever woman."

"Only if it works." She slid her hand up his thigh in apology for the pinch. "Orgustus is a pain in my neck, but he is useful. Poor Jordansson is fed up with us and broken-hearted about his god treating him so badly. If they can swap positions, it would be ideal for me."

The children ran inside from the terrace, dripping with water from the ponds. "Mummy, you're still here!"

Adele and Rainere took turns hugging the children, and then they pestered Rainere to join them outside. The day had been so tense, and Adele was tired of feeling anxious, always trying to plot a few steps ahead. She was exhausted by Jordansson's heartbreak, and

Orgustus's fury, and Sanda'hani's upset. She needed an escape, and she was going to take one.

"Don't you want me to come too?" Adele asked, tugging at Natalie's long, dark braid.

Natalie's eyes were round. "Can you really play with us?"

Adele scooped her daughter into her arms and squeezed her hard enough to make her giggle. "I have all the time in the world for you, my sweethearts," she said, then remembered Charlie had wanted to speak with her. She looked over her shoulder but realized she hadn't seen him since breakfast. "Unless I should go and find our cheeky Charlie first."

"No, *cara mia*," Rainere spoke firmly. "Come and enjoy our family."

Adele smiled. *Our family*. She felt a definite flutter in her abdomen. *Maybe this is what Dahk'hani has wanted all along.*

CHAPTER THIRTY-FIVE

"Leaving Her Lord"

Lady Olivia didn't know if waiting for Lord Orgustus in his apartment was the best idea, but she seemed to be out of good ideas right now. Her head was still pounding from the coconut rum she'd had last night, and her tongue felt dry and furry.

Groaning, she lay back on Orgustus's couch and cuddled the little black cat close. Gorrik's cat seemed to make a habit of seeking her out, and Olivia liked his company. Growing up on a farm, she'd always been surrounded by animals, and she missed that now that she lived in the Golden Palace.

"What am I going to do, kitty?" Olivia swept her hand over the cat's ears. "I wanted to upset the queen by innocently torturing Captain Lucky, not humiliate myself by getting caught in bed with her enemy."

Not that Olivia regretted her actions. She'd never been seduced by a woman as intimidating as Empress Sanda'hani, and it had been wonderful. Then Lord Orgustus had jumped in with the two of them, and things had become all sorts of fun. *Just like back on the farm,* Olivia thought, wistful. Things like threesomes just weren't done among aristocrats in the Golden Palace, or if they were, it was kept very quiet. Both women and men were expected to be restrained in their romantic associations, which were only applauded if there was a political gain for either party. Olivia could always play the game by her own rules but poor Captain Lucky was court born and bred. She knew he must have been horrified to see his intended naked in bed with anyone but him. "I guess Lucky isn't going to want to marry me anymore," she informed the cat and was rewarded with even deeper purring. "Not that I'm complaining, but what can I do now?"

There was a crash as the door flew open and hit the wall. Lord Orgustus entered, cursing. She sat up on the couch, catching the cat before he could fall. "Orgustus?"

Orgustus slammed the door closed with a heavy hand and strode to the couch, throwing himself down next to her and grabbing Olivia in his arms so fast that she yelped in surprise. He buried his face in her neck. "Olivia, I'm done for," he said with a moan.

Oh, please goddess, don't let him start crying, she thought. "Tell me what's wrong, my love."

Orgustus detached and slumped back on the cushions. "Empress Sanda'hani wants to take me to Sandar as her political hostage and damned concubine."

Despite herself, Olivia gasped. "No! The queen won't let her."

Orgustus wiped his eye. "It's done. I'm to leave tomorrow morning with the Sandarians," he said. "Unless . . ."

"Unless?"

"Unless Jordansson can talk the empress into taking him instead." Orgustus sighed gustily. "But it won't work. The queen said Sanda'hani specifically asked for me so as to cause as much heartache for Unisia as she could. Queen Adelena cannot run this kingdom without me, and Sanda'hani knows that."

"Oh, but what about me?" Olivia bit her lip to stop herself from exposing her own fear of the queen's retribution.

But of course Orgustus thought she was concerned about losing him. He stroked her cheek. "Sweet Olivia, I'm sorry that our time together has to end like this," he said. "I will always remember you fondly."

Olivia's gaze dropped to the cat still in her lap, her mind racing. "Oh, Orgustus," she whispered. "I'd hoped that you and I—I mean, I'd really only been trying to make you jealous by staying with Captain Lucky."

"I know, darling." Orgustus lapped up her lie so fast she smiled. "But if you'd like, I could set you up with my dear friend, Lord Pine? He's not nearly as clever as you, but he's handsome enough, and his Carparell bloodline will keep you in court if the queen fires you."

Olivia's smile froze and cracked.

"What is it?" Orgustus's sharp gaze didn't miss anything. "What's wrong with Pine?"

Olivia raised her chin. "As it turns out, he likes to take what isn't freely offered."

Orgustus understood the crime immediately. "I'll kill him," he snarled with enough venom to make Olivia recoil.

"Oh, no, you can't!" She hoped she hadn't taken it too far with her vague suggestion. "You'd only make a scandal, and I'll be sent back to the farm so fast no one will remember I was ever here."

"I'll make sure it doesn't lead back to you," Orgustus promised. His cheeks were red with genuine fury. Olivia was touched by his passion to defend her honor. *Maybe I misjudged Orgustus, and he's more decent than I—*

"How dare he take what's mine!" Orgustus fumed. "How dare Pine touch a woman I specifically told him was mine. I'll humiliate him, Olivia! The Carparells will all pay for what Pine did, and they'll know what happens to them is his fault."

And there's the real Orgustus. "How are you going to do anything from Sandar?" she asked spitefully.

"I'll do what I can before I leave, my love," he promised.

Olivia guessed this was the best she would get out of him, so she stood up. "I'm sorry, Orgustus," she said. "The queen is being so stupid, and I'll miss you terribly."

He reached for her hand and pulled her back down to his side. "I'll miss you too, my Olivia. I'd like to show you how much."

Olivia always liked Orgustus when he was playful. "Sorry, but right now, I have to grovel before my intended."

"Lucky is a fool not to have you in his bed," Orgustus said. "If I were him, I wouldn't take my hands off you." He kissed the back of her hand, then her finger. "And I'd put a ring right here."

"Would you?" Olivia didn't even pretend to believe him.

Orgustus frowned, as if confused himself. "Yes, I think I really would," he replied. "You are the most beautiful and conniving woman I've ever met. We'd be perfect together."

Olivia picked up the cat, who still purred at her feet. "I can't break it off with Captain Lucky now," she said, returning his surprising honesty with her own. "And I still need to know if the queen is going to accuse me of treason."

"Queen Adelena didn't accuse me, and it was the same offense," Orgustus said, his confidence, as ever, rock solid. "Anyway, I told her we were drugged and coerced into Sanda'hani's bed."

Olivia could only hope he was right.

"So, if you've already committed one infidelity?" Orgustus patted his thighs.

"I guess I'm not really in the mood to beg forgiveness on my knees," she said, and slid onto his lap.

"How about I'm the one on my knees?" Orgustus murmured, and she felt a flare of excitement. He'd never put any effort into giving her pleasure before.

Olivia let go of the cat and slipped her arms around his neck. "I would like that very much," she said.

Chapter Thirty-Six

"A Glad Farewell"

Adele woke early the next morning in the Glass Bed, facing Rainere, her head pillowed on his outflung arm, her leg hooked over his thigh. She could see that he was still asleep, even if one part of him was very much awake.

Craning her head to look out the balcony doors, she noted that it was still dark outside and snuggled back in against his chest. It was delicious waking with his smoky, spicy scent on her skin. Unfortunately, they hadn't made love last night because the children had kept them busy coming in and out, first demanding that Rainere tell them dozens of stories, then demanding their mother come and "keep the bad dreams away" while they slept. She knew that it was still early days for their recovery from all the new traumas, and she was happy to stay close if it made them feel better. It wasn't until the early hours of the morning that she finally got to keep her promise to join Rainere in bed. But her prince was already snoring, and she didn't have the heart to wake him up.

It was so quiet in her bedchamber that Adele could hear the birds chirping their morning songs out on the balcony. She rolled to her back, wondering how she'd fallen asleep. Feeding on Rainere's magic had meant that she never needed sleep, normally. She guessed that it was being pregnant that had changed things. Though it'd only been a short night, she felt rested. It was also a relief not to have the dragon magic racing around her body making her want to kill someone.

I feel normal again. She stretched her arms over her head and reveled in the thought. It had been so long since she had only herself and two magics for company. *Sleeping soundly, getting time with my family, and solving the Sandar war with hardly any bloodshed. Life is finally going my way.*

Adele sent up a quick prayer for the twelve warriors who'd been killed by her QGs yesterday and hoped they were with their god. *Oh, except that Dahk'hani is growing inside me, so how...?* She quickly pushed the thought away. She wanted one more quiet minute before the reality of life as queen of Unisia and a pawn of the gods came crashing back over her.

Rolling over, she buried her nose in Rainere's neck, licking the pulse point where it throbbed against her tongue. Rainere mumbled loudly and flung himself onto his back in a melodramatic gesture. She stifled a giggle and began moving down his body, kissing his chest and tenderly licking each nipple before shuffling further down to trace the indentations of his abdomen with her tongue. Rainere was completely unaware of just how perfect his body was and took it for granted, as if it were banal instead of beautiful. The shimmering gray insignia of the Mark rippled when she kissed it, and Rainere sat up with a sudden indrawn breath. Then he saw her kneeling between his legs and slumped onto his back again, watching her return to work on his abdomen with heavy-lidded eyes. "*Cara mia.*"

"I could do this all day." She blew lightly on the places she had just licked and giggled when he moaned.

"*Cara mia,* use your wicked magic on me," Rainere rasped, so sleepy and sexy that Adele almost took him up on his offer. "Just don't take too much—I'll need some energy to disguise myself as Odin today."

"I don't need your permission to take what I want, my prince." Adele sucked on the flesh of Rainere's inner thigh, making him groan with pleasure. "You're mine to do with what I will."

"How dare you speak to me like that," he said, and his eyes were closed now. "You'll pay for that insult—and, goddess, yes, put your tongue right there."

There was a loud knock at the door. "Your Majesty?"

"Shit, it's Mrs. Ollenby." Adele sat up. "It must be later than I thought. The Sandarians are leaving today. We'd better get ready."

Rainere was incredulous. "Adelena, finish what you started," he growled.

The knock came louder this time, and she slid out of bed, giggling as he made a wild grab for her and missed.

"Please, my darling," he begged shamelessly. "It'll only take a minute, but my balls will ache all day if you don't."

"Your balls aren't my concern right now," Adele said with a grin. She opened the bedchamber door to her team of dressiers. Lady Olivia was there too, and Adele decided to ignore her. "Good morning, everyone!"

Rainere flung a corner of a sheet over his lap just in time as Mrs. Ollenby rushed into the room. Flustered, she approached the naked and sullen prince.

"Your Highness, Prince Rainold is here, as is Mr. Grottonski. I believe they are both eager to speak with you. It was all I could do to stop them from entering Her Majesty's bedchamber just this moment."

"I had another idea for how to start my morning," Rainere sniped, and Adele laughed loudly enough to make him scowl at her.

"Er, quite, Your Highness." Mrs. Ollenby held out his robe.

Rainere sighed hugely, swinging his legs out of bed. He wrapped himself in the striped silk robe and ventured out to meet his audience.

Lady Olivia did her best to be professional, but Adele could tell the girl was suffering in the wake of her very public humiliation. Adele had no idea what Captain Lucky would look like angry. She had seen him annoyed and a bit morose, but she had never seen him actually lose his temper.

The other dressiers gossiped about the drunken party with the

Sandarian visitors like it was all so much innocent fun. No one mentioned war or the rumor that a god had created the earthquake that had destroyed the Garden Wing, which Adele thought was remarkable considering how close it had been.

"I heard that Jordansson spent last night in the royal Sandarian tent doing the goddess only knows what," Julien said as he curled Adele's hair. "And with all *four* sisters."

"I heard the empress too," Katie added with a giggle. "I wonder how they even managed. A girl just isn't made to take that much man."

"I heard he's more than Orgustus," Piers added. "And that is saying something *big*."

All three giggled and slid sidelong glances at Lady Olivia again. But Olivia raised her chin and continued selecting jewelry from the royal collection in its wooden cases, ignoring the team with a dignity that Adele found admirable, even if she couldn't say she admired the woman herself.

The sun had risen by the time Adele was dressed and heading to the dining table to see her children. Her Queen's Guard were already seated. Unfortunately, Prince Rainold and Grotto were also at the table. The prince was sitting near her children, chatting away to them. Grotto loomed behind his chair like a malevolent specter, clasping a large, dusty book to his chest. She knew Rainere had told his father about her condition last night, but hadn't asked how Rainold had taken the news. She guessed she would find out now.

"Eat, everyone, we've only got a little while before we need to say farewell to the Sandarians." She poured herself a cup of tea. "Has anyone heard what transpired with Jordansson's attempt to woo the empress?"

There was an uncomfortable silence before Ohrig answered. "It seems he spent the evening in a valiant effort to show his best features, Your Majesty."

"I hate that man. He stinks and is always sweaty," Natalie added conversationally.

"Jordansson is making a huge sacrifice for Unisia, and we will respect him, young lady," Adele said, using her firmest tone.

"Well, it remains to be seen." Ohrig frowned. "We won't know until the empress says it's so."

"That rhymes," Aaron said. "Know, says so. Rhyme."

Ohrig ruffled Aaron's golden-brown hair. "Sure, kid," he said.

"*Mummy* got a baby in her *tummy*," Aaron announced. "That rhymes too."

Adele closed her eyes and groaned inwardly. She didn't want this discussion right now.

"Mummy?" Natalie piped up. "Tell Aaron it's bad to lie."

"Well, actually, my darlings." Adele forced a bright smile for the children. "I do have a baby on the way."

"But you have Stella." Natalie was confused. "How can you get another baby? Are you going to give Stella away because she's broken?"

"Natalie, please. Stella isn't broken—she's perfect, sweetheart," Adele said, feeling her smile becoming brittle. *Why was Natalie always so caustic?*

"Who's the papa?" Leafy asked, her accent masking the word so much Natalie had to translate.

"Prince Rainere is the father." Adele was grateful when Rainere took her hand. He was holding Stella on his knee and making her giggle. The very image of happy fatherhood. "We're going to have this baby together."

As if that had been the cue he was waiting for, Grotto dropped the enormous book onto the dining table with a heavy thud. "Is the paternity verified, Master?" His voice was just a creak but carried well enough.

"By the gods themselves, Grotto," Rainere answered proudly.

Several things happened at that point. Charlie came running into the room as if he were being chased, then Jordansson mooched in behind him, only keeping up because his legs were so long. The little black cat of Gorrik's jumped up onto the breakfast table, making the children squeal with pleasure. And the baby inside Adele moved.

"Charlie?" Adele held her belly. "What is it?"

But Charlie was watching Prince Rainold instruct the children on the horrible diseases that filthy cats carried with them. He was trying to get the little cat off the table, but it was dodging among the dishes and teacups, evading capture. "Nothing, Your Majesty." Charlie took a seat and wiped the sweat of his brow. "I just didn't want to miss breakfast, that's all."

Adele accepted the lie and smiled cautiously at Jordansson. "How're you feeling, my friend?"

Jordansson only gave her a heavy look as he dropped his bulk into a chair and reached for a plate of egg-and-bacon pies. He was wearing his shirt open and his pants low enough that she could see the muscles that ran down in a deep V. Though at least he was showered and had boots on, so he was fine to see the empress off.

Distracted, Adele had only caught the last bit of what Grotto was saying. "And I will add it to the Book of Genealogy." He opened the ancient book from the back cover and flicked a hefty handful of pages over.

"No, Grotto, not the back of the book," Rainere said, angrily enough to make Stella whimper. "You will write this baby at the front of the book."

"But Master, your union with the queen hasn't been sanctified by the Church of Serena, as all royal Marchant marriages must be," Grotto said, managing to convey an air of poisonous satisfaction. "Your babe with the Unisian queen will be born illegitimate, so it goes at the back of the book with all the others."

"What others?" Adele asked. She was echoed by Natalie, who got out of her chair. Prince Rainold picked her up and held her so they could both read the page over Grotto's shoulder.

"Is this Prince Rainere's name?" Natalie asked, pointing. "And is that all the baby names? That's a lot."

"That is a lot of babies," Prince Rainold agreed. "Grotto, exactly how many babies had my son fathered before he was cursed with immortality?"

"One hundred and thirty-two," Grotto said, clearly displeased to have to respond to Prince Rainold, though it was to Adele that he gave his fluorescent glare, making her skin crawl. "One hundred and eighteen lived to their fifth birthday, and one hundred and sixteen lived to maturity, long enough to produce their own offspring."

Adele felt nausea, slimy and wrong in her stomach. "You had one hundred and thirty-two babies?" she asked Rainere.

He frowned, probably feeling the tumult of her emotions through the Mark. "I created those offspring," he clarified. "But they weren't my children, and I wasn't a father to them."

"What the fuck do you mean by that?" she snapped, not even hearing her children giggle at her curse.

"Adelena, it was my duty as the last Marchant prince to propagate the family. I had to spread the royal blood—*the* Blood—for future generations," he explained. "I got those offspring upon servants and village women and the like. It was all very banal. The women would arrive after dinner, I did my duty, and they left again. I never saw the same woman more than two or three times so no attachment could develop, and I certainly never saw them once they were pregnant."

Adele looked around the table at all the staring faces. "Why is this the first time I'm hearing this?"

"Oh, darling, don't be like that!" Rainere's light tone grated on her nerves. "I don't tell you how many meals I've eaten or enchantments I've worked, or how many frogs I've killed. Why would I tell you how many women I've managed to progenate?"

"*Progenate*?" Adele felt the anger building behind her shock.

"You kill frogs?" Aaron asked the prince, upset. "I like frogs. They have squelchy ideas."

General Ohrig was closest to Aaron and pulled the prince into his arms for a cuddle. "Maybe the children shouldn't be here for this discussion," he suggested. Adele couldn't find it within herself to give him a response, but was relieved when he gestured to the nannies, who were waiting by the nursery door. They hurried over and collected the complaining children, whisking them off to finish getting ready for the morning's event.

"It wasn't love, it wasn't even fun, it was simply duty," Rainere added, and she could see he was mystified by her anger. "I reached my maturity at sixteen, and Grotto said the time had come. I had a woman in my bed every night until I turned twenty-three and realized I could stop it. I had reached well over a hundred progeny by then, and I was allowed to rest."

"A woman in your bed every night for seven years." QG Leith whistled low. "That's something like—" The rest of his sentence withered under Captain Lucky's glare.

"It's my birthday today, but I don't think I'm getting that much action," Charlie said. If he was joking to break the tension, it didn't work.

"Two thousand, five hundred and fifty-five lays," QG Owens whispered, but everyone heard.

"Not quite." Rainere's worried gaze was riveted to Adele. "Some nights I was sick with a fever or injured from training, or—darling, are you all right?"

"Fever or injury? They were your only excuses for a night off from joyless sex with strangers?" Prince Rainold asked. He looked like he was experiencing enough emotions for everyone when he turned on Grotto, striking him on the shoulder. "You nasty, hideous elf! How dare you inflict that horror on my son! I trusted you to care for him, not turn him into a Marchant breeding stallion. Rainere, my heart's light, it must have been so awful for you."

"And for the women who were *progenated*," Adele added, wondering why Rainere looked hurt and Rainold so affronted.

"Your Majesty, my son had no choice," Prince Rainold shouted, his eyes flashing angrily. "Do not dare suggest otherwise! Rainere was only an innocent when Grotto demanded that he begin this night-mare of turning sex into a hideous labor." He turned to his son again. "Oh, please tell me there was someone lovely among all the dross, darling boy? Someone who gave you some semblance of joy along with her body?"

But Adele didn't hear his answer because Tilburn entered the apartment and announced that the Sandarians were gathering at the front gates to leave.

CHAPTER THIRTY-SEVEN

"Show of Faith"

Just as she had a few days ago, Adele stood under the hot sun at the gates of the Golden Palace. But this time she'd brought her children and full household staff out with her as a show of faith in front of the empress. For several tense minutes, she'd been afraid that Lord Orgustus might not join them, but Tilburn let her know when the young lord rode out from the stables on his dappled gray horse, a caravan of packing trunks in wagons behind him.

"He didn't pack light," she overheard Owens joke, but all she could think was that she had Jordan Jordansson, desperate to leave, on one side of her and Lord Orgustus, desperate to stay, on the other. Their unhappiness was her fault, but the power to fix it rested entirely with Empress Sanda'hani.

The Sandarians emerged in a train from the Great Stables of the Golden Palace, sunshine sparkling on the silver beads braided into the Tree Horses' manes. The children were excited to finally see the empress, whom they remembered so fondly from their trip to Sandar. She let Natalie and Aaron run to meet Sanda'hani's carriage when it stopped just inside the palace gates.

The empress and her sisters embraced the children, smiling and giving them small gifts before leading them back to where Adele stood sweating in her pale green lace gown, a fringed parasol held over her head by a member of the Household Guard. There was no shade by the gates and the men had to sweat in suits and jackets, their cheeks slowly turning rosy under the hot sun.

Jordansson immediately began fidgeting, pulling at his collar and undoing the cravat someone, probably Tilburn, had insisted he wear. He muttered something in his own tongue that made Rainere-as-Odin chuckle. Adele vaguely wondered at Rainere's mirth but put it down to his happiness that Jordansson might be finally leaving the court.

"Oi, Jordansson! C'mon, man, how many of the empress's sisters did you really bed last night?" Adele overheard QG Leith whisper and wished she hadn't. It was awful to think of young Jordansson being desperate enough to give himself to the women who'd almost killed him, simply for the chance to escape the Golden Palace.

"All of them," Jordansson answered, sounding more anxious than proud. "But not the empress."

Leith guffawed. "By the goddess' own grace, how do you feel after giving it to four women in one night?"

Jordansson muttered something in his own tongue that made Leith ask, "What's that, mate?"

"He said, 'Thirsty,'" Rainere answered for the tribesman, which set the QGs to chuckling among themselves until Captain Lucky hissed something and they shut up again.

A dry breeze carried the dust kicked up by the dozens of Tree Horses. Adele heard Lord Orgustus clear his throat. She braced herself for recriminations, but instead the lord spoke to his friend.

"Jordan."

"Yes, Orgust."

Adele was standing between them, and they could easily speak over her head, as if she weren't even there.

"Jordan, I want to thank you for trying to help me." Orgustus's usually booming voice was reduced to a sad rasp. "I know you've done your very best to keep me in my home, and whatever happens today, I will always consider you a friend. If the queen allows it, please come and visit me in my desert prison."

Adele felt tears prick her eyes at his words.

"You're a good man, Orgust," Jordansson replied. "If I have failed, and you need to leave, please have a son, have a daughter, laugh, live. Life can change in a day. I remember well one trip I made across the tundra to find an ice bear and met the strangest woman, who turned the world upside down for me."

Jordansson smiled down at her and she wanted to squeeze his hand and apologize for everything, but it was too late.

The empress had finally arranged herself, standing in the middle of the road leading out of the gates. She began a speech in her own language that Rainere said was a prayer, so he didn't bother to translate it. Adele's children were milling around, and she had to keep an eye on them until Sanda'hani called her to attention.

"Your Majesty, Sandarians do not enjoy the protocol and ceremony of Unisians, so you will forgive me if I get to the sharpest point of our farewell."

Adele nodded. Next to her, Lord Orgustus swayed against her arm.

"I do not wish to cause offense to the great and noble former regent, Lord Orgustus St. Lucidis. He is my first choice, and remains so, for the position of royal Unisian ambassador to Sandar."

Adele was sure she felt both Orgustus and Jordansson stop breathing.

"However, my sisters are my counsel, and I take their advice as grave and true. They wish for the Jordani tribesman of the Three Sisters Tribe, Jordan Jordansson, to take the position. They believe his passion for the role will serve both Unisia and Sandar well in the coming years."

"If that is your wish, Your Grace, then I acquiesce to the change." Adele had to skip out of the way as Jordansson and Orgustus clasped each other in an embrace with lots of laughter and backslapping. She lowered her voice to ask, "Are you really sure, Sanda'hani?"

Sanda'hani rolled her eyes as her sisters fell to giggling and swamped a joyful Jordansson, who embraced all of them, easily swinging the tall women off their feet. "Well, he'll be the first Unisian ambassador who isn't even Unisian," the empress said, and her lips quirked in a grin. "But my sisters have suffered so much these past days, it is good to see them smile again. Do you mind? I know he was a favorite of yours."

Adele leaned in closer, avoiding any chance of being overheard. "I find myself without much energy for favorites these days," she said. "Sanda'hani, if the worst should happen and I don't survive Dahk'hani's rebirth, please know I will do everything in my power to ensure those who come after me remain friends to Sandar. My former regent will be in your debt—hopefully, he remembers it."

Empress Sanda'hani took Adele in her arms and held her tightly for a long moment before releasing her. Adele could see a warm sincerity in her gaze. "Dahk'hani is a merciful god. Simply ask, and you shall receive his love, Queen Adelena—never forget that. His words are plain, and his actions come from a great and loving heart. Listen, and you will know him. Trust, and you will be rewarded."

Adele nodded. "He's your god—I'm sure he's much nicer to you than me." Sanda'hani laughed and embraced her again.

Jordansson managed to extricate himself from the four sisters, telling them he needed to say his goodbyes. In two long strides, he was before Adele. His clear blue eyes squinted in the bright sunshine, and sweat was trickling down his brow, but he beamed with joy. "My queen, I think our time together ends here."

"And what a time we've had, Jordansson." She looked up at the tribesman. "I'm sorry Unisia wasn't the adventure that you wanted, and I am truly sorry that I broke my promise to you. I couldn't let you stand by me with the burdens that I have to carry."

Jordansson stroked her cheek with a gentle hand. "We would not have worked as a pair anyway," he said. "You are always angry and very demanding of your men, yet you give them only empty beds and work to do."

Adele let her breath out in a huff. "Well, I guess that's true," she admitted.

"But I also know that you are a great queen, and you sacrifice much of yourself," Jordansson continued. He leaned down even further to murmur in her ear. "You must stay strong so that your men stay strong. I understand this now. And I know I am not strong enough to stand by a god-blessed queen with fire in her eyes. Though we didn't shag, I will always love you."

Adele got one look of the cheeky expression on Jordansson's face and burst out laughing.

"It's true, but don't tell your prince," he warned.

"I won't." Still chuckling, she moved back into line. "Goodbye, Jordansson, and go with our love to your new adventure in Sandar." She was suddenly very glad that he was going to get to be a father soon, even if it wouldn't be his biological child. Though after his performance the night before, it was almost certain that another child was in his future.

All that was left was for Jordansson to embrace his St. Lucidis friends, and then the Sandarians took their leave, trundling off in carriages and on horseback. The dust caused by their departure caught in Adele's throat and traced the tears down her cheeks. She could've blamed the new hormones, but they were probably tears of relief. War had been averted, and her responsibility to Jordansson was also at a blessed end.

With Mrs. Ollenby's help, she gathered her reluctant children together. They hadn't been outside the palace since Adele's return from the Ice Mountains and complained loudly about returning to their apartment. It was Rainere who suggested the children should have a riding lesson, as the new ponies had arrived for them at the stables. Adele thought it was a wonderful idea. The day was glorious, and it was time to celebrate.

Servants were sent to prepare the stables for the royal family, and the children were now happy to go with their mother and exchange their uncomfortable formal clothes for riding gear.

Of course, Adele couldn't escape her duties that quickly. Tilburn caught her on her way out of the palace and insisted she give him an hour of her time. He had an armful of scrolls for her to ratify the change in ambassador to Sandar and various other pieces of contract that had been created by the heavy threat of war, now resolved. After a parting kiss and plea to hurry, Rainere took the children down to the stables with the three nannies in tow. Adele also tried to dismiss her Queen's Guard for the afternoon but Ohrig demanded that Pepper and Lucky remained close by her and she wasn't in the mood to argue.

Adele didn't want to go all the way back up to the royal apartment when she expected to join the children very soon, so Tilburn set her up with her paperwork in a beautiful library on the ground floor of the palace. The room was big and airy, and the walls were lined with packed bookshelves. There was a wide leather couch and two match-ing armchairs set by a glass-topped coffee table in the center of the room, but Tilburn chose to put her at the big desk by the wall of win-dows. Louvered shutters shaded the room from sun and gave privacy from the garden outside, where courtiers could be seen walking in pairs or picnicking in small groups, enjoying the fine morning. Lucky and Pepper took up their stations just outside the door.

Sitting in the comfortable desk chair, Adele ran her hands over the soft maroon leather blotter on the desktop and grabbed her quill. "Right, Tilburn," she said. "I'll finish up with these scrolls then I'm done for the rest of the day."

"Very well, Your Majesty, because you've certainly earned your time off." He beamed at her so brightly that Adele wondered if she should ask for something else while he was in such a good mood, but thought it wasn't wise to be greedy. She'd no doubt be causing him another headache very soon. He waved in two servants pushing tea trolleys and announced, "Charlie Row for you, Your Majesty."

Charlie slipped in behind the servants, looking tense as he searched the room with his gaze.

"I'm over here." Dwarfed behind the big desk, Adele waved at him. "Let me get all this paperwork squared away, and then we can have that chat you wanted yesterday."

Gesturing for Charlie to take a seat, Tilburn skipped out of the room and closed the door.

But Charlie didn't settle in, and seemed oddly impatient for her to finish as he stalked around the room muttering rhetorical questions like "These paintings are so ugly, does that even look like a horse to you?" and "Why would you make couch cushions out of leather? It's uncomfortable."

Only listening with half an ear, she grinned to herself. Charlie was grumpy, fine, but she was in a great mood and was very keen to get work out of the way so she could join her family for a nice afternoon in the stables. Hopefully, she could help begin to heal the horror the children had endured at the site of their violent kidnapping.

"Charlie, why don't you pour the tea and have something to eat?" she suggested, concentrating on a scroll that she knew had been written in the King's Tongue but was still indecipherable. "Tilburn gave us a plate of those little lemon tarts that you like."

Charlie did as he was told, pouring the tea and handing Adele a cup. He leaned over her shoulder to read the scroll. "What's *heretoforandforevermore* happening about?" he asked.

"I'm guessing the position of—wait, I think it's about the war— wait." Adele read further, then signed the bottom of the scroll where Tilburn always put a little star mark. "Nope, I still have no idea what that one's about."

She picked up the next parchment with one hand and held her cup in the other. "Thanks, Charlie," she said and took a sip. "Perfect. You know just how I take it."

"It's not a hard thing to notice." Charlie shrugged off her compliment and half-sat, half-leaned on the edge of the desk near to her.

Adele skimmed another contract and signed at the bottom, then picked up the next scroll and signed at the bottom of that one too. She left the parchments in a messy pile, not bothering to roll them again, and took yet another from Tilburn's much neater stack. "Imagine if I was signing my life away," she joked.

"You could be," he said.

"Well, luckily, I trust Tilburn," she answered, then cast the brooding teen a look. "Seriously, take a seat, I won't be long."

Charlie let out a long noise of impatience and dragged a chair from the other side of the desk to join Adele on her side. He set himself a little too close for comfort and stared at her with his arms crossed while she worked. Adele skimmed another scroll and signed at the bottom, fairly certain that it was a contract to allow Jordansson the freedom to return to Unisia as long as he registered said return with the court first, and in the event of . . . blah, blah, blah. She did two more before Charlie's sighing got on her nerves again and she had to throw down her quill.

Leaning back, she held her teacup in both hands, returning Charlie's gaze. "Well?"

Charlie's dark eyes flickered, the ring of silver turning around the irises. "Well, what?" he snapped.

"Are you always this grumpy on your birthday?" She sipped more tea to hide her smile. "Or did you think I didn't hear you while I was getting the fabulous news that my prince is father to an entire empire of children?"

Charlie grunted. "Why do you care who Prince Rainere fathered?" he asked. "It was well over a hundred years ago—all those kids would be long dead and buried by now. It's got nothing to do with the bun in your oven."

Adele flinched at Charlie's honesty. "He still should have told me that he'd had children," she said. "Even from that situation."

"That *situation?*" Charlie looked indignant. "Tell me who wants their lover to know they've been used like that? In those days, they'd have loved a chance at a kid with pure Marchant blood in him. Grotto would've made a lot of money off Rainere's arse and then probably took a cut from all the babies too."

Adele chewed her bottom lip. *Damn it, Charlie's right.* "He was so young when it started," she murmured.

"Well, he was my age, and that's hardly young," Charlie said, grumpily. "But I'll tell you what makes sense to me now, though. When we were in the Slums to rescue your kids, Rip had a proper go at Prince Rainere for ignoring the plight of the poor and broken-down in Concordis. Rip said, 'How can you let them do this to your people?' And I thought, yeah, Prince Rainere, you should do something for us—we share your blood."

"What did Rainere say?"

"He said, 'These are not my people. They are human, and I am not,'" Charlie said with a fair impression of Rainere's sneer. "And I thought, you bastard! But now I know he was made to whore so hard, I know full well that changes a man's view on his fellow citizens, even if they do share his bloodline. It's tough to care about people who made you suffer like that."

Adele remembered the night Rainere had first come to her bed. He'd been so rough that she had thought he was going to force her without any pleasure for either of them. She'd never forgotten the lost look in his eyes. Only when she had touched him gently had he calmed. Maybe it was only in that moment he realized that they were going to make love instead of just "progenate."

Well, now I feel like a monster. She needed to apologize to Rainere. *And I can't blame Dahk'hani for me acting like a jerk, this is all my own jealousy.*

Charlie leaned forward, elbows on his knees. "You've gone quiet. Have I annoyed you?"

Adele sighed and gave him a rueful smile. "It's just annoying how smart you are sometimes. You always find a way to remind me that I'm an alien in this world and that I shouldn't jump to conclusions." She slurped the rest of her tea before it went cold. "Now, enough about me. What do you want for your birthday? You're seventeen today, and that's a big deal, so you get a big present." She chuckled at his shocked expression. It was rare to surprise Charlie.

"You shouldn't leave yourself open like that," he spluttered. "I might take advantage of your generosity."

"You've earned whatever it is you want," she said, reaching for his hand. She felt the calluses on his palm and noticed the butt of the knife in its holster peeking out of the cuff of his new silk shirt. *Like Rainere, there is an edge to Charlie,* she reminded herself. *He's had a hard life too.*

"Actually, I've got a present for you today." Charlie's voice had gone flat, and he had that hard glint in his eye that made him look so much older than he was. "No more lies."

Adele braced herself for bad news. "Then tell me."

She sat silently as he recounted the tale of Orestes's capture. It was only when he revealed that Aaron had been told by Gorrik's little cat where Ohren was being held that she let her tears fall.

"Your Maj, your son is very special," Charlie said. "I don't know why none of us thought that Orestes would use such an obvious place, but Aaron saved us a world of trouble."

Adele dashed her tears away, sniffling. Charlie whipped out a handkerchief, and it made her smile. "Look at you, you're a proper gentleman now, with handkerchiefs and everything."

Charlie shook his head. "I'm still me," he said. "I kept information from you that I should've shared immediately. We've got Orestes cornered, but Prince Rainold says I can't kill him. All of my running and dodging was for nothing, as usual."

Charlie was staring down at his feet, so he wasn't watching when Adele took a narrow candle from the desktop candelabra and shoved it into one of the lemon tarts. She held the plate under his nose.

"Hap-py birth-day, de-ar Char-lie!" she sang, off-key. "Quick, make a wish!"

Charlie's expression suggested that she'd lost her mind.

"Come on! Do you really think that while I was dealing with war and gods and poison that I had any time for all of the work you and the princes did to find Ohren?" she asked. "Now, am I pissed off that neither Rainere nor you thought to mention it to me even in passing? Yes, I am. Am I pissed off that for some inexplicable reason, you still chose to underestimate the evil jerk, and Orestes had a chance to put me in a near-fatal spell that allowed Dahk'hani to get at me? Yes, I am very pissed off about that."

Charlie grimaced. "I can't say it's been a great week for you," he said.

"But I'm also relieved that you are using your own brain and working with Rainere, doing the things that I can't do," she continued. "I bet you've already found out who poisoned the beer from Merrills, haven't you?"

Charlie nodded. "Orestes was the culprit. He either bribed or threatened someone in the distillery at Merrills. I've got the Lady Mayor looking into it right now."

Adele put the plate of cakes down. "Seriously, Charlie, you're amazing!" she said. "You're a huge asset to me, and I count you as my friend too. I hope you feel the same."

Charlie nodded slowly, his gaze piercing. "You and me make a good team, don't we?" But Adele had the strange impression that they might've been talking about two different things.

"If you still want to join the Queen's Guard, there's a place for you," she offered, poking him in the ribs and trying to get their light-hearted banter back. "We could use a smart boy like you in the ranks."

She thought he'd have jumped at the chance to join the QGs, but he shook his head. "You say that you like me using my brain," he said. "But the QGs all use General Ohrig's, so there wouldn't be much scope for me to scarper off and do my clever work if I was wearing the white and gold."

"Then I'll have to think of another position to keep you close," she said. "It's not right for me to just have you working with no job title or salary."

Charlie looked at the plate of tarts. "I've never had a candle before," he said. "What're you supposed to wish for?"

"It's your birthday, Charlie." She wrapped her arm around his shoulders. "You get to wish for anything you want—and don't forget you still get a present from me too."

Charlie's lips moved in a silent whisper and blew softly. As she watched the flame gutter and die, Adele suddenly heard music in her head. She leaped off her chair, yelping, "Sweet Christ, what was that?"

Charlie's arm slipped around her. "Are you all right, Your Maj?" He raised a hand to feel her forehead, like Rainere would have done. "You've gone very pale just now."

"I think so." But Adele felt a fluttering in her abdomen that took her breath away. Her head swam with a drunk feeling, but the good kind of drunk feeling, buzzy and warm.

Hands at her waist, Charlie lifted Adele to sit on the desk, her feet dangling as he stood between her knees and looked into her eyes like he was trying to find something there. "There's always been this beautiful thing between us, hasn't there, Queen . . . Adelena?"

Charlie took her hand and wove his fingers through hers. "You know, when a man has a birthday, he gets a kiss from everyone he wants to kiss."

"Mm-hm." Adele listened hard and thought she heard a tinkle of the Chime Voices again, but they were coming from Charlie. She leaned closer. "How're you doing that?" she asked. "There's that music again."

He stroked her cheek. "Can I have my birthday kiss . . . Adelena?"

"What? No!" Adele grabbed the front of Charlie's shirt, meaning to push him away, but he only came closer, his lips lining up with hers. "You're just a kid, I wouldn't do that to you."

She wasn't sure if it was Charlie who closed the gap, but in an instant his lips were on hers and his hands were in her hair. He kissed like his life depended on it, and she could taste lemon tart on his tongue. Self-loathing was screaming for her to stop, but then hunger flared, and behind her closed eyes all she could see was the glittering green magic inside of him, deep in his chest. Rainere had an ocean of power contained within him, whereas Charlie was a raging torrent of uncontrolled waves. It was delicious and wild even as it evaded her touch, but she heard the music again. *My Chime Voices are alive!*

Charlie's moan was filled with lust and pain, and the sound dragged her back to reality. She remembered to extract the tendrils of her magic carefully so as not to cause any whiplash for either of them. Opening her eyes again, she found that she had her hands inside his shirt and his mouth was on her neck. "God, Charlie, I'm so sorry." She tried to pull away. "I didn't mean to do that."

Charlie wasn't as quick as Rainere, but he was still quick when he pushed her backward on the desk and yanked her thighs up around his waist. "Do it again," he demanded, breathless as he undid his trousers. "That thing inside me, do it again."

The serpentine magic pushed her up into Charlie's arms. It was determined to capture the heady green river under his heart. The gold magic told her it was right, she needed it, and he was willing and a little magic would make everything better. The Chime Voices invited her inside him. It was only her own strength and very human willpower that made Adele push him away. But this time she wasn't gentle, and he hit the bookshelf on the wall, staring at her, shocked.

She shook her head, already denying what she'd almost done, and Charlie was nothing if not sharp to a change of atmosphere. Quickly, he was tucking himself back into his pants and doing up his shirt buttons. As he ran his hands through his hair, she saw that they were shaking. But it was the only thing that gave him away.

Adele slipped off the desk. "Birthday wish granted," she said. "Now let's never speak of this again."

Charlie gave Adele a dark look, and the silver in his eyes flashed, accusing her of being the monster she felt like right now. Anything she could say would sound like the vile excuse of every pedophile that she'd read about on Earth. *Maybe honesty would work? He deserves that, at least.*

"Charlie, that thing I just did to you," she began, and the guilt almost made her choke. "That's the magic in me that wants yours." She had to look up at him now. He'd grown so much, and she was still treating him like a child. "I'm a demon, Charlie." She watched for his reaction, but he was wearing that stone-cold expression she'd seen so often. "I'm dangerous. I'll hurt you and I won't even mean to, but it's the greed of the magic—"

Charlie pushed a strand of hair behind her ear. "Too late, Your Maj," he murmured. "Now that I know it can be like that, you've ruined me for anyone else."

"Ruined you! Sweet Christ, Charlie, what I do is evil!" Adele suddenly heard the Chime Voices shrieking again, the sound so loud that she staggered against the desk.

"Oh, no, it's coming back again. You better run." She could barely hear her own voice over the cacophony of music. She looked in his direction and saw him reaching for her. If he touched her, all her promises would be broken.

"Damn you, Charlie. Run!" she shouted, and the chandelier above them rattled with the power in her voice.

This time, he listened and ran. As soon as the door slammed behind him, Adele felt the terrible urgency drain away. Hands pressed over her racing heart, she strained to hear the Chime Voices, but in front of her there was only the mess of paperwork yet to be finished and the chirping of birds outside the windows. The door opened again.

"You all right, Your Majesty?" Captain Lucky asked. "Charlie almost bowled me over just now."

"Fine, fine!" she said and waved him away. "I'll be out in a second."

The door closed and Adele stood in the silence, concentrating on taking long, slow breaths.

"I don't want another crisis," she announced, as if the magic within her might give a damn. "I'm carrying you, Dahk'hani, but I will grow you in my own way, with love and goodness. No having sex with teenagers, no matter how powerful they are." The flutter in her abdomen returned, and so did the hunger for pure green, icy cold, metallic magic.

"I said no." Adele was firm. "Now, I want to have a nice, quiet afternoon with my family, and then a nice, quiet family dinner, and then a nice, quiet evening in bed with Rainere. His is the only magic you will ever drink again." Decided, she rushed through the rest of the scrolls and then went outside into the sunshine to find her way to the stables. In the fifteen-minute walk, nothing bad happened, and for that she was supremely grateful.

Chapter Thirty-Eight

"A Dark Side Revealed"

Leaving Queen Adelena behind in the library, Charlie made his way down to Hell. The same young guard was still at the door, and this time he didn't even spare a moment of sympathy for him, just muttered the password and took the key. He spied an old meal tray with a metal cup inside the door. The cup made an awful clattering noise as he trailed it along the bars of all the cages. He pushed open the door to the Boss's cell.

Orestes was right where he'd left him, tied to a chair with serrated metal restraints that were a specialty of Charlie's from the days before Queen Adelena came into his life. The wizard's wrists and ankles were crusted with dried blood.

"I said the more you pull, the tighter they get," Charlie chided. He pushed Orestes's chin so his head flopped back. "But it doesn't look like you believed me."

Orestes had a vacant look in his eyes that spoke of hunger and blood loss. There was also a puddle of piss under his chair, stinking up the room. "Boy, you can't kill me." His voice rasped painfully on a dry throat. "Only I will protect you from the demon queen."

Charlie released his knife from its holster and checked the blade for nicks in the dim light of the green-flamed lantern. He sliced his thumb on the edge and painted the blood on the blade. "Queen Adelena is an angel," he said. "And she's a bloody hero."

"The demon whore is no hero!" Orestes shouted. He found the strength to spit, but it only got as far as his own knee.

Charlie didn't answer; instead, he began to slice off Orestes's shirt buttons and pulled the shirttails out of his pants. He pushed the fabric down, making soothing noises when Orestes tried to struggle away from his touch.

"Ask Prince Rainold—he knows it too." Orestes was starting to panic now. "The goddess blessed me in a vision! She showed me! Adelena must die so that Unisia can live. Charlie, please, don't do it!"

Charlie lifted the knife to his ear, like he wanted to hear better. "Are you begging for your life, Boss?" he asked. "Because you always taught me that those who beg should be the first to die."

Orestes gasped, then his eyes focused on the blade that was heading for his throat.

Charlie paused in his movement just long enough for Orestes to risk looking up at him. The hope in the Boss's eyes was almost as precious to him as Adelena's kiss had been. "Remember when you did this to me?" he asked, tracing the bloody blade against Orestes's throat, scratching at the blond bristles. "Me and my mates, Danny and Gill, we botched a pickup and lost some of your blue tonic in the sewers. Wasn't our fault. Your thugs had taken us for thieves and busted our backpacks. They brought us to you, and then we sat tied to three chairs in a line, just like you are now."

Charlie pressed the blade a little deeper and watched the blood bead on Orestes's skin. "Gill was honest. He told you what happened, and so he died first. You slashed so deep his blood sprayed all over me." He pressed harder, and Orestes moaned. "Then Danny starts begging for his life, and you give your little speech about 'dignity in the gutter.' He died slow, because you enjoyed cutting us up, didn't you?"

"You scum got what you deserved," Orestes snarled.

"Then it was my turn." Charlie paused, tapping Orestes's forehead with the point of the knife. "Do you remember what I said to you?"

Orestes's head twitched to the side and Charlie was forced to relive the moment once more in front of the man who still terrified him.

"I said, 'I stole your tonic, Boss, and I'll get the money back to you. I'm so sorry.'" If he closed his eyes, he could smell the blood and horrid fecal perfume of punctured intestines all over again. "And you laughed because you knew I was lying. You said, 'I've got no use for honest thieves, so I'm keeping you, kid.' Then you gave me to your thugs as a reward for bringing me in. You said, 'Show him what my mercy feels like, and make sure he never forgets it.'"

Orestes's Adam's apple bobbed against Charlie's blade as he swallowed.

"And they tied me up too, but it wasn't to a chair, and it lasted a night and a day before my friends were allowed to come and get me." Charlie sat on Orestes's lap, rightly supposing the contact would disgust the man, who hated being touched. "Do you remember now?"

Orestes grunted. "You deserved it."

Charlie pressed closer, excited to see the blood pool on his blade. "Now, you're going to get what you deserve."

At the first slice, Orestes screamed, at the second he howled, and after that, Charlie didn't hear any more over the pounding of blood in his ears.

CHAPTER THIRTY-NINE

"Vows Under Question"

If she was very careful and didn't think about the god-baby growing in her body, then Adele could convince herself she was happy. Relaxed, even. It had been a wonderful afternoon at the stables. The children loved their little ponies, and Natalie had even taken a turn leading one around the corral, though Leafy and Aaron just played at grooming, brushing the ponies' manes and currying their fluffy gray coats. Rainere took his enormous black stallion, Titor, out for a long ride through the forest and reported that he'd found a picnic spot filled with courtiers, where Lord Orgustus was the center of attention, regaling them with exaggerated tales of his escape from slavery.

The family went back to the royal apartment just as the sun began to sink to the horizon. The children were put in the bath, and Adele sat with them, chatting and playing, until they were called to dinner. The chefs had outdone themselves preparing all the children's favorite dishes, which meant everything was covered in melted cheese or sticky sauce. She felt guilty when Charlie didn't come to eat, but still, sitting at the dining table, just the six of them, was another rare luxury she tried to enjoy. She teased Rainere about drinking too much beer until he pulled her onto his lap and kissed her, which made the children squeal in disgust and delight.

"If you're kissing, then you have to get married!" Natalie shouted, making all the children laugh as they scampered away from the table, already in the middle of another game.

Sweet Christ, marriage. Adele felt her smile wilt, but Rainere caught her chin with his thumb and forefinger. "Yes, now we *have* to," he said, and his tone held a note of warning she didn't like. "I will have my child born legitimate, *cara mia.*"

"Rainere, there's still so much at stake here," she whispered. This close she could see the shadows of every emotion haunting his forest-green eyes, and she knew his will was as strong as hers.

"It's decided." His lips touched hers and he whispered, "My child changes everything."

But this baby is not your child, she thought, panicked. *How can you claim it when Dahk'hani already has?*

Moving his face away, Rainere's top lip curled in either anger or disappointment at her silence. "You're still disgusted with me after what you heard from Grotto this morning. You assume I was given the choice to abandon my progeny." He let go of her chin and crossed his arms. "And that I don't deserve my own son."

"What? No!" Adele was shocked he would think that, but she still shifted off his lap and back to her own chair to get some space between them. "Darling, I think you're a wonderful man. My children adore you, and I trust you absolutely."

"Absolutely?" Rainere raised an imperious eyebrow. "Even though I stole Natalie from you and then lost the children in a vicious kidnapping?"

Adele was stunned to silence again.

"You'll never really forgive me, will you? What mother could forgive that?" he asked.

But Adele had already asked herself that question and she still wasn't sure of the answer. "Rainere, I love you, but now isn't the time for a wedding."

It was Rainere's turn to look incredulous. "A wedding!" He shook his head. "All I want is the crucial Marchant binding ceremony and for my son to be written under my name in the Marchant Book of Genealogy, for him to be recognized as a prince. You cannot deny me this."

"And I won't, Rainere," she whispered. Because what else could she say? She looked away, already imagining how marrying a Marchant prince would destabilize the kingdom that she'd only just put to rights. Then a hideous thought occurred to her. "Wait! Are you only here as penance for your past actions? Because of guilt? Not because you actually want to be with us?"

Rainere leaned across the table. "How dare you ask me that when I'm the one trying to bind us even tighter." Sparks dripped from his finger when he pointed it at her belly. "At the very least that baby should be born knowing its brother and sisters share a name, though they don't share blood."

She took a deep breath and let it out in a rush. "Sweet Christ, be reasonable, Rainere," she whispered. "This baby is a god and it might kill me."

"All the more reason for the children to have my name," he said just as quietly, and whatever he saw in her expression made his anger dissolve. He reached for her again. "The goddess will not let it come to that, *cara mia*. Have faith."

Faith? Is that all we can rely on now? Adele thought and had never been more relieved to hear her steward announcing the arrival of visitors.

Prince Rainold entered the room with a battered but smiling High Wizard Ohren, to the delight of the children, who re-joined the table and began sharing stories from the exciting day they'd had. Rainere poured the wizards each a glass of beer. Rainold shuddered at the sight of it, but Ohren took his glass gladly and needed a refill before he'd even put it back down on the table.

"That sounds like so much fun. I'm sorry I missed it," Ohren told Natalie. "Leafy, did you enjoy the stables too?"

The little Marchant child nodded and cuddled her blanket close. "I gotta pony of me own," she whispered.

"Of *my* own, darling," Adele corrected the little girl with a smile. "We say 'my,' not 'me.'"

"I gotta pony of my own," Leafy repeated. She covered her smile with a corner of her blanket.

"What a charming child," Prince Rainold declared. "Why did I never think to adopt a few urchins? They're great fun. You have so many, Your Majesty—would you mind terribly if I kept Leafy?"

"Nope, Leafy is ours for good." Adele pulled the little girl onto her lap for a hug. "And when her brother gets back from the mines, he can live with us too."

Leafy snuggled into Adele's arms. "I gotta bruvva of my own," she said. "And a family."

"Yes, we are a family," Rainere agreed, but his gaze lit upon Adele.

When the clock chimed the hour, the three nannies swept in and took the children away to clean them up before bedtime. The evening was still warm, and so pleasant—and because she needed to recover from her intense conversation with Rainere—Adele asked for chilled cherry wine to be served out on the terrace.

Hollis delivered the wine along with a jug of ice water. Adele dropped onto the biggest outdoor couch, the wicker one that was almost as wide and deep as a bed. Curled up in the plump cushions, she released a huge sigh. Ohren chuckled as he took a seat at the other end of the couch.

"Such a noise, Your Majesty," he said, sitting back on the cushions, careful of his injuries. "Anyone would think you had the world on your shoulders."

Adele attempted a smile. "How did I ever confuse Orestes for you, Ohren?" she asked. "I should've known something was wrong when he never made fun of me."

Ohren pulled off his charmed jewels and set them on a little saucer on the side table nearest to him. His image shimmered, and then before her sat a tall, handsome young man with electric-blue eyes and blond curls flopping over a bruised forehead. She handed him a glass of cherry wine and took a glass of water for herself. They clinked "cheers" and took long sips.

"But did you not miss me at all?" Ohren asked in disbelief. "I mean, you must've needed my sensible counsel and help with the Sandarian empress?"

"Well, Orestes really got on my nerves, so I was always glad when he left the room," she said. "I know the kids missed you a lot, though. Orestes simply ignored them. Honestly, that should've been my first warning. The next time your identical twin pretends to be you, I'll be on it straightaway."

"Well, at least pregnancy hasn't affected your sense of humor," he said, looking somewhat mollified. "And trust me, I managed to do a lot of thinking down in Hell, and I'm done treating you like a party piece. From now on, we work together as friends. If you would like that?" His expression suggested he was already sure that she would.

She rolled her eyes. "That's wonderful, Ohren, but do you want to hear what your brother did to me while you were in prison?"

Ohren finished his glass of wine in a single swallow. "Spare no detail," he said.

While Adele talked, she watched Rainere and his father wander out to the terrace. He'd stayed inside to tell his usual bedtime stories to the children, and Prince Rainold had gone with him. Seeing that she was deep in conversation with Ohren, he led his father to the balcony edge to give them some privacy.

But Adele still couldn't take her eyes off him. She thought the difference between the two princes was not as stark in the soft candlelight on the terrace. They were roughly the same height and build—it was only Rainold's constant animated movement that set him apart from his son. Rainere's shoulders were held stiff, and his hands hardly moved at all. Only very occasionally did his lips twitch up in a half smile at something his father said, but that smile was enough to heat her desire. She could see the moment that Rainere knew she was thinking about him when his hand slid over the Mark on his side. Not for the first time, she wondered what it felt like to have two sets of emotions squashed into the same body. *It can't help his sanity to have my awful powers echoing through him all the time,* she thought.

"Queen Adelena?"

Adele didn't realize that she'd stopped talking. "Sorry, Ohren, where was I?"

"Well, it sounds like the Sandarians left us on good terms."

Prince Rainold linked arms with Rainere and led him over to Ohren and Adele. "There you go, darling. I won't keep you from your lady a moment longer."

Rainere dropped onto the couch next to Adele, tucking her under his arm. Rainold folded himself onto the same large couch, cuddling into the high wizard. He and Ohren touched foreheads.

"Hello, you," Rainold said softly.

"Hello, you," Ohren repeated and kissed his nose. "Thank you again for not killing my twin."

"You're welcome," Rainold said. "Thank you for letting me rescue you from Hell."

"You're welcome." Ohren lightly kissed his lips. "Thank you for forgiving me for not being the one to rescue you from your interdimensional prison."

Rainold returned Ohren's kiss with a more passionate one. "But I haven't forgiven you for that, darling."

"This is nauseating," Rainere murmured to Adele. "Perhaps we should leave the gentlemen to their own devices?"

"No, no, we'll stop," Rainold promised, but he kept laughing as Ohren wrapped his arms around him and kissed behind his ear. "Come on, we need to talk to the kids about important things."

Adele chuckled, but Rainere only looked confused. "It's funny!" she said, squeezing his knee. "I mean, we look so much older than these two boys, yet we're called the kids."

"I suppose my father is really only sixteen years older than me," Rainere reminded her. "It's only that we were cursed at different times in our lives."

"I blame Grotto for not having you cursed earlier," Rainold said. He balled his elegant hands into fists and punched his thigh. "But I suppose he was too busy farming your bed out for gold. By the goddess Serena, I could just kill that elf!"

"Get in line," Adele growled. She caught Rainere's hurt expression. "Not about the age you were cursed, sweetheart. I think it would be weird to be in love with someone who looked so much younger than me." She stroked his thigh. "You're perfect as you are, as well as perfect for me."

"Perfect for you!" Rainere threw back his head, and Adele leaned against his chest to enjoy the vibrations of his laughter. His lips found her ear. "A perfect idiot," he whispered just for her, and she sighed out the tension she didn't know she was still holding after their fight.

Rainold gazed, wonderstruck by the beauty of a smiling Rainere. "You look so happy tonight, darling. Is it the baby coming that makes your heart so light?"

"Yes," Rainere said. "And I have this woman to thank for it." He turned her chin with his finger, and there was love in his forest-green eyes. "I can only try and be worthy of her."

"You mean *demon*," Prince Rainold corrected his son. "Adelena is a demon, darling—you don't want to forget that."

Rainere raised an eyebrow, his smile dying. "There's something you shouldn't forget, Prince Rainold—"

"So, speaking of babies," Ohren interrupted the princes. "What are we going to do about Princess Stella?"

Adele had been captivated by the charged atmosphere between Rainere and his father, but her daughter's name brought her back to reality with a thud. "What about Stella?"

"Well, since Rainold, very cleverly and with amazing ingenuity, freed the princess from the dragon flame," Ohren said, "she is common again, and being common, she is vulnerable to the Summer Influenza."

Adele felt her heart clench painfully. "Stella isn't immune after contracting it once already?"

"Immune? No." Ohren was confused by the idea. "The influenza presents with different symptoms each year. The only remedy is the Fire Orchid tonic as a preventative. Essentially, the tonic adapts to the body, giving a commoner their own tiny source of magic. The effect only lasts a few months, but that's enough to survive the flu season."

"It sounds like the Fire Orchid tonic works like the Gift of Life," Adele said. "Can they be interchanged?"

Prince Rainold gave Adele a sharp look, but his laugh was airy. "What funny ideas you have, Your Majesty," he said. "No commoner can ingest the Gift of Life. The Gift is powerful, unadulterated magic in liquid form. Only magical creatures and those with particularly pure royal blood can benefit from its effects."

"The Gift would act on the body much like the Summer Influenza, in fact," Ohren said, warming to his subject. "The green magic would dominate and destroy the central nervous system without any other source of magic to control it."

"You make it sound like the magic is sentient," Adele said, and then felt foolish. Of course the magic was sentient—she could feel it loving her releases and fighting her control daily.

"It's the nature of magic," Rainold said. "It still needs a host if it intends to grow more powerful, and all magic wants to be more than itself. It's the one directive it follows."

"What does it do with the power?" she asked, settling back into the crook of Rainere's arm.

Rainold cocked an eyebrow at her question. "Why does anything in the natural world follow its own purposes? It's magic, and it wants to grow. That's why demons are so attracted to Marchants, and vice versa." He sipped his wine, watching Adele over the rim of his glass. "Demons are powerful creatures, but they require magic to nourish them because their own is finite. The magic in a Marchant of royal descent is strong and self-perpetuating. For its own part, the Marchant magic desires to be joined with a demon's own magic, because it's transformed into something more powerful again inside the demon. The desire you two share is the same desire that Rainere would have with any other demon who came close to him."

Rainold waved his hands like doves taking flight. "I'm sure you two really do love each other," he continued. "But wouldn't it be interesting to know if your attraction was as strong without all the magic?"

Rainere was so tense Adele felt like she was being embraced by tree branches. She discreetly slipped a hand up his thigh. "And what about you two?" she asked, determined not to let Rainold get under her skin. "A Marchant prince and a St. Lucidis royal. What's the attraction there?" She instantly wished she hadn't asked when both Ohren and Rainold burst into peals of laughter.

"It was purely an intellectual attraction," Ohren said, when he'd calmed down a little. "Rainold is the cleverest wizard I've ever met."

"No, *you* are the cleverest wizard you've ever met." Rainold said, rolling his eyes when Ohren agreed with a chuckle. "But I was the only one who could understand you. Personally, I liked you as soon as I heard your constructive time wave theorem and then because you were such an excellent kisser."

Ohren's cheeks were bright red, and he embraced Rainold so tightly that the prince was tangled in his arms, laughing and protesting.

"I know you weren't asking for their life story," Rainere muttered in Adele's ear. "But they're acting like a couple of love-drunk idiots, and I'm tired of watching Ohren seduce my father."

Adele couldn't begrudge the long-lost lovers their joy, but it had to be uncomfortable for Rainere. Since her arrival in Evendaar, she'd also thought of ancient High Wizard Ohren as a surrogate grandfather type. But that illusion was shattered when he was in his true form as a twenty-something making out with his boyfriend.

"Oh, are you two leaving?" It was Rainold who noticed them

getting up. "We have much more to discuss, you know." He batted Ohren's hands away. "Seriously, Rainere, sit back down, please."

Rainere slung his arm around Adele's waist and led her to the living room doors.

"Rainere, do not walk away from me!" Rainold shouted, all playfulness gone. "You managed to get a demon pregnant, and that's a very dangerous mistake to have made. We need to discuss the consequences!"

Rainere shut the terrace doors and swung Adele up into his arms so fast she giggled. "It's not just my magic that wants you naked right now," he growled.

Adele had just pressed herself into his kiss when she heard a cough nearby. "Your Majesty?"

Oh, for fu— "General Ohrig, didn't I already dismiss you for the day?" she asked, communicating something much stronger with her glare.

"The Queen's General cannot be dismissed from duty," Ohrig reminded her. "But I've got someone you need to see."

"Is it *very* important, Ohrig?"

"It is."

Rainere let Adele's feet touch the ground again, but she held his hand and they both joined Ohrig. The general called out to Hollis, and the steward allowed the Lady Mayor to enter the royal apartment.

Bethany Merrills looked beautiful tonight. Her high-necked, violet silk gown brushed along the ground, the jet beads that fringed her waist and sash tinkling as she walked. Her hair had been curled and set in a high bun, with loose tresses cascading over one shoulder. Bethany bobbed in the most dignified curtsy Adele had ever seen. But the Lady Mayor wasn't looking at her—she only had eyes for Rainere.

"Good evening, Your Majesty and Your Highness. I apologize for intruding on you without an appointment."

"I'm sure my general thought you had a good reason for doing so." Adele gestured for everyone to sit down on a pair of fuchsia silk-covered couches separated by a gilt coffee table. She kept hold of Rainere's hand when he sat next to her.

"Your Majesty, the Lady Mayor has discovered the culprit who poisoned the beer delivered to the palace," Ohrig said, taking a seat next to Bethany.

Adele followed Bethany's gaze, which was still on Rainere. He did look particularly dashing tonight, his cheeks pink and three shirt buttons undone to expose the top of his well-defined chest.

"That's wonderful news!" Adele spoke loudly, trying to gain the mayor's attention. "Have you dealt with the matter?"

"I have dealt with the single culprit who personally poisoned the beer, Your Majesty," she replied. "Unfortunately, the problem seems to be more systemic than we first thought."

Adele held her breath so she wouldn't let out a huge "Well, of course it is" sigh.

Bethany leaned forward in her seat, directing her question to Rainere. "Your Highness, I'd like to know if you have dealt with the problem that we shared the other night."

Rainere's eyes flashed, and Adele knew she was the only who could tell that he was uncomfortable. To anyone else, he just looked furious. "As far as you're concerned, the problem has been dealt with."

"Is he dead?" Bethany's bold question made Ohrig dart the mayor a warning glare.

Rainere stared but didn't answer.

"That's a no, then," Bethany snapped. "Perhaps if you're so reluctant to do the work, you will allow me to take it on myself?"

Rainere's lips quirked up at both ends, genuinely amused by the Lady Mayor, and Adele was suddenly very curious to hear how well these two knew each other. "If only it were that simple, Lady Mayor," he drawled. "But alas, the problem seems to be more systemic than we first thought."

"But you promised me!" Bethany argued, touching a hand to her neck.

"Then perhaps incompetence is contagious," Rainere said. "You promised me something very similar and have yet to deliver on it."

Bethany pressed her painted lips into a hard line. Finding no joy with the prince, she finally focused on Adele. "Your Majesty, with the Boss incapacitated, the Underworld is in utter chaos. The poison used in the beer meant for you is a new weapon on the streets. Except instead of coming from the Slums, it's being fabricated on the clean streets of the Guild Quarter. Without the fear of the Boss looming over them, a certain clan of your finest citizens are making poison and contaminating large batches of the common blue tonic. As you might know, blue tonic is the single biggest seller on the opiate market."

Refreshments arrived, and Bethany Merrills accepted her glass of chilled wine. "Now we have poisoned blue tonic flooding the streets, and bodies are piling up at an alarming rate," she continued. "The addiction to blue tonic crosses all boundaries, Your Majesty, among rich and poor alike."

"What would you like me to do about it?" Adele asked.

For the first time since she'd entered the grand royal apartment to take a meeting with the queen of Unisia and a Marchant prince, Bethany Merrills looked overwhelmed. "I don't know," she replied. "We've never had a situation like this. For as long as I've been in office, we've always had the Boss controlling the Underworld. His ways were harsh but very effective. Without him, I fear we're vulnerable to the dangers he actually protected us from."

Bethany's fear triggered Adele's stubborn optimism. "Rubbish! We'll find a solution without returning to the old ways of the Boss. It's a new world, so we'll make new rules." She stood up. "But not tonight. If you would like to, you are welcome to stay in the palace as my guest, then we shall reconvene tomorrow after breakfast and look at this crisis in depth."

"Well, actually I should —" Bethany glanced at Ohrig, who gave her that tiny shake of his head Adele knew so well. And just like she did, Bethany acquiesced to the general. "Thank you, Your Majesty, you are too kind."

"We'll wish you a good night, Your Majesty and Your Highness." Ohrig stood and raised his eyebrow at her, but Adele didn't want to talk about this anymore, so she gave her own tiny head shake. Ohrig led the Lady Mayor from the apartment.

Adele turned to Rainere. "I don't care if someone else comes to declare war on Unisia, I am taking you to bed right now."

Rainere laughed that new laugh of his. "Well, there were several requests from the children that you were to kiss them while they slept," he said. "And apparently you have to leave proof that you were there, or Natalie said she's coming in to wake us up in the morning."

Adele winced. Morning was her favorite time with Rainere. "I'll leave them a signed document."

She went to the nursery as Rainere disappeared into her bed-chamber. Moving carefully in the dim light, she tucked Aaron's limbs back under the covers and replaced Natalie's cuddly toys from where they'd fallen on the floor. Stella was sleeping soundly in her cot, the three big puppies crowded together under her low bed. Leafy, as always, was awake the moment she heard the door open and watched Adele with round eyes.

She leaned over and kissed the little girl on the head. "Bad dreams, sweetheart?"

Leafy dropped her chin. "Imma Special," she said, and Adele knew she'd been dreaming about the mines again.

"I'm a Special too," she whispered.

"They'll hurt you," Leafy whispered back.

Adele tucked Leafy's security blanket closer to her chest. "If someone tries to hurt the people I love, then I fight," she said. "If anyone tries to hurt you again, Leafy, then I will fight to protect you."

"Why?" Leafy's voice was thin with fear, and it broke Adele's heart.

"When I was little, I was adopted too," she whispered. "My

mummy and daddy found me on the side of a desert road, and they kept me as their own daughter. My mummy always told me that she knew as soon as she saw me that I was special." Adele didn't add how her adopted mother went on to become very disillusioned with her "special" child who never did anything right in her eyes.

"Is that baby special too?" Leafy asked, pointing at Adele's belly.

"Some of our children are born in our bodies, and some of our children are born in our hearts," she said, avoiding the question. "You were born in my heart, Leafy. The minute I saw you, I knew you belonged with us. You're family now."

Leafy snuggled down in her comfortable bed. "Family."

"Family," Adele agreed. She kissed Leafy on her hot little cheek. "Now, go to sleep before I send Prince Rainere back in here to tell you more boring stories."

Leafy giggled and turned her head into the pillow, eyes already closing.

Feeling satisfied with her maternal duties done, Adele began thinking of her duty to Rainere and how she still needed to apologize for questioning him about his time "progenating" women. She wondered how to open the conversation without it turning into another fight as she crossed the quiet living room to her bedchamber. She found him wearing only trousers as he closed the double doors to the terrace.

"I heard my father and Ohren out there," he complained. "And I really wish I hadn't."

Adele giggled in sympathy and presented him with her back so he could undo the ribbons and laces of her dress, which he did with a muttered charm and soft touches. "There must be romance in the air," she said. "Charlie wanted a birthday kiss from me today."

Rainere's hands pushed her gown to the floor. "So that's what I felt in the Mark this afternoon. You were enjoying Charlie?"

Adele spun around in his arms. She could tell by the downturn of his lips that she'd annoyed him again. "God, no! Charlie just got a little excited," she said. "What I'm more worried about is why I had such a strong reaction. He's a child and—" She forced herself to say it. "And I really hurt him, I could tell."

"Is this your apology?" Rainere asked, lip curled.

"Yes, I am sorry for kissing anyone else when I'm committed to you alone." Adele was too distracted to try and be cute. "But it was only meant to be a little peck, and then I attacked him. He was so upset with me, but when I tried to explain that the magic takes over sometimes, I just made it worse. He didn't come to dinner tonight, so I guess he's still furious with me, and so he should be. I betrayed his trust."

Rainere snorted in derision. "I think you might've misread Charlie's intentions, *cara mia*."

"No matter how tall he gets, he's still just a boy," she said, grim with guilt. "But Rainere, it was the hunger that frightened me. I was swept away in it so fast."

Rainere slipped his hands low and lifted her, wrapping her legs around his hips. His sneer had disappeared now, and he looked at her lips like a starving man. "This hunger you speak of, can I feed it for you?"

She clung on as Rainere carried her to the Glass Bed. "How do you know Bethany?" she blurted before she could stop herself.

"I've never kissed her, if that's what you're asking." Rainere lay Adele among the dozens of pillows and climbed in next to her.

She pushed him onto his back and sat astride him. She ran her hands over the flat, hard muscle of his chest. "I'm sorry," she said. "I've got no right to question you when I've been acting like an arse. But we also have some very serious stuff to talk about, and it can't wait. You were so angry with me before, and I want to know where that came from. I know I was unfair to you this morning when . . ."

But Rainere groaned in exasperation and bucked his hips to move her against him. "Don't be so cruel, *cara mia*!" he said. "It's already near midnight. We've only got a few hours together before the day starts again, and you want to waste it talking. For the love of the goddess, kiss me and forget about it."

But there was something else that troubled Adele, and it tickled at the back of her mind. *What was it?* It wasn't about Charlie but something about their kiss—something it had let her do. But Rainere wasn't waiting any longer. Threading a hand through her hair, he pulled gently and pressed his lips to her neck. The sensation of his tongue on her skin wiped away thought and made her magic ignite. Yet, still, Adele resisted and the memory she was seeking almost surfaced.

"Darling, we really have to talk about our fight," she said, trying to catch his head in her hands as his lips moved over her collarbone. "I can't believe you think I don't trust you with the children. You're incredible, and you do so much for them. With this new, strange godbaby coming, we have to get any problems we have between us sorted out quickly."

"Yes, I know." But he wasn't listening as he caught her hands with one of his, clasping them to his chest. His other hand slid between her legs. "Stop your torture and kiss me before I go insane."

Gasping, Adele gave up the fight for a sensible conversation and melted against Rainere's gorgeous, strong body. "Such a romantic, my prince," she murmured, and moaned as her serpentine magic slid, coil upon coil, from underneath her heart, seeking her fingertips. "If you insist."

Adele froze solid when the sudden, shrill cacophony of the Chime Voices pounded in her head, electrifying every cell in her body for just a moment before she fell into the darkness.

*

Adele knew that she was in a dream. The clarity that came with a vision wasn't there and she didn't recognize the forest glade surrounding her. The sun shone, though she didn't feel the warmth, and butterflies fluttered their electric-blue wings, trembling on every tree branch and every green leaf, though she didn't feel a breeze. In front of her, Dahk'hani was a ball of light, floating above the ground on a fluffy white cloud.

"You're my baby?" Adele asked, and her voice was like the Chime Voices tinkling.

"Mother!" The ball of light spoke as it pulsed. "Call her!"

A sharp pain struck Adele so hard she fell, though she didn't feel the ground beneath her knees. Her insides burned and she wrapped her arms around herself. But this wasn't right. If it was a dream, Adele knew she shouldn't feel pain.

"Call her!" The voice was young, male and high-pitched with panic. "Call her!"

Adele reached out to cradle the ball of light, and it flared, searing her eyes.

*

Adele woke with a cry tearing from her throat. The bedchamber was dark, only a single candelabra on her dressing table providing a little light. She sat up in bed, not knowing if she wanted to weep or scream. Her naked body was drenched in sweat, and she stank of metal, tasting rust on her tongue.

"Rainere?" She felt around for him, shaking like she had been zapped with electricity. "Sweetheart, I had a horrible nightmare."

He was on the other side of the bed, laid out on his back, arms spread wide, and there were dark shadows bruising his chest. The pillows beneath him were also dark. When she shook him, he felt cold to the touch. "Rainere, wake up, please," she begged. But he didn't wake, though she slapped his shoulder and almost climbed on top of him.

"Oh, no, this is all wrong," Adele whispered. She lifted her hand from the pillow near Rainere's head, and it came away wet with dark green liquid. "Sweet Christ, it's his magic. What have I done?"

In a wild panic, she leaped off the bed and raced to throw open the balcony doors, screaming for Prince Rainold and Ohren to help her.

The wizards were sleeping on the large outdoor sofa, covered by one of the silk throws. For one awful moment, Adele thought that they were dead too, but Ohren was the first to rouse, startled into alertness by the sight of her, naked and shrieking at him. He shook Rainold awake. Puzzled, the two found their trousers and followed her into the bedchamber. It was only when he saw Rainere lying still that Rainold dashed to his side. He checked Rainere's eyes and felt for a pulse at his throat. "It's weak, Ohren," he shouted. "He's fading. Help me!"

Ohren repeated the same checks that Rainold had just done and listened to his heart. "It's slow," he agreed. "I'll try to massage it."

Adele had never seen anyone massage a heart through the ribcage before. It seemed such a violent way to get someone to wake up. Suddenly, Prince Rainold blocked her view of the bed, his eyes narrowed in fear and rage. "What did you do to him?" he hissed. "Tell me now, demon."

Adele sobbed. "Nothing," she tried to say. "I woke up and he was like this." But Rainold's hands were on her shoulders, and he shook her too hard for the words to make sense.

"Rainold, let her speak!" Ohren shouted from the bed as he used gusts of gold magic and his hands to thump Rainere's heart back to a normal rhythm. "We need to know what she did so we can fix it."

Rainold pulled Adele so close they were touching, naked chest to chest. Her nipples pebbled against his warm skin, and the circle of silver around his irises started spinning. Instinctively, she knew that their reactions had nothing to do with her fear or his hate. It was her magic that reached out and his that submitted.

"You did this while fucking him, didn't you?" Rainold was appalled at what he saw in her eyes. "You took all his magic, and now he's got nothing left to sustain him."

Adele tried to pull away, but his hands were like iron bands around her arms. "I just kissed him," she protested. "And then there was darkness, and I dreamed . . . but I don't know what I did. I don't know!"

Rainold's nose was close enough to touch hers. "I hate you." His whisper was filled with hopelessness. "I hate all of you damned demons." Yet he buried his head in her neck, and Adele felt his tongue.

"Rainold, get ahold of yourself!" The force of Ohren's shout shook them both. "Release the queen and help me with your son."

Adele had to push Rainold away, but this time it was easy. Despite her heart's pain, she felt vital and strong. Glaring, Rainold spat what he'd tasted of her onto the floor by her feet and joined Ohren. She hovered at a safe distance from the bed and watched Ohren try to save Rainere's mortal body. He had his hands on Rainere's head, and the wizard's eyes were closed as a golden probe connected their foreheads. When he opened his eyes again, they were filled with despair.

"No!" she shrieked. "There must be a way I can fix him."

Ohren shook his head. "It's impossible. He needs his own magic to heal from this. I've never seen anyone so strong so depleted."

"No! I can do the impossible, I do it all the time!" Adele covered her mouth with her hands, trying to hold in the hysteria.

"Blood!" Rainold turned on her in a frenzy. "Give him your blood, and your magic will feed his."

Ohren reached out for his lover, trying to pull him close. "That's not how healing works."

But Rainold shook him off. "Rainestra once told me that the Eldars drink their demon blood in a special ceremony when they want to work really powerful enchantments. She said that the demon takes the magic from the Eldar until they are almost drained, and then they bleed into a crystal glass, and the Eldar drinks it. She said they only need a drop or two of gold magic to make it stable. Try it, Ohren—try it now!"

Ohren shook his head, but Adele grabbed a water glass off her dressing table and tipped the liquid to the floor, handing it to Rainold. She found a letter opener on the little decorative desk in the corner and sliced her wrist crossways. Rainold took the glass and held it as the blood dripped in a haphazard stream. "It's too thick, the blood won't run," she shouted in frustration.

"Then cut yourself deeper, demon." Rainold grabbed the letter opener and jabbed it right into her open wound, the blood streaking down the blade and into the glass. She was so happy to see it fill that she didn't even feel the pain.

With a quick slice on his finger, Ohren added a few drops of his own blood. "Now what?" he asked as he took Adele's damaged wrist, wrapping it in a silk shawl and holding her arm above her head to slow the blood flow.

Rainold climbed onto the bed and half-lifted Rainere into his lap. He held the glass of cooling blood to his lips and tipped his head back. The three of them held their breath while Rainold dripped the blood into Rainere's mouth, sip by sip.

Then Rainere swallowed. Just a little, but it was a swallow. Adele dived forward to grasp his hand. "Oh, darling, please drink it all."

"Get away from him!" Rainold's eyes flashed at her. "He'd better live through this, demon, or you'll die by my hand next."

Adele recoiled from Rainold's paternal fury. Even when her desperate concern for Rainere would have trumped every other emotion in her body, now she felt only shame.

"Queen Adelena." Ohren slipped a robe over her naked shoulders. He leaned down close to whisper. "Go and get some witnesses, right now. Even if Rainere lives, Rainold will come at you. He'll be quick and savage."

With a sob of despair, Adele did the unthinkable. She belted her silk robe and dashed out of the bedchamber, away from her dying love and ran for the only place she might be safe.

Bursting into the apartment of her Queen's Guard, she raced across the living area and threw herself at Ohrig's door. It was locked, so she banged as hard as she could with two fists, shouting for him at the top of her lungs. It seemed to take forever before she heard any noise. Ohrig finally opened his door, naked but for a towel wrapped around his waist.

"Your Majesty?" Ohrig's voice was rough with sleep, though his pale blue eyes were alert. "What's happened?"

"It's Rainere. I think . . ." Adele sobbed, gasping for breath. "I think I've killed him!"

Then Captain Lucky was coming out of his room, dressed in a neat pajama suit. "Who've you killed, Your Majesty?"

But Adele could only press her hands to her mouth.

"She thinks she's killed the Marchant prince," Ohrig answered for her.

"Impossible. Unless you cut him into little pieces and burned him or set against him with dragon flame." Lucky thought he was comforting her, but Adele choked on more sobs.

"Lucky, get the men roused," Ohrig ordered.

Lucky rushed off to wake the other QGs. At another time, Adele might've been surprised to see Charlie coming out in his boxer shorts from a bedroom in the QGs' apartment, but tonight was not that time.

"What do you need right now?" Ohrig held her shoulder in his big, warm hand. "Tell me, and we'll do it."

Forcing away the hysteria, Adele tried to form a coherent sentence. "Prince Rainold is with Rainere now," she squeaked. "He is trying to revive him, but . . . but Ohren said that I need witnesses in case Rainold tries to kill me in revenge."

"Ohrig?" Bethany leaned in the doorway of Ohrig's bedroom wearing a man's dressing gown. "What's going on?"

"Go back to bed, darlin'," Ohrig said. "The queen needs me."

Without argument, Bethany melted back into the darkness of his room.

"You all have to come with me now," Adele pleaded. "Hurry! I need to see if Rainere is any better." She waited five long minutes, pacing the corridor, before the QGs and Charlie were mostly dressed and ready to accompany her on the mad dash back to the royal apartment.

They were greeted by Ohren at the door. The high wizard's face was gray with fatigue, but he clasped Adele's hand, giving it a squeeze. "He's all right, Your Majesty," he said. "Your blood worked very well."

Adele crept to Rainere's bedside. Rainold was nowhere to be seen, but the bathroom door was open, and she heard the sound of running water. On the night table was the empty glass, stained rust-red with her blood.

Rainere opened his eyes at the noise of the QGs' arrival, but his smile was for her alone. "*Cara mia*, where'd you go?" His voice sounded like two stones rasping together.

"God, I'm so sorry!" Adele flung herself at him and buried her face in his chest. "Are you all right, really?"

With a visible effort, Rainere forced himself upright. "Of course I am," he said. "Why are the Queen's Guard here?"

"I imagine Her Majesty thought she might need her lapdogs to keep me from killing her, my darling son," Rainold said as he came out of the bathroom.

Adele watched as Rainere's gaze traveled from her tearstained face to his father's tense one, to Ohren's gray cheeks, and then to the Queen's Guard, looking rumpled and anxious. Wrapping a bedsheet around his waist, he got out of bed. "As you can see, I'm not dead, so you can all leave. Now."

"Darling." She hesitated. "Are you sure?"

"It's the shock." Prince Rainold bustled forward to try and push Rainere back onto bed, though his son resisted. "He'll need weeks to recuperate from what you did to him, demon. I was very lucky to be close by tonight. If you'd left him like that any longer, he wouldn't have woken."

"It's no one's business what Queen Adelena and I do," Rainere protested, as he sank back down on the edge of the mattress. "Leave us."

"No, she can leave," Rainold shouted, and Adele flinched from his glare when he pointed at the door. "I'll call you if Rainere needs any more of your blood, demon. Until then, you will stay far away from my son or I'll kill you myself."

"For goddess' sake, Rainold, stop it!" But the words seemed to drain the last of Rainere's strength, and he fell backward with a moan. Rainold lifted Rainere's legs and tucked him under the covers again, crooning sweet nothings.

"What did you do, Your Maj?" Charlie sounded more curious than concerned as he watched Rainere fade back into sleep.

"I warned you," she whispered. "I told you what I can do. Except this time, I didn't stop."

"Your Majesty?" Captain Lucky shouldered Charlie out of the way and led her to a chair with an arm around her shoulders. "In the panic, you might not have noticed." He placed a gentle hand on her belly. "There's been a change."

Adele looked down to see a new roundness to her abdomen. "The baby grew?" She couldn't comprehend it. "It's growing after what I did?"

Lucky dropped into a crouch beside her chair. "When we were in the Ice Mountains, Dahk'hani usually came to you in a vision, Your Majesty." His voice was gentle and slow. "Did that happen again tonight?"

Adele nodded. "We were kissing, then I blacked out, and I dreamed of Dahk'hani but it wasn't real enough to be a vision. He was asking for something, he wanted me to . . ." But she couldn't remember what it was.

Ohrig muttered a string of expletives under his breath, and Adele felt a wave of guilt swamp her.

"I'm so sorry," she told him as tears leaked down her cheeks. "Just when we think life will get quiet, I go and fuck it up again."

Lucky took Adele's hand in one of his and felt for the pulse on her wrist. "The most important thing you can do now is stay calm, Your Majesty," he said.

"The most important thing she can do is stay away from anyone with Marchant blood, the filthy demon," Rainold said, his hands chopping the air in his fury. "It's clear she's going to feed that unnatural baby of hers with our pure magic. Mark my words, she won't stop until we're all dead and her monster is the only one alive."

Adele's hands snaked around her abdomen as if to protect the unborn god from Rainold's awful truth. Yet even now she found herself taking in the beauty of Prince Rainold's shirtless body. Just imagining the depth and strength of his magic made her shiver.

"Shut up, my love. These are the Queen's Guard, and they will not tolerate any murderous speeches from you," High Wizard Ohren said, embracing Rainold with one arm as he addressed the group. "Rainere is healed and needs rest to recover fully. I think we should leave him alone now. I, for one, could do with a stiff Firewhiskey, if anyone wants to join me in the living room?"

Only Rainold stayed behind, dragging an armchair to the bed to watch over his sleeping son. Everyone else followed High Wizard Ohren out to the living room, where Mrs. Ollenby was wringing her hands and waiting with trays of hot tea and whiskeys already poured for everyone.

"Your Majesty, I overheard the shouting," she said. "Is everything all right? How is Prince Rainere?"

Still reeling from the shock of nearly killing him, Adele only shook her head. She dropped onto a couch and curled into herself.

High Wizard Ohren sat next to her, wrapping his arm around her shoulders and pressing his lips to her hair as he whispered, "It was the god who forced you to do that to Prince Rainere. Please don't blame yourself."

Ohrig took an armchair close by. He sipped his Firewhiskey, looking between Adele and High Wizard Ohren. "So, we're all friends again, High Wizard?" he asked. "Charlie filled us in on your little adventure with Orestes."

"I still don't know how we could have been so blind as to confuse you both." Lucky shook his head.

"Exactly! Orestes has no sense of humor, and I'm the life of the party," Ohren said, in an attempt at levity that was ignored by all.

Adele took a cup of hot tea from Mrs. Ollenby. "It's horrible to think that he was so close to all of us, but especially the children."

Ohren patted her knee. "Well, I'm back now. Charlie and Rainold saved me, and I will be eternally grateful to them both."

"Charlie said you've got Orestes in Hell," General Ohrig said. "You think it's wise to keep him there?"

"He's been effectively neutralized," Ohren said as he took a glass of Firewhiskey from the tray offered to him.

"But we'll need a more permanent solution soon." Adele frowned. "If you can be rescued, so could he. What if Pere Raven tries to break him out? He's got into the Golden Palace before without us knowing, and so did Rip when he disguised himself as a steward."

Charlie sat on the arm of the couch close to her. "Maybe one of those containment spells that Prince Rainere does, Your Maj?"

"Yes, that's a great idea," Adele said, relieved that someone was helping her fix problems instead of finding more. "I'll talk to Rainere about it when he feels better."

Charlie looked down at her, and she thought he looked so handsome when he smiled like that. The silver ring was spinning around his irises, and his gaze dropped to her silk robe that had opened a little at the front. Adele felt the magic's hunger bite her, fierce and greedy. "Charlie, if you could take a seat somewhere else," she murmured. "I'm finding it hard to concentrate."

"Because I'm so irresistible, my queen?" he asked with a chuckle. "It's funny how you've changed your tune since this afternoon."

Adele risked a glance up at Charlie, and what he saw in her eyes only made his smile grow. "I said, move away!" she hissed, and the cup in her hand cracked to pieces, splashing tea everywhere.

Still smirking, Charlie got up and found another seat.

"Your Majesty?" Lucky was at her side with a handkerchief to mop up the tea. "You've gone very pink just now. Do you feel overheated?"

Mrs. Ollenby rushed to give Adele a glass of water and another cloth for the mess on her robe. "The baby, Your Majesty," she said, and her lavender eyes glistened with tears. "It's grown so much just tonight. Is it making you hungry? Would you like something else to eat?"

Adele was starving, but not for food. Lying in bed next door was her perfect meal. Just imagining Rainere and Rainold together, writhing under her hands, had her salivating. *I need to get out of here now,* she thought, desperate to hide somewhere safe and not have to deal with these depraved urges.

"Well, I hope the drama's over for tonight," Adele said to the crowd of friends all watching her with a wariness that made her want to cry. "But we've still got the Lady Mayor here, and she'll want to keep that meeting I've made with her in the morning."

"The Lady Mayor is in the Golden Palace?" Mrs. Ollenby was surprised. "I'm so sorry, Your Majesty, I wasn't asked to prepare one of the guest suites for her. Goddess, I'm so embarrassed! Who arranged her accommodation?"

"It's fine. Bethany is in with Ohrig." Adele stood up, flinching as the skin of her stomach pulled over the new baby bump.

"Oh. She's *staying* with General Ohrig." Mrs. Ollenby buttoned her lip. "I see."

Adele knew she had probably dropped Ohrig into deep trouble, but she was too tired to cover for him. "I'm going to stay in the QG quarters too," she said. "Please tell the children and Rainere when they wake up that I'll be back for breakfast."

"Of course, Your Majesty." Mrs. Ollenby tilted her head, confused, but too professional to question her queen. "I'll make sure one of the spare rooms is made up for you."

"Charlie, you stay here and sleep in Rainere's room on the other side of the nursery," Adele said. "I can't have—it'll be easier for both of us."

Charlie tried to smother his smirk. "Sure, Your Maj, but I have a guest in my room at the QG quarters, and I should really let her know."

Adele was hit by a wave of exhaustion and gave up the pretense of being in control. "Whatever," she said, "I just really need to lie down somewhere before I fall over."

Captain Lucky stayed close to her on the walk back to the QGs' apartment, his arm sliding around her waist whenever she stumbled, then quickly releasing her again. A sleepy maid entered after the group and went directly to set up one of the empty bedrooms with clean sheets and towels. Adele took a seat in the lounge area but groaned when she found the armchair was damp with something that smelled like sour wine. She moved to the couch and waited for Captain Lucky to return with his medical kit to stitch the cut on her wrist.

Charlie nipped into his bedroom with a promise of leaving soon, but Adele couldn't help but watch the door, all the while telling herself to look away.

"Earlier we had a bit of a birthday party for Charlie, Your Majesty," QG Leith said, distracting Adele from her dark thoughts.

Lucky arrived with his square leather satchel full of medical supplies and sat close to her side. She gave him her wrist and he got to work on removing the bloody shawl. "Oh, yes?"

"We thought the kid needed a celebration for the big day. Seventeen, and he's finally a proper man. He can get married, have kids, buy property, all that insanely boring stuff. He's got Siobhan in there with him now for his official birthday kiss," Leith said, chuckling.

"Watch yourself, Oleitham. I taught you better manners than to gossip like that." Bethany was still dressed in Ohrig's robe, her long black petticoats peeking out underneath. She approached Adele and knelt before her. "Are you all right, Your Majesty? Is there anything that I can do to help?"

"No, thank you." Adele tried to present a brave front, though Lucky was sewing silk thread through her skin. "I'm sorry to have disturbed your evening."

Bethany frowned, but her eyes were soft. "Can I make you a cup of tea, or get you something for the pain in your arm or the . . . ?" She gestured at Adele's unmistakable baby bump.

Adele felt her eyes fill with tears again for no reason other than it was nice that Bethany cared. "I just need sleep, I think," she said. "I'm not in pain, just really uncomfortable."

The maid announced that Adele's room was ready, and it was Captain Lucky who accompanied her down the hallway, holding her glass of water and a lantern to light the bedroom. The covers were already pulled back, but Lucky shifted the pile of pillows for her and watched as she slipped herself into bed. She lay down with a gusty sigh and felt like she could sleep for a hundred years.

Even behind closed eyes, Adele could sense her young captain hovering. "Are you going to stand there all night, Lucky?" she murmured.

"Would it trouble you if I did, Your Majesty?" he asked. "I wouldn't suggest anything improper, it's just where Dahk'hani is concerned—well, honestly, it's everything about the whole god business. I'd like to keep an eye on you in case you have another vision, or the baby grows again, or you find yourself unable to stay away from the Marchant princes."

"Sure. Whatever," she muttered. "But lie down next to me. There's no point in you missing out on sleep if, by some miracle, none of those things happen."

She heard him swallow and would've rolled her eyes if they hadn't been closed already. "Lucky, it's no worse than sleeping next to each other by a campfire," she said. "But suit yourself. I'm not forcing you."

She felt the gentle motion of the bed dipping down on one side, and then she fell into a deep, untroubled sleep.

CHAPTER FORTY

"The Morning After"

Adele woke up feeling warm and comfortable. She snuggled into the firm chest she was lying on, and it took a moment before she remembered where she was. Peeking up through her lashes, she saw that Lucky was awake and staring at the ceiling. From what she knew about her chaste captain, she thought this was probably the first time that he'd ever woken up next to a woman. She was just sorry that it had to be her and not someone more fun. She rolled off him and onto her own side of the bed.

"G'morning," she said with a yawn and burrowed into her pillows. "What's the time?"

Lucky checked his pocket watch on the bedside table. "It's just before normal muster." He stretched out on the bed, his shoulders popping as he worked out his stiffness.

"I probably should have warned you that I cuddle when I sleep, but you could've pushed me off."

Lucky shrugged. "You needed the rest, and it was nice." His expression froze when he realized what he'd said. "Not in an improper way, of course. Just to say that I wasn't uncomfortable."

Adele opened her mouth to tease him but then the hideous memories of last night came flooding back. She rolled onto her back, breathless with guilt at what she'd done to Rainere. *I almost killed the love of my life,* she thought. *I am a monster and I'm growing another one.*

"Your Majesty, don't do that to yourself."

Surprised, Adele turned her head. Lucky had pushed himself up on an elbow, his short, blond curls were rumpled, and his blue eyes were intent on hers. "Prince Rainere knows you would never intentionally hurt him," he said. "The love between you both is clear to everyone. It's . . . well, it's beautiful."

Adele wanted to talk about anything else. She figured they were already in bed together, so intimate questions would be allowed.

"I know it's your private business, Lucky," she began. "But how are things with Olivia?"

Lucky's chiseled jaw flexed. He dropped his gaze to the pillow, but not before she saw the flash of pain in his eyes. "I had decided that I was willing to overlook a single indiscretion, especially one caused by narcotics and an old flame leading my lady astray," he said. "But Olivia feels so much shame over the matter, and it's made things difficult to resolve. As it stands, we're still intended for each other—a commitment neither of us entered into lightly—and if our love is true we'll get through this."

With nothing to say that didn't make her a hypocrite, Adele decided to quickly change the subject. "Hey, what's up with Ohrig and Bethany? Is Leith all right with them being together?"

Lucky smiled at her gossipy tone, which was just the reaction she wanted. "Well, they've been on and off for years," he admitted. "I'm sure the general won't mind me telling you he and the Lady Mayor were quite the infamous couple about town back a decade or so ago. They are both very concerned with politics and helping the less fortunate citizens of Concordis, though when they're together, they do argue all the time." Lucky dropped his head to the pillow, facing her. "Leith told me he gets tired of the fighting, but as long as Ohrig doesn't include him, he doesn't really mind what the two of them get up to."

"Oh, I see." Adele rolled to her side, mirroring him by tucking her hands under her cheek on the pillow. "But isn't Ohrig having a 'thing' with Mrs. Ollenby?"

Lucky's eyes widened. "What?"

Adele nodded. "I've caught the pair of them a couple of times—giggling and flirting, Ohrig trying to work his magic."

"His magic?" Lucky looked mystified. "But the general is a man of integrity. I'm sure he wouldn't be leading on two women at the same time."

Adele laughed but then saw Lucky was serious. "Sure, of course," she said, then yelped, "Ouch!"

"Your Majesty?" Lucky was up and leaning over her, eyes scanning for injuries.

"It's the baby." Gingerly, she stretched out her legs, testing the stomach muscles that had just spasmed. Parting her robe and using the bedsheet for modesty across her hips, she revealed the skin of her belly. The baby moved again, but this time the muscles moved with it, and Adele could see a tiny bulge rise and fall.

"Grace of the goddess, it's grown again," Lucky said, worry making his words sound like a curse.

"It's very weird to have this much movement so early," Adele said. "But I guess everything about this pregnancy is going to be weird."

They both watched as another little bulge rose and fell on her abdomen. "You can touch it if you want to," she offered. "I know you've had a lot of medical training, but a pregnant demon with a god-seed inside her is probably not going to come up in your studies very often."

Lucky gently stroked her belly and froze when the baby pushed up under his hand. He gave it an experimental pat, but the baby was still again. "Is this tattoo the Dahk'hanian diagram you told us about?" He traced a line that curled under her belly button, surprising them both when it shimmered at his touch. "I hate that it's marked you like this," he murmured.

"Lucky, this thing in me, do you think that you could get it out before . . . ?" Adele stared into Lucky's eyes, silently begging him not to make her finish that sentence.

"My poor queen." Lucky understood. His warm hand slid over her belly and scooped her closer to him. "If only we could be sure the fetus's removal wouldn't kill you, or kill the wizard who performed the—"

"Of course," Adele said. "It's a god not a baby."

"It's a small comfort for the rest of us, but you are certain to meet Serena in her Garden in the Beyond should it come to that," Lucky murmured. "If you would allow me, it would be an honor to call the final blessing of the goddess for you at the . . . end. I know the rites. I did them for my mother."

Adele bit her lip and could only nod.

Lucky wiped her tears away with a gentle hand, a hand that drifted down to the side of her neck, under her hair. "I'm sorry this is happening to you, my queen," he whispered and she could feel his breath cool on her flushed cheeks. "You don't deserve any of it."

Adele closed her eyes so she wouldn't have to look up and see the wide band of gold turn in his. "Lucky, I'm a demon and a monster," she said. "It's Rainere who didn't deserve what I did to him."

"The Marchant prince is a different kind of monster," Lucky whispered, and his hand felt so nice moving down to her shoulder, squeezing it. "Perhaps you need a human man to balance your goddess-given power. Someone's whose love is untainted by dark magic. Someone who loves you for the woman you are and not the queen you have to be."

Despite her misery and self-loathing, Adele finally caught the change in atmosphere. She opened her eyes to see that Lucky's muscled torso was leaning over her, his hand still stroking her shoulder, his golden head tilted to hers, his smile dreamy. *Fuckacat, the poor guy's got caught up in the pull of my magic,* Adele thought, and cursed herself in exasperation. *He'll be so upset with himself when he realizes*

I can do this to him too. She resisted her own wicked urge to give him the kiss he was aiming for and instead put both hands on his broad chest, pushing lightly. He didn't budge. "Lucky, we should get up."

On the bedside table, Lucky's watch chimed the hour, distracting them both enough that Adele could wriggle out and away from temptation. She made it to the edge of the bed but was embarrassed to note that her robe looked rather more tea-stained and transparent than it had last night. "I think I'll just wait for you to leave first, Lucky," she said, slipping back into bed to get under the covers. "Could you bring me something to wear, please?"

"Of course, Your Majesty, of course, of course," Lucky said in a rush, sounding oddly husky. He kept his back politely turned from her as he hustled out of bed, but he stopped at the door and threw her a last glance. "I'll bring you one of my shirts while you, uh, shower."

"Thank you, Lucky," Adele called out, but Lucky had already closed the door behind himself. She slapped her forehead, hating herself all over again. "And I'm sorry that I'm such a disgusting demon that I almost bewitched you."

Heaving a huge sigh, Adele rolled out of bed for the second time and made her way to the adjoining bathroom. Unlike her palatial bathing room, there was only a narrow shower, a little sink with a mirror over it, and a white porcelain toilet bowl. The two brass towel hooks on the back of the door were the only decoration.

As the ordinary, unperfumed water cascaded over her shoulders, Adele cradled her new pot belly in her palms and remembered how she always used to speak to her babies when they were inside her. *How are we going to keep going like this, little Dahk'hani?* she wondered, feeling a shiver despite the hot water. *And why have you stopped talking to me now that you're in my body? We really should get to know each other if I'm going to be your mother. That is, if I survive that long?*

But Dahk'hani didn't answer and Adele had to get on with her day, no matter how reluctant she was to do that. Wrapped in a towel, she left the bathroom and found that Lucky had made the bed too, the blanket corners sharp and tight, the pillows stacked neatly, and laid one of his white dress shirts at the end for her. Adele buttoned the starched shirt that fit her like a dress, happy that it hung well away from her baby bump. Though, she thought it was probably a moot point when the queen of Unisia paraded herself through the corridors on a walk of shame from the night before. She debated sending for her clothes, but then figured it would be quicker just to run back to her apartment like this.

Entering the communal loungeroom, she saw Pepper busy in the kitchen. He greeted her with a mug of tea, milky and with too much sugar. "How're you feeling this morning, Your Majesty?"

"Well, thanks, Pepper," she said. "At least now I feel strong enough to face this day."

There was a knock at the apartment door, and Lucky went to answer it. General Ohrig came in from the terrace, blowing out his last puff of cigarette smoke. "Mornin'," he grunted, and took his mug of tea from Pepper with another grunt of thanks.

"Sleep well?" she asked but didn't worry when he ignored the question. He was always extra grumpy in the mornings. She wondered if Bethany was still in his bedroom and hoped she could avoid her.

Adele looked over when Lucky sounded like he was getting very annoyed with the person at the door. Then she choked on her tea when Benjamin Belvoir pushed passed the captain with a smile and mouthful of excuses. He lit up when he spotted her. "Your Majesty, I've been looking for you!"

Adele couldn't speak. Her mouth was watering, and the hunger growled in her gut, fierce and needy. Benjamin was wearing his usual stable hand uniform, a white shirt with sleeves turned up to the elbows and black denim trousers with leather patches on the knees and inside the thighs. Nothing special at all, but he looked delicious.

"Why, Ben?" Pepper asked.

"Why, what?" Benjamin slowly dragged his gaze from Adele to the red-haired QG.

"Why're you looking for Her Majesty?"

"He wouldn't say." Lucky had no love for the handsome stable hand, and she hoped he didn't know even half of the rumors or truths about Benjamin and Lady Olivia.

"It's just that I had to find my queen." Benjamin crossed the floor, and Adele was suddenly afraid that he meant to embrace her. Ohrig must have thought the same thing because he stepped in between the two of them and held his hand to Benjamin's chest.

"State your business, kid, or get out of here," the general growled. "The queen's a little busy today."

Benjamin was confused. His handsome face screwed up in a way that worked to make him look both endearing and thoughtful, though Adele knew there really wasn't much going on behind his pale green eyes. "I needed to see the queen," he managed to say. "I thought, or I think, she needed something from me."

Adele took a step toward the tall stable hand. Black curls fell over his forehead and brushed against his long, black eyelashes. "I didn't call for you," she said. "But now that you're here—"

"Your Majesty," Ohrig interrupted. "Your children will be wanting you, and there's the Marchant prince to check on."

"Yes, of course." Adele flinched from his stern expression. "I'll meet the rest of you at the royal apartment for breakfast."

"And I'll walk you back, Your Majesty," Benjamin offered. She thought of all the little side passages between the QGs' quarters and her own.

"No, I'll do it," Lucky insisted. "You can go back to work, Benjamin."

Benjamin gave Adele one last longing, confused look before he was pushed out the door by Lucky.

"Damn it, they're like bees to honey, aren't they?" Ohrig said, unimpressed. "That kid didn't even know why he wanted to see you, he just knew he had to."

"And I'm a honey trap," she agreed, miserable. "Because they want me, and then I try to kill them. I guess I don't have to say it, but your main task today is to keep me away from anyone with obvious Marchant blood, or any proper magic. I will not give in to this hideous hunger."

"But, Your Majesty, the baby needs to be fed somehow," Lucky said. "We should ask Prince Rainold what to do. He was with his demon wife, Rainestra, when she was pregnant with you. He will know how she sustained herself and the baby."

"I'll ask, but he'll probably just spit at me again," Adele said.

"Mornin', darlin'." Adele felt a hand on her low back as a half-dressed Owens lurched past her, heading for the kitchen and the teapot.

Lucky, Pepper, and Ohrig stared, silent, until Owens noticed them and then looked down at Adele.

"Fuckacat, my apologies, Your Majesty! It's usually Charlie's little lady, Siobhan, parading around here in the mornings wearing his shirt, and I know she spent the night," Owens said, by way of excuse. "And you're wearing your hair down your back, and you're the same size. Fuck it, I'm very sorry."

Adele was learning so much about her QGs' romantic lives that morning. It was like a little mental holiday from the insanity she was currently involved in.

"Owens, you know how you do that thing where you never speak?" Ohrig's frown was fierce.

"Yes, General."

"Keep doing that."

"Yes, General." Owens nodded, relieved.

"It's all right," Adele said, trying to save her QG any more embarrassment. "I was just leaving."

Lucky was already dressed and ready to accompany her back to the royal apartment. He seemed to be willing to ignore their weird intimate moment from earlier and for that she was grateful. Adele also ignored Benjamin, who was still loitering in the hallway outside the QG quarters, chatting with a couple of giggling maids.

Back in the royal apartment, the children were up and stirring for the day, more energetic than their two nannies, who were both a little red-eyed and pale from Charlie's birthday party. Mrs. Ollenby was supervising preparations for breakfast and was happy to see Adele looking alive and well, if very inappropriately dressed in her captain's shirt.

Adele stood by and waited for Mrs. Ollenby to check with the Marchant princes if it was safe to enter her bedchamber and go into her wardrobe. Lady Olivia slipped in the front door of the apartment, still yawning, and didn't see Lucky until it was too late to avoid him.

"Oh, good morning!" Olivia looked from Lucky to Adele, down to the gold captain stripes on the breast pocket of her shirt, and back to Lucky again.

"Good morning, Lady Olivia," Lucky said, and even Adele shivered from the chill in his tone.

Olivia tossed her long, blonde curls. "It seems you've had an eventful night after our *conversation*, Captain," she said. "But I wonder if the queen would like to get dressed in her own clothes now."

"Yes, she would," Adele said, irritated to be stuck between her clueless captain and Olivia's wrong conclusion. "I'm just waiting for Mrs. Ollenby to clear my room."

Olivia was clearly dying of curiosity but only nodded. "Of course, Your Majesty."

In the awkward silence, Adele heard both the princes shouting, then quiet, and then more shouting. Then Mrs. Ollenby threw open the bedchamber door with a grand flourish. "You may enter your own chamber as you wish, Your Majesty," she announced loudly.

When Adele peeked in, she saw the scene was much the same as it had been last night. Rainere was sitting up in bed, Prince Rainold occupying the armchair next to him.

"*Cara mia*," Rainere croaked, but his smile was vital, and it warmed her heart.

"Rainere," she whispered as stabbing hunger pains stole her voice.

"Go on, then, Your Majesty!" Rainold pointed at the closet. "Get dressed, but do not get any closer to us. I can see what you're thinking from here."

Miserable because she couldn't deny the hunger making her hands shake, Adele went into the dressing room with Olivia and got dressed as quickly as her lady-in-waiting could work. She had to leave her hair down, as neither Julien nor Katie or Piers had been allowed into the room by Prince Rainold.

"Should I ask what's going on here, Your Majesty?" Olivia asked, maybe taking pity on Adele sitting in abject shame, or maybe it was seeing her clearly pregnant bump protruding under her slip.

"No," Adele said.

"And is it Prince Rainere's baby, Your Majesty?" Olivia persisted. "I understand how hard that must be with the hatred against Marchants. I mean—"

"It's actually all a big fucking mess, Olivia, so can we leave it?" Adele was close to tears again, cursing her pregnancy and the awful things it was making her want to do. "I've still got to work today."

Olivia closed her mouth, but Adele could see the young woman thinking at a mile a minute. "But you and Captain Lucky would never do anything." She tossed her hair again. "I mean, if it was for revenge because I kissed your prince, I could understand, but I don't know how you could even convince Lucky to look at you that way."

Adele raised a hand for Olivia to shut up. "I have *never* and would *never* do anything with Lucky," she said. "And seriously, Olivia, I have bigger problems right now than you kissing Rainere a few weeks ago." She didn't even pause to let herself feel the relief that hearing only a kiss had passed between Rainere and Olivia gave her.

Then Olivia actually giggled. "Sorry, Your Majesty. We're friends again, I promise."

Adele almost told Olivia where she could shove her friendship but then bit her lip. There was no point in making another enemy just now.

Finally sheathed in a flattering burgundy gown that sat loosely under her bust and draped her abdomen, Adele was determined to maintain her dignity as she crossed her bedchamber and checked on Rainere.

"My darling, I'm so sorry for all of this," Rainere called out.

She stopped by the door, keeping a safe distance from her sweet prince and his furious father. "Darling, you've nothing to be sorry for," she said. "I'm just so grateful that you're still . . ." She couldn't say "alive" with Olivia hanging on their every word. "You rest, and we can talk later."

"Do you promise?"

Adele didn't know if Rainere was joking. He always accused her of breaking every promise she'd ever made. "No," she said. "But I'll try."

"Well, I promise you'll see me," Rainere said. "I'm feeling better already."

She tried to return his smile but it felt like her heart was being pulled to pieces as she forced herself to walk away from him.

While she'd been getting dressed, the dining table had filled up considerably. Her four children, their nannies, the Queen's Guard, Charlie, the real High Wizard Ohren, Lord Orgustus, and Mrs. Ollenby were already seated when she took her place at the head of the table, having to shift the three dogs who were trying to crowd themselves by Aaron's feet.

Thankfully, Lord Orgustus was in a bright mood that morning after his brush with exile in Sandar the day before. As Adele fed Stella her porridge, she filled him in on the problems in Concordis that the mayor had brought to her last night: the chaos caused by the disappearance of the Boss, the fatal new drug that was circulating through the streets and killing addicts, and the news that the Lady Mayor was sure the poison was being manufactured by a cohort in the Guild Quarter.

"I know nothing about any of this," Orgustus said. He'd stopped eating, and his expression was narrow with fury. "This is my city, and someone has been keeping secrets from me."

"I'm not looking for answers from you, my lord, but I do want you in the meeting with Bethany after breakfast," Adele said as she mopped Stella's chin with a napkin.

"Your Majesty, might we not talk about something more cheerful?" High Wizard Ohren asked, looking pointedly at the children. "This really hasn't been a subject for little ears."

Adele felt a flare of anger at the high wizard's judgmental tone. "One day, my children will rule this kingdom, Ohren," she said. "God forbid they'll ever be as clueless as their mother is right now. They must learn from the cradle how to keep the peace and stay alive."

"Well said, Your Majesty!" Orgustus was always pleased to get a point over Ohren.

Adele didn't want anyone to think she was on side with Orgustus and was about to say so, when Charlie suddenly appeared at her shoulder, leaning down to whisper, "My queen, you smell amazing." And she completely lost her train of thought.

Adele didn't even allow herself to glance at him. "Charlie, go and see Prince Rainold, but then I want you back here for the meeting with the Lady Mayor."

Charlie dashed away. Adele looked down the table to her general. Ohrig gave her a nod of approval, and she clung to it like a life raft. But that was just for now. What was she supposed to do about this hunger that burned her insides like acid all day?

Adele pasted on a smile and accepted a piece of toast from Natalie. "Now, what're you kids going to get up to this morning?" she asked her family and let herself fall under their noise and normality.

CHAPTER FORTY-ONE

"Two Princes and a Pauper"

Charlie knocked once, then entered Queen Adelena's enormous bed-chamber without waiting for an answer. The room smelled like the same perfume that had grabbed him with a raging desire at the table and didn't help to cool the heat between his legs.

"Oh, look, darling, Charlie's come to visit." Prince Rainold cried out, delighted. "Hello, Charlie!"

Charlie grunted a greeting and wandered over to the two princes, trying to pull his jacket down over the front of his trousers. He stood at the foot of the bed. "So, what did she do to you, Your Highness?"

"Charlie, that demon sucked all the magic out of my son." In a flash, Prince Rainold had flipped from happy to miserable. "She almost drained him of his life energy, and I had to force her to give up some of her blood just to revive him."

Charlie wrinkled his nose in disgust, though he was completely fascinated. "Is that why the queen's got a bandage on her wrist?"

"Yes," Rainold said. "Believe me, it was all I could do not to stab her in the heart instead of just slicing her arm."

"Father, you overstep," Rainere growled. "It was an accident. She didn't mean to hurt me. She never does." Pushing Rainold out of the way, Rainere climbed out of bed. Charlie watched him take a few weary steps to a narrow couch by the balcony doors. The prince was only wearing pajama pants, and his tattoo rippled across his back as he reached for a large flask of Firewhiskey, poured himself a double, and sat down again.

"So it really hurts, does it?" Charlie knew he was pushing his luck, but he kept going. "I mean, it didn't hurt me when she slid that vine of magic deep inside me. Goddess, it felt like she was sucking my cock from the inside."

"No, Charlie!" Rainold was appalled. "I never thought the demon would go after you too."

"Her name is Adelena, not 'demon'!" Rainere glared at the pair of them. "She told me about how you tricked her with your birthday kiss, boy, and you'll have my thoughts on that when I've recovered."

"She seemed to enjoy herself." Charlie decided to give a nonchalant shrug just to see if Rainere would try and have a proper go, but the prince remained slumped in his seat. "In fact, she worked very hard just to hold herself back from me. If I hadn't left, it definitely would've gone further." He grinned at Rainere. "You're welcome."

"For my *cara mia*, that was just foreplay." Rainere lapsed into a dreamy smile. "Having Adelena inside me this time was like being fucked by the goddess herself. It was like having my soul ripped out through a tunnel of orgasms. The pleasure kept coming and coming until I wanted to die, but never wanted it to end."

"That sounds like a pretty decent way to go to the Beyond." Charlie moved to pour himself a Firewhiskey that he had no intention of drinking. He just wanted to show Rainere that he could handle his spirits at breakfast time too.

"You're both talking like idiots," Prince Rainold said. He took the drink out of Charlie's hand, only to slug it back himself. "A demon is a terrible creature, but what's worse is that we Marchants are like dumb beasts to the slaughter. All our incredible intellect and spell craft cannot defeat the call of that suicidal lust. I barely survived one pregnant demon—I have no interest in being at the mercy of another one."

"But you did survive," Charlie prompted. "How?"

"We were at the Gray Palace, and there was a village on the outskirts of the estate," Rainold said, like there was an obvious connection.

"I know the one," Charlie said. "With the mud brick houses, and cats running around everywhere. Sorry to tell you, but it's dead now. Every kid got taken to the mines, and that's where Pere Raven got his hands on me too."

"Yes, well." Rainold sighed at the news. "It was much busier in the old days, and therefore I had a steady supply of my father's progeny or various other descendants lurking about. Rainestra was talented, so she could drain and not kill quite well. It's clear that Adelena doesn't share her mother's skill."

"They're bringing all the workers back from the mines soon," Rainere mused. "There are sure to be some young adults among the rabble who are strong enough to sate her."

"Are you fucking insane?" Charlie asked, sounding calm, though his heart dropped into his stomach. "She would never abuse children like that. She isn't a monster!"

"She will die if she doesn't eat magic," Rainere said, and groaned as he shifted his sore body. "Unless we want to sacrifice ourselves, we'll need to sacrifice someone else."

"Queen Adelena said that when she was on her way to find the dragon, it was Dahk'hani who brought her magic with the ice bear and then the river of magic in the sky," Charlie said. "Maybe he'll do the same again if she's starving him."

"Don't be stupid, Charlie." Rainere shot the rest of his Firewhiskey. "As far as Dahk'hani is concerned, our queen already lives in a field of cows, so why would he send her milk?"

"I'm not a cow," Charlie muttered as he watched Rainere stagger back to the bed and slide himself under the covers.

"No, of course not, you're a big boy." Rainold moved across the room and wrapped an arm around his shoulders. "But there is still this constant pull of the demon's power on our magic, and we need to be very careful of it. The lust is what drives you crazy, until you just don't care how dangerous she is anymore. Then you will go to her. You will need to fuck someone else, a lot."

Charlie recoiled from Rainold's embrace. "I don't want to do anything with you—I said that already."

Rainold shushed Charlie, irritated. "I have Ohren to keep me satisfied. I was hoping that you still have your little girl too?"

Charlie nodded.

"Good! She is going to get very lucky, very often, while you fight this demon's call," Rainold told him. "I know it sounds a little barbaric, but I tried all sorts of potions and poisons to counteract the effects of the call. Yet every night I found myself back at Rainestra's feet, waiting for her to finish feeding on another man and then take me." Rainold shuddered. "It was so degrading."

"What about Adelena's children?" Charlie asked.

Rainold's hands fluttered like sad doves before coming to rest on his chest. "I found out too late that, even before she was pregnant, Rainestra had been casually feeding on Rainere when he was just a tiny baby, not quite a year old," he said. "Demons are ruthless savages when it comes to sating themselves."

Charlie just couldn't imagine a world in which Adelena would eat the magic out of her own children and wards.

"So, you have the high wizard, I have my girl—who does Prince Rainere have to keep him away from the queen?" he asked, nodding at the snoring prince.

"I'll find him someone," Rainold murmured. "Hopefully, last night will be a lesson, though somehow I think he will be difficult to convince where his demon is concerned."

He turned his teary gaze to the bed. "Oh, Charlie, I know there's a reason the goddess Serena wanted me back in Evendaar but keeping my darling son alive is more important to me now."

Charlie pulled out of Prince Rainold's hug. He really didn't want to be around this unstable prince and all his emotions when he had so many of his own to deal with. "Right. Well. I'm off," he said, but at the last moment he relented and handed the weeping prince a handkerchief.

Back in the living room, Charlie could see that breakfast had finished already. Siobhan had Aaron on her hip and sent him a little wave, but he pretended not to see her as he caught up with Ohren. "Your sweetheart's in there crying his eyes out, High Wizard," he said. "In case you wanted to know."

Ohren looked to the ceiling as if searching for strength. "I forgot how melodramatic Rainold can be," he muttered, but he still headed to the queen's bedchamber. "Tell Her Majesty I'll join the meeting a bit later."

"Charlie, you're with us," QG Leith called out from across the living area, and he fell into step with the rest of the QGs following the queen to the Lavender Meeting Room.

They met Benjamin outside the royal apartment. He lit up when he saw the queen, but she rushed past him. Charlie had no sympathy—Ben was too good-looking and had it too easy. Charlie grabbed his arm and told him that Prince Rainold wanted a word in the queen's bedchamber. He figured it'd be a laugh to throw the stablehand in there while Ohren and Rainold were together. Just to stir them all up.

Ohrig, who seemed to hear everything, heard that too. "What's all that Prince Rainold business about, Charlie?" he asked, frowning like usual.

Charlie fell into step beside him. "Benjamin's got a freakish amount of Marchant blood and needs to get the warning," he said.

Ohrig stopped Charlie with a hand on his chest. The rest of the group swung around them and moved on. "You have thirty seconds to tell me what Prince Rainold is saying about the queen to you Marchant boys."

Ohrig wasn't playing around, so Charlie confessed what Rainold had told him. Of course, he didn't mention that he had kissed Queen Adelena. He didn't imagine Ohrig would find that very amusing.

"Tits of the goddess, this is getting worse by the minute," Ohrig said. "We've got to keep an eye on the queen at all times, especially when she's with the children. Not that she'll do anything, but just in case."

Charlie was surprised to be included in the plan. "You remember that I've got green blood too, General?" he said. "Maybe I should keep my distance when it comes to the queen."

"Don't be funny, Charlie." Ohrig threw an arm around his shoulders, pulling him along the corridor to catch up to the others. "We all know that the queen won't crack onto you. You're like one of her own children."

Charlie ground his teeth and didn't say anything, but he really, really wanted to.

Chapter Forty-Two

"A Meeting of Minds"

Adele had feared that morning's meeting would be another parade of bad news and impossible problems for her to fix. She was delighted that, for once, this was not the case. The Lady Mayor took charge of the room right away. Bethany Merrills had clear ideas and was vocal about how to deal with the problem of a poisoned opiate in her city. However, she wasn't prepared to compromise on her demand that "street justice" be allowed to punish the perpetrators. Adele really enjoyed hearing a woman take on both an angry Lord Orgustus and an appalled High Wizard Ohren—especially when it wasn't her.

Though, to their credit, the two men were maybe a little less patronizing than they usually were with Adele. It was clear that Lord Orgustus knew Bethany to be a formidable opponent and took the chance to agree with her as often as he could without conceding his own view that all crimes should be dealt with by the court. Adele thought it was also interesting how little Ohren seemed to know about how either the Topworld or the Underworld of Concordis were run. More than once, Bethany was frustrated enough to ask, "Didn't your brother, the high magistrar, explain any of this to you, High Wizard?"

Like Adele, the QGs and Charlie stayed quiet. Only Tilburn was called upon to detail how certain strategies might affect the treasury.

The morning meeting continued until midday, and lunch was brought in, but there was no pause in the discussions.

"How're you feeling, Your Majesty?" Ohrig murmured, softly elbowing her in the ribs. He was clearly getting bored, as indicated by the doodles of swords and birds on the notepad in front of him.

Adele felt hollow and desperately hungry despite devouring a plate of miniature meat pies. "Fine," she whispered back. "But my presence seems to be very unnecessary. Do you think I could leave?"

"If I know Merrills, she's hoping that you will," Ohrig said, angling his shoulders so that no one at the other end of the table could see his lips move. "I couldn't believe it when she started bringing out financial statements from the largest businesses in the Traders Quarter to prove there is no money in the city to pay for the suggested task force. She's clearly trying to bore you to death."

Adele suppressed her amused snort. "And Orgustus?"

"He's afraid of her," Ohrig said, looking sideways at the young lord. "You'd do well to change the conversation if you want to get out of here by midnight, Your Majesty."

"Ending meetings is one of my favorite things to do," she whispered. "Just hold your girlfriend back when she gets annoyed with me."

"Merrills isn't my girlfriend," Ohrig growled back. "We're just friends."

"You and I are friends, Ohrig." Adele made sure to smile in a way that had him rolling his eyes. "You and Merrills are *special* friends."

"General Ohrig, if you have something to say, I'm sure we'd all love to hear it," the mayor called from down the table. "We haven't yet been privy to any of your practical suggestions for how to solve this problem facing our city."

General Ohrig stared Merrills down, refusing to rise to her bait, just as she refused to look away.

"Rest assured, my general gives me his best counsel, Bethany," Adele said, interrupting the two of them. She wondered if the mayor was jealous of Ohrig whispering with her, then decided it was irrelevant. Hunger was cramping her stomach, and she wanted to be back with her family. "Now, the primary problem on the table seems to be a lack of funds needed to form a task force to clean up the streets of both the Traders Quarter and the Guild Quarter."

"How very astute of you to ascertain that, Your Majesty," Bethany said, her tone noticeably crisp.

"What do you have in mind, Your Majesty?" Orgustus shot Bethany a warning glance. "The Crown budget is taxed to its limit."

"Well, can someone tell me how much the royal family costs to keep?" Adele asked.

Tilburn frowned. "I don't understand, Your Majesty."

"I just had a delivery of ten new pairs of shoes encrusted with crystals and precious metals," she explained. "I know I didn't order any new shoes, Tilburn, and the reason I know I didn't order them is because I already have an entire closet full of very similar shoes. Let's stop the delivery of new shoes until further notice and put the money in the pot for the task force."

"Your Majesty?" Tilburn was still confused.

"And my dresses keep changing, sometimes without me having worn them even once," she continued. "That's got to cost the court a fortune. So let's stop ordering new dresses as well."

"But no!" Tilburn blurted quickly. "The artisans who make your shoes and garments have come from the same families for generations, and they all live in the Golden Palace, Your Majesty. To stop your weekly orders would crush their businesses."

Adele was feeling light-headed, and it made her a little reckless. "Then they can open shops of their own in town," she snapped. "Stop the orders and use the money for the task force. In fact, I want five more regular, pointless costs that are incurred by the royal family stopped and the money put toward security in Concordis."

"But, Your Majesty, that will cost jobs!" Tilburn almost shouted. "Your courtiers' careers are at stake."

"Tilburn, you've only had a royal family for a few months

now—how can these costs be so entrenched already?" She didn't wait for an answer. "In fact, I think we could do with fewer courtiers running around the Golden Palace and partying on the Crown's coin. Evict at least fifty of them by the end of the month."

"Your Majesty, these courtiers are royal by blood and marriage—they have a right to live in the Golden Palace," Tilburn argued.

"If you don't want to ask them to leave, you could always tell them to start paying their own bills," Adele suggested.

Tilburn squinted so hard his eyes disappeared, so she knew he wasn't in the mood to banter.

"Well, I've probably caused enough scandal for the day!" She stood up. Tilburn, her Queen's Guard, and Charlie followed a moment later. "Right, I found you a pile of money for the task force, Lord Orgustus. Now you can work with our mayor to find an effective strategy to spend it. If you'll excuse me, I have other matters to attend to today."

Both the Lady Mayor and Lord Orgustus stood up, and she heard him say, "Such an inventive solution, wouldn't you agree, Lady Mayor? Fortunately, I already have a few ideas on which courtiers to evict first."

But Bethany had jumped out of her seat. "Your Majesty, if I could have a word?"

Adele heard Bethany call out just as she made it to the end of the Hall of Portraits. In a surprise move, Bethany lurched forward, catching her arm to spin her around.

"Tits of the goddess, Your Majesty, what're you thinking?" Bethany hissed. She used her superior height to crowd Adele's back against the wall. "Are you insane? Do you realize the power you've just handed that lordling? Or how little your contributions will mean with him in charge of the funds for my city? Have you any idea how incompetent Orgustus is?"

Adele blinked at the barrage of questions. "I thought I was helping." She instantly felt foolish and cleared her throat, yanking her arm free. "You needed money, I found you money, Bethany."

"And back off her," Ohrig growled. "Remember who you're talking to and where you are, Merrills."

Bethany Merrills looked to the ceiling, as if searching for divine guidance, but she didn't get out of Adele's personal space. "Look, I know you're not a politician, Your Majesty," she whispered. "But I am, and I'm telling you it is a mistake to leave Orgustus as financial liaison to my office. He's court bred and more interested in drinking in my establishments than dealing with me."

"Right, so I'll appoint Tilburn as the financial liaison," Adele interrupted. "Do you have a problem dealing with him?"

Bethany looked down at the petite majordomo standing by Ohrig's elbow, her surprise melting to a pleased expression. "Not at all," she said. "His impeccable reputation precedes him, of course."

Adele grinned at Tilburn's fierce squint. "There you go, Tilburn, you wanted that job anyway."

"Your Majesty, I don't want to overstep, but if we're going to be effective in solving this crisis, then we need to work together as equals—and honesty is a part of that," Bethany said. "I don't play court games, and I don't manipulate with flattery and veiled threats. What you see is what you get with me."

"Adelena."

Bethany's eyebrows couldn't have gone any higher. "Pardon?"

"My name is Adelena," she said. "If you want to work as equals, then you can call me by my name."

Bethany smiled, and Adele smiled back. *Brilliant, I've finally done something right,* she thought.

"Adelena," Bethany agreed, but her expression changed to concern. "Honey, you don't look so good. You've gone very pale."

"No, I'm completely fine," Adele said. Then the Chime Voices screamed in her head and everything went black.

*

It felt like only a moment had passed when Adele opened her eyes again and found she was lying on a tweed-covered sofa in an unfamiliar bedroom. The rough fabric scratched her cheek as she twisted to look around. The room was small, and every wall was lined with packed bookshelves. The air smelled of their polished leather covers—like beeswax and dust. Heavy velvet curtains had been drawn over the single floor-to-ceiling window, leaving the room in near darkness. A pair of men's slippers poked out from beneath the fringed counterpane of a four-poster bed. Adele wanted to sit up, but her head felt too heavy.

"Your Majesty?" Ohren's young face swam into view, his eyes startlingly blue even in the dim light of the room. "How're you feeling?"

"Fine," she croaked. "A little thirsty."

"I don't think you're fine at all," Ohren replied, because, of course, he knew everything.

She was just about to snap back, *Then why did you ask?* But the high wizard had disappeared, and she was too tired to be angry. Ohren reappeared with a tall glass of cold water and helped her sit up to drink a little.

"I think you should have a dose of the Gift of Life, Your Majesty," he said without preamble. "I know you can't take any more magic from your Marchant prince, and any moral stance you have against the Gift will be moot because those who suffered to make the stock I have, well, they're already dead and gone." He seemed to stop talking with an effort and took a deep breath. "I think you absolutely need to do something before this baby eats you alive."

"Damn, I must look terrible," Adele muttered. She slumped back on the couch cushions.

"You know I think you're beautiful, Your Majesty." Ohren took her temperature with his palm and frowned. "But there's no denying that you're fading."

"Well, I can't afford to lose my looks on top of everything else," she said, refusing to allow herself to feel the panic hovering at her shoulder. "Can I use one of your disguise charms? A long, gray beard should cover lots of sins."

"If Her Majesty's making fun of you, she can't be feeling too bad," Ohrig said from the door, and came in, followed by the rest of the Queen's Guard.

"Hey, lads, where are we?" she asked.

"You're in my chambers," Ohren replied. "I thought you might want a little peace and quiet when you take, uh, your medicine."

"For being the High Wizard of the Court of the Golden Palace, your room is pretty poky," she noted.

Ohren shrugged. "I prefer to call it cozy."

Adele caught her general's eye. "Ohren wants me to take the Gift of Life."

Ohrig crossed his arms and leaned his bulk against a narrow dressing table making all the small glass pots and jars tinkle together. "But you're thinking about Leafy."

"And Charlie, and Rip, and all the children who've died in those evil mines," she said. "It'll be like I betrayed them. How can I say I'm better than Orestes or a Marchant Eldar if I take that hateful potion to save myself?"

"And to save your baby, Your Majesty," Captain Lucky said. He was crouched by the end of the sofa, studying her intently.

Adele didn't have an answer to that. *Normally I would do anything to keep my baby alive. But is it really my baby?*

It was oppressive, lying in a dark room with seven men all breathing and thinking at once. She asked for someone to open the curtains, but when the light hit her, Bear was the first to say it. "Oh, shit, Your Majesty!"

She groaned. "I guess I probably look as rough as I feel."

"You didn't even look this bad when I squashed you like a bug after the ice bridge collapsed," Bear said, raising his hands to deflect Captain Lucky's glare.

"Glad you didn't sugarcoat it for me, Bear," Adele said.

"And excuse me, but isn't the baby bigger now?" Pepper asked.

Adele molded the fabric of her gown over the baby bump and measured it with her hands. "Sweet Christ, that looks like five or six months now."

"You know, I was just being polite asking your permission to give you the Gift, my queen," Ohren said. "You'll probably collapse again very soon, and I'll give it to you intravenously while you're unconscious."

"Ohren, the queen said no," General Ohrig warned him.

"The queen is so caught up in her web of hypocritical morals that she's going to very self-righteously die in a very short time," Ohren said, and she heard the wobble of fear in his voice. "Has anyone but me wondered what Dahk'hani is going to do when his host dies? Because I don't think it will be the end of him, just the end of Queen Adelena. Then we'll be left with no demon queen, no power of her prophecy, and one angry, almost-formed god."

"I want Rainere," Adele said. "He'll know what to do."

"Ah, but I promised Prince Rainold that I wouldn't bring you two together," Ohren said, apologetically. "And I don't want to break another promise to him this soon after we got back together."

"And why're we supposed to care about your romantic relationship?" Ohrig snapped.

"Anyway, Prince Rainere hasn't recovered his strength yet, so he'd be no good to her," Ohren hurried to add.

"I just want to talk to him, not eat him," she said. "Someone get him."

"Not here," Ohren said. "Take her back to her bedchamber, and when Prince Rainold finds out, tell him I said it was a bad idea."

Captain Lucky was nearest, so he scooped Adele up into his arms, holding her to his chest. The shiny golden buttons of his jacket dug into her arm, but she didn't have the energy to shift herself.

"Hurry, Lucky," she whispered, and then blacked out again.

CHAPTER FORTY-THREE

"A Walk Between Worlds"

Rainere had made it out of bed and was stretched out on the peacock-blue velvet couch in the living room. He was reading the history of Marchant horse husbandry to Aaron, who was cuddled on his lap. The little girls were copying spell diagrams from a beginner's textbook at a low table nearby. Stella was in the nursery, napping. He was just wondering if he could take a nap too, when the Queen's Guard were announced and felt his heart seize in terror. He leaped to his feet, racing to take Adelena from the captain's arms. "What happened?"

"Her Majesty looked well enough in the meeting this morning, but then she fainted as we were returning here, and High Wizard Ohren insisted that we take her to his quarters. She slept for three hours and then woke looking as she does now," Lucky reported, much calmer than the rest of the QG's looked. "Once awake, Her Majesty became upset when Ohren suggested that she should ingest the Gift of Life to feed the baby, and then her energy faded again. She asked us to take her to you and fainted."

Rainere stared down at Adelena. Her skin was chalky, and her breathing was shallow.

"Is Mummy dying?" Natalie tugged at Rainere's shirtsleeve, her eyes wide with fear.

"Not at all." He forced himself to look calm for her. "The baby is making her very tired. She fainted because she needs medicine and magical food."

"Should we put her to bed, Your Highness?" Lucky asked.

"I will," Rainere said. He turned his back, making for the bed-chamber. "The Queen's Guard is dismissed."

Captain Lucky jogged until he stood in the doorway of the bed-chamber. Rainere raised an eyebrow and felt a frisson of excitement. He would enjoy hitting Lucky across his too-perfect face.

"With all due respect, Your Highness," Captain Lucky said, in that calm way of his. "You have no authority over the Queen's Guard. You cannot dismiss us. We'll see to Her Majesty's safety."

Rainere was about to respond, but the captain had already stepped aside, so he contented himself with a powerful glare as he made his way to the Glass Bed and laid Adelena down. Checking her vitals, he found her pulse was weak and her forehead hot. The adrenaline in his own body suddenly petered out and he was forced to sit on the edge of the bed.

"We need a more experienced doctor than me," Rainere croaked. "Go and get my father and the high wizard. Tell them to hurry."

Someone left to do as he bid, but he didn't see who. Adelena's breathing hitched like she was in pain, and he held his own breath until hers let go again. Exhausted, he climbed up on the bed, burying his face in her neck and slipping his hand between her breasts. He only had a trace of magic left inside of himself that he could draw on, but he couldn't give it to her—she had to take it from him. "Don't leave me," he whispered, his lips brushing the hot skin under her ear. "Don't you dare leave me, *cara mia*."

Dazed, Rainere didn't know how much time had passed before he felt his father's presence at his shoulder, murmuring comforting nonsense and stroking his back.

"Sweet boy, I came as soon as I heard that the demon had col-lapsed," Rainold whispered. "She looks awful, doesn't she?"

Ohren tapped Rainere's shoulder. "Prince Rainere, there are grave choices to be made."

Rainere rolled over to sit on the edge of the bed, surprised to see Mrs. Ollenby, Captain Lucky, and General Ohrig had joined them. He tried to make his tired mind focus. "What decisions?" he asked.

"She needs the Gift to feed that baby before it kills her," Ohren said.

"What're you waiting for?" Rainere asked. "Give her everything you've got."

General Ohrig's eyes were red-rimmed but his glare was still fierce. "The queen despises the Gift. She was thinking of Leafy and all the other children who suffered to make it. She'll hate you giving it to her."

"If she lives, then Adelena can hate me for as long as she likes," Rainere said. "I helped make all those damned Marchant brats—they can finally give me something in return for what I suffered."

Charlie had slunk into the room and Rainere watched him join the group of concerned idiots who kept talking while Adelena's breaths became even shallower.

"Prince Rainere is right, give her the Gift," Charlie echoed.

Rainere stepped forward and socked the kid so hard in the jaw that he spun around and fell to the floor like a wet rag. He tensed when General Ohrig took a step toward him, but Captain Lucky already had a hand on his general's arm, holding him back.

"Charlie knows what that was for," Rainere told them.

Charlie held his jaw and adjusted it to make sure it still worked, then climbed to his feet with a hand from Ohrig. "You pulled your punch, Your Highness," he said, wiping blood off his lip and still managing an infuriating grin. "Surely you can hit harder than that."

Rainere sneered. "But like she keeps telling me: you're only a *child*, Charlie."

Now Charlie was furious, the silver circles in his eyes flashing. *Finally*, Rainere thought. *It's time I taught him some limits.*

"Gentlemen, if you've finished measuring cocks, can we decide how to save the queen's life?" The high wizard waved his hands to get their attention. "I've got the intravenous apparatus and the first dose of the Gift here."

"What does Mrs. Ollenby think?" Prince Rainold asked, slipping an arm around the lady's shoulders. "It might help to have a woman's perspective."

Mrs. Ollenby dabbed at her tears. "I say do it," she said, resolute. "I'll tell the queen myself that I supported the decision."

Ohren set up the intravenous injection equipment with Prince Rainold by his side, criticizing and fussing over it, but it was Rainere who insisted that he be the one to actually put the needle in Adelena's arm. The entire group stood silently watching as the first trace of the silver liquid traveled from the glass jar, down the transparent tube stuck into the joint of her elbow, and then into her vein. Rainere's breath came out in a rush when he saw Adelena's chest lift. The Gift worked quickly. In a little less than a minute, her temperature dropped to normal and she lost the protruding bones from her cheeks. Even her hands resting on the white sheets looked normal again.

"Why isn't she waking up?" Ohren asked, fiddling with the device that controlled the flow of Gift into the tube. "It's clearly working."

"Because it's going straight to the baby, darling." Rainold pointed at Adelena's abdomen, which had swelled noticeably.

"It's taking too much," Rainere said. He couldn't believe it. As soon as the jar of Gift was emptied, Adelena started shriveling again. Ohren quickly attached another glass jar. "Do we even have enough Gift to sustain her if she absorbs it this fast?"

Ohren took Rainold's hand and let him be the one to say it. "We'll do our best, my sweet boy," Rainold said. "I'll go and retrieve the stocks at the Gray Palace to help supplement the little that Ohren has in his laboratory. Then we'll just have to wait and see."

Rainere looked down upon his fragile lover. *Serena, don't let her die,* he begged silently. *Tell me what I need to do and I'll do it. Anything. Everything. Just don't let her die.*

But Serena wasn't listening to prayers, so there was nothing to do but watch the silver liquid drip into Adelena's veins, keeping alive the baby who was killing her.

Chapter Forty-Four

"For Fire and Glory"

Charlie couldn't stand there watching Adelena recover, then fade, then come back just a little bit less alive. He had to get out of her crowded bedchamber. Only Ohrig saw him leave, and the general raised his finger to his lips.

Like I'm going to tell anyone the queen is dying—what kind of idiot does he take me for? Charlie's heart squeezed in his chest, and that pain was much worse than the bruise on his jaw. He tried to find some satisfaction in Rainere needing to retaliate for the kiss. *Maybe he could tell that she loved it through that Mark of his,* Charlie thought as he scuffed his feet through thick carpet, following a wavy pattern in the threads. *Maybe he could tell that she loves . . .*

But he couldn't quite finish the thought. It felt like blasphemy, as it had when he'd heard Ohren say, "I can't stand to see another baby kill a woman I love in this damn Glass Bed."

That'd been the last straw.

"Now fucking Ohren is in love with the queen!" Charlie muttered, turning a corner and dodging a group of courtiers gossiping and laughing in the hallway.

Tonight he just wanted to be alone in a dark place and not think about Adelena's face sinking in on itself as the god-baby leeched her life away. Turning another corner, he walked down a much quieter hall. Out of habit, he stuck to the shadows.

How can she die like this? he wondered, descending a stone staircase. *How can this be what the goddess wanted for her?* His jaw throbbed again, and he knew he should've put some ice on it.

Rainere only got a quick one in because he could, he thought. *I bet he'll go crazy and kill everyone if she dies.*

Charlie needed to run. He picked up his feet, dashing down dark hallways and each darker staircase. He stopped when he got to the door to Hell. Leaning in the corner next to the hypnotized guard, he wiped off the tears, telling himself it was sweat. He gave the guard the password and went in.

Orestes was staring at the wall of his cell, his mouth slack and his shoulders slumped, but his blue eyes were sharp when Charlie entered. "Come to try and torture me again, have you?"

"No, I've come to release you," Charlie said, waving his knife. "The queen has fallen ill and needs your magic to heal her."

Orestes's mouth snapped closed at that. Charlie moved behind the Boss and took his wrists in one hand.

"I'm not going to give her any magic voluntarily," Orestes said, and the malice in his voice made Charlie want to stab him. "Unless she drinks my blood, and I don't think they're about to let her do that. How sick is she, anyway?"

Surprised to hear this idea for the second time in as many days, Charlie stopped pretending to cut Orestes's bonds and moved in front of the Boss. "Adelena doesn't need blood. She goes through your skin to drink the magic."

Orestes looked horrified. "She just sucks it out of you against your will?"

Charlie couldn't even imagine wanting to resist an experience as incredible as Adelena taking his magic with a kiss. He grinned and felt a twinge in his swollen jaw. "Hey, would it work on me if I drank your blood, Boss?"

Orestes snorted. "Of course it would, you stupid boy!"

"And for a man tied to a chair, you're pretty arrogant." Charlie didn't think, just palmed his knife and sliced it across Orestes's neck. He was careful not to hit the jugular, but there was a lot of blood pouring down the wizard's neck. He fought his revulsion and licked a tongueful, thinking it was going to taste like his own coppery, metallic blood. But as he swallowed, he could taste honey and tiny fizzing spots of gold magic. He went back in for another lick, and then another. Finished, he wiped his mouth with a handkerchief from his pocket. His jaw wasn't sore anymore. The swelling had gone down, and he would bet that even the bruise had disappeared.

"Well, what d'you know?" Charlie grinned, sure he was showing red teeth. "Your blood works just fine on me."

Orestes's head rolled to the side, and the wound on his neck was still bleeding profusely. Charlie pressed it with his handkerchief, and then used Orestes's own cravat as a bandage. "It's a pity you golden boys don't heal as fast as a Marchant," he noted, tying off the ends of the cravat.

Orestes blinked slowly. "The goddess protects her Favored, you filthy Green Blood."

"Is that why I'm doing so well, then?" Charlie licked the last trace of blood and honey from his lips. "Now, about that torture?"

Orestes started trying to rock in his chair, and his howl was feral.

"That's it." Charlie moved in with his knife. "Lie back and take it like a good boy."

CHAPTER FORTY-FIVE

"The Sleeping Beauty"

Morning sunbeams filtered through the chiffon curtains on the balcony doors, moving across the cream-and-gold carpet to reach the cut-glass columns of the Glass Bed before refracting and tossing rainbows all over the room. Slumped in an armchair, Rainere was caught in the twilight between sleep and waking and tried to bat them away from his face. Rousing a little more, he remembered that he was dozing by Adelena's bedside. A female giggle made him open his eyes.

"Your Highness, good morning." Lady Olivia dipped a curtsy. She was wearing a low-cut gown that hugged her figure, so just that tiny gesture was quite a show.

He sat up, alarmed to see her holding Adelena's hand. "What're you doing?"

"I'm just going to give Her Majesty a little bed bath, and then I'm going to change her dress." Olivia smiled like they might've been at a picnic instead of Adelena's sickbed. "What's wrong with her anyway? Is it the pregnancy that's making her ill?"

Rainere stood up, rolling his tight shoulders, and trying to stretch the crick in his neck. "I'll do it," he said. "Leave her."

"No, you won't, darling!" Prince Rainold appeared from behind his chair. "I said you can sit by the queen, but you cannot touch her—it's too dangerous."

428

"But—"

"I said no, darling." Rainold patted his back. "Please don't make me cross. I don't want to have to force you from her room too." Rainold's pats became soothing circles. "Now sit back down and rest."

Rainere looked at the intravenous pole and noted the half-empty bottle of silver fluid draining into Adelena's tube. The very last bottle was waiting on the bedside table next to a pile of fresh needles and an ornate clock ticking away the moments that she slept. Thankfully, the baby had stopped growing after midnight, so in the morning light, she looked healthy again. Her cheeks pink, her breathing deep and easy. Yet she still didn't wake.

Lady Olivia was stripping Adelena, careful to cover her swollen breasts with a towel but exposing the rounded baby bump. Rainere saw the skin of her belly move and jump.

"Prince Rainere?"

Rainere hadn't realized that he was on his feet, reaching to touch his baby. At Olivia's call, Rainold came racing over and wrenched his hand back again. "Rainere, I'm sending you out, now!"

"No, you can't." Rainere sank back into his armchair and put his hands up in a gesture of peace. "I'll sit. I won't touch her."

"I said out!" Rainold narrowed his eyes, and Rainere saw the ring of power turning in his father's eyes, as if he really was going to force him to go.

In a desperate move, he tried what Aaron always did when he'd been disobedient. Dropping his chin, he looked up at the prince, using a soft voice. "Please, Father."

And Rainold melted into smiles again. "You're so much trouble, darling," he said, smoothing his hand over Rainere's stubbled cheek. "I'm still trying to make the queen a tonic that might help the Gift last a bit longer in her system, so please stop distracting me."

Rainere nodded. "So, no progress since last night?"

"We're using your idea and Ohren's blue tonic recipe now," Rainold answered as he went back to the potions paraphernalia set up on a dressing table. "I think we're going to need more space for our hardware though."

Rainere grunted. Clearly, they needed his help but he didn't trust Olivia so near his queen. The lady had started washing Adelena with wet cloths, squeezing them out into a porcelain bowl of scented water. He was just about to protest that she was being too rough when Ohren arrived to check on the intravenous drip. The high wizard was wearing his disguise charms, and Rainere idly wondered if it just felt like clothing after so many years. Personally, he found wearing Odin's face uncomfortable and slightly nauseating.

"I know what you're thinking, Your Highness," the high wizard said, and Rainere was surprised enough to be distracted from his thoughts. "You're thinking that if you ingest all of this tonic, then you'll be strong enough to feed her again."

That wasn't what he'd been thinking, but of course it had crossed his mind.

"But she wouldn't be strong enough to resist killing you," Ohren promised him. "And then we would have no resources left, either tonic or your magic."

Rainere was just about ready to tell Ohren what he could do with his opinions when the high wizard leaned over to snatch the wet cloth from Olivia's hand. "For the goddess' sake, girl, you must be gentle," he said. Shouldering her out of the way, he resumed washing Adelena himself, wiping her arms with long, gentle strokes. "I did this for my own sister once, you know, before she—"

"If you don't mind me asking, High Wizard?" Olivia's voice was meek, but her expression was vivid with curiosity. "Prince Rainere is immortal—how can the queen kill him?"

"She wouldn't kill his body, dear one." Rainold joined them. Between two fingers, he held an injectable vial full of silver-and-blue liquid that swirled and popped. "But she would suck out all his magic and leave him as a bag of sloppy skin filled with bone dust and liquidized organs. His brain would falter, and his mind might escape, or it could get stuck inside him. Then he would live forever as a disgusting puddle, unable to function or speak, and no magic to heal him. Quite hideous and something I'm very keen to spare him from experiencing, though he keeps trying to push my patience."

Ohren took the vial from Rainold and examined it closely. "You think it's ready now?"

"It has stabilized," Rainold said, his brow furrowing. "I've nullified the opiate effect, which will decrease the rate of absorption, and she will sleep more deeply, but I can't promise there won't be hallucinations. I've never tried this on a demon before."

As soon as Ohren shut the block over Adelena's drip, Rainere saw her cheeks pale and the flesh hollow again. He watched closely as Ohren poured the potion into the glass jar. The blue liquid mixed with the silver and raced down the tube into her bloodstream. Color instantly returned to her cheeks.

"It works!" Ohren kissed Rainold with a loud smack. "You're still such a marvel with potions, sweetheart."

Rainere felt light-headed and realized that he was holding his breath. He let it out in a rush. "Thank you, Father."

But Rainold looked troubled as he gazed down at Adelena. "She's so little, isn't she?" he said. "Rainestra was much taller, and fuller in the breasts and, everywhere, really. She's not at all like her mother when you compare them."

"I remember Rainestra's laugh," Rainere said, trying to recall the woman he'd always called Mother. "Did you dance with her in the hallways? I think once, I was sitting on the stairs when I was supposed to be in bed, and I remember you two dancing, and there was always music in the house."

"Yes, we danced quite often." Rainold sniffed, and his eyes filled with green-tinted tears. "And now I'm thinking of you sitting on those stairs in your little nightshirt, watching us with your big eyes. It breaks my heart that I missed everything, Rainere. I missed your birthdays, your first enchantments, the night you were made immortal. I wasn't there for any of it. And now you're this adult man who keeps looking at me like I'm some freak who has no business loving you. I almost can't stand it, darling!"

On an unfamiliar impulse, Rainere stood and folded his father in a tight embrace.

"I love you more than anyone else alive, Rainere," Rainold whispered, his tears flowing down his young face. "But I'm still grieving for what I lost when the Eldars took me away. Our life together would've been wonderful."

"And it will be now," Rainere promised. "We can have those days again when my son is born. As soon as I've married Adelena, he can take the Marchant name, and we'll raise him in the old ways." He had thought he was giving his father a wonderful gift, but Rainold only dissolved into more miserable tears, burying his face in Rainere's shirtfront.

"I was thinking about the name Rainfred," he added, but was confused when Rainold sobbed even harder. Ohren finally rescued him by taking Rainold in his arms, both wizards looking at him with such profound pity that Rainere had to turn away. Thankfully, they left the bedchamber together without another word.

"Your Highness, are you all right? I could stay with you." Lady Olivia was hovering by the bed.

But Rainere felt suffocated by too many emotions, and grief made him cruel. "Get out, you filthy whore," he growled.

He enjoyed a rare moment of satisfaction when Lady Olivia dashed from the room, but then Aaron crawled out from under the bed with his enormous puppy, Hero Boy, next to him. Swallowing another curse, Rainere dropped into his armchair and held his hand out, hoping the little boy wouldn't be afraid. "I shouldn't have called Lady Olivia a whore, that was . . . unkind," he said by way of apology.

But Aaron came readily into his arms. "Olivia says it all the time to my nannies," he said. "Why is your shirt all green and wet?"

"My father was crying on me," Rainere said.

"He's very sad a lot," Aaron said. "Like the baby."

Rainere frowned. "Does the baby talk to you? Does he sound like your dogs?"

Aaron chewed his bottom lip, thinking this through. "He's loud," he said. "but he's not a dog, he's a baby."

Checking the door to make sure it was closed, Rainere dared to lift Aaron and sit him next to Adelena, yet even that close encounter made the hair on his skin rise, and he wanted to touch her so badly. "Can you listen to the baby for me?" he asked, stepping away from the bed. "See if he's all right?"

Aaron put his hands on his mother's naked belly and listened. "He says call her," Aaron said. "Call her *Mother*."

Rainere didn't know how to ask a four-year-old to determine if the fetus was viable except in the most basic terms. "Is he hungry?"

Aaron listened again. "Nope," he said. "He's saying, 'Call her.'"

Rainere sighed in relief.

"He wants to feel you," Aaron said.

Checking the door again, Rainere reached for Adelena. The baby was already moving, but when he placed his hand over the bump, it pushed into him and then stopped.

"He wants you to call her," Aaron reminded Rainere.

"Adelena, darling," Rainere said, softly. "Come back to us, *cara mia*." He slid his hand over her warm skin, her belly taut as a drum. "Come back to us, please."

"What's a *cara mia*?" Aaron asked.

"It means 'my beloved' in the Old Tongue," he replied, his voice rough with suppressed lust. "It is the sweetest name to call your lover."

"What's a lover?" Aaron asked.

Ignoring the question, Rainere stepped back from the bed and smoothed Aaron's hair back off his face. "You need another haircut, son," he said. "Your bangs are already in your eyes."

"I don't think I'm your son," Aaron said, frowning again.

"But I want you to be." Rainere cupped Aaron's chin. "I love you like a son, like this baby will be."

Aaron shrugged. "Natalie says our real daddy is on Earth. He's called Justin, and I don't remember him," he said. "But do you love me like Mummy loves Leafy, like an adopted?"

Rainere nodded.

"We're all adopted, then—even this baby will have to adopt us." Aaron hopped down off the bed, Hero Boy instantly by his side, and they walked to the bedroom door.

There was a loud knock, and Rainere cursed when Charlie stuck his head in. "Your Highness, I need a word."

"Hi, Charlie," Aaron greeted the teenager. "The baby says call her."

"Good to know, kid." Charlie ruffled Aaron's hair and shut the door behind the little prince.

Rainere was feeling exhausted after a night with little sleep. His magic was still worryingly depleted and he wasn't in the mood for Charlie's games. The boy wandered to the opposite side of the Glass Bed, looking Adelena over with greedy eyes. The damp towel over her breasts showed the outline of her nipples, and her sex was barely covered by another small towel. "That baby got big."

Rainere felt a possessive growl build in his chest. "Fuck off, Charlie."

Charlie raised an eyebrow. "Aw, be nice, Your Highness. I've got a present for you."

Rainere crossed his arms over his tearstained shirt. "What?"

With a sharp toss, Charlie sent a tiny, sparkly thing arcing over the bed. Rainere's reflexes weren't as fast as they should've been, but he managed to catch the vial in the tips of his fingers. He turned it this way and that, letting the metallic sparkles in clear liquid catch the light. "What is it?"

"God Dust."

Rainere fumbled the tiny vial in horror.

"Ah, be a little careful, Your Highness."

"Charlie, this is a potion form of the Summer Influenza!" Rainere shouted. "How the fuck do you have something this dangerous in your damned pocket?"

"I found it in the Boss's bedroom, tucked in a drawer," Charlie said, keeping up the nonchalant act that made Rainere grind his teeth.

"This is the most dangerous weapon in all of Evendaar," Rainere said. "And you threw it at me, across the queen's own body."

Charlie grinned wider. "I trusted your reflexes."

"This is not a game, Charlie! If the vial had broken, the consequences for Princess Stella would've been fatal."

"It's unbreakable glass, Your Highness." Charlie enunciated each word as if he were speaking to an imbecile. "The seal can only be broken with a drop of Orestes's blood." He pulled out another glass vial filled with a dark red liquid. "Like this," he said.

Rainere clasped the vial of God Dust to his chest as if just looking at Orestes's blood would open it. He swore viciously.

"Rainere, language, please!" Prince Rainold and High Wizard Ohren had returned to the room, followed by Mrs. Ollenby. "Now, what is all the noise about?" Rainold asked. "We could all hear you through the door."

Rainere and Charlie exchanged a loaded glance, and both slipped the vials out of sight. "Charlie wanted to give the queen a dose of his magic," Rainere said. "But I told him it was too dangerous."

Charlie rolled his eyes as Prince Rainold launched into his most disgusting description of what would happen to him during and after he was drained by a magic-starved Adelena.

"So how about a St. Lucidis wizard, then?" Charlie asked, surprising everyone with the question. "Why can't Ohren give her magic? Her Majesty is a demon—surely she can tolerate any type."

Rainold glanced at Ohren for confirmation, but he was already shaking his head. "What you say is technically true, but to distill gold magic from blood takes a very long time in a very delicate procedure. We just don't have that kind of time."

"Give her your blood then." Charlie kept arguing. "Just pour a nice old glass of blood down her throat and see what happens."

"No." Ohren was firm. "I won't take that risk."

"Adelena told me that she took magic from you once," Rainere said, feeling a wild surge of hope that there might be another solution right in front of them. "She said that she ended up on your lap and you almost—"

Ohren blushed red. "No, that isn't what happened. I tried to read Queen Adelena's power before I knew she was a demon and accidentally gave her access when she followed the psychic tracer back to me. There was no—I mean—we didn't get physical."

"Why are you blushing, then?" Prince Rainold asked, eyes narrowed with suspicion. "Don't lie, Ohren, just tell me if you had sex with Queen Adelena."

"What? No! That's disgusting!" Ohren protested, then caught the expressions on the faces of the Marchant princes, Charlie, and Mrs. Ollenby. "Sorry, I don't mean that it would be disgusting to have sex with her—I'm sure it's very nice. But I was always wearing my old-man charms, and—"

"All right, calm down, we believe you." Rainold patted Ohren on the arm.

"But I don't." Rainere raised his voice over his father's. "Adelena told me you reacted to her and got excited, as any wizard might."

Charlie faked a retching noise.

"Magic is magic," Ohren agreed finally, his cheeks pink. "I won't deny that the sensation of Adelena's internal touch was very interesting."

"And she took magic from you with that touch, or you wouldn't have liked it so much," Rainere said stubbornly. "So it can be done, and we should try letting her touch you."

Ohren looked uncomfortable. "I refuse to take that risk," he said. "I'd rather give her my blood."

"Charlie, grab Ohren. We'll do it now," Rainere said.

Charlie rushed to do as instructed.

"Ah, let's be as sterile as we can, please!" Ohren was a complete child about having blood extracted from his forearm, but eventually they had half a jar of his sparkling, red-gold blood.

"It's even lighter than Orestes's," Charlie said when he saw it.

While they arranged the transfusion, Mrs. Ollenby dressed Adelena in a long, white satin nightgown with multicolored ruffles over the chest and shoulders, satin bows dotted around the hem. The fabric was thin enough that they could all see the moment the baby started jumping in Adelena's belly.

Stopping the flow of the modified Gift and swapping it for untried blood suddenly felt very risky. Rainere apologized over and over to his sleeping lover as her cheeks went gray. Ohren's blood went into the intravenous tube and raced into her. They all watched as the skin on Adelena's arms shriveled against the bone and the baby sucked the strength out of her body to sustain itself.

"Turn the Gift back on now," Rainere shouted as Ohren fumbled, trying to take the block off.

"No, she needs more blood," Charlie was shouting. "Give her more blood, High Wizard."

"Charlie, it didn't work." Prince Rainold was the calmest of them. "The blood did nothing."

Rainere held his hand on Adelena's belly to calm the baby and took her bony wrist in his other hand, feeling for a pulse. The silver liquid of the Gift was pouring down the tube as it helped her recover from the shock of being given Ohren's useless blood.

Dismayed, he watched as the jar went from half full to near empty in less than a minute. "Damn you, she's worse than she was," he growled. "Why did I listen to a stupid fucking boy?"

Charlie stood at Adelena's feet and reached out his forefinger and thumb to twitch a bow on the hem of the nightgown. "She would hate this ugly dress," he mumbled.

Mrs. Ollenby let out a little sob, and Rainere's temper exploded.

"Fuck off, all of you!" His shout rattled the windows and doors. "Get out and leave us alone!"

The room darkened as the sun was suddenly covered by clouds, and a chill wind blew through the room, condensation coalescing on every glass surface. Droplets of rain fell from the clouds hovering on the ceiling. The only place rain didn't fall was on Adelena.

"This isn't how it was meant to be!" Rainere shouted as thunder rumbled and shook the chandeliers. "This can't be what the goddess wanted for her." He was going to lose Adelena, and nothing could eclipse his grief. "Serena, I never wanted a son at the cost of my love," he whispered and dropped to his knees by her side.

CHAPTER FORTY-SIX

"For Love of His Queen"

Charlie lay on the bed in his chamber in the Queen's Guard quarters. The room was exactly like all the other QGs' chambers—very fancy, with clean, white walls and a nice gray wool rug on the polished floorboards. He had a bathroom too, all to himself. It was pure luxury, and he'd never had it so good in his life. He would've preferred to have a window as a second exit, but Captain Lucky had explained that there were no windows in the chambers because normally QGs worked in shifts, and they had to be able to sleep at any time. Not that there were enough QGs to work in shifts for this queen, but traditions being what they were in the Golden Palace, the lads just took their dark rooms and burned through a lot of candles.

Charlie had come back to change out of his soaking-wet clothes after Rainere's sudden inside rainstorm, but when he got down to his boxer shorts, he lost the energy to put another shirt on and get back to the chaos in the royal apartment. The Queen's Guard were out in the training yards, taking out their frustrations on a bunch of defenseless wooden objects with their swords. But Charlie didn't want to join them, though he'd been invited. The guards fought in lines, following patterns and instructions. That wasn't how a fight really worked, so he didn't see the point in learning how to hold a sword when he'd always been in much closer quarters—hand to hand, eye to eye, knife against knife.

Charlie remembered the four men he had killed in his life. Three had been trying to kill him, and one was a young friend who'd been asleep in the bunk next to his. The orders had come from the Boss to end Leon, and he'd sliced the boy's throat. He always told himself that Leon hadn't felt a thing, that the pain had really been his, living with himself afterward.

But seeing Adelena lying half-dead on the Glass Bed had woken too many ghosts. It was like all the grief was now piling on together to crush him. Shivering, Charlie rolled the vial of Orestes's blood in his fingers.

"I'd kill anyone if it meant Adelena didn't have to suffer," he murmured, "but how can I help her?"

It was the chills that finally drove him to the bathroom. He turned the shower on as hard as it would go and stepped under the pounding water, but it didn't wash away his confusion or his anger. He took himself in hand as he pictured the queen lying on her bed, covered only in skimpy towels, but this time, she wasn't still as death. This time, she opened her eyes and laughed her smoky laugh. She reached out, inviting him in as her towels dropped away . . .

Charlie gasped at his too-fast finale, and it was so unsatisfying. Lust tainted by grief; love curdled by fear. He turned off the water and sloshed through the puddle on the floor to the sink. Wiping steam from the mirror, he studied his reflection. The silver circles were still turning around his irises after the recent orgasm, and his chin seemed darker than usual. He should've been delighted to have his beard finally come in, but today that kind of joy felt hollow.

"I'm not a stupid kid," he told the face in the mirror. "Rainere is the idiot, starting storms and smashing the place up when he should be working trying to find a cure for her."

Charlie smoothed back his dark hair with pomade that he'd stolen from Captain Lucky's room. It smelled like almonds and flowers. He guessed from the fancy tin that it must've been expensive. "Maybe I should find out about this blue tonic problem?" he murmured. "Adelena'll be so grateful when she finally wakes up that I didn't just sit around crying over her. She'll respect that I had to keep busy." He frowned at his reflection. "Now how about you stop talking to yourself like an idiot, and get going."

Thanks to Mrs. Ollenby and the Golden Palace tailors, Charlie could dress in his second new suit. This one was a burgundy velvet with brass buttons, and the trousers were a light wool that tucked into his boots neatly, the fabric tight yet flexible in case you had to climb out of a window. He attached his watch chain to a vest button and read the inscription that always made him smile, then dropped it into his pocket. He strapped the knife holster to his wrist and tucked a couple of handkerchiefs into his pockets. He seemed to be giving out the white cotton squares like party favors lately and didn't know the etiquette for getting them back once they'd been offered. It was an expensive business being a gentleman.

Deciding to take the long way to Orestes's bedchamber, via the always-busy corridors where the Carparell family had their apartments, he was amused to be greeted by many courtiers. Clearly they thought he was one of them. It was only when he hit a large group gathered at the mouth of a hallway that he was forced to stop and interact.

"Excuse me, I need to get through." He made his voice a little higher than usual, faking a Golden Palace accent.

All talking in the group stopped, and Charlie started counting heads like he would in a fight. But this was the Golden Palace, and battles were fought with words, not knives. He recognized the soon-to-be-evicted Lord Pine. The Carparell family had caught the worst of the evictions, as Lord Pine had fallen out of favor with Lord Orgustus over an incident with Lady Olivia, or so said the rumor mill.

"And who's this?" Lord Pine asked, and Charlie decided he was going to have fun mimicking that snotty tone later. "Go the long way round, why don't you?"

"That's the queen's pet Marchant," a tall, blond courtier with big, horsey teeth said. "I heard she found him in the gutter at the Home for Recovered Slummers."

"Orcello, you are wicked! My sister lived at Belvoir Estate just last summer." The lady was fluttering her eyelashes at Horse Teeth, but he just laughed a big hee-haw.

"And your sister is a slut for Green Bloods, so that makes sense, Onidia!" Horse Teeth shouted, and even Onidia joined in to cackle at her unfortunate sister's reputation.

Bored now, Charlie tried to slip through the crowd, only to feel Lord Pine's hand grasp his shoulder, surrounding him in a cloud of sweet cologne. "If I may inquire, what is your name, sir?" He was asking Charlie but directed his question at the still-tittering courtiers.

"I'm Charlie, Lord Pine." He hunched, trying to appear submissive now he'd been caught.

"Charlie?" Lord Pine guffawed at that one. "As in 'any old charlie will do'? That's the name your mother gave you, is it?"

"Yes, sir, Lord Pine." Charlie hung his head and reached internally to grab his magic.

"Well, Charlie, do you like parties?" Lord Pine asked.

"Of course I like parties!" Charlie thought he might've been overdoing it with the stammer, but the buffoon didn't notice.

"Oh, no, Pine, that's not a good idea." Horse Teeth, Orcello, seemed nervous about something and Charlie's interest was piqued.

"Rubbish!" Lord Pine clasped Charlie in a one-armed hug. "The queen takes my home away, and I can take her pet away."

"Away?" Charlie was genuinely confused this time.

"My lord, it won't be safe," Onidia chimed in.

"And I say Charlie deserves a party and it will be fine," Lord Pine snapped. "Now, Charlie, I have a little crash pad in the Guild Quarter, where we're all going tonight for a party. Why don't you come along, say around the tenth hour? It's going to be great. You'll also see some of your Green Blood friends there."

Inside Charlie was gleeful but forced himself to look confused. "Which house in the Guild Quarter is yours, Lord Pine? They're all so big, I'm sure to get lost." That got a laugh from the crowd, and Charlie smiled too, like he thought he'd been clever.

Lord Pine bent down much lower than he needed to look Charlie in the eye. "It's the really big one with pine trees out in front and Pine Estate in gold letters, six feet high, on the gate," he said. "I don't think even you could miss it, Charlie."

"No, you're right." He chuckled along with the lord. "I won't miss it. The ninth hour, you said?"

"The tenth hour!" Lord Pine gave him a hearty slap on the back, which would've sent him sprawling if he didn't have the reflexes of a cat. "Now, off you go and do the queen's bidding, little Green Blood."

Charlie moved through the crowd with as many "excuse mes" and "thank yous" as he could. *What a bunch of arses*, he thought. When he was out of hearing, he laughed aloud at his good fortune. *Thank you, Serena! If I was going to get involved in one of the Boss's conspiracies to kill off Green Bloods with poisoned blue tonic, I'd sure as hell be more discreet than these shoddy idiots. By the goddess herself, I'm going to burn that Pine Estate to the ground. And I know just the perfect person to help me get at these damn aristocrats.* Charlie instantly started planning the caper. He would need a crew, just a small one to run interference, and he'd need explosives—lots of explosives.

He dodged out of the way of a group of gossiping maids, who curtsied as they would to any other gentleman, and he was reminded that he was far too well dressed to run this caper himself. He added disguises to his list. *This Charlie needs to look like any old charlie.*

He was still chuckling to himself when he walked into Orestes's bedchamber. He hadn't had the nerve to use the portal in the wardrobe by himself before, but now it seemed ridiculous to be frightened of the same magic that rested within himself. Nevertheless, he still held his breath and braced as he walked through and out into the Boss's office in The Magician's Wand. He sighed with relief then quickly replaced the magical lock on the wardrobe with the charm he'd copied from Rainere. Stepping out of the Boss's office, he stood on the balcony, surprised. Below him on the pub floor was a mess of construction. Dozens of workers were scrubbing walls, sanding floorboards, and generally fixing things. QG Leith had told him that Adelena had claimed the place as her own, but he had no idea that the Boss's old headquarters was getting refurbished. He spotted the Lady Mayor further down the balcony, holding a large scroll of building plans in her hands and talking with several surly-looking guys dressed in black denim.

Distracted as she was, Merrills was easy to sneak up behind. "You think you'll get this place open soon?" he asked. The Lady Mayor gave a surprised yelp, but he didn't let her see how amused he was. "The queen will be pleased."

"Charlie." Merrills recovered from her shock quickly and waved away their audience. "What're you doing? And how did you get in here?"

"Queen's business on both counts," he said. "We need to talk, my Lady Mayor."

Charlie could see the bruises on Merrills's neck that she had tried to hide with a scarf and she saw him looking.

"I have a temporary office up here." She opened the door to the room next to the Boss's office. "Come in."

Renovations were clearly continuing in here too. The wall had four different velvet fabrics tacked to the woodwork, and there was a large leather couch shoved into a corner, piled with table linens. A desk covered in invoices and paperwork was parked in another corner. Charlie locked the door, quickly charming it. It wouldn't be soundproof, because he hadn't perfected that bit of the spell yet, but it would make their voices more muffled, even to magically enhanced hearing.

Merrills took a seat at the desk and offered him a padded foot-stool to sit down. "This is going to be a gorgeous private room for more discreet gatherings if Her Majesty should need them," she explained. "Do you think she'll like it?" She poured two small glasses of clear liquor. Charlie thanked her but left his on the desktop. "So you do mean business today, Mr. Charlie?"

He thought Merrills was amused by his sobriety, and it rankled a little. "The last room on the balcony row is to be reserved for the queen and the queen only," he said.

"The one that used to be the Boss's office," Bethany clarified. "Certainly, but may I ask why?"

"No." He kept his expression neutral. "The room can be decorated, but the wardrobe in the corner must be left untouched. I've put a rather nasty enchantment on it, so warn your workers to stay away."

Merrills wasn't smiling now. "Very well."

Suddenly, Charlie was comfortable again—back in the Slums, with dangerous work to do. This was the world he understood, the one he'd grown up in. The Lady Mayor was a woman he'd always seen in passing on his way to doing other things, but he knew good people that she'd helped, and he knew she had integrity that others in her family didn't. The Merrillses were a mixed bunch of rogues and thugs, but they'd made themselves rich enough to buy Bethany the office of mayor and help her keep it year after year. Any other mayoral candidate often found the need to go on a long trip before the election or simply didn't turn up on the day. He didn't blame Merrills. It wasn't her fault that her parents and siblings used her as a front woman.

"My concern today is the problem in the Guild Quarter with the bunch of aristos trying to poison blue tonic," Charlie said. "I'm here on orders from the queen to fix that issue."

Merrills's expression was guarded, but her tone was polite. "The queen has already promised me very generous funds to form a task force to combat this very problem."

"And unless we're very careful, most of that money is going to end up in the pockets of corrupt bureaucrats and thugs instead of trained police guards," Charlie said. He spotted a smudge of building

445

dust on his trousers and brushed it off. "She's asked me to help you with a more discreet solution to the problem while the funds are still being gathered."

Merrills took a moment, then asked an irrelevant question. "How is the queen faring with her pregnancy?"

Charlie frowned. "I'm sure I don't know what you mean."

"Oh, I see. It's like that." Merrills cocked her head to the side, nodding for him to continue.

"I need to know if you've heard any rumors about who might be behind the manufacture of this poison," Charlie said.

Bethany reached for her throat but didn't quite touch it. "It's common knowledge that I get a very mixed crowd at Merrills's restaurant, and I've had my servers listening out for any tidbits of news, but so far they've given me nothing," she said. "What've you heard?"

"Enough," he said.

Bethany's glare could cut glass. "Charlie, the people dying of this poison are *my* people. I want to know what you know."

Charlie let the silence stretch between them, wondering how much to reveal. "It seems that your problem and our problem are one and the same," he said finally.

Bethany's eyes widened. "But how?"

"Did you suppose the Boss of the Underworld would let a little thing like his incarceration stop the good work of killing Marchant scum?"

It was Bethany's turn to let the silence stretch between them. "What do you need from me, Charlie?" she asked finally, and he told her.

CHAPTER FORTY-SEVEN

"Unwelcome Guests"

"She looks terrible, doesn't she?" Olivia smirked.

Orgustus nodded, as his gaze roamed the queen's huge belly. *How in the name of the goddess can she be so pregnant already? This must be the work of dark magic,* he thought, surprised at how much pity he felt for her. *But she's brought this horror on herself by shagging a Marchant prince.* His boots squelched on the carpet as he moved closer to the Glass Bed. "Why is it so wet in here?"

"Oh, you'll never guess!" Olivia was carrying Gorrik's cat in her arms, and it stared at him intently. "Prince Rainere made a storm inside this morning. Thunder and rain, everything. Of course it was miserable to clean up the mess afterward, but not a drop fell on the queen. How does he do these incredible things?"

Orgustus frowned at her enthusiasm. "He's as dangerous as he is unhinged, Olivia," he said. "But you told me that he's working with that other Marchant wizard. The one who appeared from nowhere and he calls Father?"

"Prince Rainold *is* his father." Olivia sounded exasperated to have to explain herself again. "I've told you, the prince was freed from his interdimensional prison by the high wizard and Rainere. Prince Rainold admitted everything to me. He's actually quite charming when you get to know him."

"But who is the father of this thing?" He pointed at the baby bump.

"The queen practically told me that it was Rainere," Olivia said. "It definitely wasn't good news."

"Maybe she knew it could do this to her?" Orgustus mused, leaning down over the queen. This close, he could see the gray tint of her skin and hear her breathy whimpers. "Whatever is growing, it looks like it's killing her to do it."

He felt Olivia's hand on his shoulder. "And when she's gone, you'll be regent again," she said.

Oh, goddess, could it be that easy? He straightened and took Olivia's hand in his. Her wide blue eyes were filled with a mix of steely ambition and pure hope, probably reflecting his own. "The throne will be mine, and the future of Unisia will be back in my capable hands," he said. "I promised you I'd put a ring on this hand, and I will deliver, Olivia. But we will be a regent family with royal heirs. You must be sure to ingratiate yourself with the queen's children if we are to control them as they come of age."

Olivia's pretty nose wrinkled in disgust. "They're such spoiled little brats," she complained. "And that Natalie is the worst of them all, always shouting at me when I punish the nannies. How about instead of keeping them, we give them to Prince Bertie at Belvoir Estate? Then we can work at making our very own family." She dropped the cat from her arms and pushed herself against him, molding his hands over her breasts.

Orgustus had to chuckle at her audacity. *This woman has ice in her veins,* he thought, *and she'll make a perfectly ruthless ally while I get myself repositioned. I'll just have to be careful not to string her out too long before I cut her loose.* "I'll consider it," he said with an indulgent smile.

"And don't worry, Orgie," Olivia said, tossing a scornful glance at the queen. "I won't get so fat when I carry your son."

As if I'd ever let a viper like you have my child, he thought as he offered her his arm. "Let's go and get you a ring to announce our intentions before the court," he said. "Can I be the one to tell Captain Lucky that you two are over?"

A flicker of uncertainty, or maybe shame, crossed Olivia's face, and she forced a little laugh. "I'll do it," she said. "The poor man will be in such a state—better to let him have his moment of privacy before we tell the court about us."

Orgustus sniffed, displeased as much by her disobedience as by any show of loyalty to a rival. "Tell him today," he ordered. "Whenever we have to announce the queen's death, it will be nice for the people to have our wedding to cheer them again." *And afterward, the drama of our divorce due to your inevitable infidelity will keep them all entertained,* he thought.

With a happy squeal, Olivia rose to kiss him, then pulled away before he could take it further.

"We'd better go," she said. "Prince Rainere could come back at any minute, and he's in a foul mood. From the look on his face, you'd think the queen was dead already. Now, Orgie, I know exactly the sort of ring I want. I've already got a design for the jeweler."

Orgustus wasn't surprised by that at all. He followed her and opened the door, throwing a glance back at the queen. *I'm almost sorry it's going to end for us this way, Adelena,* he thought. *Even though you're a demon and Marchant sympathizer, you made one hell of a queen.*

He closed the door.

"Are they gone? D'you hear them?" A voice whispered from beneath the bed.

Three little faces peeked out from the silk flounce and scanned the room.

"S'okay, c'mon." Leafy was the first one brave enough to crawl out. She held the fabric so Aaron and Natalie could follow.

"Hi, Master," Aaron greeted the little black cat curled up at his mother's side. The cat winked and gave a little mewl of pleasure. "He said 'hi, royal children.'"

Natalie pushed a step stool up to the side of the bed, and they all clambered up, the girls pulling up Aaron by both hands.

"Now, Aaron, we have to hurry," Natalie said. "Sera will come find us soon."

"Them nannies are all talkin' 'bout boyfriends," Leafy told her. "They won't even know we're gone."

"Shh, I'm asking Master to help us, and he talks very quietly." Aaron frowned in concentration as he locked eyes with the cat.

The little cat began making odd noises, mewling like he might have been in pain.

"Okay." Aaron nodded. "Master said Natalie has to take Leafy's magic and give it to Mummy. I'll tell the baby to not eat it all."

Leafy held out her hand, and a ball of green magic coalesced over her palm. "It's my biter," she warned Natalie. "It'll hurt you when you touch it."

Natalie whimpered in fear and looked down at her mother. "But I have to do it," she said. "Mummy'll die if she doesn't get magic."

She placed her palm on top of the sparkling green ball in Leafy's hand. "Oh, it doesn't hurt," she said, pleased. "I can take it myself." She pulled magic out of Leafy until her whole arm was surrounded in a green cloud.

"Ouch," Leafy whispered. Sweat now streaked her forehead, and her cheeks were pink with the effort of letting go of so much magic.

"Stop, that's enough," Aaron warned his sister. "I'll tell the baby to leave Leafy's magic alone when you give it to her." He placed Natalie's other hand on their mother's chest, then he put his hands on the baby bump. The magic channeled through Natalie and into Adele. All the children grinned when they saw her chest rise with a deep breath and the baby started kicking.

"Yay! Let's do that again!" Natalie cried. She was still shaking little green sparkles off her fingertips, delighted with the effect.

"I'm too tired." Leafy wiped tears off her cheeks with the back of her hand. "Can we do it later?" She fell into Natalie's arms, and the little girl squeezed her and kissed her hair, just like a miniature Adelena.

"The baby says call her," Aaron told them. "He wants Prince Rainere to kiss her all the time, he wants all his magic. He wants him to call her."

Natalie stroked Leafy's hair. "I'll tell Prince Rainere to kiss Mummy like she's Sleeping Beauty. He's her true love, so it's all right they aren't married yet."

The children climbed down off the bed and ran across the wet carpet to sneak through the door to the living area. Natalie held Leafy's hand as they ran to their nursery, and they were still giggling as they crept back into bed.

Chapter Forty-Eight

"A Forest of Pine"

Charlie took a moment of grim satisfaction to watch the flames as they reached up to the sky like angry wings, spreading their orange light over the hysterical crowd of partygoers. There was another loud explosion and only Charlie knew that it came from the illegal tonic kitchen in the garden behind the mansion. *Pine is dead, and his estate is burning. Let's see Prince Rainere do that.*

The party at Pine Estate was as he had expected it to be. Lots of lords and ladies from the Carparell family drinking copious amounts of alcohol and complaining loudly about the whore queen who'd destroyed all their lives by evicting them from the Golden Palace. Charlie was amused to hear that Lord Orgustus had used the opportunity to oust his least-favorite courtiers. None of these evictions had happened yet, but the courtiers had all whined as if they were already living in the Slums and not, in reality, moving into their very own family estates in the city or the outer suburbs of Concordis.

As far as Charlie was concerned, tonight they all got what they deserved.

There were no carriages or wagons to be had so late, and Charlie had to leg it back to The Magician's Wand. Bethany had given him a key to the kitchen door at the back, and it was an easy matter to be in and up the stairs to the wardrobe portal in the office. Sprinting like he was being chased, Charlie ran through the Golden Palace and straight to the royal apartment. Standing in the hallway outside her door, he was so excited to see Adelena that he tricked himself into believing she was already awake and ready to listen to his new adventure.

I've dealt with that little poisoned blue tonic problem, he was going to say, very casually. *Oh, you want to know how I did it? It was nothing. I killed three people and who knows how many others died in the blaze that's destroyed Pine Estate. Of course, Pere Raven was behind it all, and he got away from me, but I'll . . .* Charlie froze, his boots stuck to the carpet.

"Mr. Row?" Hollis, the steward, was staring at him. "Shall I announce you, sir?"

Charlie couldn't focus on the question. *I have no idea how many people I killed tonight.* He felt sick. Adelena wouldn't think killing innocents had been a brave and clever thing to do. Not even a guilty aristocrat. *She'll hate me.*

"Mr. Row, Prince Rainere Marchant was looking for you earlier," Hollis said. "He's inside the royal apartment now."

"Sure, I'll go see him." Charlie followed Hollis into the living room and was announced, but no one noticed. There were thick clouds of magic hovering on the ceiling as Ohren, Rainere, and Prince Rainold argued over what should be done to save the queen. The dining table had been turned into a temporary laboratory and the scent of dark magic hung heavy in the air.

"Father, please, it's our only option now," Rainere was shouting. "I'm begging you."

"No, darling, I won't, I can't," Rainold shouted back. "You can't ask that of me."

"It's not for me," Rainere bellowed. "It's for my son! Your grandson!"

"Rainold, it's all we have left to try," Ohren said, and took the prince in his arms. "My love, you're our only hope to save her."

Not interested in hearing any more, Charlie went to the

bedchamber door and slipped through. *It'll be this easy,* he thought as he kicked off his shoes and shucked off his jacket. Undoing the buttons of his shirt, he felt the crust of Lord Pine's dried blood on his skin and wished he'd cleaned up for her. Then he climbed onto the bed and lay on his side, right next to the queen. His heart pounded, but he clung to the knowledge that it wouldn't hurt when she killed him.

The queen looked healthy but was sleeping as still as death. She was lying on her back, and her hair was brushed over her shoulders, clinging to the rise of her breasts. Her drip had been taken away, and she only had a little bandage on her hand to show where the needle had been.

"By the goddess, you're beautiful," Charlie whispered. He leaned in to inhale the special scent that was Adelena's own, a mix of roses and metal. "Now wake up, my love."

Like it was one of his fantasies, Adelena smiled in her sleep.

CHAPTER FORTY-NINE

"Dreams Realized"

The dream was short, frantic, and very loud. Adele woke to the same words echoing in her ears: *Mother. Call her!* The perfume attracted her first—it smelled delicious, like smoke and rich spices. Instinctively, she turned toward it, and he was lying on his side, hand propping his head up, staring at her.

"Charlie?" She was confused, wondering if this was another dream.

Charlie's shirt was unbuttoned, and he had streaks of blood marbling the white skin of his chest. "Your Majesty, you're looking gorgeous."

Adele turned away from the vibrant, magic-drenched boy. "Shut up, I look awful."

"You're dying," he said simply.

Call her! Adele tensed as the voice in her head grew more desperate. *Call her!* "Call her. What're you doing? It's too dangerous to be near me."

Charlie moved and suddenly he was on top of her, holding his weight with his hands by her shoulders. "I'm good with dangerous," he said, and laid a soft kiss on her cheek. "If one of us has to die, I've decided that it won't be you."

Adele took a deep breath. The fragrance of his magic was

intoxicating. *Call her!* "No," she whispered. "You have your whole life ahead of you—call her! I won't be the one to take it."

"You can't fight me, Adelena," Charlie said. "I deserve to die because I've done terrible things." He flicked his bangs off his forehead and grinned. "Anyway, who're they going to miss more? Their goddess-blessed queen or some ol' charlie?"

Adele could hear the Chime Voices tinkling. It would mean everything to taste his magic and sate her hideous hunger. "Call her," she whispered helplessly. "Call her."

Charlie dropped his hips between her legs and rested his forehead against hers. "I love you, Adelena."

"I love you too." Adele tried to turn her head, but his face followed her. "That's why I can't do this."

"You can and you will," Charlie promised. His lips touched hers.

"Call her!" The plea tore at Adele's throat, but her hands trapped the back of his head.

"Do it now, love," Charlie whispered. "I know you need me."

Adele slipped a hand down to his naked chest, her fingers already sizzling with green sparks. Her hunger was ferocious. The need for magic overwhelming. She teetered on the edge of releasing her tendrils into his body.

"No," she moaned. She rolled Charlie onto his back and swung her leg over his hips. She looked down and touched his trembling jaw, running her hand down his throat. She squeezed hard enough to make his breath catch. "Charlie, I can't—"

"Please take me," Charlie begged, but he didn't mean it.

It's only because he loves me, Adele thought. She closed her eyes to see the magic churning just below the surface of Charlie's skin. She leaned in and the Chime Voices began to chant, reassuring her this boy was hers to take. His sacrifice was necessary and honorable. "But you're just a child," she murmured. "Just a little boy . . ."

"Adelena, darling?" Soft, strong hands pulled at her shoulders and she followed the movement to be cradled against a wide chest. She inhaled his cold, spicy scent and wanted to weep in relief. Rainere's magic was as deep and wide as an ocean. The Chime Voices sang louder, urging her to find salvation within him. Eyes shut tight, Adele climbed off Charlie and buried her nose in his neck, savoring the familiar warmth of the man she loved. He wanted to save her and their child. The Chime Voices demanded that she dive deep into him and take what he offered.

"Charlie, run." She heard him growl but was too far gone to care about anything except the pain and hunger wracking her body. She pressed her hands against the hard packed muscle of Rainere's chest and released her tendrils of magic.

Magic. Glorious, life-giving magic flowed into her limbs. The baby began tumbling under her ribs and they both drank deeply until they were saturated with magic.

The Chime Voices shrieked their pleasure but Adele cautioned herself to listen for any hint of Rainere's pain. She was determined not to black out this time but could feel the evidence of his excitement pressed against her stomach. This pleasure, she would never deny him. Groaning, Rainere fell onto his back beneath her hands, her face still buried in his neck to inhale his gorgeous scent. She kept one palm pressed to his chest and with the other she took him in hand. "Darling, now," she commanded, and the song of the Chime Voices echoed in her voice.

"No, I can't," he whispered, but his hands were on her hips guiding her home and when he entered, they gasped in unison. "Yes! *Cara mia*, don't stop. Please, don't stop."

"Rainere, darling, I love you," she told him. "Thank you for feeding us." With her magic inside him and his body inside her, the union was complete. Behind her eyes, Adele could see nothing but the deep, raging waves of Rainere's magic. She heard his heartbeat in her ears, the vibration of it racing with his orgasm and then slowing as she reached his limits. Her orgasm was a thing of incandescent beauty. Directing her Chime Voices, she insisted both her magics, green and gold, return a little of the flow back into him, swirling together under his heart. His body quaked in another orgasm beneath hers, and he shouted his second release.

Adele pulled back the tendrils of her serpentine power and felt Rainere's magic settle in her bones. She draped herself over his torso and felt the baby kick out where their bodies were connected. She licked at the sweat trickling down his neck, tasting honey and metal. "My love," she murmured. "No one can do what you do, Rainere, no one." Then she fell deeply and peacefully asleep.

*

Rainere looked up when his father left Adelena's bedchamber. Rainold was still trying to do up his shirt but his hands were shaking too badly to fix the buttons. Ohren handed Rainold a glass of Firewhiskey and he threw it back in one swallow.

"Father?"

Rainold didn't look at him but limped to the open balcony doors, holding Ohren's arm for support. He was pale and still sweating profusely, his skin tinged greenly on his forehead where the magic had leeched out.

Rainere went to join them. "How is she?"

"She's asleep." Rainold's voice was hollow with fatigue.

"Did you fuck her?" Rainere hated how much he needed to know.

He saw Rainold's expression suffuse with despair before he forced a smile. "Darling, she took all I had to give her. She's well again and she's sleeping."

With a nod, Rainere accepted the answer that didn't tell him what he feared to know. "Father, I cannot express my gratitude."

Rainold rolled his shoulders and groaned in response.

Rainere knew the sort of pain his father must be in, still, he couldn't help but defend the sleeping Adelena. "At least you're walking," he said. "At least she left you with enough to—"

"Rainere, stop it." Rainold turned to collapse in his Ohren's arms. "You know what it cost me to do that for your demon. Let me rest."

Ohren led Rainold away and Rainere went out onto the terrace to stare up at the night sky. "It was worth it," he muttered, though guilt twisted his gut that it wasn't him who had made the sacrifice. "When she wakes up, it'll all be worth it."

*

Adele awoke with a start and it took a moment to realize that she wasn't in any kind of pain. Relieved, she sat up in bed and ran her hands over her enormous baby bump.

"Hey, kid, you got big," she whispered and mentally scanned herself again. Her magics responded quickly and her body felt strong. "It looks like we might be out of the woods. What do you think?"

Trying to move was difficult, but she managed to wiggle then lever herself out of bed. As she slipped on her robe and slippers, she could hear voices next door in the living room and hoped the children were there.

Out in the dining area, she discovered the four kids, Prince Rainold, and Mrs. Ollenby all sitting down to afternoon tea in the lounge area. A buffet had been set up on the coffee tables, probably because the dining table looked like a chemistry lab had exploded all over it. Rainere and Ohren had their heads together working on a potion. Through the balcony doors, she could see her Queen's Guard huddled in a group, discussing something with serious expressions.

"Good afternoon, everyone!" Adele called out and laughed when the four children came running to her. Distributing hugs, she led them back over to the couches.

"Your Majesty!" Ohrig had run in and threw his arms around her in a flying bear hug that made her giggle.

"Easy, Ohrig," she said. "I'm going to start thinking you were worried about me."

A wave of exhaustion hit her as she greeted her QGs and

Mrs. Ollenby, but as the children were bouncing in their armchairs with excitement, she was determined not to let them down. Then Rainere wrapped her in his arms, swinging her off her feet, until Ohren insisted he be allowed to give her a quick exam.

"Darling, I'm all right," she promised Rainere when he refused to let her go. "I'm not sure why, but honestly, I feel amazing."

"I bet you do," Rainold muttered from his seat on the couch. He looked terrible, his cheeks pallid and there were dark shadows under his eyes. But his glare was vivid enough to make her shiver and turn away from him.

Strangely, Adele found that if she didn't think about the baby, she could chat and laugh like nothing was wrong. Happy to join the party, she ate an enormous plate of tiny quiches and butter pastries, and another plate of cakes. Her hunger felt bottomless, and it seemed to delight everyone to see her eat. The Queen's Guard joined the meal at the children's insistence, but Adele could see they were still all very tense and only became more so when Tilburn came in dragging Charlie with him.

"Oh, Your Majesty! I'm delighted to see you out of bed!" But her majordomo was squinting like he was looking into the sun. "I wouldn't trouble you so early in your convalescence, but something very urgent must be brought to your attention."

Adele grinned at the idea that Tilburn would think her being out of bed for ten minutes meant that she was in recovery from growing her god-baby. Then Ohrig surprised her by standing up, eyebrows beetled. "No, Tilburn. She doesn't need to be bothered with this. I told you I'd handle Charlie."

"Oi! No one's handling me," Charlie protested. "I did what I did on the queen's behalf and solved a massive problem. You're fucking welcome!"

"Shut it, kid," Ohrig snapped at the same time Tilburn screeched a wordless noise of fury and unfurled a scroll.

"The Lady Mayor has handed me invoices to cover the costs of three sets of clothing, the services of two dressiers serving three customers, private hotel costs, and seven pounds of illegal munitions. Then there is a hefty note of compensation for the life of one pickpocket named Timothy, to be paid out to his benefactor, and a tidy sum of gold coins. Shall I go on?"

For some reason, Charlie looked across the table at Rainere. "I fixed a terrible situation, and bad people died. It happens, doesn't it, Your Highness?"

"The Pine estate has been burned to the ground!" Tilburn shrieked. "Respected courtiers of royal bloodlines have been assassinated, and you dare lay blame at the feet of the queen. You foolish boy, if it gets out that you were—"

"Oi! Shut it, Tilburn." Charlie's expression was ferocious. "I did what was necessary. What've you done to help her lately?"

Everyone looked to Adele, and despite not knowing what they were talking about, she weighed in. "It's easy enough to blame the demon queen for anything horrible," she said, attempting a bit of gallows humor. "I probably won't be around to suffer the consequences."

Charlie deflated a little. "Sorry, Your Maj," he said. "I didn't mean for them to blame you. I'll cop to it—I just want you to know that I did something right by you."

Adele couldn't quite seem to make herself attach any importance to the conversation. She was more interested in Aaron cuddling close to her. He rested his two hands on her baby bump, and his expression showed he was listening hard.

"What is it, sweetheart?" She tried to smooth the frown from his little forehead.

"He says call her," Aaron said. "Call her. That's all he says, but I think now . . ."

"What do you think, darling?" She felt light-headed again just asking about the baby.

"I think he is very scared that you won't," Aaron said. "He really wants you to *call her*."

Adele stood up, holding on to the edge of an armchair to steady herself. "I have to—call her," she whispered as she felt a huge gush of liquid fall from between her legs. "God help me, it's time."

Rainere's chair fell back in his rush to get to her. "I will not leave you," he growled, and his fingers dug into her arms. "We'll do this together."

"Call her." Adele folded over, the pain wracking her abdomen. "Call her."

There was a flurry of movement, but she only saw colors as her vision blurred.

"Rainere, hurry, she's fading!" Rainold shouted.

She knew time had passed because now she was on her back on a couch and Rainere's face was hovering over her. The fragrance of magic was thick on her tongue and her vision was clear again. "She's back!" Rainere shouted. "She's taken a breath!"

"Someone get the children out of here!" General Ohrig yelled, and Adele guessed her end was close. The baby was moving frantically.

Captain Lucky held her hands in his cold fingers. "Your Majesty, as I promised, I will say the last prayer of our goddess Serena."

Adele moaned internally screaming *Call her!*

"Our blessed goddess Serena, we beseech you humbly as your servants upon this world of Evendaar, heed our prayer. We call you to our beloved queen, your faithful angel, who leaves us to enter your Garden. We call you, sweet goddess Serena. Take this angel under your wing and into your heart. We call you, sweet goddess Serena—"

The light in the room dimmed as all the candles guttered. A rumble of thunder shook the windowpanes.

"Darling, please." Rainold shook his head at his son. "Don't make it rain on these sweet people. Not now."

Rainere was frowning at the rattling balcony doors. "That's not me," he said.

Captain Lucky continued his prayer, and at his next words—"We call you, sweet goddess Serena, she who is the mother of us all"—a huge gust of wind opened every balcony door, blowing back the curtains and revealing the light of the setting sun. Adele felt a surge of electricity powering her to pull out of Rainere's arms. The baby was tumbling under her ribs and she could swear he was screaming inside her.

The magic, the pain, the love. It all became clear now.

Captain Lucky was leaning over the back of the sofa above her, his head bowed. She grabbed his shoulder. "Lucky, it's Serena! It's been Serena all along. We have to call her!"

"Of course!" Lucky was desperate to give her anything she wanted. "We need the chapel. The spire will carry our voices to Serena's ears."

Adele struggled off the couch and to her feet. Natalie darted to her side and she hugged her daughter hard. "Come on, sweetheart, today we're going to face the gods."

Natalie raised her little chin. "Will they keep you alive?"

"We'll fight them if they don't!" Adele shouted over the noise of the wind. "Now run, we're going to church."

Rainere scooped Adele up in his arms and raced out of the room as fast as an immortal wizard could run.

The Church of Serena was on the ground floor of the palace, in an annex off the enormous Throne Hall. They were the first to reach the richly appointed chapel, with Ohren and Prince Rainold close behind. Adele paid no attention to the sweeping stone arches of the ceiling or the intricate stained-glass windows set high in the walls, their colors lit by flashes of lightning outside. The cast iron candelabras lining the carpeted aisle flickered on as they dashed by, illuminating the rows of long, cushioned pews.

"Quickly, say all the prayers you can think of to call Serena," Adele instructed as she knelt at the rosewood altar at the front of the chapel. Behind it was a ten-foot-tall stone statue of Serena, naked but for the flowers and vines draped over her chest and between her legs. Carved baby animals sat by her feet, and her stone lips smiled down on them. Rainere knelt on Adele's right side, his father next to him, and the Marchant princes chanted in unison, beseeching the goddess to heed them. Ohren surprised Adele by grabbing one of her hands in his and quietly begging forgiveness for a litany of sins, promising to be a better man if Serena would listen to him now. Kneeling in a row behind her, their seven voices raised together, her Queen's Guard and Charlie recited the same simple prayer over and over again. Behind them, Mrs. Ollenby, her four children, and Tilburn sat in the cushioned pews, eyes wide, praying loud and hard.

Adele raised her gaze to Serena's stone face. "You owe me, lady," she whispered. "I've been your Hidden Child and the servant in your terrible Prophecy of the End of the World. I have grown your brother in my body but come and take him now. Serena, come get Dahk'hani, please!" The baby turned under her ribs. "Serena, he's ready for you," she said, teeth gritted against the pain. "Come and get this kid before he kills me." Then the ground moved, and she was thrown onto her face, prostrate before the stone goddess. "Serena!"

The world continued to shake and tremble around them, statues falling off their pillars and the tapestries fluttering like sheets to the floor. Adele heard a shout and found herself squashed under Rainere's body, the baby still pummeling her from the inside.

"Oh, no, it's happening!" Prince Rainold screamed, hysterical. "I didn't stop anything. We are destroyed."

"Rainere, get off!" Adele tried to struggle out from under the prince. "Protect the children, not me." A large chunk of stone fell next to them, and through the hole in the ceiling, she could see the Gottessteppen above them, purple, green and golden clouds writhing across the inky blackness like the sky was on fire with magic.

"Mummy, you called her." Aaron dropped to his knees, tugging on her hand. She scooped him against her while Rainere staggered off to get the other three children, the stone floor cracking under his feet. More of the roof was torn off by a great gust of wind, and plaster rained down, making the children scream. Then, suddenly, all was quiet. Adele risked a glance up and felt the baby struggling in her belly. In her bones and in her heart, she knew—it was time.

Adele stood with her children holding on to her skirt of her nightgown. "He's ready for you, Serena," she called.

And Serena came.

The goddess was the image of every woman created. She was tall and voluptuous and lithe. Her skin glowed white, then deepened to the darkest black, then melted into gold an instant later. When Serena smiled, Adele wept tears of joy. The voice of the goddess was her beloved Chime Voices—her words were their songs.

"My sweet little angel." Serena enclosed her in an embrace that felt like being cocooned by pure love. "You called for me."

Adele could have stood in that hug for an eternity, but the kicking of the baby god shook her out of the ecstasy. "Serena, Dahk'hani has journeyed from his home beneath the earth to be with you again."

Serena's hands slid over Adele's protruding belly. "My true love and brother, Dahk'hani?" she asked.

More than anything, she wanted Serena to hold her again, but she managed to answer. "Yes, Serena, he is yours."

Adele thought that Serena's gaze was as deep and wide as the universe, and probably just as insane. "You have carried Dahk'hani well, my angel," the goddess sang. "I will see him enter this world."

Adele reached for Rainere's hand and held it as she touched the heads of her children. "I love you all so much." Then she let them go and walked forward with Serena to lie on the velvet cloth at the top of the altar steps. Her gown disintegrated in a cloud of fabric feathers, her naked body and shifting baby bump bared for all to see.

"Dahk'hani, my love." Serena closed her eyes and sang a song with no words, but Adele felt a deep, gravitational pull between her legs. Serena's hands parted her thighs. As the goddess's song became high and fierce, Adele fought hard against the fear that threatened to claim her sanity, but Rainere had crept to her side. She held his hand

and could only whisper the words, "I love you, Rainere Marchant." Then she had to push.

There was an almighty flash of white light, and Adele's body heaved with a powerful surge. The contraction gripped her, and she screamed her agony in one long, unbroken howl. Dahk'hani slipped from her body like her three babies had before him. It was over.

Then two gods were at the altar, the broken statue of Serena at their feet, each gazing upon the other with a love that could change time and warp the worlds.

"Dahk'hani, you chose mortality to preserve our beautiful world," Serena sang to the babe she cradled in her arms. The goddess had red hair cascading down her naked form, her breasts and bottom huge as she knelt next to Adele and transferred the babe into the crook of her arm. "He chose you, mother angel."

Adele looked down into the baby's wise, old-innocent eyes. They were a pale, pearlescent gray, and he had a thick patch of black hair still wet with birth fluids. The skin of his tiny body was a shade of olive so deep it was almost green. He was beautiful. He was perfect.

"Wait, no. He's yours," Adele told Serena, but the goddess was already on her feet, arms raised, the air shimmering around her.

"Angel, you are the mother Dahk'hani has chosen. Keep him safe and loved," Serena sang. "I will return when he realizes his godhead once more."

In a sound that shattered reality for just a moment, the goddess was gone, leaving behind the gasps of the human witnesses.

"I thought Serena said not to let this happen," Prince Rainold said to no one in particular. "I really thought she *didn't* want this destruction."

Adele felt Rainere's arms slide around her as he pressed kisses to her dusty, sweaty hair. Natalie, Leafy, and Aaron clambered on top of her, and Mrs. Ollenby brought Stella over, crowding in close to see the new baby.

"Eeew, he's got blood on him." Natalie wrinkled her nose. "And so do you, Mummy."

Rainere shucked off his jacket and covered Adele's naked torso. "You're incredible," he said, touching his forehead to hers as they both looked down at the baby. "And he's beautiful."

"Rainere—"

"No, you heard Serena, *cara mia*," he said, and his face shone with happiness. "Dahk'hani is a god no longer, but mortal. You're his mother and I'm his father—he's our son."

The baby reached a little hand up, and she could see the swollen wrinkles on his palm. *See, he is just like a normal baby,* she told herself, trying to settle the terror in her chest. The baby touched her breast, and green sparkles coalesced at his fingertips, dragging a string of magic from her body.

"Look, darling, he's feeding from you!" Rainere crowed, delighted, as Dahk'hani's little face relaxed, eyelids drooping, looking exactly like a contented newborn drinking milk. Only a moment later, the baby fell sound asleep and Adele felt his pull on her release.

Sweet Christ, he's nothing like a normal baby, she thought, panicked.

"Was that it?" QG Bear asked, making Adele look over at him from Rainere's arms.

"Next time you get to have the god-baby, Bear," she croaked. "I'd like to see where Serena drags it out of you."

Bear shrugged. "Seems like the Golden Palace got its arse kicked, but we're all good."

"The queen did all the work by herself. Again," QG Owens said with some disappointment.

"I guess we can go back to being decorative," QG Leith added, and men grunted in agreement.

"Are they always like this?" Rainere asked.

Adele nodded and sent her brave guards a smile. "They like to play it cool after an adventure," she said. "In case anyone noticed that they were scared shitless."

"Mummy, swearing." Natalie giggled, then the other children joined in.

Rainere scooped the baby into his arms, and Mrs. Ollenby helped Adele get to her feet, doing up the buttons of Rainere's jacket for her. Adele's legs were shaking, and she felt blood trickle down the inside of her aching thighs. "I don't feel very good," she whispered.

"We're going to put you to bed with a nice cup of tea, Your Majesty," Mrs. Ollenby said, but it was General Ohrig who wrapped a supporting arm around her waist and let her lean against him.

"Congratulations on your son, my queen." His pale blue eyes were bloodshot, and he lowered his voice so only she could hear. "And you survived, darlin'. Fuckacat and bless the goddess that you're still with us."

Adele managed a shaky smile for him. The rest of her QGs and Charlie moved in to catch a glimpse of the god-child as Rainere rocked him in his arms. "I really need to get cleaned up," she said. "Do you think you'd mind carrying me back to the apartment?"

Ohrig bent to put his arm behind her knees and kept the other at her back, then lifted her up while watching her expression closely. "You're not all right, are you?"

Adele leaned on his wide chest, too tired to hold her head up any longer. "I'm fine," she lied. "I didn't die, and Rainere got the son he wanted, and Dahk'hani is still in Evendaar. Seems like a good result." She felt Ohrig's chuckle rumble through his chest, and she knew why he was laughing. *Because my life is completely ridiculous!*

"Your Maj, look!" Charlie shouted. "It's—"

A man was climbing over a pile of rubble in the doorway of the Throne Hall. He clambered to the top of a large chunk of ceiling arch and stood tall, pointing his finger at them. "You!" he shouted. "What the fuck have you done?"

Adele met Rainere's gaze with a cold snap. "Rip!"

Ripenzo Shale was clearly enjoying making an entrance and took his time descending from his high point, then picking his way through the destroyed pews to Adele. "So, there I am, trapped in the Eeyrie, chained to a wall in a very small prison, when what should happen?"

Adele groaned, leaning back against Ohrig's chest. "Someone shut him up, please."

"He's gorgeous." Rainold giggled. "Who is that?"

"That's my half brother, Ripenzo Shale," Adele said, talking over Rip so loudly that he stopped his little outraged speech. "He's the son of King Octavius and Queen Olivia St. Lucidis and was the baby you gave to the Marchant Eldars instead of me. The Eldars kept him and raised him as some sort of weird science experiment. He's my very own bad-luck charm."

"Oh, that's rich, coming from you, Adelena! You're like the bloody queen of bad luck." Rip was furious. "What did you do?"

Adele frowned. "When? Be more specific, Rip. A lot's happened since you ran away."

Rip looked pained at the interruption and began his story again, enunciating each word through clenched teeth. "So, there I am, *trapped,* when the ground shakes, the sky shatters, and we're falling. The Eeyrie dropped out of its dimension and entered Evendaar's atmosphere. Its magic failed because the bridge between *this* dimension and *that* one collapsed, pulling it through."

"Oh." Adele tried to make her very tired and still-shocked brain take in this information, but she came up blank. "The Eeyrie is in the sky?"

"The Eeyrie exists in a separate dimension," Prince Rainold explained to her. "Sort of like my interdimensional prison, except the natural laws of existence still apply there."

"Then how can it fall?" Adele wasn't sure who to direct the question to, Rip or Prince Rainold.

"Exactly!" Rip was pleased she'd finally got it. "It can't fall, but it did fall. You broke it!"

"So now we're going to have Eldars flying through the sky again?" Charlie demanded to know.

All Adele wanted was a soft bed in a dark room, so she didn't mince words. "Look, Rip. Dahk'hani finally found a way to make me pregnant, and then, about five minutes ago, Serena helped me to give birth to him, and now she's disappeared. No thanks offered. No questions asked. No answers given."

"Shit, I had no idea." Rip lost his attitude and closed the distance between them. He only then seemed to notice that she was in a bad way. "Where is Dahk'hani now, darlin'?" When he followed her gaze to the babe in Rainere's arms, his mouth opened, and he made an odd, strangled noise. "That's . . . the . . . that's the *god*?"

"He is our son." Rainere's voice vibrated with pride, and his chin was high. "He is mine and Queen Adelena's."

Adele drooped against Ohrig's chest again. "Rip, I'm really, really tired. Can we continue this discussion after I've slept for about a hundred years?"

"Like Sleeping Beauty," Natalie agreed before taking Rip's free hand. "I'm glad you're back, Uncle Rip. We didn't know where you'd gone. We have a granddaddy now."

Still stunned, Rip managed a half grin for Natalie, but his indigo gaze flicked back to Adele. "I heard that Rainere's dad escaped prison. He's in a lot of trouble with the Eldars, and that'll come to you too."

Adele made a huge "but of course it will" sigh.

Rip stood in front of her and didn't move. "There's another storm coming," he whispered. "I'm sorry to tell you this, darlin', but it's going to be bad."

Adele leaned forward to lay her hand on Rip's whiskery cheek. His eyes were filled with anxious love, and he smelled like warm honey. "Aren't they all, brother?" she said. "Aren't they all?"

To be continued . . .

ACKNOWLEDGMENTS

As always, a huge thank you to my dearest Reader. You are always there for me and Evendaar. I treasure you.

Thank you to Monica Hall, the best First Reader a writer could have.

Thank you to the amazing team at the Artful Editor. As an independent author I could not have written this book without your professional and artistic support. Thank you to the brilliant Ernesto Quiñonez for his excellent advice and the always wonderful editor, Denise Logsdon, for her wise guidance and incredible attention to detail. If there are any errors it is not the fault of the extraordinary proofreader, Robin Samuels, but my own for constantly wanting to change things.

Thank you to all the friends and family who supported me in writing this novel in the trying times we shared together this last year.

To find out more about the author A. R. Winterstaar or the World of Evendaar please visit:
www.evendaar.com
or follow
A. R. Winterstaar on Facebook for regular writing updates.